Also by Jill Mansell

Miranda's Big Mistake
Sheer Mischief
An Offer You Can't Refuse
Millie's Fling
Perfect Timing
Rumor Has It
Take a Chance on Me
Staying at Daisy's
To the Moon and Back
Nadia Knows Best
A Walk in the Park
Thinking of You
Don't Want to Miss a Thing
The Unexpected Consequences of Love
Making Your Mind Up
Falling for You
Good at Games
The One You Really Want
You and Me Always
Three Amazing Things about You
Solo
Meet Me at Beachcomber Bay
Head over Heels
This Could Change Everything
Fast Friends
Maybe This Time
Kiss
Mixed Doubles
It Started with a Secret
Two's Company

and now you're back

JILL MANSELL

sourcebooks landmark

Published by Sourcebooks Landmark, an imprint of Sourcebooks
P.O. Box 4410, Naperville, Illinois 60567-4410
(630) 961-3900
sourcebooks.com

Simultaneously published in 2021 in the United Kingdom by Headline Review, an imprint of Headline Publishing Group, a Hachette UK Company.

Library of Congress Cataloging-in-Publication Data

Names: Mansell, Jill, author.
Title: And now you're back / Jill Mansell.
Other titles: And now you are back
Description: Naperville, Illinois : Sourcebooks Landmark, 2021.
Identifiers: LCCN 2020053711 (print) | LCCN 2020053712 (ebook) | (trade paperback) | (epub)
Subjects: GSAFD: Love stories. | Humorous fiction.
Classification: LCC PR6063.A395 A83 2021 (print) | LCC PR6063.A395 (ebook) | DDC 823/.914--dc23
LC record available at https://lccn.loc.gov/2020053711
LC ebook record available at https://lccn.loc.gov/2020053712

Printed and bound in Canada.
MBP 10 9 8 7 6 5 4 3 2 1

This book is dedicated to my brilliant readers.
Thank you so much for buying—or borrowing—my books.
You're all wonderful! xxx

chapter 1

"My God, my ears." The person in the corridor outside their hotel room was cracking up. "What's that *horrible* noise?"

Didi, wearing only a bath towel, pulled a face at the closed door and shouted back defiantly, "It's called singing." Honestly, here they were in Venice, one of the most miraculous cities on the planet, and there always had to be one comedian trying to bring you down.

"You can call it singing," her critic observed. "Some might call it caterwauling."

They heard the sound of his footsteps fade as he clattered up the rickety staircase to the boys' rooms on the top floor.

Didi said, "Shay Mason thinks he's *so* hilarious."

"You were a bit out of tune," Layla told her. "To be fair."

Layla was always fair; it was really annoying.

"I don't know why you invited him. He doesn't even go to our school." Well, she could hazard a guess. As Layla carefully applied a second coat of turquoise mascara, Didi met her friend's gaze in the age-spotted antique mirror and raised an eyebrow.

"Don't go giving me one of your looks," said Layla. "He's been kind to me, that's all. I told you about the time those other boys were making fun of me, and he stopped them doing it. I don't fancy him."

"Not even a bit?"

"No!"

"OK, I believe you. Thousands wouldn't." Didi broke into a playful grin and turned up the radio as her favorite Elton John track began to play. "I only asked." Grabbing her hairbrush and holding it like a microphone, she sang off-key at the top of her voice, "I'M STILL STANDING, YEAH YEAH YEAH."

"He'll be able to hear that." Layla pointed at the ceiling.

"Oh, I'm counting on it," said Didi.

....

What had just happened? Didi's eyes snapped open; something had woken her. Turning her head to one side to check the alarm clock, she saw that it was 3:10 in the morning.

"Don't put the shrimp on my feet," muttered Layla from the other bed.

Right, OK. Now she knew what had interrupted her sleep.

"Just get into the washing machine," Layla mumbled. "You're all blue."

Didi smiled to herself, because listening to Layla talking in her sleep was always fun. But that was it; after an irritable "*Not* the dog biscuits," Layla turned to face the opposite wall and began snoring gently once more.

Wide awake now, Didi saw an eerie grayish light and flickers of movement filtering through the gap in the curtains. Sliding out of bed, she crept across the room and peered out the window. Incredibly, it was snowing outside, fat flakes falling like feathers from an inky sky. Snow in Venice, during February half-term break; who'd have thought it? When they'd come upstairs to bed four hours ago, it had been bitingly cold, but still no one had expected this to happen.

She pressed her nose against the icy glass and peered left and right, drinking in as much of the view as she could see. But there really wasn't much of one; Calle Ciati was a winding backstreet, dark and silent. She'd be able to see so much more from the front of the hotel, which overlooked the canal.

Venice. In the snow. But what if it all disappeared by morning?

Layla was completely out for the count; she might no longer be actually snoring, but her lips were making a small *pfff* noise with each regular exhalation. She loved to sleep and couldn't bear being woken even a minute before it was time to get up.

Five minutes later, bundled up and clutching her yellow bobble hat, Didi crept down the ornate staircase, reaching the deserted vestibule and silently letting herself out of the hotel. Oh wow, it was amazing; the snow was already several inches deep, soft and creaking underfoot as she turned left and made her way along the narrow street. A couple of other people had taken the same journey earlier, their footprints already disappearing as the snow fell faster, but there was no one else in sight. Didi was alone but felt entirely safe, although she took care to keep away from the potentially slippery edges when the next pathway led her to one of the backstreet canals.

Then she made the final turn and there it was, the vast expanse of St. Mark's Square stretching out before her. Her heart soared at the sight. It was spectacular enough in daylight, but now, blanketed in white and with the snowflakes tumbling down, it was utterly magical. St. Mark's Basilica, topped with gold and fronted by the ornate sky-high flagpoles, looked like an illuminated wedding cake. Over to her right, a couple were locked in each other's arms, kissing. To the left, someone else was building a snowman. A few other people, drawn by the snow, were taking photographs, and a woman in a full-length white faux-fur coat carried a dachshund in her arms as she made her way diagonally across the square and passed the Campanile before disappearing from view.

Didi pushed her hands into the pockets of her own rather less glamorous outfit, more of a knee-length padded anorak than a coat, but at least it was warm and waterproof. Having observed the energetic creator of the snowman for a couple of minutes, she found herself moving closer before realizing with a jolt who it was.

Oh, great. Instinctively, she spun around, facing away and catching her breath while working out what to do next. A part of her was furious with Shay Mason for ruining this once-in-a-lifetime experience, because up until five seconds ago, she'd been so blissfully wrapped up in the wonder of it, and now she was going to have to head back to the—

Whoomph! A snowball hit the ground just to the left of her, skidding past before disintegrating like powdered smoke.

Ha, not as clever as he thought he was. With an air of triumph, Didi turned and said, "Missed."

Across the ten-meter distance separating them, Shay Mason called back, "I meant to miss."

"Of course you did."

"Don't move," he ordered, reaching down to scoop up and swiftly pack together another snowball.

Didi stayed where she was, wondering if it was going to hit her in the chest. Like a fast bowler, Shay took aim and threw the snowball. The first had landed two feet to her left. This one landed two feet to the other side of her. Shay did a small bow, then broke into a grin. "If I'd wanted to get you, I could. But I'm a gentleman, so I wouldn't do that."

"You're never going to win a snowball fight." Didi found herself reluctantly smiling in return.

"I'm a lover, not a fighter." He paused, then shook his head. "That's probably the wrong thing to say. All I really want to do is finish building this snowman. You could give me a hand if you like."

"Could I?"

His eyes were bright. "You can even sing."

"Oh dear," said Didi. "You had to go there."

"I was only teasing earlier." The grin broadened. "You have the voice of an angel."

"The voice of an angel who sometimes sings off-key. It's OK. I know it's not always great. I just love doing it anyway."

He tilted his head. "So are you going to stay and give me a hand?"

"May as well." Snowflakes were landing on his hair and lashes, settling on the shoulders of his navy jacket. "Seems like you could do with some help from an expert."

It took them a good thirty minutes, but at last their snowman was completed and looking magnificent. Standing five feet high, with twenty-cent coins for eyes, an abandoned stripy scarf wrapped around his neck, and Didi's yellow bobble hat providing the finishing touch, he wore a jaunty smile fashioned from discarded bottle caps.

A group of Spanish tourists applauded their efforts and offered them a swig from their bottle of prosecco. Spotting another unopened bottle protruding from the overcoat pocket of one of the men, Shay asked in broken Spanish if he could buy it and offered him a twenty-euro note.

When the Spaniards had left, they collected two chairs from the dozens laid out in front of the café behind them and planted them next to their magnificent creation. As the snowflakes continued to tumble helter-skelter, Shay removed the wire cage from around the bottle's cork and passed it to Didi, who used it to give their snowman a nose. Then he popped the cork, and they took turns drinking from the bottle before setting it down in the snow between them. Then together they sat back, side by side, to properly take in the beauty of their surroundings.

"So here we are." Shay's bare fingers were loosely clasped as they rested on his chest. "I know your name and I know where you live but not much more than that. Why don't you tell me something fascinating about you?"

Didi considered the question. They both lived in Elliscombe and were in their last year at school, but the social circles they moved in were entirely different and seldom overlapped. She and Layla attended Stonebank Hall, several miles north of the town, and their parents were able to afford the fees, plus such luxuries as holidays abroad. By way of contrast, Shay Mason was in his final year at the local high school at the opposite end of town, his mum had died six years ago, and his dad was currently in prison. Again.

But those facts alone might give a stranger the wrong idea about Shay, who didn't appear to feel remotely hard done by and who'd always brimmed with confidence. As Didi thought this, it occurred to her that she appeared to know more about him than he did about her, probably because his upbringing had been that much more interesting to observe and other people had loved to gossip about him. Over the years, while his father had spent varying periods of time languishing at Her Majesty's pleasure, Shay had convinced his social workers that he'd be staying with the parents of various school friends before stealthily moving back into the family home and looking after himself while working hard at school and simultaneously holding down two or three part-time jobs during the evenings and weekends. He and his clothes were always clean. He had charm, coupled with confidence and the ability to chat easily with anyone at all. He was tall and lean, built like an athlete. And of course it didn't do any harm that he possessed the kind of glowing good looks that made him irresistible to far more than his fair share of admirers.

Charisma, that was the indefinable quality. People either had it or they didn't. It would be easy to feel sorry for anyone else whose upbringing had been so chaotic and unpromising, but you wouldn't feel sorry for Shay Mason.

Anyway, he'd asked her a question. "I can pick up a pencil with my bare toes," said Didi.

"Useful."

"It *is* useful."

"And you can actually write messages with it?"

"Of course, but I'm not going to do it now. Your turn. What's fascinating about you?"

Promptly, he replied, "I can fit a whole crumpet in my mouth in one go."

She nodded, impressed. "Equally useful."

"Can I ask you another question? Why did Layla invite me along on this trip?"

It had been one of Layla's father's typically expansive gestures. He'd asked her how she'd like to celebrate her eighteenth birthday, and Layla had said she'd always wanted to visit Venice, thinking it would be a family holiday. Instead, her dad had told her to pick nine friends so she could celebrate with them in style, creating memories that would last a lifetime. To avoid mayhem, her parents had come along too, in order to pay for everything and keep the party under control.

"She told me you were kind to her," said Didi. "Something about a group of boys making fun of her one night in town. But you stepped in, sorted them out, and walked her home." She paused because Shay was observing her closely. "Why are you looking at me like that? Did it not happen?"

"Oh yes, it happened. And it was really good of Layla to ask me along. It was just…you know, unexpected." His brief smile indicated what he meant. Out of the ten of them here in Venice, nine were from the two local private schools and socialized together. Shay was the only one from the public high school and certainly the only one with a jailbird dad.

"She wanted you here." Didi brushed away a snowflake that had landed like a feather on her nose. "She likes you."

"What kind of like?" Shay's silver-blue gaze was unwavering. "That's why I'm asking you. Does she just like me as a friend because I'm an awesome person—which I definitely am, by the way—or does she fancy me?"

"And you're asking me this because you *want* her to fancy you?"

"I don't want that. She's a lovely girl, but…no." He shook his head. "But I don't want to hurt her feelings either."

They paused while an elderly man drew closer in order to admire their snowman, then smiled and nodded before continuing across the square.

"I asked her this evening, before dinner," said Didi. "And she said no, she just likes you as a friend. No plans for anything more."

"OK. Well, good to know." Clearly relieved, Shay raked his damp blond hair back from his forehead. "Out of interest, any other reason you can think of for her inviting me?"

Didi recalled sitting in the kitchen of Layla's house while she'd been compiling her list of invitees. When Shay's name had come up, Layla's mum, Rosa, had said, "Would he get along with your other friends?" and Layla had replied, "Of course he would. Shay gets along with everyone. And I bet he's never had a holiday in his life."

Was that what he was asking now? She wasn't about to tell him he'd been added to the list as an act of charity. Instead, she said, "No other reason. She's just grateful you rescued her from the idiots that time. And I can't believe you aren't even wearing gloves." She changed the subject and pointed to his hands. "Aren't they freezing?"

In response, he reached across and briefly rested his fingers against her left cheek. They were unbelievably warm. "I have excellent circulation. Second to none. Another of my talents."

Didi bent down to collect the bottle of prosecco wedged upright in a mound of snow. She took another fizzy swig, passed it across, then watched him drink before resting the base of the bottle on one knee.

"I can't believe we're sitting here at four in the morning in front of the Basilica." Her gesture encompassed the white marble, the Byzantine architecture with its ornate gold detailing, blurred now by the steadily falling snow.

Shay nodded in agreement. "When I woke up and looked out the window, I had to come outside and see it properly for myself."

"And build a snowman."

"Sometimes these things just have to be done."

Didi found herself wanting to learn more about him. "What A levels are you taking?"

"Math, physics, chemistry, English. You?"

"English, history, and art." She paused. "You must miss your mum."

Shay took another glug of prosecco, then passed the bottle back to her. "Of course I miss her. But it's been six years now. You kind of get used to the way things are."

Here, in this moment, it seemed as if a connection had been forged between them; Didi felt as if she could ask him anything. "What's it like to have your dad in prison? Sorry, tell me if I'm being too nosy."

"No worries. People always ask me that question. It's the kind of thing they want to hear about." He shrugged. "Again, I don't really know any different. It's like me asking you what it's like to have two honest, law-abiding parents who live and work together and own a luxury hotel. That's your life, and you don't stop to wonder how it feels because you're used to it."

He was right; she lived a privileged life and took it for granted. She said, "It must be horrible for you when he…goes away."

"It is. But again, I'm used to it. And then I'm glad when he gets out. It's always great to have him home again." Shay shrugged easily. "I know he's a bit of a nightmare, but he's still my dad and I love him. He's all the family I've got."

Didi still couldn't believe she was having this conversation with someone she barely knew. She found herself really looking at him for the first time, at his relaxed body, his damp blond hair, and his carved cheekbones. "You're doing so much better than most people would in your situation."

"I know."

"Modest too."

He smiled. "When everyone in town expects you to go off the rails and follow in your father's footsteps, it kind of makes you want to go the other way, just to prove them wrong. And now I have another question. What's Didi short for? Or is it a nickname?"

"My name's really Danielle, but when I was little, I couldn't say it. When my mum and dad tried to teach me, it came out as Didi instead. Started off as a family joke, then after a while, it just kind of stuck." She shrugged. "I've been Didi ever since."

"Cute."

"It wasn't my fault. I blame my teeth."

"Of course it was their fault." He grinned and sang teasingly, "Guilty teeth have got no rhythm."

"You're hilarious." But she was smiling too.

"Are you getting cold now?"

Didi was starting to shiver. "Tiny bit."

"Well, we can't go in without taking a few photos." He reached into the pocket of his navy padded jacket and pulled out a disposable camera. She took a snap of him standing in front of the Basilica with his arm flung around the shoulders of their magnificent snowman. Then it was his turn to take one of her in the same position, followed by another as she twirled with her arms outstretched and her head tilted back, catching snowflakes on her tongue.

Finally, having beckoned a passing Venetian across to do the honors, they had a photo taken of the two of them together, standing on either side of the snowman with the bottle of prosecco clutched to his snowy chest.

"*Grazie mille, signor*," Shay called after him as the Venetian trudged away in the direction of the Campanile, and Didi was quietly impressed by his facility with languages, seeing as this was his first trip abroad.

"My toes have gone numb," she said as they returned the chairs to the café and prepared to set off through the narrow streets that would lead them back to the hotel.

"Don't forget this." He grabbed the yellow bobble hat from the snowman and gave it a shake.

Didi pulled it on. "That's just making me colder." Her teeth were starting to chatter now.

Shay removed the hat, grinning as she brushed melting snow from her hair. "Can I just say? This has been fun. I'm really glad we did it."

He was standing directly in front of her, his breath warm on her face. The fingers of his left hand made brief contact with her cheek as he lifted aside a wet strand of hair. Didi felt her own breath catch in her throat. His mouth was only inches from hers, and all of a sudden, it seemed as if he might be about to kiss her.

More to the point, all of a sudden, she found herself wanting it to happen with every fiber of her being.

But it didn't.

"Come on. Let's get back," said Shay.

Didi nodded in agreement, because what else could she do? Fling her arms around his neck and wail, *But I thought you were going to kiss me! I was waiting for you to do it!*

No, that would be the opposite of cool.

As they began to make their way back to the hotel, he said, "Are we going to tell the others about this?"

"I was just wondering that." If they did, would everyone assume they'd sneaked out together? Would they be teased unmercifully for the rest of the trip and possibly for months to come? "Might be easier not to."

"I think so too. And tomorrow when we come to the square, we won't say anything when they see the snowman. It'll be our secret."

When they reached the hotel, he paused in the narrow street, and Didi's foolish heart did another skip, because maybe *now* the kiss was going to happen.

But no, double disappointment; all Shay did was slide his key card out of his jeans pocket and use it to open the front door of the small hotel. Then, having brushed the snow from their jackets and wiped it off their sneakers, they made their way silently up the stairs.

On the third-floor landing, he whispered, "See you tomorrow. Our secret."

"See you." Baffled, Didi wondered why it hadn't happened. What was *wrong* with him, for heaven's sake? Shay Mason should be flattered she'd wanted him to kiss her; he should have jumped at the chance.

Three hours later, she was woken by a whoop of delight followed by a great thud as Layla bounced onto the end of her bed.

"Oh my God, you have to get up!"

"Why? *Ow,*" said Didi as her feet were landed on.

"You aren't going to believe this," Layla shrieked. "It's been *snowing.*"

chapter 2

Thirteen years later

SOMETIMES, YOU HAD A FEW MINUTES TO CATCH YOUR BREATH before starting work. Other times, you didn't.

Sylvia, the assistant manager, beckoned her over to the reception desk. "Didi, the American guy in the Midsummer Suite's kicking up a fuss, something about too much noise. He's demanding to see whoever's in charge."

Didi shook her head; last night, Myron Miller had complained loudly in the restaurant that he'd asked for chips to be served with his steak but had been given french fries instead, necessitating a gentle explanation that over here in the UK, chips were crisps. Needless to say, he'd found this un-American and frankly unacceptable.

And this morning he was at it again; something about the finest suite in the hotel was clearly irking him. Such were the joys of keeping the customer satisfied. Didi said, "I'll go and see him now."

She took the narrow stairs two at a time and reached the Midsummer Suite on the third floor. As their pernickety guest flung open the door in response to her knock, she began, "Mr. Miller—"

"You gotta major problem with the electricity supply in this place." Myron Miller shook his bearlike head. "Like, you guys need to call a professional in to sort it out before someone gets electrocuted."

The thought ran through Didi's head: *If only it could be you.* But because she was a professional, she put on her concerned face and said, "Mr. Miller, I'm so sorry about this. Why don't you show me what's wrong?"

"Because if someone dies, you guys are gonna get your asses sued,

I'll tell ya that for nothing. Come on. Get yourself in here, and you'll see what I'm talking about." He ushered her inside, then gestured with an air of triumph. "Hear that? And even if it isn't dangerous, it's still totally unacceptable. You can't expect people to sleep with that kind of racket going on."

The last time a guest had complained about a terrible racket, it had been the sound of blackbirds singing in the trees outside their window. This wasn't birdsong though; it was a muffled, low-level buzzing sound of an electrical nature. As Didi made her way around the suite, it soon became apparent where the noise was coming from.

Oh, please, not that.

"I don't think it's a problem with our electricity supply," she told Myron.

"It's been going on for three hours now." He glared at her. "So whatever it is, you need to sort it out pretty damn quick."

Well, when you put it that way. Crossing the room, Didi bent down and listened, then rested her fingertips on the lid of Myron Miller's gleaming Samsonite suitcase. She turned and said pleasantly, "It's coming from inside your case. Do you want to deal with it, or shall I?"

It could have been a lot worse; luckily, it wasn't. With a sudden bark of laughter, Myron unearthed the sonic toothbrush that had presumably managed to turn itself on when he'd jammed it back into his bag. He switched it off, and the buzzing stopped. "Well, wouldja believe that? It didn't sound like my toothbrush from all the way in there."

An apology was clearly too much to hope for, but Didi was used to this by now. She said cheerfully, "Glad that's sorted out. And is there anything else at all I can help you with?"

But Myron Miller had already lost interest. Engrossed in his phone, he said absently, "No, I'm good. You can go."

As she let herself out of the room, the voice of another American male inside the Midnight Suite directly opposite said, "Miss? What *was* that infernal noise?"

The door to the Midnight Suite remained closed. Didi called out, "It's fine, nothing at all to worry about. It was just an electric toothbrush."

"Are you quite sure about that? Because it was kinda hurting my ears, lady. Almost sounded like someone was…I don't know, trying to *sing* or somethin'…"

Didi had already stopped dead in her tracks. *No*, it couldn't be.

Surely not.

Could it?

She stared at the Midnight Suite's closed door and felt the *thud-thud-thud* of her heart, like a fat pigeon trying to take off inside her chest.

"No, sir. It definitely wasn't singing." She paused. "Or any other kind of caterwauling."

Another second passed. Then the door was pulled open and there he was, standing before her. Almost thirteen years after he'd left.

"Hey," said Shay.

"Hey." Didi swallowed; she never normally said *hey*. But this was one of those peculiar situations, and she couldn't work out how to react. Normally greeting an old friend again after so long apart, there'd be a hug and some sort of kiss. But Shay wasn't an old friend as such; he was an ex-boyfriend.

More than that, he'd been her first love.

And the way in which they'd parted company had been tricky to say the least.

"Well…fancy seeing you here." There was a glimmer of a smile, which was something.

Didi's brain was working overtime, racing ahead. She said, "Do you know Mr. Miller? Did you set up the whole toothbrush thing?"

He shook his head. "No to both questions. I was half expecting to bump into you at some stage, but there were no plans to engineer it. I overheard the guy earlier on his phone, calling down to reception to complain about the noise in his suite. Then I heard someone come up to deal with him and realized it was you." Another glint of amusement in his silver-blue eyes. "You remember Venice, then?"

Of course she remembered Venice, every last second of it. How could she ever forget?

"Your American accent is terrible," she said.

"Almost as bad as your singing." He smiled and raised a hand. "That was a joke. You know I don't mean it."

"What are you doing here?"

"Flew in last night, rented a car at Heathrow, arrived at midnight, managed to get the last room." He gestured at the suite behind him, which cost as much as any suite in a boutique four-star hotel, then said, "Don't worry. I can afford it. Just about."

The dig was there; of course it was. Ignoring it, Didi said, "What would you have done if we'd been fully booked?"

"Who knows? Slept in the car, I expect." He paused. "I can still rough it if I need to."

There was so much unspoken, so many things she'd wanted to say to him over the years. When he'd left, Shay had done a thorough job of it; short of hiring a private detective, there'd been no way of tracking him down, finding out what he was doing with his life and how things were going for him. And even if she had been able to pay for a private detective, it would have been a pointless exercise, seeing as she was the reason he'd left in the first place.

But now he was back.

She found her gaze flickering around the outline of him, as if direct contact was too intense, like looking into the sun. At thirty-one, he was aging as well as she'd always guessed he would and was as athletically built as he'd been at eighteen. He was wearing faded jeans the exact silver-blue shade of his eyes and a plain white polo shirt with no visible logo, which meant it was either super cheap or designer and very exclusive indeed. Tanned skin. A fine scar that hadn't been there before, across his left cheekbone. And streaky blond hair still wet from the shower. He wasn't wearing any jewelry, she noted, neither a watch nor a ring on his left hand.

Damn, he'd caught her looking at his hand.

"No, still single. Unlike you, I see." He inclined his head in the direction of her hand just as Sylvia rounded the final bend in the steep staircase. "So you've found someone who wants to marry you, then. Well done."

Sylvia said brightly, "Ooh, do you two know each other?" She turned from Didi to Shay. "Actually, she found three someones who wanted to marry her! Not bad going, eh? Didi, did you manage to sort out the gentleman in the Midsummer Suite?"

"I did."

Shay chimed in helpfully, "It was an electric toothbrush."

"Oh, right! Excellent! Well, I just popped up to see if you were free to have a chat with the Carter-Laceys. They want to talk to you about booking the hotel for their daughter's twenty-first. They're waiting in the orangery."

Didi, whose palms were damp, was glad of an excuse to escape. "Of course, I'll see them now." Work took precedence over catching up with long-lost ex-boyfriends, and she needed a break in order to get used to the idea that Shay was back in Elliscombe. Meeting those oh-so-familiar silver-blue eyes, she said, "Might bump into you later."

"Might do." He nodded in agreement. "Maybe."

"Well now, this *is* interesting." Sylvia gave her a gentle nudge as they descended the narrow staircase. "He's a bit of all right, isn't he? What a body…and how about that smile!"

Sylvia was sixty. She was also fascinated by people and incorrigibly nosy. Didi thought back for a moment. "He wasn't smiling."

"Maybe not for you," said Sylvia as they reached the ground floor. "But he definitely smiled at me."

Fifty minutes later, Didi was checking table bookings in the restaurant when some sixth sense made her look up from the computer screen just as Shay passed the open doorway and made his way across reception.

Maybe it wasn't a sixth sense; in all likelihood, she'd subliminally recognized the sound of his footsteps on the stairs. She waited for him to turn his head and notice her, but it didn't happen. Instead, he reached the main entrance and left the hotel without looking back.

Without pausing to think, she hurried across the hallway and pushed open the ancient wooden front door, discreetly poking her head around it so she could see which direction he'd taken. There he was, having turned right, heading toward the market square and—

Thirty yards away, he suddenly halted and looked over his shoulder, causing Didi to leap back in alarm before he could catch her spying on him.

"*Oof,*" yelped Marcus, their newest and most nervous waiter, and *crash* went the silver tea tray he'd been about to carry upstairs. Scrabbling on the floor to collect the silver teapot, the toast slices, and the broken crockery, he said in a tremulous voice, "Oh no, oh God, I'm so sorry."

Shay Mason had been back in her life for less than an hour, and already he was causing trouble.

Poor flaming-cheeked Marcus. "Not your fault," Didi said. "Don't worry. I'll help you clear it up."

....

"OK, you're not going to believe this, but guess who I've just seen getting out of a blue Audi outside my office."

Didi could hear the excitement in Layla's voice over the phone; she was practically bursting with the thrill of being able to pass on such a riveting piece of gossip.

"I don't know. Is it someone really good-looking?"

"Yes," Layla cried. "Yes!"

"Fit body?"

"*So* fit."

"Small scar on left cheekbone?"

"I wasn't close enough to see a scar."

"Was he wearing a white polo shirt and faded jeans?"

"Oh, I hate you." Layla let out a groan of realization. "You already know."

"I bumped into him this morning. He's staying in the Midnight Suite."

"Are you kidding? And you didn't even think to tell me?"

"I was going to, as soon as I had a second. We've been crazy busy, and I've been rushed off my feet."

"And was he…you know, OK with you?"

"Pretty much." Apart from one or two iffy moments.

"So what's he doing back here now? Where's he been living, and what's he been up to all these years?"

"I don't know. I didn't ask. It was so weird seeing him again."

"Good weird or bad weird?"

"No idea. *Weird* weird," said Didi.

"I might see him tonight then, if he's around. D'you think he will be?"

"You keep asking me questions I can't answer."

"Sorry! But it's exciting, isn't it? After all this time, he's turned up again out of the blue and… Oh bum, my clients are here. I'm going to have to go."

"No worries," said Didi. "I'll see you and Rosa at eight."

"He's still looking good though, don't you think?"

"Who? Oh, you mean Shay." Didi grinned. "Is he? I didn't notice."

"Of course you didn't. Why would you?" said Layla.

At three o'clock, Didi was in her office when she glimpsed the blue Audi pulling into the hotel parking lot. She watched as Shay reversed into a narrow space, getting it right the first time, before emerging from the driver's seat. Yes, of course he was still looking good. Better than good. And he could park brilliantly too. Some people just had too many talents.

A minute later, there was a light knock at the door, and she rose to answer it, first tipping her head forward then back again to add extra bounce to her choppy, dark bob.

Well, it looked better that way.

"Hi. The receptionist told me I'd find you in here. What are you doing this evening? Are you on duty?"

"No…"

"Good. How about dinner?"

"I can't."

"Why not? Jealous fiancé?"

"My fiancé isn't jealous. And he works in London during the week."

Didi paused, then said, "It's Rosa's birthday. We're having a little party for her this evening in the orangery."

"Rosa. How is she?"

"Doing OK, considering. I don't know if you know Joe died?"

"I heard. Three years ago, wasn't it? She must have been devastated."

Didi nodded. "Layla too. It was awful. How did you hear about it? Has someone been keeping you up-to-date with what's been happening in Elliscombe?"

"No. There's this thing called the internet… It's easy enough to find out what goes on."

"You aren't on social media."

"Aren't I?" There it was again, the faint smile signaling his one-upmanship, because now he knew she'd been searching for information about him.

"Well, Layla spotted you earlier in the high street," Didi said. "If you're around the hotel this evening, I'm sure they'd love to see you."

But he was already shaking his head. "Thanks, but I'll leave it for now. Will your father be there?"

"Yes." *Would that be an issue?*

"Let Rosa have her birthday party in peace. I'm sure I'll bump into her at some stage. You have fun."

Didi couldn't help herself; she took a deep breath. "How long are you back for?"

Shay studied her in silence for a couple of seconds, and she felt a surge of adrenaline whoosh through her veins. Finally, he said, "I don't know, haven't decided yet. There are things that need to be sorted out."

chapter 3

There had to be more dignified ways of concluding your fifty-fifth birthday celebrations, but sometimes the call was just too great to ignore. Having changed out of the yellow sundress she'd worn for the party into a long-sleeved black T-shirt, jeans, and ballet flats, Rosa Gallagher left her cottage for the second time that evening and made her way along Barley Lane. It was midnight and pretty quiet by now, but she kept to the shadows just in case, turning left, then right, until she reached the high wall she'd become so well acquainted with over the course of the last two years.

There on the other side of the Cotswold stone was the garden she'd known for far longer than that, and beyond it in the darkness, Compton House, her old home, the place she'd loved with all her heart, almost as much as she'd loved Joe.

Pausing on the sidewalk, she waited for the all-too-familiar wave of sadness to pass while mentally gathering herself for the climb. She knew the footholds by now, but there was always that tricky bit over to the left where it was perilously easy to lose your footing.

OK, coast's clear. Over we go.

Up she went, pausing at the top to double-check that all was quiet before swinging both legs over and launching herself into the garden she wasn't permitted to enter. The trick was to land like a cat, silently and gracefully, and not break an ankle or jar her knees. So far, she'd managed this, but she was aware that at her age, it was increasingly likely to happen. Either that or the Colettes might one day surprise her by acquiring a ferocious, snarling guard dog.

Sliding with practiced ease behind the garden shed and through the shrubbery, Rosa finally reached Joe's tree and gave the trunk a hug. Yes, she knew anyone witnessing this would think she'd lost her marbles, but there was no one to see her, so sod them. Who cared? It wasn't remotely like hugging Joe, but it still felt like the right thing to do. She'd scattered his ashes around the base of the trunk, and that night it had rained hard, which meant that they had sunk into the earth and been absorbed by the roots of the Japanese maple. In her mind, the essence of Joe was now instilled in the tree he'd planted over twenty years earlier, and being here, touching the branches and the leaves, felt like being close to him.

She seated herself cross-legged on the dry grass and whispered, "Hi, darling, I'm here. How're you doing?"

Joe didn't reply, of course; he never did. But she felt better just being here, could feel herself relaxing in his imagined presence, and that was good enough. Stroking the rough bark of the tree trunk, Rosa said, "I'm fifty-five, can you believe it? You always used to be older than me, and now I've overtaken you. It feels so strange."

In her mind, she pictured Joe's eyes crinkling at the corners as he replied, "*So does that mean I'm your boy toy now?*" Because this was exactly the kind of thing he would have said if he were able to say it.

"Oh, Joe, is it ever going to get easier? Because I still miss you as much as I ever did. I miss you *so much*."

Rosa knew that a lot of people wondered why she would, considering the unholy mess he'd left her in, but there was no way in the world she could have stopped loving him even after the whole sorry story had come spilling out. She'd been lucky enough to spend a quarter of a century with the absolute love of her life, and that was a damn sight more than most people could say. Meeting Joe Gallagher when she was twenty-four had felt like all her Christmas wishes come true. He'd been a dynamic character who embodied the meaning of the word *entrepreneur*, a cockney chancer unafraid to take a risk, leaping from one start-up business to the next, endlessly striving for more and often getting it. A string of serendipitous deals had followed their first weeks together, and Joe had declared her his lucky charm. Two months later, she'd been stunned to discover she was pregnant and petrified that Joe would be appalled and instantly take off. But he hadn't. He'd been over the moon, and a hasty courthouse wedding had been arranged to appease her parents, who'd nevertheless pursed their lips and sourly predicted that the marriage wouldn't last.

But it had, gloriously and in thrilling, uproarious fashion. Growing up in a silent house, Rosa had always dreamt of meeting the kind of man who'd dance with her in the kitchen, and in Joe, she'd found him. He worked and played hard, they danced often, all over their little flat in Bermondsey, and when she gave birth to Layla, their happiness knew no bounds.

Life continued to be perfect, Joe's various businesses boomed, and they moved out of London in order to give Layla the kind of semirural upbringing Joe had always planned for his family. Compton House had been owned for decades by an ancient widower who didn't believe in modern conveniences, and they'd lived in chaos for eighteen months while the property was repaired and renovated around them. The four-story Georgian villa faced onto the market square, and at the back, there was a long garden that Joe had restored himself, planting new trees and nurturing rare plants. Extroverted and endlessly hospitable, he threw huge parties and invited an eclectic mix of friends from London and everyone he liked the look of in Elliscombe. As newcomers, they were nouveau riche and a bit flashy, which meant some locals had been dubious at first, but it hadn't taken long for Joe and his irresistible charm to win them over.

It was so easy to conjure up the happy memories, here in their old garden. Rosa ran the flat of her hand over the grass beside her; as well as Joe's ashes, it covered the graves of a dozen or so of their beloved pets, sadly lost over the years. Albie the Cairn terrier, Jennifer the nervous whippet, Beano and Biggie the cats, as well as various rabbits and guinea pigs belonging to Layla and a tame magpie called Gerald who'd met a sticky end thanks to the combined stalking skills of Beano and Biggie and whom Layla had insisted be buried with honors because they couldn't just put him in the trash; magpies deserved proper funerals too.

Smiling now, Rosa recalled the burial service. Layla, aged seven at the time, had made them gather around the grave and sing "All Things Bright and Beautiful" before reading aloud a poem she'd composed herself that went:

Gerald, you were my favorite magpie
How I loved the way you looked at me with your beady eye
I really hope you didn't cry
When Beano and Biggie catched you and made you die.

Rosa hadn't dared to glance across at Joe, who'd been standing next to her with his hands clasped before him, his lips pressed tight together as silent tears of mirth rolled down his cheeks. Layla had finished the poem with a reverent "Rest in peace, Gerald. Amen." Then she'd turned to look at her father and said consolingly, "Daddy, don't cry. He's in heaven now."

Oh goodness, such memories. Rosa found herself having to squeeze her own eyes shut; she mustn't cry either. Today had been a good day; the little party this evening at the hotel had been lovely, and so many kind people had given her flowers that she'd had to borrow two extra vases from her neighbor. There'd barely been enough room for them all in the cottage.

Click.

The familiar sound of the lock being unfastened was followed by the metallic swish of the french doors as they were pulled open. At the bottom of the garden, twenty-odd meters away, Rosa held her breath and fought the primal urge to make a run for it. That would be the worst thing she could do. Far better to stay put and pray they weren't coming outside because they'd already spotted her.

She heard the staccato click of high heels on the flagstone terrace and winced; high heels meant it was Ingrid, and Ingrid was scary. There was also the sound of her murmuring into her cell phone, probably busy conducting some vital business deal with a client in Tokyo or New York while simultaneously—

"*Bleurgh*," Rosa squeaked, kicking out wildly as something small scurried over her foot.

"Hang on. I just heard a noise. Not burglars, I hope." Ingrid wasn't sounding terrified, and the sound of her stilettos was growing closer. Frozen to the spot, Rosa closed her eyes and pretended to be invisible.

From fifteen meters away, she heard the footsteps stop and Ingrid say, "No, probably just a fox or something. Maybe a badger. I keep telling Benny we should install security lights, but it hasn't happened, of course, because he doesn't want to scare the wildlife."

Rosa knew the snuffly, grunty kind of sound a badger made. If she imitated one, would it encourage Ingrid to hurry back into the house? Or come closer in order to investigate and maybe take a few photos of the creature in her garden? Torn by indecision, she heard another tiny rustling noise and realized that the mouse or vole or whatever it was that had run over her foot was still in the vicinity.

"OK, I'm going inside now. Call me tomorrow after eight thirty. If I don't answer, it's because I'm in the car. I love you. Yes, bye…bye…"

The clicky footsteps receded, the french doors swished open and shut, and the key was turned in the lock. Rosa exhaled with relief; phew, that had been close.

"Right, I'd better be off. You're going to get me into such trouble one day." She whispered the words to Joe as she patted the dry grass, then rose cautiously to her feet. Creeping across the lawn and through the shrubbery, she made her way back to the familiar stretch of wall shielded from the house by the trees.

Up, up, and over, then down onto the sidewalk on the other side without snapping an ankle. There, done.

"Bye, sweetheart. Love you." She was aware that this sounded ridiculous, but once you got into the habit of blowing a kiss and saying it, it was kind of hard to stop. In the darkness, she headed back toward Frog Cottage on Barley Lane.

It might not have been the best ever birthday, obviously, but overall, it hadn't been the worst either. Each year of widowhood was slightly easier to bear than the last, and she made sure to count her blessings. Yes, she'd lost Joe, their beautiful home, and all their money, but she had her health and her friends, and of course her daughter. Among the inner loneliness, there were still pockets of happiness to be found.

chapter 4

From her bedroom window at the back of the hotel, Didi had a clear view over the patio. It was two in the morning, but she could just about make out someone sitting at one of the wooden tables and knew instinctively who it was.

Since she couldn't sleep either, she threw on a cotton jersey dress and made her way down there.

Letting herself out onto the patio, she approached Shay. "I saw someone down here, didn't know who it was."

The glint in his eye told her that he suspected otherwise, but he raised his glass and said, "I helped myself to a brandy. It's OK. I left a note in the honesty box."

Another tiny dig.

"Please don't keep saying things like that," Didi murmured. "Are you OK?"

"Me? I'm fine."

The thing was, she might not have seen him for the last thirteen years, but before that, she'd known him so well. Plus, there'd been that barely detectable emphasis on *I'm*.

"But someone else isn't."

He dipped his head in agreement.

"Is it your dad?"

"Well done on those mind-reading classes."

"He's in big trouble?"

"Yes, but not in the way you mean." His tone was even. "For once."

"Is he ill?" said Didi.

"He is. And it's not good."

"Oh no, I'm so sorry." Shay's father, known to all as Red, had been a nightmare in many ways, but she'd always had a soft spot for him as a person, such was the power of his charm. He'd been the ultimate lovable rogue.

"The doctors have given him one to two years."

She winced in sympathy. How old must he be? Late fifties? It was too young to die. Didi said, "That's awful. And where is he now?"

"Not in jail, if that's what you mean. He's put all that behind him now, doesn't have the energy for it anymore. He's been living with a lady friend up in Edinburgh for the last ten months, but it sounds like that's not going well."

This was par for the course. As long as Didi had known Shay's father, he had spent time in and out of prison, and there had always been plenty of women eager for his company. When he'd moved away from Elliscombe seven years ago, he'd rented his house out to friends of friends, and it had made sense to assume that since then, he'd been spending his free time at the home of the current woman in his life.

"He's pretty weak nowadays, not able to do a great deal." Shay waved away a large moth that was fluttering in front of him. After a pause, he said, "He wants to come home. Spend whatever time he has left here in Elliscombe. In his house."

The white solar lights strung through the branches of the trees were still glowing like stars. Didi's eyes had grown accustomed to the darkness, and she could see his features more clearly now. "So that's why you're back, to get the place ready for him?"

He raised an eyebrow. "Have you seen the state of it lately?"

Of course she had. Hillcrest, the Masons' old family home, was situated on the outskirts of the town, on the road to Moreton-in-Marsh, which meant it was hard to miss. "The garden's a bit…overgrown."

"It's a jungle." Shay's tone was curt. "And if you think it looks bad from the outside, you should see what it's like on the inside. Absolute carnage."

"There was a bunch of people living there, about ten of them." Didi wrinkled her nose. "They looked a bit…"

"That's because they were squatters. Any other property owner would use a leasing agency. But not Dad. Oh, no, that wasn't his way. All he wanted was tenants who would pay rent each month via his mate Baz. But when they left and Baz went to Spain, the squatters moved in. He's only just told me about this, by the way. I had no idea about any of it."

"And no one knew where your dad was. If they had, they'd have told him what was going on. The squatters left a few months ago."

"It's in a hell of a state. I mean, I know it was hardly a palace before, but now…" Shay grimaced. "I thought I was coming here to give the place a quick tidying up, maybe mow the lawn and put the vacuum around. I called Dad this afternoon to tell him what's happened, and that was when the story came out. Then he asked me if I'd stay and sort it out."

Didi said, "No wonder you can't get to sleep. What did you say? Are you going to?"

He looked at her. "I told him it'd take months. Easier to put the place up for auction and find somewhere else for him to live."

"So is that what's happening?"

"You'd think it would make the most sense, wouldn't you? But he doesn't want to do that. The only place he wants to live is in the house where we grew up together as a family."

"People do that, though, don't they? Go back to their roots because that's where their memories are." Didi nodded; she could understand the longing to return. She watched Shay's gaze follow the silhouette of the rooftops against the sky. "Does it feel strange, being here again?"

"Strange and familiar at the same time." He indicated the hotel in front of them. "This place smells exactly the same as it always did."

She nodded. "I know. Woodsmoke, old stone, beeswax polish, and fresh laundry. It's my favorite smell in the world."

"I'm going to have another drink. Can I get you one?" Shay emptied his tumbler and rose to his feet.

"I'll have a red wine. Thanks."

Waiting for him to return, Didi stretched her legs out in front of her and studied the stars overhead. Beneath her clasped hands resting on her rib cage, she could feel her heart thudding slightly faster than usual. Why had she come down here? Professional concern for a guest at the hotel? Or was she bursting with curiosity, longing to learn more about Shay and the man he'd become? She already knew the answer to that. It was an unnerving sensation, being thirty and feeling like an eighteen-year-old again.

Through the open side door, she heard the clink of a bottle, followed by the discreet sound of the lid being opened and closed on the wooden honesty box. When he returned, Shay leaned over her shoulder to place her glass of Montepulciano on the table.

"This might sound weird," he said, "but you smell just the same too."

Her stomach flipped, but she said lightly, "Am I supposed to say thank you for that?"

He smiled. "I'm talking about in a good way. Just saying, if I were blindfolded in a crowded room, I'd still recognize you."

Didi took a sip of wine, then a bigger sip to give herself a moment to calm down. "I can't believe you haven't been back before now."

"It was easier to stay away."

"Where did you go?"

"Did you ever ask my dad?"

"Yes! He wouldn't tell me."

"Amazing. He said he hadn't, but I never really knew for sure. I went to Australia."

"Australia!" She'd imagined a lot of destinations but never that one.

"I applied for a working holiday visa. Worked in Melbourne for six months, then Sydney for another six. When I came back to the UK, I took jobs in construction around the country."

"Construction." Didi digested this. Out of everyone in their year at school, he'd ended up with the best A-level grades and had received unconditional offers from three of the top universities in the country.

Shay shrugged. "Nothing wrong with that. It taught me a lot. I also set up an IT consultancy in my spare time, which did well. I moved to London and carried on with that for a few years, building up the business. Then I developed an idea for a dating app, which took off."

A new surprise at every turn; she'd definitely never imagined him doing anything like that. "But I searched for you online...*really* searched. And you aren't *anywhere*."

He nodded patiently. "You searched for Shay Mason. And what did you find?"

"Just loads of results in local newspapers about your dad getting arrested, going to court, going to prison again. But it was always him, never you." Shay's ancestors might have left Ireland a century ago, but the name had been faithfully passed down through the generations.

"And any potential business clients looking me up would have found exactly the same thing. So call me a pessimist, but I did feel it might put them off the idea of dealing with me. Can you remember my middle name?"

What a stupid question. She'd spent months silently saying his full name to herself, doodling it in the margins of exercise books and on notepads. "Stefan." At the risk of sounding like a complete stalker, she said, "I looked up Stefan Mason too."

"I changed it to Steven. Kept it simple."

Didi nodded. "OK. So do we call you Steven now?"

"No need. Shay's fine."

She had to know. "Did you ever look me up?"

Another glimmer of a smile. "I looked up this hotel. And there you were."

Didi spread her hands, *ta-daaa.* "Here I am."

"Looking good."

Only good? Not great? Or incredible?

"Thanks." She took a drink. "I still can't believe you started a dating app. Do you use it yourself?"

Shay shook his head. "No."

"But it's going well?"

"Yes."

"What's it called?"

"Fait."

"You're *kidding.*" A small electric shock zapped down her spine. Fait was an app everyone knew. It was an app she'd used herself. It worked on the premise that although looks were obviously important when you wanted to meet someone new, how they sounded played a significant part too, so along with submitting a photo, users were invited to upload a ten-second audio file of their voice. If another subscriber then liked what they'd seen and heard, they shared their interest with you.

"I was on Fait for a while, a couple of years ago," she said.

"Were you?" His innocent eyebrows made her wonder if he'd already been aware of this. "And how did that work out for you?"

"OK. I mean, I didn't meet the love of my life, but I met a couple of nice guys. Hang on though. Didn't I see something recently about it being taken over by You-Me?"

"You did. I sold the company to them. The deal went through a fortnight ago."

You-Me was the biggest dating app on the planet. Didi took another gulp of red wine as what Shay was telling her began to sink in.

"So did they pay you…a fair amount?"

The laughter in his eyes was the same as it ever was. "I think we can safely call it a fair amount."

Blimey.

"Could you buy this hotel outright if you wanted to?"

"I could."

"How does that feel?"

"Feels great," said Shay.

It must. She felt compelled to say it. "Mum and Dad never really thought you had anything to do with what happened."

He looked skeptical. "I don't think that's quite true, is it?"

"It is!"

"They were never completely sure. There was always that niggle of doubt. Be honest."

"But they liked you. They *employed* you."

"That's what your father told me when he called me into his office." Shay paused. "Then he said, 'And now this happens.'"

Oh God. Didi winced at the implied betrayal of trust; she

remembered that terrible afternoon as clearly as if it had happened yesterday. Obviously he did too. "I'm sorry."

"And if you're honest," Shay went on, "you'll admit that a tiny part of you wondered if I was lying to cover myself too."

She wouldn't admit it. Then again, there was no need to.

They both knew it was true.

"Right." Having made his point, Shay rose to his feet and raised his hand in farewell. "I'm off to bed."

She'd thought they'd been sharing a friendly catch-up chat, whereas in reality, Didi realized, he'd been teaching her a lesson for ever having doubted him.

Well, in all honesty, you couldn't blame him. Revenge was sweet. And who could resist it, being in his position now?

I'm Shay Mason, I'm back, and I'm richer than any of you. And don't go thinking I've forgotten what you thought of me because I haven't, and I never will.

chapter 5

Benny Colette had just surreptitiously made himself a mug of instant coffee in the large silver-and-marble kitchen of Compton House when Bill the gardener tapped on the side door and let himself in.

"I was shifting a load of earth and almost ran this over with my wheelbarrow." He held up a fine silver bracelet studded with charms. "Just managed to spot it in time. Your wife's, I'm guessing. She'll be pleased to have it back."

Benny took the bracelet from him; it was a pretty thing, the charms catching the light as they swung from the narrow chain. It was also the kind of jewelry that Ingrid wouldn't be seen dead wearing.

"What's this?" High heels came clicking across the marble floor, and Ingrid appeared behind him. "Eww, tacky. Not mine. Where did you find it?"

"Just at the edge of the lawn, by the flower bed against the south wall." Bill looked disappointed; clearly he'd been hoping for cries of gratitude and relief, maybe even a finder's fee. "Next to the lupins and hollyhocks."

She grimaced. "Well, it's cheap. I expect someone was so horrified at having been given such an awful bracelet that she threw it over the wall into our garden to get rid of it."

"It might belong to Birgitte," said Benny. "Or one of her friends." He turned apologetically to Bill. "Thanks for bringing it in anyway."

"Hot out there. Finished my water," said Bill. "Could I refill my bottle?"

"Let me do it for you." Ingrid's glance had taken in the state of his work boots. "We don't want mess all over the kitchen floor, do we, like last time? Oh, Benny, not again." Her eagle eye had landed on the jar of Nescafé he hadn't had time to put away. "The Gaggia's right *here*." She was pointing at the complicated machine that hissed and snorted like a dragon before finally conceding the world's tiniest dribble of espresso.

"I prefer instant," said Benny for possibly the thousandth time. He couldn't be bothered faffing about with those beans.

....

"Come on, come on, where *are* you?" Fragments of feathers flew up into the air as Rosa energetically stripped the bed, whipping off first the pillowcases, then the duvet cover and checking every last corner. She'd already searched the rest of the cottage, retraced her steps from last night's party at the hotel, and checked with Sylvia at reception that the bracelet hadn't been found and handed in.

This meant it had either fallen off while she'd been visiting Joe last night and was now lying in the garden of Compton House, or it was gone forever.

Which in turn meant she was going to have to either find or replace it before Layla discovered that the lovely, thoughtful birthday present she'd chosen for her mother had lasted twelve whole hours on her wrist before getting lost.

No, no, it couldn't happen again, not after last year and the debacle with the turquoise pendant.

An hour later, by a great stroke of luck, as Rosa was leaving the corner shop with a new jar of coffee, she saw Benny and Ingrid go past in their gleaming gray Mercedes, heading away from Compton House and out of town.

For once, fate was on her side. Seizing the moment and hurrying back along the high street, she reached the side of the property within minutes. She was forced to linger on the sidewalk, pretending to be busy on her phone, but at last the coast was clear. She stuffed the jar of Gold Blend down the front of her T-shirt and clambered like lightning up and over the wall before dropping down to the other side. Oof, the glass was cold against her skin; she retrieved the jar and placed it on the grass, then spent five minutes methodically searching the flower bed, the lawn, and the area around the base of Joe's beloved Japanese maple.

But no, fate had had enough and abandoned her. There was no sign anywhere of the charm bracelet. Of course there wasn't; that would be too easy, wouldn't it? Having given the grass one last sweeping search, she made her way back to the wall, double-checked that the coast was clear, then climbed back over and headed for home.

It wasn't until she went to switch on the kettle in the tiny blue-and-white kitchen that she realized she'd left the unopened jar of coffee on the lawn of Compton House.

OK, she definitely couldn't risk going back again to collect a jar of Gold Blend, even if it had just cost her four pounds thirty.

Karma's way of telling her she should have settled for a cup of tea in the first place.

....

Shay had left Elliscombe early to drive up to Birmingham airport, and by 10:30, he was waiting at Arrivals. He watched as a small boy of maybe three or four broke free from his mother and came hurtling through the gate, throwing himself into his father's arms with a whoop of delight.

He wondered if he himself had ever done that. He must have, surely? He loved his own father and had happy childhood memories of playing in the garden, being driven in the car with all the windows down, wild games of hide-and-seek around the house. He remembered being taken by his mum to visit his dad in prison on several occasions but knew there hadn't been any throwing himself into his arms allowed there. He also remembered his mum first becoming ill and feeling the need to pretend to everyone that he was fine, convincing himself that everything would be OK and there was nothing to worry about.

Well, he'd been wrong about that, but during the years of her worsening illness, he'd been able to mentally prepare himself for the inevitable and had also learned how to cook and clean and generally become more capable than the average child. By the time his mum died when he was twelve, he'd felt more like an adult.

And his grieving dad, to his credit, had also made a concerted effort to step up and carry out his fatherly duties. For almost eighteen months, possibly more by luck than judgment, he'd managed to stay out of trouble before inevitably giving in to the temptation to make some easy money and getting caught offloading a truckload of fake designer leather jackets for a fake friend.

This was when Shay had really needed to learn how to think on his feet and take care of himself. Having persuaded a local family to reassure the authorities that he'd be living with them, he had returned to his own home and looked after himself. It had become a matter of pride to make a good job of this and not let the side down. On the first occasion, eking out the money from the tin kept under the floorboards, he'd eaten mainly burgers, instant ramen, oven fries, and toast. After that, chiefly out of sheer boredom, he'd begun to cook properly, as his mum had taught him. He'd also honed his skills at fixing and mending things around the house while also taking care of the cats and still maintaining excellent grades at school. The tin under the floorboards probably contained stolen money, which wasn't ideal, obviously, but what alternative had there been? Shay had reminded himself that as soon as he was allowed to work, he'd be earning his own money, but until that time came, he'd just do what he had to do in order to get by.

And now a girl in her twenties was rushing toward him with her arms outstretched, shouting, "Yay, you're here!" Still lost in his memories, it took Shay a moment to realize she wasn't coming for him. He took a step to one side as she swerved past him and began enthusiastically kissing her boyfriend.

Enthusiastically and noisily. As he moved farther away to escape the assault on his ears, he spotted a familiar figure emerging from the corridor, held up behind a family of vacationers battling with oversized cases.

"Dad." It was finally Shay's turn to embrace his father, and he was glad of the excuse to hide the shock on his face. Red had always been a fine figure of a man, glowing with health, tall and rangy, with glittering dark eyes and a killer smile. Now, in the few weeks since Shay had last seen him, he was visibly thinner and moved more slowly, and there were violet shadows beneath his eyes, more lines creasing his once-handsome face.

"Good to see you, boy." Red held Shay at arm's length and broke into that old familiar smile. "Where's the car?"

"Close by, don't worry. Not far to walk."

"Let's get out of here then, shall we? Before those sniffer dogs figure out what I've just smuggled through customs."

"Don't try and give me a heart attack." Shay grinned; those days were hopefully long behind his father now. "If you're caught with something you shouldn't be carrying, you're on your own."

Red gave him a reassuring pat on the shoulder. "So how does it feel being back in Elliscombe?"

"Pretty strange. Dad, the house is a mess."

"I know. You already told me. Where are you staying?"

"At the Wickham."

"Are you, now? Well, well. Very fancy."

"They're fully booked, but if you want to stay over, you can share my suite. There's an extra bed."

"And have them frisking me every time I try to leave the building? No thanks. Anyway, I'm heading back this evening." As they made their way to the short-stay parking lot, Red added, "Have you seen her yet?"

"Who?" As if Shay didn't know.

"Come on. Doesn't she run the place these days?"

"Has anyone ever called you a nosy old man?"

His father's bark of laughter turned into a cough. "I've been called a lot worse than that in my life, I can tell you. Is that a real Cartier watch or a copy?"

"The fact that you can't tell the difference," Shay said with affection, "is the reason you spent so much time in jail."

An hour later, they were in Elliscombe. As they drove along the high street, Red nodded at the Wickham. "What was it like, then? Seeing her again?"

"Can you give the inquisition a miss?"

"I always liked that girl. You did too."

"That was thirteen years ago. We're all different people now."

"Still the same deep down."

What was his father playing at? Shay took the turn that would lead them to their old home and said firmly, "She's getting married."

Red raised his eyebrows. "And? You could do something about that."

Shay looked at him. "Why would I want to?"

"Fine, I get it." Red mimed zipping his mouth shut.

Minutes later, they reached their destination.

"Bloody hell, you weren't kidding."

Shay helped him out of the passenger seat. "It's worse than it looks."

His father insisted on the full tour. The out-of-control garden was fixable, but the terrible state of the inside of the house indicated the need for more extensive repairs. There was black mold on the walls and ceilings, rising damp everywhere, rotten window frames, broken doors, boarded-up windows, and missing floorboards. Ivy was growing in the kitchen; there were scorch marks on the interior walls and flood stains on the ceilings and floors. What remained of the furniture was no longer fit for purpose. In the main bedroom, a grubby mattress covered in cigarette burns occupied the floor. Someone had spray-painted *PEACE AND LOVE* on one wall, and someone else—presumably—had scrawled *FUCK THE WORLD* in even bigger letters beneath it.

"If I could get my hands on the bastards who did this…" Red shook his head in disgust. "What possessed them? It's *my* house, not theirs."

Shay didn't comment on the double standards his father was blithely employing. "I did warn you. It's all fixable, but it's going to take time. Look, I called into the real estate agent's yesterday, had a quick chat. Why don't we head back there now so you can see what's on their books? If moving back here is what you want to do, it'd be a lot easier to buy or rent somewhere else."

"*Easier*," his father mimicked.

"Quicker too. There's a fantastic house on Comer Street, newly renovated, everything you could ask for. Walls, roof, electricity supply, the whole lot. There's no conditions involved; you could be in there by the end of the month."

"And that's what you think I should go for?"

"Dad, it's up to you. I'll go along with whatever you decide. I was just thinking of...you know, the time factor."

"You mean if it takes six months to get this place sorted, it's going to be bloody annoying if I kick the bucket the day before I'm meant to move in?"

His father was treating the awfulness of his situation with characteristic flippancy and humor. Following suit, Shay said, "It wouldn't be that annoying. I'd just put it straight on the market."

Red's laughter turned into another bout of coughing, followed by the need to lean against a peeling wall to catch his breath.

"Come on," said Shay. "Let's get out of here and find ourselves some lunch."

"I'm not hungry."

"You need to eat."

"I'd rather have a drink."

"Dad..."

"Don't look at me like that." Red was unrepentant. "Right now, the healthiest part of my body is my liver. I reckon it deserves a reward for good behavior, don't you?"

Emerging from the post office, Didi was so busy waving at Rosa waiting at the bus stop that she had no idea who was to the left of her until she turned and ran into them.

"Oof, sorry! *Oh.*" She ricocheted off Shay's chest, which was simultaneously a bit of a thrill but also mortifying because what if he thought she'd done it on purpose?

"Here she is, then. Good to see you again! And looking so well. Come here, girl." Next to his son, Red Mason stepped forward and enveloped her in a hug, and Didi found herself having to hold him for an extra couple of seconds to give herself time to conceal her shock because he was so changed.

"It's OK," he said. "You don't have to tell me I look well. That'd be stretching credibility too far."

Her heart melted; he was still the same character on the inside, as self-deprecating and quick-witted as ever. "It's lovely to see you. Shay tells me you're thinking of moving back."

"We've just been in to see Maurice Welsh." Red indicated the real estate agency behind him, then the sheaf of papers in his hand. "Picked up a load of property details."

"Oh!" Didi was surprised. "I thought you had your heart set on your own house."

He looked regretful. "I did, but my boy's not so keen. Reckons it's too much hard work."

"I didn't say it was too much. I'm just thinking about how long it would take," said Shay, evidently not for the first time.

Diplomatically, Didi nodded at the details in Red's hand. "Any that look promising? There's a sweet little place on Windsor Street that's had a For Sale sign go up this week."

"We're just heading over to the Prince for a drink." Red's tone was genial. "If that boss of yours lets you have a lunch break, fancy joining us?"

"Dad's retired now. I'm the boss," said Didi.

He winked at her. "I know. Shay told me. So how about it? Can you give yourself twenty minutes off? My round."

"Go on, then. Just the one. Let me run back and tell Sylvia where I've got to."

Red was peering across the high street. "Is that Rosa Gallagher over there? What on earth's she doing waiting at the bus stop?"

"Yes, it's Rosa. Joe died three years ago," said Didi.

"Shay told me that too. Bloody old people." Red shook his head. "Falling ill and dropping dead all over the damn place, it's downright depressing. But I still don't understand what Rosa's doing catching a bus."

By the time Didi caught up with Shay and Red, they were seated in an alcove in the main bar of the Prince of Wales. The table was littered with details of potential properties, and the manager of the pub had just brought them a bottle of prosecco in an ice bucket, together with three glasses.

"Never used to drink this stuff, but I've begun to get a taste for it recently." Red clinked his glass against theirs. "Any excuse to celebrate, eh?"

"Absolutely." Didi took a sip, aware of how close her elbow was to Shay's.

"And congratulations."

"What, on running the hotel? Oh, it's brilliant. I love it."

"Well actually, I meant the engagement. Quite a rock you've got there." Red reached for her left hand. "Who's the lucky chap? He's got good taste in diamonds, I'll say that for him."

Last night, Shay had steered clear of the subject. To conceal the fact that she was feeling suddenly self-conscious, Didi said, "He's brilliant too. His name's Aaron, and he has good taste in girlfriends as well."

Red laughed. "Touché! Of course he does. I wouldn't expect anything less. So how did you two get together?"

"It was the Christmas before last. He came along to a wine-tasting event that was being held at the hotel, and we got chatting. Then he asked me out. That was it really."

"Romantic," said Shay.

"It *was* romantic actually." She bristled.

"Ah, don't tease her. You never know how these things are going to happen. But they always do, don't they? Sooner or later." Red gave Shay a nudge. "Have you told Didi how you met that last girlfriend of yours?"

Shay said steadily, "No, I haven't."

Red took a swallow of prosecco, then leaned toward Didi. "He was in a hurry at the bank so he asked if he could go ahead of her in the queue. And she said he couldn't because she was in a hurry too. Which annoyed him, obviously. Then when he left the bank, there she was, waiting outside for him, and she asked him out on a date. And he said yes."

"Wow." The sarcasm in her voice might be barely detectable, but she made sure it was there. She raised her eyebrows at Shay. "That's wildly romantic."

"What can I say?" He shrugged. "Real life isn't always a Richard Curtis movie."

Red was unperturbed. "How long were you and Rebecca together? Was it three months? I can't remember now why you broke up. Was it because she was obsessed with sudoku?"

"Dad, can we change the subject?"

"Oh, I've got it now. You finished with her because she was obsessed with spreadsheets, that was it."

In defense of both Shay's ex-girlfriend and being properly organized, Didi said, "Nothing wrong with a good spreadsheet."

Watching her, Red's eyes were bright above the violet shadows beneath them. Then he reached for the slew of property details. "OK, let's take a look at these. Didi, you can give me your expert opinion. I wouldn't trust that slimy bastard Maurice Welsh further than I could throw him."

Which, when you compared the size of Maurice with Red's current frailty, wouldn't be far at all.

Twenty minutes later, she pushed back her chair. "I need to get back. Definitely have a look at the bungalow on Bray Hill and the cottage behind the garden center. Don't bother with this one." She pointed to the house Shay had liked the look of. "The family who've moved in next door are causing all sorts of trouble on Comer Street, and the last thing you need is nightmare neighbors."

"If anyone's going to be the nightmare around here," Red told her as she gave him a goodbye hug, "I'd rather it was me."

....

It wasn't how Rosa had planned to spend her day, but these things happened. At lunchtime, she'd caught the bus to Cheltenham, a slow, meandering journey that had taken an hour and a quarter. Then she had made her way to the independent jewelry shop where Layla had bought the bracelet. Having selected the thin silver chain and begun picking out the charms Layla had chosen, it wasn't long before the woman serving her said, "That's a coincidence. Someone went for those exact same ones last week!"

"It was my daughter." Rosa wondered if a bit of a discount could be in the cards. "All the charms have special meanings for us, you see. She gave me the bracelet last night for my birthday, and I loved it, obviously, but by this morning, it was gone. I think the clasp might have been faulty."

"Oh no, definitely not. We don't have faulty clasps." The woman shook her head so vigorously her chins wobbled. "We've never had a faulty clasp; you just didn't fasten it properly."

So much for hoping for a discount. Rosa had been forced to bite the bullet and pay almost two hundred pounds she couldn't afford for a new bracelet to replace the lost one. Which meant economizing in other areas to make up for it. Lots of toast, basically. And putting in extra hours on the orders for dolls, preferably those placed by customers who'd actually pay for them.

Anyway, never mind. At least Layla wouldn't find out she'd been careless enough to lose the bracelet within hours of putting it on. And the bus was now wending its way back home, returning her—poorer but wiser—to Elliscombe.

At long last, it drew to a halt at the bus stop on the market square, and Rosa queued behind an elderly couple to disembark. As she did so, she noticed that the impressive gates to Compton House were open, and Benny and Ingrid had just returned from wherever they'd been headed earlier. In the time it had taken her to travel to Cheltenham and back, they could have been to London…or Devon…anywhere, which just made you think how—

"*Oof.*" Missing her footing on the last step, she landed with a splat on the sidewalk and felt pain shoot like a knife through her knee.

"Clumsy," tutted the old woman in front of her. "You want to watch where you're going, you do."

The woman's husband huffed with irritation. "She almost landed on my foot."

Ow, ow, *oww*. Rosa's knee now felt as if it were on fire. Mortified and unable to get up, she clutched her leg.

"You OK?" called the bus driver.

Reassured that at least someone cared, she found herself summoning a bright, oh-so-British smile. "Fine, thanks. Absolutely fine!"

"That's all right, then." The bus driver released the brake and drove off, only narrowly missing her handbag, which was lying upturned in the gutter.

"Hello? Could you just get my bag for me?" Rosa called after the old couple, but they were trundling off along the sidewalk, grumbling to each other about people who didn't bother to look where they were going. Then she heard rapid footsteps approaching.

"I can't believe they just walked off and left you! Can you move? Or should I call an ambulance?"

"No need for an ambulance." Rosa shook her head at Benny Colette. "I'll be OK in a few minutes. But my bag might not be so lucky."

Crouching at the roadside, Benny lifted the upturned bag like a man, then cursed when half the contents flew out. Hastily, he collected together her purse, lipstick, phone, house keys, and the deep-blue gift-wrapped box from the jeweler's, stuffing them back inside. "There you go. I think that's everything. Let's get you up now, shall we?"

The irony of the situation didn't escape Rosa. Eighteen months of climbing over the high wall into Benny's garden without mishap, and now here she was having managed to wreck her knee slipping off one small step. Worse still, it had only happened because she'd been craning her neck in order to gawp at him and Ingrid, with their designer clothes, top-of-the-range car, and perfect lives.

"Benny, what are you *doing*?" Ingrid's crisp, Swedish-accented voice betrayed her impatience. "I need to get into the house, and you have the keys."

A middle-aged woman who'd seen Rosa's fall came bustling over waving a packet of tissues. "You poor thing. I can't stand the sight of blood, makes me come over all queasy! But you can have these if you need them… Oh no, there's some on your hand. I can't look…"

Rosa, who hated being the center of attention, took the proffered tissues, and the woman hurried off. Other people were now stopping to watch from a distance; this was like one of those dreams where everyone stared at you in the street and you suddenly realized you were naked.

"Benny, hurry *up*," Ingrid ordered as Benny, crouching awkwardly, attempted to haul Rosa upright.

Then another voice said, “Rosa, is that you? Anything I can do to help?”

Turning, Rosa summoned an embarrassed smile of recognition. “Hello, Shay. I heard you were back. Red, hi.” Goodness, he’d lost weight.

“*Benny*,” snapped Ingrid.

Between them, Shay and Benny helped Rosa to her feet. Putting weight on her knee elicited a small yelp of pain.

“It’s fine. I’ve got her now.” Shay’s arm was firmly around her waist.

“Are you sure?” Visibly relieved, Benny said, “Hope you feel better soon,” before hurrying back to Compton House.

“Who *are* they?” Clearly baffled, Red stared after him. “Do they work for you? Because if they do, you need to sack them. Bloody hell.”

“I don’t live there anymore. They do.” Rosa flushed. A gaggle of tourists were taking photos of her now, evidently delighted by the blood trickling down her shin. “Look, if you could help me over to that bench, I’ll just sit down and wait until the pain wears off…”

But Shay was already shaking his head. “Where are you living now? I’ll give you a lift. My car’s right here.”

Anything was better than being pointed at in the street. “Well, if you’re sure. That’d be really kind.”

chapter 6

"Frog Cottage. I can't believe you're here now." Red's eyes lit up as they drew up outside. "Fond memories of this place. Had a bit of a thing going with Julie at one time."

"To be fair," Shay pointed out, "you had a bit of a thing going with most of the women around here at some stage or other."

"Julie moved to Cape Town with her sister," Rosa explained. "I was lucky; there wasn't much I could afford, but this came onto the market just at the right time. Another couple were desperate to buy it but made the mistake of saying they'd have to repaint the living room. Well, Julie was furious and told them to take a hike. She knew how much I liked what she'd done, so she sold the cottage to me instead."

"So the mural's still there? I loved that mural. I'm in it," said Red.

"You are?" Rosa frowned; this was news to her.

"Don't believe me? Let me show you." Opening the car door, he carefully levered himself out.

"Oh, it's OK! Thanks for the lift, but..." Rosa winced as Shay helped her from the passenger seat.

"Don't trust me in the house, is that it? Worried I might make off with the family silver? It's all right. You're safe. I'm a law-abiding citizen these days. Can't run fast enough to make it worthwhile." Red paused. "That was a joke, by the way. I never did break into people's houses or nick stuff from anyone I knew."

"I know that." He'd been more of a smuggling-suitcases-filled-with-tobacco-through customs opportunist. Rosa leaned against Shay for support and found the keys in her bag. "And of course I trust you. Come on. Let's get inside." As an afterthought, she added, "I don't have anything worth taking anyway."

The hand-painted mural, covering one entire wall of the living room, had been Julie's pride and joy. Over a period of three weeks, she had recreated a quirky, colorful version of Elliscombe, complete with houses, gardens, shops, and inhabitants. Everyone she'd known had been featured, and most were recognizable.

Red surveyed the mural with satisfaction. "There it is. As beautiful as ever. She was one talented lady."

"I've worked out now where you are." Rosa leaned against the table to give her knee a rest. "I didn't know you and Julie had a fling. That's you, isn't it?" She pointed to the painted version of Frog Cottage, with its pretty garden, tiny pond complete with leaping frogs, and the shadowy figure of a visitor emerging from what had once been Julie's bedroom window and was now hers.

"You didn't know because we were discreet. And yes, there I am, making a hasty exit because her dad was on his way over. See, there he is." Red pointed to the police car rounding the bend in the lane, with Julie's father behind the wheel. "What with him being a cop, he wasn't too keen on me."

Shay said, "And who could blame him?"

Now that she knew who Julie's escaping visitor had been, Rosa could see the deliberately vague hint of a likeness. She indicated a detached house in another section of the mural, over on the road leading to Bourton-on-the-Water. "And look, you weren't the only one up to no good; there's someone else here, creeping out through the back garden gate… Oh!" She started to laugh when she saw the expression on Red's face.

"Yes." He looked rueful. "That was me too. Julie's way of letting me know she was aware of what I'd been getting up to while she was away."

Rosa sent up a prayer of thanks that Julie was no longer around to portray the town's ongoing secrets; imagine if she were to find herself immortalized in the mural, guiltily skulking in the farthest corner of the garden of Compton House.

With Shay's assistance, she settled down in her red velvet armchair next to the fireplace. She carefully flexed her knee, then cleaned away the dried blood with warm water and tissues. The swelling wasn't too bad and the pain was beginning to ease. With a bit of luck and a pressure bandage, she'd soon be on the mend.

"Anyway, enough of my shady past." Red's attention had been drawn to the items on the dining table over by the window. "What's all this about? Sorry…"

When he'd stopped coughing, Rosa said, "If you don't need to rush off, why don't you sit down? I can make us a pot of tea."

"Hey, you two invalids stay where you are." Shay put out a hand to stop her before she could haul herself upright once more. "I can make the tea."

He disappeared into the tiny kitchen. Red collected two of the dolls from the table and carried them over with him before taking the blue armchair opposite her. "Did you make these?"

"I did. I do."

"And people buy them?"

She smiled. "That's the general idea, what with having to earn a living and pay the bills."

"I was so sorry to hear about Joe. He was a great guy."

Rosa nodded, glancing down at the wedding ring she hadn't yet felt able to take off. The emptiness never lessened; she missed Joe as much as ever, but as time passed, she had grown more proficient at navigating the void. "He really was. I was so lucky."

"I haven't heard what happened"—Red's tone was sympathetic—"but it can't have been easy, having to move out of that big house."

Compared with having to carry on living without the man she'd loved with all her heart, moving out of Compton House and into Frog Cottage hadn't been hard at all. But the practically overnight reversal of fortune had obviously not been ideal. It wouldn't be at the top of any newly bereaved widow's wish list.

"I'm getting used to it." Not feeling up to the full explanation, Rosa simply shrugged. "But yes, the reason I started the doll thing was to try and make some money. A friend of mine had a granddaughter with a port-wine birthmark on her face and neck, and she asked why none of her dolls looked like her, so I made one that did. And she loved it. That was what gave me the idea to set up a website so people could request dolls to be customized with the exact features they asked for."

She pointed to the boy doll with spiky blond hair and glasses and an above-the-left-knee amputation. Wearing a stripy blue-and-white top with red shorts, he had freckles and a lopsided grin. "This one's for a four-year-old named Robbie who lives in New Zealand and lost his leg in an accident. And the other doll is for a little girl named Jade who lives in London. She has vitiligo, and her mum sent me a photo so I could get the patterns of depigmentation to exactly match the ones on her face and body."

Red marveled at the detail on the dolls. "They're brilliant."

"It's a lovely thing to be able to do. I often get sent photos of the children with their new dolls. And last week, I was emailed a link to a video of a five-year-old being given the parcel with her doll inside. She had an arm and a foot amputated after a bout of meningitis. When she opened the parcel, she couldn't stop hugging it and shouting, 'My dolly's just like me!'" She didn't tell him she'd watched the video clip over and over again and had welled up every time.

When they'd drunk their tea, Shay said, "How's the knee feeling now?"

Rosa flexed it this way and that. "Much better, thanks. Nothing broken. I'll be fine." Although it was going to be a little while before she clambered over a high wall and jumped down into someone else's garden.

"Well, that's good. Dad, we need to head back to Birmingham or you're going to miss your flight."

Red nodded. He was looking weary now as he levered himself to his feet, but while his face might be thinner than it had once been, his smile was as disarming as ever. "Yes, we must go. It's been wonderful to see you again, Rosa. And thanks so much for showing me the mural." His eyes glinted with mischief. "Happy memories of times past. Take care of yourself," he added, bending to plant a brief kiss on her cheek. "Mind that knee of yours, and don't do anything I wouldn't do."

It was almost as if he knew what she'd been up to. In addition, this was someone clearly very unwell, yet here he was urging her to look after her dodgy knee. Feeling like a complete fraud by comparison, Rosa said, "It's lovely to see you again too."

....

His father slept in the passenger seat all the way back to the airport on the outskirts of Birmingham. Having parked the car and woken him, Shay said, "So what do you think, now you've seen the house?"

"Whose house? Rosa's?"

"Your house, the one you wanted to move into. The one that's completely uninhabitable."

"But it's the only place I want to be. We were happy there," said Red. "It's where I want to spend however long I have left."

Shay suppressed a sigh. He knew from experience that once his father set his mind to something, there'd be no changing it, regardless of whether the plan made an iota of sense.

"OK, well, I'll speak to a few local builders and see what they have to say."

"I want you to do it."

"That's not practical. I can't do everything myself."

"But you can do some of it. And you can be there and project manage the whole thing, oversee the rest of the work."

"I was going to take a holiday," Shay reminded him. "I was due a break, remember? After working nonstop for the last few years."

"I'm dying."

"Oh, so now we're on to the emotional blackmail, are we?"

"Now?" A glimmer of a smile. "It's been that way ever since I first thought of it."

Of course it had. If imminent death didn't allow you to play your trump card, what did?

"Wouldn't you rather stick with Angela in Edinburgh?" Although Shay already knew the answer.

"No. Every time she looks at me, she starts crying. I can't spend the rest of my life comforting her because she's upset about losing me." His father shook his head resignedly. "And I don't want her coming down here either. Easier if we call it a day. All I want to do now is go home to Elliscombe, back to our place. And spend more time with my boy, to make up for all those months we missed out on."

Months? Years more like. Shay said drily, "It's not my fault you kept getting slung back in jail."

"And I know that only too well. Which is why I can't make you agree to do this. It's your choice, Shay. If you don't want to do it, you don't have to. You're allowed to say no." He coughed gently. "God knows, it's not as if I can force you."

They both knew that. Just as Shay already knew there was no way in the world he could refuse.

Oh, the irony though. Red had spent years of his life risking so much just to make a bit of money. And now that Shay had amassed so much more than his father had ever succeeded in making, it could be too late to grant Red's final wish.

Once he'd accompanied his dad into the airport and left him at the departures gate, Shay headed back outside into the sunshine. A crimson Bentley Continental was now parked next to his car, and a female chauffeur was lifting cases out of the trunk while a couple in their seventies stood behind her clutching their passports and boarding passes.

"Oh sorry, pet, we're in your way. We'll be gone in two seconds…"

"It's fine," Shay told the elderly woman as she flapped a hand apologetically. "Take your time. Don't worry."

"I can't believe we came here in this beautiful car." Her eyes were bright as she confided, "It's not ours. It's a real Bentley! This lovely young lady collected us from our house in Solihull and drove us here… I kept waving at people in the street, like the Queen! And you'll never guess where we're going…"

"Marjorie, you're doing it again, love." Marjorie's husband was shaking his head. "This young lad doesn't want to know where we're going; he just wants to jump into his car and get out of here."

"Oh, sorry! I'm just excited," said Marjorie.

"I can see that, and why wouldn't you be?" Shay was charmed by her enthusiasm. "I'd love to know where you're off to."

"Well, it's a present from our children for our golden wedding anniversary." She beamed with pride. "All my life I've wanted to go to Venice, but we could never afford it, what with the kids and everything, but now we're going to stay there for a whole week! In a proper hotel! I keep pinching myself to make sure I'm not dreaming. We both do, don't we, love?"

Her husband said, "You keep pinching me, I'll tell you that much. You're like a woman possessed."

Shay said, "You'll have an amazing time."

Marjorie nodded happily. "Ooh, I know we will. Have you ever been to Venice, love?"

And that was it; in a flash, he was back there in the Hotel Ciati, making fun of Didi's off-key singing, followed by their serendipitous nighttime encounter in a snowy St. Mark's Square, where they'd built a snowman together, shared a bottle of cheap prosecco, and experienced that first jolt of mutual attraction.

"I have," he told her. "It's a place you'll never forget." In front of him, Marjorie was nodding happily, but in his mind's eye, he was back there now, watching Didi twirl around with her arms outstretched and her head tipped back as she caught snowflakes on her tongue. Would she even remember doing that? Probably not. Whereas he had never forgotten it, just as he'd never forgotten the realization that he'd never felt like that before, which meant there was a chance it could be the start of something—

The blond chauffeur closed the now-empty trunk of the Bentley with an expensive click, having already lined up her clients' suitcases, ready to push them in tandem. "I'll take these in for you and show you where you need to go. You'll be on your way before you know it!"

"Thank you, love. You've been so kind. Ooh, could we have our picture taken with you? Is that allowed?"

"Let me do it," Shay offered as Marjorie produced her phone.

"We're going to take so many photos over the next week." She passed it over to him and clapped her pudgy hands together with delight. "Hundreds! Me and Bob want to remember every minute of this holiday for the rest of our lives!"

"For the rest of our lives." Bob nodded in agreement. "Just got to hope the plane doesn't crash."

chapter 7

After work on Friday evening, Didi showered and changed into a gray silk camisole and jeans. She brushed the tangles out of her wet hair, quickly redid her makeup, and reached for her favorite scent. OK, no, not that one. Bracing herself slightly, she took the lid off the bottle of perfume Aaron had bought her for Christmas, then aimed the nozzle at her neck and wrists. It wasn't the type of scent she went for, but Aaron had chosen it for her from an esoteric perfumier in Covent Garden because he'd liked it so much he'd known she would love it too. Then last weekend, he'd commented on the fact that she wasn't wearing it, and when she'd fibbed about having worn it all week, he'd looked at the almost-full bottle on the chest of drawers and said meaningfully, "It's lasting you a long time, isn't it?"

Because that was the annoying thing about perfumes you weren't keen on: the tiniest spray seemed to lurk around forever.

Now she held the bottle out the window and gave twenty or so energetic squirts that would hopefully dissipate into the fresh air outside rather than fly back into her bedroom. Her phone went *ting*, and she glanced at the text from Aaron:

> Can you pick me up? Arriving on time at 19:30 hrs.
> Missed you xx

She replied:

> No problem, see you soon.

Then belatedly realized her mistake and sent a second one:

Sorry, thumb slipped, missed you too xx

It was only just past seven, but she jumped into her car to make her way over to Moreton-in-Marsh. The train journey from Paddington took ninety minutes, and Aaron always said the weekend couldn't start until she'd met him at the station and greeted him with a kiss.

As she rounded the bend on the outskirts of Elliscombe, she saw up ahead the blue car parked on the overgrown driveway of Hillcrest. Instinctively, she slowed, then felt her heart do a double thud at the sight of him coming around the side of the property, speaking into his phone. He paused and looked at her.

To stop or not to stop? That was the question.

Her foot hit the brake, making the decision for her.

"Hi," said Shay as she climbed out of the driver's seat.

"You can carry on talking." Didi indicated the phone in his hand. "I just wondered how things are going."

"I wasn't having a conversation, just making notes as to what needs doing. Which is pretty much everything."

"That bad?"

"Want to see?"

She nodded and followed him into the house she hadn't been inside for almost thirteen years. Back then, it hadn't exactly been luxurious, but Shay and his dad had kept it clean and well furnished, if a little lacking, understandably enough, in the feminine touch. They might not have gone in for cushions and candles and color-coordinated towels in the bathroom, but then again, nor had she ever encountered a dead rat in the living room like the one currently lying beside the fireplace with its legs in the air.

"I know. Don't look." Interrupting her horrified glance, Shay said, "This whole place is a health hazard."

Didi followed him through to the kitchen. "It's an everything hazard. Mind your head."

The warning came in the nick of time; he ducked to avoid the thick cobweb festooned between the door and the wall, and she saw him shudder. Nothing else—not snakes, rodents, nor any other kind of insect—had ever bothered Shay, but spiders were his absolute nemesis; they'd always freaked him out.

And it looked as if they still did. To divert his attention from the one lurking ninja-style on the wall next to the cobweb, Didi said, "So what are you going to do?"

"Well, as you know, the plan was to show my dad some great little properties in the area that are good to go so he can move straight in." Shay wagged a finger. "But no, that would be far too simple. He still has his heart set on this place."

"The Harris brothers are good; we use them when we need work done."

"He wants me to oversee the project myself. Move down here and stay with it from start to finish."

"Oh." Bit of an adrenaline rush.

"I know. Not how I'd planned to spend the summer."

"Could you tell him you can't do it but someone else can?"

"Apparently not. He played the dying card, big-time."

"I'm sorry." The air of flippancy was something of a front, Didi knew. Inwardly, she was equally conflicted. Seeing Shay again was stirring up all kinds of emotions, ones she'd put to bed over a decade ago.

"Sorry about what?"

"Your dad being so ill. I can't imagine what it must be like for you." There'd only been the two of them, father and son. It was twenty years since his mother had died. When Red went too, Shay would have no family left.

"These things happen." He shrugged, pointed to the staircase. "It's all pretty grim up there too. You don't need to see it."

Didi shook her head, relieved to be spared that awkwardness. He had to be as aware as she was that his old bedroom upstairs was where they'd spent so much time during those idyllic months together. It was where, six weeks after that first night in the snow in St. Mark's Square, she'd lost her virginity to Shay Mason. He'd been her first love and she'd been his.

A quiver ran down her spine in response to the pictures currently being stirred up in her mind. Was he remembering it too?

When she heard his breathing quicken, she thought maybe he was until he took an abrupt step away from the spider that was now galloping at speed across the wall toward him.

"You should have hypnotherapy."

He suppressed a shudder. "It wouldn't help."

"But this is quite a spidery house. I mean, it's not ideal, is it? Maybe if you think of them as dear little pets, give them names. You could call this one Fenella."

He was almost smiling, shaking his head. "Still no."

"Come on. Give it a try. Fenella's lovely! She's a Gemini, a mother of two, and her hobbies are knitting, catching flies, and watching *Coronation Street*. Well, she used to watch *Coronation Street*." Didi gestured sadly at the ancient TV with the smashed screen lying on its side on the floor. "Her dearest wish is for this house to be done up and made beautiful again so your dad can move back in and buy a new telly and she can catch up on all her favorite soaps."

Shay was laughing now, and with a fizz of joy, Didi remembered how much she'd always loved making him laugh, seeing the sparks of light in his eyes and hearing—

DDDRRINNGGG! Her phone rang and she jumped, brought back to earth with a bump. Whoops, it was Aaron.

"Hi, I'm here, and you're not."

"Sorry, sorry, I got held up at work… On my way now. I'll be there in eight minutes."

"Boyfriend?" said Shay when she'd ended the call. "I mean, fiancé?"

"Yes. I have to go." Mortified that she'd forgotten him, Didi pulled her keys from her jeans pocket.

"Let's hope he doesn't have a tracker on your car."

"Why?"

"You told him you were held up at work."

Didi cringed; why had she even done that? "Force of habit. I spend my life being held up at work."

"I'm sure he'll wait for you," said Shay.

"Of course he will." To cover her embarrassment, Didi added flippantly, "I'm worth waiting for."

"Sorry I'm late." Didi jumped out of the car.

"Stop apologizing. It's fine. Come here, you." Aaron enveloped her in a hug, right there in the middle of the station parking lot, and kissed her as if they were in a movie, which was nice in one way but also a bit embarrassing. He'd once told her that as a child, he'd watched the film *The Truman Show*, starring Jim Carrey, and had become enthralled by the idea that maybe his entire life was secretly being documented too. Didi guessed that it still, on occasion, crossed his mind. Aaron was demonstrative, fond of big romantic gestures, and sometimes when he was in a social situation, listening to other people speaking, she suspected that he was arranging his facial features in the most advantageous way, as if in readiness for his next close-up.

But then maybe lots of people did this, like when you first ventured onto the dance floor at a party. When it suddenly occurred to you that others were scrutinizing you, taking notice of your face and body, wasn't it normal to become self-conscious and suddenly hyperaware of yourself?

"Ah, look at them two, all lovey-dovey." A woman trundling past with a tartan shopping bag on wheels gave her friend a nudge. "Why doesn't my Derek do that to me, eh?"

"Because you've been stuck with the old bugger for fifty years," her friend snorted, "and if he tried it, he'd only do his back in."

"I wouldn't even want him to kiss me, not with his teeth. They're in a right state."

"Pot kettle, Maureen. Let's face it. You've both let yourselves go."

The two women carried on across the parking lot, cackling like hyenas.

Aaron murmured, "I'm telling you right now, when we've been together for fifty years, I'm still going to be kissing you every day."

"Even if I let myself go?"

"You wouldn't."

Once they were in the car, he heaved a sigh of relief. "You've no idea how much I've missed you. It's been a pig of a week." He worked crazy hours.

Didi said, "Well, you're here now. All you have to do is relax."

"That's the plan." He rested his right hand on her left knee. "It's good to be back. How have things been with you?"

"Great. Busy. The hotel's full; we had to turn away a few walk-ins yesterday." She hesitated, keeping her tone casual. "Bit of a blast from the past, actually. One of my exes from years ago turned up out of the blue. So weird; the last time I saw him, he was eighteen. And now he's grown-up."

See? Casual but not too casual. Not so casual it ended up looking suspicious. As they drove along Moreton-in-Marsh's main street, she pointed to the newly opened French restaurant with the wooden tables and chairs outside. "I'm hearing good things about this place. We'll have to give it a try."

"Flying visit?"

"Well, we'd stay for a meal."

"The ex, I meant. What's he doing back here?"

"Oh, it's really sad. His dad's dying and wants to come home to spend the time he has left in their old house."

"Don't go feeling too sorry for him," Aaron said teasingly. "So how was it seeing him again?"

"Like I said, weird."

"And you were eighteen? What was it, first love?"

"Nooo." Didi wondered if her nose was growing. "We weren't together for that long. It was in our last year at school. Then we broke up and Shay went off to Australia." She shrugged, realizing that she needed to say it. "And now he's staying at the hotel."

"His loss, my gain. I bet he's kicking himself now. How long's he here for?"

"No idea." Didi accelerated past an elderly man cycling along with a sheepdog on a lead.

"Well, let's hope he doesn't go getting any ideas." Aaron was chuckling. "You're mine now."

"Are you actually from Victorian times?"

"Don't worry. Just joking. Is he better looking than me?"

"Why? Are you jealous?"

He laughed and patted her knee. "Maybe a bit. Should I be?"

"No. Haven't you ever bumped into an old girlfriend from years ago?"

"Ha, it happened once. I was invited along as a plus-one to a wedding, and the bride turned out to be an ex from university. I had no idea until she came walking up the aisle and we suddenly recognized each other."

"Oh my God, that's brilliant. What happened?"

"She said, 'Aaron?' and I said, 'Jules?' then she threw her arms around me, burst into tears, and said, 'How can I marry him? You're the one I love. It's only ever been you!'"

Didi grinned. "Very good. What really happened?"

"She got married to the guy waiting at the end of the aisle. And later on, during the reception, she came over to me and said, 'Hi, I knew I recognized you from somewhere… You're Richard, yeah? You used to work in the gas station on Falcondale Road.'"

"Ouch. And what did you say?"

"What else could I do? She didn't remember me at all, and I was mortified. I had to pretend to be Richard from the gas station for the rest of the night."

Didi burst out laughing. This was what she liked about Aaron. Every now and again, he might do or say something a bit cringey, but he meant well, was kindhearted, and had the endearing ability to veer from overconfident to self-deprecating in the blink of an eye.

No, she didn't like him; she loved him. And he loved her. She flexed the fingers of her left hand on the steering wheel, admiring the way the diamond glittered in the sunlight. It still startled her sometimes to see it there. But she'd get used to it soon, would be wearing it for the rest of her life. And in December, she and Aaron would be getting married.

When Hillcrest came into view, the blue Audi was still parked in the drive, with Shay leaning against it. This time, Didi put her foot down on the accelerator.

"Look," Aaron marveled. "Signs of life at that place at last. At least he doesn't look like a squatter."

Time for another split-second decision: to let Aaron know who it was or not? Shay turned and raised his hand in friendly recognition, nodding and smiling as they approached. Didi couldn't help wondering if he'd estimated the time it would take her to return from collecting Aaron at the station and had come outside in order to see them drive past.

"Someone you know?" said Aaron.

OK, so she was going to have to say it. Her foot pressed harder on the accelerator. "That's Shay."

chapter 8

OK, SO FAR, SO SURREAL.

Layla had flirted with dating apps before of course, but nothing had ever really come of it, apart from finding herself on the receiving end of incredulous messages from men who flat-out refused to believe she wasn't lying to them. The general consensus was that she had to be a prostitute catering to nerdy types.

Basically, over the course of the last ten years, if she'd had a pound for every time someone had expressed surprise that she was an accountant...well, she wouldn't *need* to be an accountant; she could just sit back and live off the proceeds instead.

But she wasn't going to change the way she dressed or did her makeup; this was her, and it would just feel weird to wear plain clothes, discreet lipstick, and sensible shoes. She couldn't help her magpie tendencies; practically her whole life, she'd found herself drawn like a magnet to the kind of outfits that other people automatically rejected because they were just too much.

As far as Layla was concerned, too much was never enough. And she knew perfectly well that it didn't always work in her favor either professionally or personally, but wearing the clothes she did and looking the way she did meant more to her than conforming in order to please other people. It was her hobby and her passion, so she did it anyway.

And today, for the first time in many months, she had an actual date with a man who looked and sounded perfect. Which, if everything worked out, would mean she owed it all to Shay Mason, because if it hadn't been for Didi telling her the astonishing news about Shay's just-sold business, she would never have redownloaded the app.

Leave it all to Fait was the company's advertising slogan, and now she was starting to feel as if it was all meant to be. OK, maybe it wasn't realistically likely that tonight's date would turn out to be The One, but it had to happen at some stage, and they were off to a good start because she'd searched for someone within a ten-mile radius, and like magic, there he'd been, a mere seven miles from Elliscombe.

Fingers crossed he'd live up to expectations.

Her phone buzzed with a text to let her know that Will had arrived and was waiting outside. Bang on time, as always. Layla grabbed her bag and all but danced out of her flat.

"All dressed up," Will observed. "Looking good."

"Thank you. Feeling good!" He probably didn't mean it, but she didn't care. Thanks to her aversion to driving, Will Osborne had been ferrying her around for years. A couple of years older than Layla, he'd spent his teens and early twenties caring for his widowed mother, who'd finally succumbed to her long-standing heart disease. It couldn't have been easy for him, but he had never complained. He was the quiet, steady kind. Now he lived alone in the family's small cottage on Comer Street and devoted himself to running the most efficient one-man taxi service in the Cotswolds.

"Off out somewhere nice?"

"Don't faint." Layla lovingly smoothed the cherry-printed satin skirt over her lap. "I'm going on a date!"

"Excellent. Where'd you meet him?"

"Well, I haven't yet. That's going to happen in, ooh, about fifteen minutes from now."

Will frowned. "You're off on a date with a complete stranger?"

"He's not a complete stranger. I used a dating app. This is how these things happen nowadays." Layla laughed. "Don't tell me you've never tried it." Will had had a couple of girlfriends in the last few years, she knew that, but it wasn't a subject they tended to discuss.

"Too busy working." He shook his head and expertly reversed the taxi to execute a three-point turn in the driveway. "Doesn't sound very safe."

"You sound like my mum," she retorted. "I'm not stupid, Will. If this guy invites me back to his place, then tries to persuade me to climb into that big cooking pot on the stove, I'm planning on saying no."

He wasn't smiling. "I know you think that's funny, but it really isn't. You shouldn't be going back to anyone's place if they're a stranger."

"Hello?" Exasperated, she spread her hands. "I'm not going to be doing that because I'm not an idiot. He's new to the area, just moved down from Manchester, and we're meeting on the little bridge next to the Kingsbridge Inn. Then we're going to go for a walk along the riverside in broad daylight, have a nice chat, and get to know each other. You never know, we might even go completely wild and pop into the pub for a drink. Then, when it's time for me to come home, I'll give you a call and ask you to pick me up."

"OK," said Will. "Don't let him get you drunk."

She rolled her eyes. Honestly. "I won't get drunk."

"Have you emailed his details to anyone?"

"No."

"D'you want to email them to me?"

"No, Will. And this is supposed to be a happy time for me, OK? I'm actually hoping he's going to turn out to be a nice guy and not a serial killer or a homicidal maniac."

"Sorry." He raised a hand from the steering wheel. "I'm sorry, I just…"

"You don't want to lose a good customer, I know." Layla smiled to show he was forgiven. "You've been reading too many psychological thrillers, that's what's got you thinking. I'll be fine."

As he dropped her off in Bourton-on-the-Water, close to the Kingsbridge Inn, Will said conversationally, "Given any more thought to those driving lessons?"

"No." Honestly, was he trying to put himself out of business?

"Well, the offer still stands if you change your mind."

That was never going to happen. "OK."

"Text me when you're ready to head back."

"I will." She climbed out of the passenger seat.

"Have a good time."

"Thanks."

She waited until he'd driven off before taking a deep breath and preparing to turn to look at the low stone bridge across the River Windrush. She'd never been flat-out stood up before, but it was always a possibility; it could be about to happen now. If her date wasn't here, she'd just have to walk up and down for a bit and pretend to be admiring the scenery before slipping away and sending that text to Will. Oh God, the humiliation…

But when she turned, he was there. Better still, he was watching her and smiling broadly, as if genuinely delighted by what he saw.

Best of all, he looked every bit as good as he did in his dating profile. Like, seriously good. Bonus!

Layla stepped off the sidewalk and narrowly avoided being mown down by a familiar car. Will, having turned around and come back along the high street, braked sharply and gave a pay-attention shake of his head as he drove past her.

Then he really had gone, and it was safe to cross the road.

"Hello," said Harry Gray.

The butterflies were going crazy in her chest. "Hello."

"It's you." He had an irresistibly infectious smile.

"I know."

"No, I mean it's you." He gestured toward her hair, her outfit, her shoes. "I was in Elliscombe last week, and I saw you from a distance, walking down the street. I just felt…you know, it was one of those moments that catches you by surprise. I had this incredible urge to chase after you and find out who you were, but then you turned the corner and I lost my nerve, because what if you thought I was a complete lunatic and couldn't get away fast enough? So I let you get away and spent the rest of the day kicking myself."

"Oh, wow." Layla was speechless. It was astonishing enough discovering she was capable of evoking such a reaction from a stranger in the street, let alone a stranger of this caliber looks wise.

"Then this morning, I took a quick look at Fait and nearly dropped my phone when I saw you on there. Well, I was almost sure it was you; I couldn't be a hundred percent certain."

"And it was me?"

He nodded. "It was. If this isn't fate, I don't know what is."

"I know the person who invented the Fait app!" Did that make her sound like a terrible name-dropper? Oh, but it was so relevant! "His name's Shay, and he came to my eighteenth birthday trip to Venice… He's staying in Elliscombe right now!"

Harry grinned. "Well, whoever he is, I owe him a drink."

They walked side by side along the water's edge, which felt easier than having to sit opposite each other in a pub and make potentially staccato face-to-face conversation. This way, there wasn't a hint of awkwardness, and it was all Layla could do to stop herself casting covert sideways glances at him as they chatted away. Harry was a personal trainer and it showed; he was wearing jeans and a tight-fitting white T-shirt that clung to his biceps and clearly delineated abs. He had tanned, lightly freckled skin and green eyes, and his dark hair was cut really short, enhancing neat ears and the excellent shape of his skull. His cologne was fresh with a hint of pine, but in a good way rather than a bathroom-freshener one. His mum was from Yorkshire, his father Scottish. He'd been living in Manchester for the last six years.

"And I talk too much," he concluded with a wry grin. "Sorry about that. It's only because I'm so nervous. Anyway, enough about me. Tell me about you. What do you do for a living?"

Layla hesitated. It hadn't taken her long to learn that if you wanted to get positive responses on dating apps, it helped if you didn't announce from the word go that you were an accountant. Bracing herself slightly, she said, "I'm an accountant."

"What, seriously?" He did a jokey double take. "You don't look like one. And I suppose you're sick to the back teeth of hearing people say that to you."

"It happens quite often."

"Amazing. God, I love it though. I love surprises. And I love what you're wearing. Imagine looking the way you do and being able to fill in tax forms."

Phew. Layla felt the last remnants of anxiety receding. He wasn't put off by her profession, and everything was going to be fine.

"Tell me more," he said. "Any other surprises I should know about?"

Now he was putting her on the spot. "Umm…I love Beyoncé?"

"That's not a surprise. Everyone loves Beyoncé."

"Let me save the rest of my surprises for now." They'd walked the length of the village on one side of the river, then back again on the other, and Layla's high-heeled butterfly shoes were turning her toes numb. "Shall we stop and get a drink?"

"Definitely. I want to know everything about you. Are you into fitness?"

May as well get it over with. She shook her head. "Not really, no." Was this going to put him off?

But Harry was smiling, showing no sign of being horrified and wanting to run a mile or maybe ten. "That's fine. It makes a nice change. There's more to life than body sculpting and sit-ups."

Phew. Thank goodness for that.

Two hours later, sounding bereft, he said, "Are you sure you have to go?"

Layla wasn't at all sure, and she definitely didn't want to go, but she was under strict instructions from Didi to leave him wanting more. Which was pretty rich, considering Didi had slept with Aaron the first night she'd met him. But Layla was the one who'd asked Didi's advice on this occasion, and she had promised to do as she was told.

Besides, everything seemed to be going fantastically well so far, and it felt kind of empowering to be the one in charge for once, being all assertive and saying no.

"I do have to go." One-upmanship was such a buzz. She leaned forward and planted a brief kiss tantalizingly close to Harry's mouth. "I need to be in my office by seven tomorrow morning, and my taxi's going to be here any minute. But it's been great."

"When am I going to see you again?"

Yeehaw! "I don't know. You haven't asked me yet."

"I'm asking you now. Tomorrow night?"

The urge to yell *yes, yes, YES* was almost irresistible. This was all working like magic, going exactly according to plan. But she had to keep the upper hand. As instructed, she said casually, "Sorry, can't do tomorrow."

Even though it nearly killed her.

"Right." He looked crestfallen. "OK, no worries. Well, tonight was fun."

But he'd pulled back a fraction, and the tone of his voice had flattened. Panicking, Layla blurted out, "I can do Sunday!"

"Sure?"

"Yes, I'm sure!"

"OK. Sunday it is." And now he slid his arm around her waist and drew her toward him. This time, it wasn't a peck; it was a proper kiss, a meaningful one, long and slow and bursting with promise.

Layla swooned; it had been quite a while since she'd found herself on the receiving end of something like that.

By the time they finally broke apart, she was breathless and trembling.

"Sure you don't want to change your mind?" Harry murmured. "My place is just up the road."

She knew where it was. He'd already pointed out the bijou second-floor flat above one of the touristy shops catering to visitors who yearned to buy crockery, paintings, light shades, and tea towels…anything at all, basically, so long as it featured scenes from the Cotswolds.

"I can't…"

Smiling, he lightly stroked an index finger along the line of her collarbone. "You could if you really wanted to."

chapter 9

Layla's phone buzzed. "That's my taxi," she said and twisted around, expecting to see the car making its way along the high street. Moments later, she realized it was one of the ones parked opposite. "Oh, it's already here." Well, that was a tiny bit embarrassing. "Better not keep him waiting. I'll see you on Sunday."

Harry grinned at her. "Can't wait."

She made her way over the bridge and across the dry grass. Had Will been sitting there all this time watching her get kissed to within an inch of her life? But when she reached the taxi, Layla saw that he was engrossed in typing something into the iPad on his lap.

As she opened the passenger door, he switched off the iPad and slid it into the glove compartment.

"What were you writing?"

He fired up the engine. "Nothing."

She hoped it wasn't a Facebook post to accompany a luridly incriminating photo, broadcasting to all and sundry: *Look at Layla Gallagher with her blind date tonight, snogging like a teenager outside the pub. Talk about desperate!*

She fastened her seat belt. "Been waiting long?"

"I was only two minutes away when you texted me."

"You should have buzzed me when you got here."

Will said mildly, "You seemed busy. I didn't want to interrupt."

As they pulled away, she turned to wave goodbye to Harry, but he'd already disappeared. Still euphoric after such a ragingly successful evening and unable to resist a quick boast, Layla said, "Well, thanks for asking. We had a brilliant time."

Will expertly swerved to avoid a fox that had darted into the road. "So I gathered."

The thing about Will was that he had the kind of sense of humor that was so dry it was sometimes hard to detect. Rather than retaliate, Layla took out her phone and pretended to be engrossed in incredibly important business of an accountanty nature instead. When they arrived back in Elliscombe, she glanced up and said, "Here's fine," as he was about to drive past the Wickham Hotel.

"I'm glad you had a good time," Will said as she climbed out of the car. Presumably his way of apologizing for being dry before.

She hoisted her silver bag over her shoulder and gave him a fleeting half smile to let him know he'd overstepped the mark. "Me too."

The night air was warm, and a buzz of conversation and laughter drifted across from the back of the hotel; plenty of guests were still gathered outside in the garden. When she reached it, Layla paused to admire the scene. The trees were strung with solar fairy lights, there were silvery uplighters tucked away in the shrubberies, and tiny candles flickered in glass jars on every table. The mingled scents of honeysuckle, roses, and nicotiana filled the air. The assembled crowd was drinking, socializing, and chattering away, and she spotted Didi in a violet shift dress and emerald heels talking to a party of hotel guests.

"Layla," said a male voice behind her, and she swung around, recognizing him at once.

"Shay!" Goodness, the beautiful boy of thirteen years ago had grown into a stunningly attractive man. Along with all the other girls at school—and probably a few boys—she'd had one of those low-level crushes you never even admitted to because you just knew there was no chance of anything happening with the person involved. Shay had been as out of reach and unattainable as a rock star. The fact that he'd had a criminal father and a highly unconventional upbringing hadn't put anyone off him at all. If anything, those factors had only added to the attraction.

Then Venice had happened. Shay and Didi had struck showers of sparks off each other, and that had been it, a fait accompli. At the time, it had been like being shown an extraordinary chemical reaction in the school science lab. It had almost felt like a privilege, Layla remembered, to be able to witness the magical connection between them. And their relationship had continued for the next six months, invincible and unbreakable, right up until the end had come, suddenly and explosively, and Shay had disappeared.

Now he was back, more wildly unattainable than ever, and having a little crush on him would be even more of a pointless exercise than before.

Oh, but it was so lovely to see him again. Plus, she couldn't wait to witness his interactions with Didi. How must she be feeling now?

Let alone Aaron…

"You look amazing." Layla gave him a huge hug.

"So do you. And you're an accountant, Didi tells me. That's incredible."

"I'm an excellent accountant. So if you ever need someone to take care of your millions…"

Shay laughed. "I'll remember that."

"No, but seriously, I owe you one. Didi told me about you and Fait. I can't believe it was yours." Unable to resist sharing, she gabbled, "I've just been on a date tonight with someone I met on there!"

"And you're looking pretty happy, so I hope that means it went well."

"So well. Best first date ever. And it's all thanks to you."

"We aim to please. Not that it's my company anymore. I saw your mum earlier, by the way."

"Oh, I know. She told me on the phone about you and your dad coming to her rescue this afternoon. She was so grateful to you both."

He shrugged. "It was nothing. Glad to help. How is she now?"

"Not too bad. Apparently wrapping a bag of frozen sweetcorn around her knee has worked wonders. She'll be fine." Layla paused. "I was so sorry to hear about your dad. Horrible for him and for you."

"Thanks." Shay's voice softened. "And I'm sorry about yours too. You must miss him so much."

"We do." Layla nodded. Her father and Red Mason had been unlikely friends, both of them opportunists who shared a sense of humor and a fondness for a few drinks in their favorite local pub, the Prince of Wales. "It was hard for Mum especially, having to move out of the house. None of us had any idea what the situation was like financially when Dad died, so it came as a massive shock. Mum's battled through it—she takes little part-time jobs wherever she can—but it hasn't been easy, getting used to not having any money. And of course she won't let me help her out."

"We saw the dolls she's been making. They're fantastic," said Shay.

"They are, but for every one she sells, there are two more she makes for people who tell her how much they want one but can't afford it. Mum's so softhearted, she can't bear to turn them down."

"Ah, she didn't mention that."

"You know what she's like." Layla changed the subject. "So anyway, does it feel strange seeing Didi again?"

And there it was, that bewitchingly enigmatic half smile she remembered so well. "I don't know that I'd call it strange. Interesting, perhaps. We're all older now, aren't we? Everything changes. Didi's running this place, got herself a fiancé. I'm glad she's doing well."

"Mum says you're going to be doing up your old place for Red to live in. So that means you'll be around for a while."

"Well, it wasn't how I'd planned on spending the summer, but he's talked me into it." Shay gave her a wry look. "That's my father for you. Always did have the gift of the gab."

"And will you stay on here in the hotel while you're working on the house?"

He shook his head. "Dad's keen to get away from his current lady friend in Edinburgh. He wants to move down as soon as possible. So I'm going to rent a place for the two of us. I've found a couple to look at tomorrow." He glanced past her. "Here comes Didi. I'm guessing that's the fiancé with her now."

"His name's Aaron." Swiveling, Layla waved to them. "She'll be wanting to hear all about my date."

Shay said, "If you two end up together, I'm going to be taking all the credit."

Layla remembered the giddy-making kiss, the sensation of Harry's warm fingers sliding through the hair at the nape of her neck. Jokingly—but not completely jokingly—she said, "You'll be guest of honor at our wedding."

....

The arms of the doll had to be stuffed in exactly the right way, and Rosa was in the middle of a tricky maneuver, wrestling to replicate the angles, when her landline rang. Not recognizing the number of the incoming call, she was tempted to leave it. But curiosity, as always, won out.

"Hey, how's the knee?"

She did a mini double take. "Red, hello! Who gave you my number?"

"No one. I looked it up online. You aren't unlisted."

"Oh, right. I know that. Sorry, I just meant I wasn't expecting to hear from you."

"You probably should get unlisted." He sounded amused. "Stops you getting calls from weird people."

"You aren't weird."

"I know I'm not. I'm talking about crank calls and scammers. Knee?"

"Bit painful, not too bad. Are you in Edinburgh?"

"I am. Now listen. I've had an idea. But all I'm going to do is suggest it to you, and it's fine if you want to say no. In fact, you don't even have to do that. I'll just say it and put the phone down. Then you can have a good think about it, and if you want to say yes, you call me back. If you don't want to say yes, it ends there. And there won't be any awkwardness, I promise."

Rosa frowned, puzzled. "Do you want me to make a doll for someone you know? Because it's not a problem. I'd be happy to do that."

"Rosa, that's very kind of you, but it isn't a doll I'm after. I'm more interested in that spare bedroom of yours."

"Oh..." Well, she hadn't been expecting that.

"Just for three months, until my own house is habitable again. I'd pay you a decent amount, of course. Shay said we could rent a place together, but he'll be out working all day, and I'm used to spending my time with other people. I don't much enjoy being on my own. So I thought maybe you wouldn't mind a bit of company, and I promise I wouldn't be a nuisance." He paused. "There, that's it, I've said it. If the idea horrifies you, that's fine. I completely understand, and we'll never mention it again. I'm putting the phone down now."

"Wait—" Rosa blurted out, but it was too late; the line had already gone dead.

She rose to her feet, limped through to the kitchen, and poured herself a small glass of wine. Back in the living room, having made herself comfortable once more on the sofa, she returned the call. Red answered on the third ring.

"Sounds like an excellent plan to me," she said.

"Really?" The delight was evident in his voice. "You're sure?"

"Absolutely sure. Soon as you like. When were you thinking of moving in?"

"Tomorrow? Or maybe the next day." She heard him stifle a cough. "This is the best news."

"I think so too." She meant it. She had plenty of friends here in Elliscombe, and Layla's flat was only up the road, but living alone wasn't something she'd ever really learned to enjoy. A bit of undemanding day-to-day company could be just the thing she needed to cheer herself up. In a purely platonic way, of course.

"Thanks," said Red. "And it's only going to be for three months, max. I'll try not to die on you."

"You'd better not. If you do, I'll kill you," said Rosa.

chapter 10

Didi's fiancé, Aaron, had introduced himself to Shay with one of those crushing I'm-so-manly handshakes before launching into a manly conversation about cars.

Shay, not remotely interested in cars, was nodding along and half listening instead to Layla, who was excitedly regaling Didi with details of this evening's date with Harry, which couldn't have gone better.

"I mean, have you tried the Mercedes AMG GT Coupé? Got some poke behind it, that one. Eight-cylinder biturbo engine with dry sump lubrication. It's the bomb, I'm telling you." Aaron shook his head in admiration.

"It's just so incredible… When he looked at me, it was like he wanted to know every single thing about me," Layla gushed happily. "I can't wait for you to meet him!"

"Upright radiator grille and electronically extending rear airfoil… silver brake calipers…memory package…"

"And he has the most amazing elbows! I have such a thing for really good elbows, don't you? They make all the difference."

"Oh, wrists are my favorite thing." Didi was nodding. "I love wrists."

Shay fought the urge to glance at Aaron's wrists.

"And if you go for the GTS, you get another forty-six horsepower. With adjustable sports suspension."

Never in his life had Shay been so glad to get a phone call. Pulling out his cell, he said apologetically, "So sorry, it's my father. I'm going to have to take this."

"Go ahead. Don't mind me." Aaron gestured that he understood. "I'll get us another drink, shall I? Won't be long."

Oh God, another drink meant another twenty minutes listening to the contents of a car manual, but Aaron had already disappeared in the direction of the bar.

"Dad, everything OK?" Because each time you received a call from the phone of a parent who was terminally ill, you instinctively prepared yourself for the worst. One day, the voice at the other end might not be Red's; it might belong to a paramedic, a doctor, or a stranger in the street.

"Never better," said Red. "Listen, I've got some news. You don't have to find us a place to stay for the next few months."

Oh God, now what? Did this mean he'd decided to stay in Edinburgh with Angela after all? Had the plan to renovate their old home been abandoned, meaning that Shay could put the place on the market and spend at least part of the summer relaxing on holiday somewhere exotic?

The thoughts raced through his brain; this was what he'd wanted more than anything. But now that it seemed likely, there was a curious lack of elation. "You've changed your mind about getting the house done up and moving into it?" This was crazy; now he was actually feeling disappointed.

"What are you talking about? Of course I haven't changed my mind," said Red. "I'm coming down on Monday, catching the late-morning flight."

"I don't understand. So what's the news?" Shay frowned. "And where are you going to be staying?"

"I'm moving in with Rosa Gallagher."

"What?" This was quick work, even by his father's standards.

"Don't sound so shocked." He heard wheezy laughter. "This is a platonic arrangement, what with me being on my last legs, pretty much. Rosa has a spare room, and she could do with the cash. It means I don't have to spend most of my time on my own, and you don't have to feel guilty about it. You can stay on at the hotel and work on fixing up the house. Doesn't it make sense?"

"Have you asked her yet?"

"Of course I have. It's all arranged. Right, I'd better go. Need to break the news to Angela. Can you pick me up from the airport on Monday?"

"I…guess so."

"Look at me, becoming quite the jet-setter in my old age. Bye!"

"You look shocked," said Didi. "What's happened? Is he all right?"

"Seems fine." Shay turned to Layla, who had stopped telling Didi about her date and was now waiting to hear about the phone call. "That was my dad calling to let me know that on Monday, he's going to be moving in with your mum."

Layla's eyes widened. "Are you serious?"

"It's what he says."

"But…if that was true, she'd have told me." As Layla put down her wineglass, her phone made a chirping sound in her bag. She took it out. "It's a text from Mum: 'Hi, darling, how's the date going? Guess what, Red Mason's going to be my lodger until his house is ready! Money for me, company for him! Call me tomorrow.'"

"Wow," said Didi.

Shay realized he was glad the old house still needed doing up.

The next moment, he caught himself glancing at his left hand as he reached for his almost-empty glass. Did he have nice wrists? What made them special? And for God's sake, why was he even asking himself this question?

It almost came as a relief to see Aaron threading his way back from the bar with a tray of fresh drinks.

"I'm going to have to speak to her." Layla had turned away from him, was murmuring the words in Didi's ear, but Shay still heard them. "I mean, this is Red Mason we're talking about."

Here was something he'd had plenty of practice dealing with over decades. Hearing the faint edge in his own voice, Shay said, "You can trust him. He wouldn't take anything belonging to your mum."

"Oh my God, I didn't mean anything like that." Clearly mortified, Layla blurted out, "I meant his reputation with women, I swear! Nothing to do with the other stuff. It's just that there hasn't been anyone else for Mum since Dad died, that's all…"

"Sorry." And now Shay felt terrible too. He'd gone there, had addressed the elephant in the room, only it had turned out to be the wrong elephant. "Of course you didn't mean it that way. And if it helps, Dad's already told me this is going to be a platonic relationship." He rested his hand on Layla's shoulder. "I really am sorry. I guess I've gotten used to apologizing for him over the years. But all those bad habits are behind him now, I promise."

"I feel as if I'm missing out here, coming in late and only hearing half the story!" Aaron, who evidently hadn't heard the other half from Didi, began handing out the drinks. When it came to Shay, he said, "And it's my turn to apologize now. I just bumped into some American guy up at the bar, and he happened to mention that you weren't interested in cars."

Ah, Myron from the Midsummer Suite had attempted to engage him in conversation last night, and that time, he'd been honest from the word go.

"As long as they get me from A to B, that's all I care about," Shay admitted.

"And there you've been, putting up with me boring you to tears for the last twenty minutes. You should have said!"

"It's fine. Thanks for the drink."

"Hey, no worries. Let's forget cars," said Aaron. "What do you want to talk about instead?"

Oh, I don't know. Your fiancée, maybe?

Didi, her eyes bright, waggled her fingers playfully in the air just to the left of Shay's shoulder. "Well, he likes spiders…"

chapter 11

"LOOK, SORRY ABOUT THIS. I FEEL LIKE ONE OF THOSE AWFUL PEOPLE the week after Christmas, dumping a puppy at the dogs' home and making a quick getaway." As he carried his father's cases upstairs, Shay said, "But the guys with the van are going to be waiting for me outside the house, so I really need to..."

"Make a quick getaway." Rosa followed him. "I know. It's fine. You go ahead."

"Woof woof," said Red. "Dump and run. Don't mind me."

Shay placed the cases on the bed and swung around. "The rest of his things are going into storage until the house is ready. This looks great." He admired the bedroom Rosa had hastily decluttered, taking in the view over the garden from the diamond-leaded windows, the blue-and-white curtains and matching bed linen, the paintings on the sky-blue walls, and the bijou en suite bathroom. "Dad, you've done well. Try not to get yourself kicked out."

"I'll do my best." In the doorway, Red was recovering his breath.

"I have to go. See you later." Shay grinned at Rosa. "Let's hope he behaves himself. Any problems at all, let me know."

They watched from the window as he jumped into his car and sped off. Rosa said, "I'll put the kettle on, leave you to get yourself settled in."

"Hang on." Red unzipped the smaller of the two cases and took out two bottles of prosecco. "Stick these in the fridge, would you? We'll have a proper drink in a bit."

"OK, but I mustn't have more than one glass. I've got a doll to make this evening, and it wouldn't do to amputate the wrong leg."

By five o'clock, the second bottle was almost empty, and it had been mutually agreed that there should be no doll making tonight.

Oh, but the last couple of hours had flown by. Red was wonderful company and a natural raconteur. Up until today, most of what she'd known about him had been acquired via hearsay and gossip. But hearing his stories in his own words was proving completely fascinating. Here they were, sitting outside in the shaded part of the garden, and it was light-years more fun than chopping potatoes and onions while half watching *Come Dine with Me*.

"It was the adrenaline rush that got me hooked." Having checked the time on the watch that hung loosely around his wrist, Red took a couple of packets of pills from his shirt pocket and washed the tablets down with water followed by a glug of prosecco. Which probably wasn't advisable, but he was almost sixty years old, and it was his body, his decision.

"I don't like adrenaline rushes," said Rosa. "They make me feel sick."

"Oh, come on, not always." His eyes glinted with mischief. "How about when you buy a two-hour parking ticket and don't get back to your car for three hours?"

"That would never happen, I'm telling you now." The very idea made her skin prickle with panic. "If I thought I was going to be there for three hours, I'd buy a ticket for six hours just to be on the safe side. *Would* have," she amended, "back when I had a car."

"You see, that's the difference between us. I'd never even buy a ticket in the first place, and the thrill would be in wondering if I was going to get caught. Best of all, heading back to the car and reaching it just before the traffic warden gets there. That's the kind of adrenaline buzz I'm talking about."

"I don't know how you can do it."

"Ah, I reckon it's in the genes. When I was a kid, my parents were that way inclined too. What was your favorite TV show when you were at school?"

Rosa blinked. "Um, *Blue Peter*, I guess."

"You see? Mine was *Robin Hood*. And the Cary Grant movie *To Catch a Thief*. There was also an American TV series called *Alias Smith and Jones*. Then when I was about eleven, my dad smuggled me into the cinema, and we saw *Butch Cassidy and the Sundance Kid*. Everything I loved was about lawbreakers, people who got a thrill out of beating the system. To me, it was glamorous and exciting and the best fun in the world. Some people get that kind of rush from…I don't know, scoring a goal at Wembley or singing onstage in front of a massive audience or riding a motorbike at a hundred miles an hour." He sat back and spread his palms. "I always got mine from getting away with something I shouldn't have been getting away with."

"I can see that," Rosa protested. "But the thing is, half the time, you didn't get away with it, did you? You kept getting caught and sent back to prison over and over again."

He shrugged. "It was the risk that made it exciting. The thrill of the gamble."

Gambling. Well, she knew all about that. Maybe this was why Red and Joe had always gotten along together so well; Joe might never have done anything illegal, but he'd been the ultimate entrepreneur and risk taker. In order to build up his businesses, he'd juggled money with great success, right up until that success had—without her knowledge—disintegrated and turned to disaster.

"Sorry." He raised a thin hand by way of apology, and Rosa realized she'd been staring off into space. "Is that the reason you had to move out of Compton House? I haven't asked anyone what happened…"

She nodded. "It's fine. It's no secret. There was a problem with one of the businesses getting into trouble, and Joe did what he'd always done, borrowing from the others in order to shore it up. But this time, the situation didn't sort itself out, and he found himself getting deeper and deeper into debt. He didn't want to worry me, so he kept it to himself and worked on finding new ways to make it better…loans, a second mortgage, a few evenings in the casino. Except that didn't go according to plan either, and the more money he lost, the more he had to gamble to try and make it back, because sooner or later, it had to come good, didn't it? He didn't tell me any of this," Rosa went on. "A couple of his friends did, months later. And the thing is, he only did it because he loved me and wanted to protect our family. We meant the world to him."

"Of course you did."

"He was trying to get himself out of a financial hole, but the hole kept growing deeper. And I still had no idea about any of it. Then he had the heart attack, and it must have been the stress of it all that caused it to happen." Rosa's throat ached at the memory, but she forced herself to carry on. "He was about to be taken into surgery to be operated on, and I think he knew he wasn't going to make it. He kept telling me he loved me and was sorry over and over again, but I didn't know why he'd need to say it."

"Terrible for you." Red nodded in sympathy.

"It really was. I was in a complete daze for the next couple of weeks, but it was still really bothering me, not knowing why he hadn't been able to stop saying sorry. I mean, I always knew he loved me, and it had never even occurred to me that there could have been anyone else. But I actually began to wonder if he'd been having an affair."

"Joe? Never."

"I know. I wondered if some glamorous mistress might turn up at the funeral. Anyway, that didn't happen, and we had the service, and I was *still* waiting for the mistress to turn up. Then a couple of weeks later, I was called in for a meeting with Joe's accountant and his solicitor, and that was when the truth came out. That was when I discovered the mistress was actually the bank."

"Shit."

"Nearly all the money was gone. And the bank wanted our house because it no longer belonged to us. It was their house then."

"I can't imagine how awful that must have been." Red was reaching across, topping up her glass. "After everything else you'd been through."

"It *was* awful because it had been our beautiful home. When they told me, I burst into tears."

"I'm not surprised."

"But what they didn't realize," said Rosa, "was that they were tears of joy because all of a sudden, I knew why Joe had been saying he was sorry. There hadn't been any secret affair. Our marriage *had* been as happy as I'd always thought it was. Compared with what I'd been terrified of, losing the house was nothing."

Red nodded. "There you go. Money isn't everything." He paused, then winked. "Still nice though."

He'd lost his wife twenty years ago, and now his body was riddled with cancer, but he was utterly lacking in self-pity, still able to make her smile. Rosa said, "Shall we talk about something more cheerful? You must be so proud of Shay."

"Oh, I am, I am. My brilliant boy, who somehow managed not to inherit the criminal gene. You know, after he sold that company of his, a financial adviser told him he could move his money into an offshore account…all perfectly legal but it would save him a fortune in tax. And he wasn't even interested!" Red shook his head in disbelief. "No idea where he gets it from. Must be his mother's side of the family. God knows it wasn't mine." Laughter turned to coughing, and Rosa heard the effort it took to regain control of his breathing once he'd stopped. Then his phone began to ring and he said, "Let me guess, Angela again," because she'd called twice already, in floods of tears. Answering, he sighed, "Ange, you have to stop this. I'm in bed, about to go to sleep. No, it's the truth. I'm switching the phone off now. It's been a long day. Yes, I promise you, I'm fine. But you mustn't keep calling, OK? It's time to let go. You need to get on with your own life now."

"She's still crying," said Rosa when the call had ended. Sitting there while he told his sobbing ex that he was in bed had made her feel weirdly guilty.

"To be honest, for the last couple of weeks, she's hardly stopped. It's too much. It's exhausting." Red shook his head. "And quite boring too."

"She's upset. She loves you."

"She wants to marry me."

"Oh no, poor thing."

"Don't feel too sorry for her. Angela's all about the drama. And she only latched on to the idea of a wedding after finding out just how much my son was worth."

"Oh," said Rosa. That put a different slant on things.

"Quite. I think she likes the idea of being Shay's tragically widowed stepmother. Anyway, that's not going to happen. And I'm looking forward to a drama-free existence down here." He reached across and clinked his glass against hers. "Do you think we can manage that?"

"I'm sure we will. I'm not the dramatic type."

"Perfect. Cheers."

"Cheers." They clinked again.

"Nice bracelet."

"Thank you." Rosa shook her wrist, giving the charms a cheery jangle. "It was my birthday last week. This was my present from Layla."

"Well, happy birthday for last week. And lucky you, having a daughter who buys you such nice things."

"I know I'm lucky. Although actually, she didn't buy me this one." Afternoon prosecco had gone to Rosa's head and loosened her tongue, but if anyone was good at keeping secrets, it was Red. "She chose the charms specially because they all meant something to us and gave me the bracelet on the night of my birthday. By the next morning, it was gone."

"You mean someone took it?" Red looked outraged.

"No, not at all! It just fell off my wrist at some stage, and I couldn't find it anywhere. Last year, Layla gave me a turquoise pendant, and I accidentally dropped it down the waste disposal, so there was no way I could tell her I'd managed to lose the bracelet too. Which meant I had to travel over to Cheltenham, find the shop, and get another one made up with all the same charms. When I arrived back, that was when I missed my step getting off the bus and landed on the sidewalk. And you and Shay rescued me."

"I don't mean this to sound bad," said Red, "but I'm glad you fell off that bus."

Rosa smiled. "Now that it doesn't hurt so much, I'm glad too. Apart from having to shell out for another bracelet."

"Maybe it'll turn up. Then you can take this one back."

For a split second, she almost told him about her midnight visit to the garden of her old home. But no, he'd think she was deranged. "Fingers crossed."

He paused. "Can't be easy, though, going from living a comfortable life to having to downsize and start all over again."

"It had its moments. I'm getting used to it. When Joe was alive, he used to whisk me off to Milan for the weekend to buy beautiful designer outfits. Now I get most of my clothes in charity shops. But that's fine. It's exciting when you pick up a bargain." She plucked at the material of her lilac dress. "Like this one, three pounds fifty from the local hospice shop."

"You look great." Red nodded with approval. "No one would ever know."

"Except last December when I wore it to the Christmas fair in the town hall and Ingrid came up to me and said, 'Oh my goodness, look at you. I gave an identical dress to the charity shop!' So I had to confess that it was hers, and she said, 'Well, isn't that incredible? I'd never have thought something of mine would fit you!'"

"Charming. Who's Ingrid?"

"You saw her the other day, getting cross because her partner came over to try and help me to my feet while she was waiting to be let into their house. Which used to be our house."

"Ah, got it. Tall, skinny, long blond hair. Just your average nightmare."

"Ingrid isn't really a nightmare, just...blunt. She runs an international interior design company and is quite high-powered, says what's on her mind." Rosa paused, remembering the sternly worded letter she'd received from Benny Colette's solicitor in response to her own handwritten one: *I'm afraid my clients feel extremely strongly that your request is inappropriate and unworkable, and they are unable to grant any form of visitation rights to their property or its grounds.*

"What are you thinking now?" Red didn't miss a trick.

"Nothing."

"Have you been to the house since they moved in?"

She shook her head because, technically, she hadn't entered the house. "No, but I know it doesn't look anything like it did in our day. People who've seen it say it's very minimalist and Scandinavian, very *taupe*."

"Not my style." Red grimaced.

"Nor mine, but plenty of people love what Ingrid does. She's very in demand. Are you hungry, by the way? I can heat up a cottage pie if you fancy it."

"That sounds nice. I don't eat a lot nowadays though. You mustn't be offended if I can only manage a few mouthfuls."

"I'll put it in the oven, and you can have as much or as little as you like." Layla popped around after work a couple of times a week, but it would be nice to have someone else to cook for after all this time.

Rosa headed into the kitchen, but when she returned to the garden several minutes later, Red had fallen asleep in his chair. His hands were loosely clasped together in his lap, his head was tilted to one side, and a lock of dark hair had fallen across his tanned forehead. The shadows and lines on his face had lessened, leaving him looking several years younger, more like his old self. He'd always been a good-looking man.

His phone rang, making them both jump. He opened his eyes. "Whoops, dozed off there. Shay, hi. No, no need to come over. It's been a long day, and I'm exhausted." When he'd switched off his phone, he looked at Rosa. "Sorry, I don't think I can manage any food. Is it OK if I just go up to bed?"

"This is your home. You don't have to ask. You can do anything you want."

For a moment, there was a glint of something in Red's eye, as if he were about to make some teasing comment before stopping and thinking better of it.

"Thank you," he said instead, getting slowly to his feet. "I'm tired, that's all. But I'm fine."

Harry was up early on Wednesday morning, clattering around in the kitchen. After waiting for almost ten minutes to see if he was bringing her a mug of tea in bed, Layla made her way through the flat and found him eating a bowl of Shreddies with a tablespoon.

"Morning." He greeted her with a dazzling smile.

"Oh." Having found a clean mug and a tea bag, she scanned the contents of the fridge. "Where's my milk?" She'd brought a fresh carton of partly skimmed over with her yesterday.

"Isn't it there? Sorry, maybe I finished it." He looked baffled.

"You mean it's all in there?" Layla pointed to the oversized bowl in his left hand. "But…why didn't you use your soy milk?"

He shrugged. "I ran out."

"So what am I going to do?"

"I don't know. Drink it black?"

"But…I don't drink it black. That's why I brought a carton of milk over."

"Sorry, babe." He put the bowl down and gave her a kiss.

"You could run down to the co-op and pick up some more," said Layla.

"Haven't got time. I need to be out of here by eight thirty. And so do you," he reminded her.

She ran the cold tap and glugged down a glass of water instead, facing the sink.

"Oh dear, are you cross with me now? I'll buy a carton of milk for you next time. I know, I'm a bad boyfriend." Harry gave her his most beguiling smile. "But I don't mean to be, and I do I—" He stopped abruptly and closed his eyes. "No, I mustn't say that."

"Say what?" Her heart flipped.

"Nothing. How can I say it when I don't even deserve you?" He heaved a regretful sigh. "I really am sorry about the milk. Do you hate me now? Are you going to dump me? Please don't dump me." His tone was playful as he moved closer and inhaled. "God, you smell amazing."

How could she resist him? "OK, I won't dump you. This time." Layla said it teasingly; it might only be six days since they'd first met, but their time together had passed in a whirlwind of excitement and emotion. Having initially planned to make Harry wait for a fortnight, she'd rapidly amended that decision just in case he grew tired of waiting, and also because…well, why shouldn't she change her mind if she wanted to? When the chemistry was there, fizzing like champagne bubbles, what was the point in saying no just because advice columnists told you it would pay dividends and make your partner keener on you in the long run? Sometimes these things did need to happen sooner rather than later. Which they had, and it hadn't spoiled their relationship at all.

He laughed. "Thank goodness. Will I see you on Friday?"

"Not tomorrow?"

"Can't. I've got a new client booked in." His arms were around her now. "I'd rather be with you though."

"Well, how about coming over to my place on Friday? You haven't met Didi yet; we could meet up with her and Aaron."

"Look, I'm sure your friends are great," said Harry, "but I have to spend my days making small talk with clients. When I'm not working, I'd rather just relax. You and me alone together, here in my flat. I'm sorry if that's too boring for you, but it's my idea of heaven."

Against her better judgment, Layla felt herself melting, because when someone so beautiful to look at was saying those words, it was impossible to resist. He was stroking her hair now, running a thumb along the line of her collarbone, and the look in his eyes was just—

"Shit, is that the time? We need to get a move on." He gave her a brief kiss, filled with longing and regret, then pulled away. "Time to go."

She'd prebooked for Will to collect her at 8:45, but when she left the flat at 8:30, the taxi was already parked across the street, and he was sitting on one of the benches at the water's edge, enjoying the morning sunshine. Layla watched as he tore small pieces of bread from his sandwich and threw them to the ducks, then took a sip of something hot from a takeout cup.

When he saw her, he jumped to his feet and tossed the rest of the sandwich into the river.

"Oh, you didn't need to do that." She blurted the words out in protest. "Sit back down and finish your coffee. I'm early."

"Only if you're sure. I just got back from taking a family up to Heathrow." He took a gulp of his drink and fanned his mouth. "Sorry, bit hot."

"Coffee?"

"Tea."

Layla's mouth watered.

"Actually, I'll leave it," said Will. "I've had enough for now."

"Don't throw it away," she yelped as he leaned toward the bin.

He looked at her. "Why not?"

"It's a waste! I mean..."

"Do you want it?"

"I wouldn't mind."

"Didn't he make you a cup of tea this morning?"

"We ran out of milk." *We.*

"Here, help yourself. It's got sugar in it. Can you cope with that?"

"Perfect." For years, she'd tried so hard to get used to tea without, but it was never as nice. Not caring that it was hot, she glugged it down. God, it was like nectar. She wiped her mouth with the back of her hand. "Better than perfect. Thanks."

"You're welcome."

"Can I just...sorry, you've got crumbs..." She brushed them off the collar of his white shirt where he couldn't see them.

"Thanks. Let's get you home now, shall we?" He gathered up the iPad that had been lying on the bench next to him.

"You're always tapping away on that thing," said Layla. "I'd love to know what it is you're doing."

Will smiled, took the empty cardboard cup from her, and dropped it into the recycling bin next to the bench. "Nothing interesting. Come on. Let's go."

chapter 12

"Now, darling, just tell me this," Didi's mother had said over the phone the other evening from her seafront apartment in Marbella. "When you picture yourself in your wedding dress, what exactly do you *see*?"

Didi marveled at the way her mum's mind worked. She said patiently, "I don't see anything. I haven't found it yet."

"Well, we can't have you walking up the aisle stark naked, can we! When's your next day off?"

"Thursday. Why?" A split second later, Didi realized she'd fallen into a trap.

"Right, I'm booking my flight over. I'll see you on Thursday morning, and we'll make a start."

"A start on what? I'm not getting married until December." Another even more terrifying thought struck her. *Oh, please don't say I'm getting a surprise wedding and it's actually happening next week.*

"Sweetheart, December's no time at all. This isn't like picking up packs of panties in M&S, you know. Choosing the right dress and getting it altered to fit properly can take *months*."

Didi was already aware that she appeared to be lacking in some indefinable dress-selecting gene. She couldn't envisage anything worse than trying on endless variations of wedding outfits, but at the same time, she accepted that her mother probably had a point.

There'd be no stopping Maura anyway, once her mind was made up.

And now it was Thursday, and here was her mother, fresh off the plane and leaping out of Will Osborne's taxi, swathed in a flowing multicolored silk dress and trailing a cloud of perfume in her wake.

"Darling, are you quite sure you're ready?" She looked at Didi askance.

"How are you, Mum?" Didi gave her a hug. "And yes, I'm sure. Let's get this thing done."

"I meant is that what you're wearing?"

"It's my day off."

"Yes, but jeans? Hardly ideal when you'll be taking them on and off all day."

"I can keep them on," Didi reassured her, "and just try the dresses on over the top. You won't be able to see them under the skirt."

"Oh my goodness, you don't have a clue. Thank heavens I'm here to sort you out. Now let's get going, shall we?"

She was gesturing, attempting to lead the way back to the taxi. Didi dug her heels in like a dog and waved her car keys. "It's OK. I'm driving. We don't need a cab."

"Don't be ridiculous. You won't be able to drink if you take the car."

"Why would I want to drink?"

"Because they always give you glasses of champagne in bridal boutiques!"

"Can't I just say no?"

It was Maura's turn to look shocked. "No, you can't because that would be incredibly rude."

If customers had to have drink forced on them, choosing a wedding dress was clearly a major ordeal. Didi said, "I could tell them I was pregnant."

"Oh my darling! Are you?" Her mother's eyes lit up.

"*No*, Mum."

"Ah well, that's probably a blessing. Otherwise, it'd be a nightmare getting you fitted for your dress. Come on. We can't cancel the taxi now. I've already told Will he's got us for the next few hours. Let's have some fun, shall we? A proper mother-daughter day!"

By one o'clock, Didi was all frocked out, and her mother was just getting started. The wedding shops—no, not shops, always either boutiques or showrooms—were scented and glamorous and contained a dizzying selection of dresses. Will drove them from one to the next, waiting patiently in the taxi with only his iPad to keep him company while

Maura knocked back flutes of champagne and cried, "Oh, no, darling, that's so *plain*," every time Didi dared to try on something that didn't look like one of the showstoppers from *The Great British Bake Off*.

After a whistle-stop tour of Oxford, Cheltenham, and Stroud, Didi said, "This is torture, and if we don't stop for something to eat, I'm going to faint."

"You girls today, honestly. No stamina. Now, how about this one if we had extra Swarovski crystals sewn around the neckline and the hem?"

The dress was a monstrosity, and sparkling crystals were Didi's worst nightmare. She shook her head. "Mum, no. You can't make me choose something like that. If you're so desperate for a Disney princess dress, *you* get married. All I want right now is a plate of pie and chips."

"And that's why you couldn't do up the zip on the last dress you tried on," said Maura.

They didn't go for pie and chips; that wasn't her mother's style at all. Instead, they went to a glamorous new bistro in Minchinhampton, and Maura took a dozen or so photos of her starter before settling down to eat.

"So, how is everyone? All good at the hotel? How's Aaron?"

It was the first time she'd mentioned his name. With Maura living in Marbella and Aaron in London, they'd only met twice but had liked each other well enough. Didi said, "The hotel's fine. Aaron's great. He's busy at work but comes up most weekends."

"Show me your photos of him, darling. And has he sorted out what he's going to be wearing for the wedding?"

"Not yet, but he will." Aaron was keener on buying clothes than she was, and the walk-in wardrobe of his apartment in the Barbican was stuffed with designer outfits. Didi scrolled through the photos on her phone until she found the most recent ones of Aaron and herself.

"You do make a lovely couple. I prefer his hair like that, shorter at the sides. The first time I saw him, it was a bit...you know, bleurgh. He'll have it short for the wedding, won't he?"

"Mum, he's a grown-up. If he wants to dye it bright orange and wear it in a mohawk, he can."

"If he tried that, I'd wait until the registrar launched into the lawful impediment malarkey, then I'd stand up and say, 'Yes, I object. His hair is ridiculous, and I refuse to let my daughter marry such a plonker.'"

Didi laughed. "No one says plonker anymore."

"No one wants to marry one either." Maura grinned and gave her a playful nudge. "It's fine, I'm only teasing you. I like Aaron very much. And I promise I'm not going to turn into one of those nightmare mothers-in-law. I won't even come along with you on your honeymoon. Well, not unless you really want me to!"

They looked at a few more photos of Aaron, then chatted about the hotel staff Maura had known before Didi brought her up-to-date with various goings-on in the town and the happy news about Layla's blossoming romance with Harry the personal trainer. Finally, as their main courses arrived, she said casually, "Oh, and guess who else is back? Red Mason."

"Really?" Maura put down the fork she'd just picked up.

"And Shay." Didi wondered why she'd waited to tell her in this way. It felt as though her attempt at making the news seem less important had backfired.

Her mother took a sip of wine and dabbed at her lipsticked mouth with a napkin. "They're both back? Why?"

"Red has cancer. He doesn't have long to live. Shay's doing their old house up for him to move back into. Red's moved into Rosa's spare room until it's ready."

"And the boy?"

It was strange to hear him called that. Didi said, "Shay's staying in the Midnight Suite until the work's finished."

"The Midnight Suite at the hotel? But that's ridiculous. How can he afford that?" Her mother shot her a warning look. "If you're letting him stay without paying, you're—"

"I'm not doing that. He is paying."

"Well, in that case, I wonder whose credit card's going to be taking the hit."

"Mum, you—"

"And you've seen him, have you? I mean, has he spoken to you?"

"Yes, he's—"

"How about Red? You've seen him too?"

"We met up for a drink last week at the Prince of Wales."

"Oh, you did? So he's well enough to go drinking in pubs, is he?" Maura raised her eyebrows. "He's probably not even ill. It's just another of his stories."

"Trust me, he's ill."

"Well, just try not to have anything to do with them. I'm sure they're only back to cause trouble. And why on earth is Shay staying at the hotel anyway? Why would he even want to do that?"

"Because he can," said Didi. "Mum, he's rich."

"Hmph. Well, I suppose these things happen. Those king prawns look delicious."

They looked like king prawns. Didi said, "I mean, seriously rich. He invented Fait, the dating app, and just sold the company for, like, zillions. I asked him if he could afford to buy the hotel outright if he wanted, and he said he could."

She watched as this information sank in. At length, her mother said, "And is that his plan?"

"Pretty sure it isn't. It's our hotel, Mum. He can't buy something that's not for sale."

"Good. Well, I suppose he always was a smart boy."

Didi shook her head. "He never did have anything to do with what happened."

"Is that what he told you? Well, he's bound to say that, isn't he?"

"He would never have done anything like that. You know he wouldn't."

"And yet he up and disappeared." Her mother shrugged. "And no one else was ever caught. Anyway, never mind all that now. The best thing you can do is just keep well away from the pair of them. I know you were keen on Shay back when it happened, but it's all in the past now. You've got Aaron, you've got this little beauty"—she tapped Didi's engagement ring—"and five months from now, you'll be married!"

Lunch over, Maura took out a credit card and said, "My treat." She skimmed over the itemized bill, then looked up.

"Oh dear, excuse me?" She beckoned the young waitress over. "I'm sorry, this isn't right."

Didi winced inwardly; after years of working in the industry, she had a Pavlovian reaction to customers' complaints. It was even more awkward when the person doing the complaining was your own mother.

Maura tapped the bill and said briskly, "You've made a mistake here, charged us twenty-three pounds for the wine when it should have been thirty-two."

"Oh, gosh, I'm so sorry about that. Thank you for noticing."

"You also forgot to charge for the asparagus and the wild mushrooms, so you need to redo the bill."

Blushing and stammering, the waitress did as she was told. When the amended bill had been paid, she said, "Thanks again. Not many people would have done what you did."

"Darling, don't mention it. I wouldn't have wanted you to get into trouble. We've had a wonderful lunch, and that's the important thing. Me and my girl"—Maura gave Didi's hand a squeeze—"having a perfect day out together."

chapter 13

Rosa was waiting in line at the post office to send a just-finished doll off to Connecticut when a voice behind her said, "Hello there, how's that knee of yours? Better, I hope?"

It was Benny Colette, clutching a couple of small packages of his own. Rosa beamed. "Much better, thanks. It was sore for a few days, but all mended now. Thank you for coming to the rescue when you did."

"Not that I did much, but glad to hear you've recovered. That's a big old parcel you've got there. If it's heavy, want me to carry it for you while we're queuing?"

"I'm fine. It doesn't weigh much. I make dolls," Rosa explained, puffing a strand of hair away from her cheek. "This one's off to its new home in America." The hair was still there, so she transferred the package to one arm and used the free hand to clear it. Sitting waiting for her a couple of meters away, Red was observing the exchange with amusement.

Benny said, "Well, that's a coincidence."

"What? Don't tell me you make dolls too." She laughed. "Because I won't believe it."

"I don't. I just noticed your bracelet. Let's have another look?"

Feeling her cheeks heat up, Rosa raised her arm again, and Benny studied it more closely.

"Mouse…parrot…Eiffel Tower…little dog…yes, all the same charms, isn't that amazing? Last week, our gardener found a bracelet exactly like this in our back garden."

"Oh." Her mouth was dry, she knew she was blushing, and her brain, caught off guard, couldn't work out what to say without landing her in a world of trouble. "Well, this is…um, mine."

"Sorry, I'm an idiot. Of course they're the same." Benny shook his head. "I was thinking the charms had been chosen separately, but it must just be the way the bracelets are made and sold in the shop."

The perfect solution. Relieved, she exclaimed, "Yes, that's it. They all have the same charms!"

"Well, it looks very nice anyway."

"Thank you." Hooray, she could breathe again.

"Time for the lass to set off on her big adventure," said Benny.

Rosa was so steeped in guilt that for a split second, she thought he meant it was time for her to climb over the high stone wall into his garden. But Benny was pointing to the cashier waiting behind the glass.

"He's ready to take your parcel off you, send that doll on her way."

"Yes," she said faintly. "Thank you."

Five minutes later, with the parcel dispatched, Rosa said goodbye to Benny and left the post office with Red. As soon as they were safely out of earshot, he said, "Well, that was educational."

Her heart sank. "Was it?"

"You lied to him." Red tilted his head and gave her a side-on speculative look. "And you gave up the opportunity to get your two-hundred-pound bracelet back. I'm just wondering why you'd choose to do that."

It was no good; she was going to have to confess. She took a deep breath. "OK, you really want to know? Joe's ashes are scattered under his favorite tree in Benny's back garden. If I'd known we were going to have to sell the house, I'd never have done it. But I didn't know until afterward, and by then, it was too late." She paused, fiddling with the strap of her bag over her shoulder. "I wrote to the new owners, Benny and Ingrid, asking if I could possibly be allowed to…you know, occasionally visit the tree, because I missed Joe so much and it was the only place I could feel properly close to him. But the solicitors wrote back and said it wasn't possible. I mean, I suppose it sounded a bit pathetic. And I'm sure they've forgotten all about it by now. So anyway… Oh, don't laugh at me."

"Hey, I'm on your side." His eyes were bright. "I'm not laughing *at* you, I'm laughing with you. Go on. Tell me the rest."

He'd already worked it out for himself of course. But he was enjoying it so much, Rosa carried on. "Every week or so, when I really feel the need, I change into dark clothes, sneak out at night, and climb over the wall into their garden. I hug the tree, then I sit down and talk to Joe."

"And you've never been caught?"

"Never." *Obviously.*

"No security lights? No motion detectors?"

"I think they have them closer to the house, but not in my section."

"They really should."

"Please don't tell them that," said Rosa.

He was grinning now. "I won't. But I must say I'm impressed by your trespassing prowess after everything you told me about how law-abiding you are."

"I feel guilty every time."

"But isn't it a tiny bit exciting too? Doing something you aren't allowed to do and getting away with it?"

"Maybe." Rosa managed a faint smile. "Once I'm home safe."

"So falling off the bus last week can't have helped."

"I haven't been able to risk it since that happened." She flexed her knee, double-checking that the pain was negligible.

"But you're better now. When's it going to happen next?" He gave her a complicit nudge.

"Your appointment at the health center is for eleven fifteen." Rosa tapped her watch. "It's already ten past."

"And you're trying to change the subject."

"If you must know, I was thinking of paying a little visit tonight."

Red laughed. "Good for you."

"It won't be good if I get caught."

"Want me to act as your lookout?"

"No thanks. I was going to wait until you'd gone to bed."

"Come on. How can you expect me to get a wink of sleep? I'll be wide-awake and worried sick waiting for you to come back."

They'd reached the health center. Rosa pointed him in the direction of the entrance. "Off you go. I'll see you later. Give me a call if you want me to walk back with you."

"No need for that. My body might be decrepit," said Red, "but I still have all my brain cells. I know the way."

....

It was midnight when they set out along Barley Lane. Having slept from six until ten, Red had insisted on accompanying her.

"There's only the landing light on," Rosa murmured when they reached Compton House. "That means they're asleep."

"Over you go, then. And look after that knee of yours. If you hear an owl hooting, that'll be me warning you not to move. Well," Red amended, "unless it's an owl."

"I feel like Bonnie and Clyde."

His teeth gleamed white in the darkness. "You aren't allowed to be both."

Rosa located the familiar footholds and clambered over the high wall, dropping silently to the ground on the other side. Her knee took the strain without any trouble.

Oh, it was good to be back. Of course she could speak to Joe anytime she wanted, but it was only here that she ever felt truly close to him. Reassured that no one could see her, she gave the trunk of his tree an overdue hug and stroked its bark, murmuring, "Hello, sweetheart. It's OK. I'm here," into the warm night air. Then, sitting down on the ground and running her fingers over the neatly mown grass, she imagined Joe seating himself opposite her, his dear face wreathed in a smile of anticipation as he waited to hear her news.

And since there was rather more of it than usual, she wasted no time in regaling him with everything that had happened since her last visit. For a good fifteen minutes, she chatted away in a low voice, knowing that Joe would be entertained by the various goings-on. Then, mindful of poor Red having to wait for her on the sidewalk, she whispered, "Right, I'd better go now. Love you so much, sweetheart. Now that my knee's better, I'll be back again soon."

Thirty seconds later, just as she was in the process of hauling herself over the wall, a faint swish of bicycle tires on dry pavement reached her ears, and something bat-like loomed out of the darkness. The bike's rider jammed on the brakes and squealed to a halt in the middle of the road. Rosa, her heart crashing against her ribs, ducked out of sight and dropped back down into the garden with a thud.

"May I ask what's going on here?" The stentorian tones of Beryl Thomsett rang out, and Rosa squeezed her eyes shut in dismay because Beryl was bossy, nosy, and afraid of no one.

"Nothing at all. I—"

"Oh good heavens, it's *you*. I heard you were back in town, Red Mason. Well, I suppose that answers my question," Beryl barked. "A leopard never changes its spots, does it? And don't think I didn't see your accomplice about to climb back over the wall either. Right, that's it. I'm calling the police."

"Oh no, shh, no no, you don't want to do that... It was jusht a shilly game, that'sh all. I was messing around... Honest, I don't do bad stuff anymore, I promise..."

Rosa cautiously opened her eyes and listened because all of a sudden, Red sounded completely plastered.

"Don't be ridiculous. I know who you are, remember. *You*, on the other side of the wall." Beryl's voice rose to address the intruder. "Get yourself over here this minute. I'm not afraid of you, whoever you are, and I have a blue belt in karate."

"OK, OK, no need to shout," Red slurred. "All I did was try to throw the housh keysh over Rosa's head for a joke... I didn't mean for them to go into the garden, and then I couldn't climb over and get them, so she had to—*hic*—do it. Rosa? Rosa, come and tell Beryl not to arrest me... I'm shorry I threw the keys... Did you manage to find them?"

Hooray for quick-thinking ex-criminals. Rosa called out, "Yes, just found them now, thank goodness! Hang on..." She clambered back up and over the wall like a black-clad ninja, dropped down onto the sidewalk, and took her house keys out of her jeans pocket. "Here they are, *phew*, and you're never going to do anything like that again."

"I'm shorry." Red staggered and swayed convincingly. "They weren't shupposed to go over the wall. I thought you'd catch them."

"Hello, Beryl!" With a bright smile, Rosa waved the keys at her. "We really weren't trying to break into Compton House. Red just had a bit too much to drink and did a silly thing. Don't worry. I'm taking him home now to sleep it off."

"Well." Beryl sounded disappointed; she'd evidently been looking forward to carrying out a double citizen's arrest. "I hope you know what you're doing, letting someone like him move into your house. If you want my opinion, it's just asking for trouble."

"Shorry." Swaying again, Red said, "I'll behave myself, I promish."

With a humph of disgust, Beryl got back on her sturdy bicycle and pedaled off, her black Burberry mackintosh billowing out like bat's wings behind her.

"You make an excellent drunk," Rosa told him.

"Thank you." No longer swaying, he bowed.

"And thanks for getting me out of trouble too. If she'd caught me there on my own, I wouldn't have been able to think of an excuse fast enough."

"Rules for life. Always have an excuse at the ready. You never know when you're going to need one."

Rosa laughed. "You have your uses. I'm learning more and more."

"Oh, you're lucky to have me. I'm practically indispensable," said Red.

chapter 14

"What are you thinking?" said Harry, appearing in the bedroom doorway.

What was she thinking? Layla had no intention of answering that. Telling a brand-new boyfriend that you were imagining how you'd write your new name once you were married to him would be terrifying enough to send anyone running for the hills, if not crashing through the bedroom window.

Oh, but it sounded so perfect though. Layla Gray! In her mind, she'd already been practicing her new signature, especially loving the underlining flourish of the final *y*. Of course, plenty of professional women preferred to keep their own surname when they married—and there was nothing wrong with Gallagher—but equally, wasn't it nice sometimes to have a change?

"I'm thinking it's far too early to be getting up yet." Lying back against the pillows, she patted the empty side of the bed in a seductive manner. "I hope you weren't thinking of leaving me alone in here."

"I wish we could stay in bed all day." He looked regretful. "But I have to work."

"What? It's half seven on Saturday morning."

"And I have a client waiting for me to knock on her door at eight fifteen. Hang on. Kettle's just boiled." He disappeared into the kitchen and returned two minutes later with a red-and-white-striped Arsenal mug. "Here you go. I've made you coffee."

Layla preferred tea, but she said, "Thank you!" and took a cautious sip, ducking her head so he wouldn't see her mouth curl in a grimace because he'd made it with cheap granules and soy milk again.

"Is it OK?"

"Lovely!" She beamed because no one liked a finicky girlfriend. It wasn't his fault he preferred soy milk to the normal kind.

While Harry was in the shower, Layla thought back over the past nine days, which had passed in a haze of happiness.

Anyway, a perfect weekend now lay ahead of them. Throwing back the duvet, she raced through to the kitchen, tipped the contents of the Arsenal mug down the sink, and jumped back into bed with the empty mug just as the shower was switched off.

When Harry emerged from the bathroom wearing only a sky-blue towel around his hips, Layla said, "I've been thinking. Rather than meet up later, why don't I wait here while you visit your client? Wouldn't that be easier?"

"It would be easier." He threw her an apologetic smile. "But I've got another client booked in at midday, and I'll be stuck with her for three hours at least." Reaching over to retrieve the mug, he added, "And she's keen to introduce me to her friend who might hire me too, so who knows when I'll be able to get away? Oh, baby, don't be sad. I'd much rather be with you than them, but building a client list is kind of important right now."

"I'm not sad," said Layla, which was a lie, but she didn't want to sound needy. "Actually, it's for the best. I have a ton of work to catch up on."

"Well, you do that, and I'll get on with my schmoozing, and we'll see each other this evening."

Leaving her with an entire empty day. *Bum.* Aloud, she said, "Perfect," while wondering if he would be missing her as much as she was going to miss him.

"You're amazing. Come here." Breaking into a slow smile, he put the mug down on the bedside cabinet and bent over to plant a kiss on her mouth. Which just made it worse because she didn't want the kiss to end.

"I'm going to ask you a question now," he murmured against her lips. "And I want an honest answer."

"OK." Heavens, what was he about to ask?

"Did you throw away the coffee I made you?"

Oh. Crestfallen, Layla said, "Yes."

"Why?"

"I can't stand soy milk." She might as well be honest. "It's rank."

He started to laugh. "Oh, babe."

"How did you know I'd thrown it away?" Please don't let there be hidden cameras.

"You don't taste of coffee."

Well, that was a relief at least. Layla nodded. "Excellent detective skills."

"And excellent abs." He flexed proudly. "Don't forget the abs."

"I don't think anyone could forget your abs."

"Right, we need to get out of here." Dressing at the speed of light, Harry scooped up the clothes she'd left in an untidy pile on the chair in the corner of his bedroom. As he handed them to her, he leaned forward and kissed her again. "You're gorgeous, do you know that?"

She ran the flat of her hand over the front of his white T-shirt, her fingertips bumping over the impressive six-pack. She didn't usually have this much confidence, but he was making her feel like a goddess. Kissing him back, she said playfully, "Of course I do."

When they'd left the flat and Harry had headed off on his bicycle, Layla sat down on one of the riverside benches and took out her phone. Telling herself she fancied a change, she called Alan's Taxis instead, but Alan was taking a family to Gatwick, and his brother was sleeping off a late night and probably wouldn't be awake before midday.

The third and worst taxi company in Elliscombe wasn't even answering its phone.

She heaved a sigh, texted a request to Will, and received a prompt reply:

> I'll be there in ten minutes.

She sat back on the bench to wait. He hadn't made any more barbed comments since that initial evening, but she sensed he was still thinking them. Well, if he came out with some sarcastic remark, he'd get an earful in return.

On the sidewalk behind her, she heard the *clip-clop* of two pairs of high heels, and a girl said with a snicker, "See that one over on the bench? Looks like a Christmas tree."

Which was fair enough really, considering the way the multicolored sequins were glittering on her emerald taffeta jacket.

"Imagine having to go home dressed like that, so everyone knows you hooked up last night." The other girl spoke with more than a touch of schadenfreude. "Embarrassing, innit?"

Layla imagined having the kind of confidence to turn and say to them, "Actually, I'm not embarrassed at all. It was great."

When Will's taxi pulled up, he didn't utter a word as she climbed into the passenger seat. Not until they were a couple of miles down the road did he say easily, "It's going to be a nice day."

"It is. Except I'll be busy working in my office."

Several seconds passed before Will continued, "Looks like it's all going well, then. With the new guy."

Here it came. Layla braced herself. "Very well, thanks."

They paused at a junction. "Has your mum met him yet?"

"No, because I'm not living in an episode of *Downton Abbey.*"

"Don't you think Rosa would like him?"

She gave a *pfff* of exasperation. "Of course she'd like him."

"Sorry, I'm sure she would." Will accelerated out onto the main road. "I was just wondering why it's always you going over to his place rather than him coming to yours."

"Because I prefer it this way." Layla's tone was crisp. *Not that it's any of your business.*

"Fair enough." He grinned, unperturbed. "Well, more business for me."

Back in Elliscombe, she stepped out of the taxi and heard a piercing wolf whistle from across the street. Oh no, not more comments. She ignored it, but as she was letting herself into her flat, a hand landed on her shoulder. "And where have you been, you naughty girl?"

She turned. "I think you can probably guess. Was that you whistling just now?"

"Yes, it was me. I saw the cab pull up and there you were. You stayed over again last night, then? I've got five minutes," said Didi, "for you to make a quick coffee and catch me up with all the gossip."

Upstairs, in the flat above her office, Layla switched on her shiny black coffee machine and made two proper coffees with real, fresh milk… oh, bliss.

"So? How's it going?" Didi's eyes were bright.

"Great. Really great."

"And how many times last night?"

"Twice last night. No time this morning because he had to go to work."

"Right, but it's still good?"

"It was fantastic. Everything was fantastic," said Layla, "apart from the soy milk he puts in coffee."

"Oh, gross. Tell him to get some proper milk in."

"Already have." She changed the subject. "Are you and Aaron around this evening?"

"Aaron can't make it this weekend." Didi was already checking her watch, sipping too-hot coffee in her haste to get back to the hotel. "He has a work thing on. How's your mum getting on, having Red as a lodger?"

"Loving it so far. She's enjoying the company. Slightly worried he's going to teach her how to steal a Lamborghini, but…"

"He's a reformed character," said Didi. "And your mum's an angel who'd never do anything naughty."

"Of course she wouldn't. And speaking of Red, everything going OK with you and Shay?"

"We're fine. He's a guest at the hotel, and I'm the manager. We see each other in passing, chat for a bit, that's all."

"Really?" Layla raised an eyebrow as Didi finished her coffee. "You don't look at him and get butterflies, then start remembering the old days when you two were crazy about each other?"

"No." Didi tried not to smile.

"Well, I don't know why you wouldn't because it's not as if he got ugly and turned into a complete *troll*—"

"I need to get back to work." Laughing, Didi rose to her feet and headed for the door. "I have a fiancé, remember? Shay has his work cut out fixing up his dad's house. And you have your new boyfriend to keep you busy. So no more troublemaking, OK?"

The door closed behind her, and Didi clattered down the staircase. Alone once more in her pride and joy, the little flat she'd decorated with such love and care, Layla gazed around at the beautiful curtains, soft rugs, comfortable furnishings, and perfect lampshades. The kitchen might be small, but it was fitted out with all modern conveniences, and in the bathroom—which was spotless—she never ran out of posh toilet paper. She'd described her flat to Harry, had even shown him photos of it on her phone. He'd seen for himself how warm and welcoming it was.

So why, each time she suggested he might like to come over to Elliscombe, did he end up persuading her that it would be easier if they met up at his place instead?

chapter 15

"Come upstairs." Shay was holding his hand out, beckoning for her to follow him. "I've got something to show you."

Which if anyone else were saying it would have prompted a smart reply. But right now, Didi's mouth was too dry to utter a single word because the look in Shay's silver-blue eyes, framed by those dark lashes, was having far too much of an effect on her. He meant business, serious business, she could tell. When they reached his old bedroom, he was going to kiss her, just like old times, and her body was already quivering with joyful anticipation, because she wanted it to happen, it had been so long...

Oh, but why did there have to be so many things in the way, cluttering up the staircase? Struggling not to lose her balance and stumble over the bags of rubble, Didi clung on to Shay's hand.

"It's OK," he said like a man in absolute control. "You're safe. I've got you."

But when they finally reached his old bedroom, it was full of drifting snow and penguins—

"Whoops, sorry," said Sylvia as Didi's eyes snapped open. "I didn't know you were asleep. Slight problem downstairs."

Didi blinked, realizing that she was in her apartment, having dozed off on the sofa in front of the TV. On the coffee table was a plate containing a slice of cheese on toast with just one bite out of it, alongside her untouched mug of tea. She swung herself upright and felt the last vestiges of Shay's warm grip on her hand drift off into the ether as the dream full of promise was replaced by tedious reality.

"Give me a second." She slurped a mouthful of tea and grimaced because it was stone cold. Then she shook her head to clear the fuzziness and looked up. "OK, ready. What's happened?"

"Brace yourself," said Sylvia. "It's a tricky one."

....

Tricky was an understatement, and the lingering memory of that dream wasn't making the situation any easier. Parking up on the overgrown verge outside Hillcrest, Didi took a deep breath and climbed out of the car. Having edged past the almost-full dumpster on the driveway, she entered the house through the open front door and found Shay levering up rotten floorboards in the living room.

At least he wasn't upstairs in the bedroom, surrounded by drifts of snow and dancing penguins.

"Hi." He sat back on his heels. "When I heard the car pull up outside, I wasn't expecting it to be you. Everything OK?"

That voice, those hypnotic eyes and thick lashes...and now he was wiping his hands along the faded denim that was stretched across his thighs, with absolutely no idea of the effect it was having on her fevered imagination, purely because less than twenty minutes ago, his hand had been holding hers as he led her upstairs to see whatever it was he needed to show her.

"No, everything isn't OK." Didi gave herself a mental shake; she really must stop thinking about that dream. "And I need to ask you a massive favor."

"Right. Interesting." He rose to his feet. "Should I say yes straightaway or wait until I hear what it is?"

"A couple have just turned up at the hotel. She's eight and a half months pregnant."

"Hang on, is this Christmas Eve? Did they arrive by donkey?"

"It's their wedding anniversary," Didi went on. "They got married a year ago at the Wickham. Four months ago, the husband booked the Midnight Suite for tonight as an anniversary surprise."

"You mean someone at the hotel messed up and double-booked the room?" Shay raised an eyebrow. "Oh dear, was it you?"

It was good that he was joking, but not so good that the way he was looking at her was turning her insides to jelly. She said steadily, "It wasn't me. He arranged it online through a booking agent without realizing they were scammers. The agency reserved the suite with us, sent him the confirmation, then kept the money he sent them. When we didn't receive the payment, the booking was automatically canceled. The first this guy knew about any of it was half an hour ago when he and his wife turned up for her surprise stay. Which turned out to be more of a surprise than either of them were expecting."

"Right." Shay nodded slowly.

"She burst into tears."

"Poor woman."

"And she's…" Didi spread her arms, miming a vast pregnancy bump swelling out in front of her.

"So you're wondering if I'll do the gentlemanly thing and give up my suite for the night."

"Yes."

"Go on then, you've twisted my arm." His mouth turned up at the corners. "I'll move to another room. All in the name of romance."

Didi took a deep breath; she hadn't finished twisting his arm yet. "Thanks, that's great. The thing is, we're completely booked up, so there isn't actually another room for you to move into."

"Right. Maybe they could share my suite," said Shay. "I'll sleep in the bath."

She broke into a grin. "You're a hero, but it doesn't have to be that drastic. I thought you could move into my place for the night and—"

"Are you serious? Does Aaron know about this?"

"I thought," Didi continued, "that you could move into my apartment for the night, and I'll stay over at Layla's."

Shay considered this for a second. "What about Aaron? Does Layla have room for both of you?"

"He's had to stay in London this weekend. Busy with work."

"OK." He nodded, then gestured around the living room. "Well, I was going to put in a couple more hours here, but should I go back now and move my stuff out?"

"Are you definitely happy to do this?" Didi double-checked.

"Not a problem."

Phew, relief. "Thanks so much. You're a star." Pulling out her phone, she said, "And we can take care of everything if you'd rather carry on here for a bit. I'll just give Sylvia a call and let her know."

"How about you? Are you on duty tonight?"

"No." She shook her head. "Why?"

"Would your fiancé object, do you think, if I asked you to have dinner with me?"

A zing of adrenaline shot through her body. Aaron might not be deliriously happy about the prospect, but he was off to a ridiculously glamorous event this evening at the Goring in Belgravia, and she knew for a fact that two of his ex-girlfriends who worked for the same company were going to be there too.

So he could hardly object, could he?

"Hello?" said Sylvia, answering the call. "And?"

Didi exhaled. "Shay's happy to do it. Can you let the couple know, then get his things moved into my apartment?"

"Oh, thank heavens for that! I knew he wouldn't disappoint us." Sylvia's delight was evident. "I could kiss him!"

"No need to go that far." Ending the call before Shay could overhear anything even more inappropriate, Didi looked at him. "Aaron isn't the jealous type. He won't mind at all."

"Good. Was that Sylvia? What else did she say?"

"That she could kiss you."

"Wow." His mouth twitched. "Sounds like it's my lucky day."

Rosa finished rereading the letter that had arrived earlier and heaved a sigh. She put it down on the kitchen counter, and the breeze through the open window sent it gliding to the floor.

"Don't worry. I'll get it." Bending, Red retrieved the handwritten letter with the attached photo. "What is this, another order?"

"Yes. Well, kind of."

He gave her a quizzical look. "Can I read it?"

She wavered, already knowing what his reaction would be, then shrugged. "Fine."

Red studied the photo for a couple of seconds, then began reading aloud:

Dear Rosa,

Here is a photograph of my darling little granddaughter Maisie who I love more than life itself. She is six years old and gets bullied by all the other children at school because she has to wear glasses and also has a big birthmark on her neck, and it just breaks my heart.

Maisie is a dear sweet girl, and she cries every day because she has no friends and says nobody else in the world looks like her. Well, last night I saw a video on Facebook of a little boy opening a parcel from you, and it was so wonderful. I was in floods of tears when he saw the doll you'd made for him. It would just be so lovely if my little Maisie could have a doll that looks like her. I would do anything to make her smile again, but the sad thing is, I can't afford to buy one of your dolls. I am an old-age pensioner and a widow with hardly enough money to get by, so I was wondering if you ever made dolls for free out of the goodness of your kind heart. If you could do this, I would be so grateful, and you would make my darling Maisie the happiest little girl in the world!

Bless you in advance.
Yours sincerely,
Pamela Baker

When he had finished reading, the room was silent apart from a bumblebee bashing itself against the window, unable to comprehend why it couldn't get through the glass.

"Well," Red said drily, "full marks to her for trying. She must think you're a complete pushover. Do you want to chuck it in the garbage or shall I?"

"No!"

"Oh please, the woman's a con artist. If it's even a woman." He shook his head. "It's probably some bloke who'd rather spend his cash on beer and women than use it to buy his kid something for her birthday."

"Don't say that," Rosa pleaded.

"It's a begging letter. Somebody wants something but they don't want to pay for it. They're trying to find out just how much of a soft touch you are."

"You think that, but what if you're wrong?" Maybe she was a bit of a soft touch, but wasn't that better than being endlessly suspicious and cynical? Her vivid imagination meant she'd instantly conjured up mental images of Maisie and her kindhearted grandma. She said, "It could be genuine. And that poor little girl, being bullied at school, sobbing her heart out..."

"If I'm right," said Red, "they'll start targeting you for money next. Trust me, I know what these people are like. I've met enough of them in my time."

Rosa knew deep down that he was probably right. "OK, I won't make the doll. I'll pretend I never got the letter, it was lost in the mail."

"So does that mean I can get rid of it?"

She swallowed and nodded. "Go on, then."

"Well done. Gold star for you." Red lifted the lid of the garbage can and dropped the balled-up letter inside. "Right, I'm going to go and sit in the garden."

Rosa waited until he was safely settled outside with his cup of tea and a newspaper, then stealthily retrieved the crumpled ball and wiped away the stains left by Red's tea bag. Just because she wasn't going to make the doll didn't mean she had to throw the letter away.

chapter 16

It was seven in the evening, and the room swaps had been implemented. Up on the top floor of the hotel, the anniversary couple were happily ensconced in the Midnight Suite. Here in the private quarters, Didi's room had been tidied up, the linen had been changed, and Shay's case lay open on her beloved king-size bed. She'd already wheeled her own overnight case across the high street and left it in Layla's flat. And Layla, getting ready to meet up with the new love of her life, had given her the spare key because she'd be staying over—*again*—at Harry's place tonight.

It was more bed-hopping than Didi was used to but worth it to keep good customers satisfied. Now, having demonstrated to Shay how her temperamental shower worked, she let herself out of the flat before he could emerge from the bathroom stark naked.

Ooh, imagine…

Not that it was likely to happen, but better to be on the safe side. It made sense to wait for him downstairs.

Finding herself a comfortable rattan seat in the orangery, she opened a text from Aaron.

> There are speeches. No one warned me about the speeches. They're going on and on and ON.

She smiled and texted back:

> You poor thing, how you suffer for your career. Have some more champagne.

Thirty seconds later, he sent her a photo of himself looking suitably cheerful, brandishing a condensation-speckled bottle of Laurent-Perrier. The accompanying text said:

> I'll survive. How about you? Doing anything nice tonight?

She hesitated, then typed:

> Quick catch-up with Shay before heading over to Layla's.

Which was technically true but—she hoped—also made the Shay part sound reassuringly insignificant.

Ting. Aaron's reply flashed up on the screen:

> Have fun. But not too much fun! X

"There you are." Shay appeared, his hair still damp from the shower. He was wearing navy trousers, a purply-blue shirt the color of blackberries, and the aftershave she would always associate with him for as long as she lived.

"Hi. Sorry, I was just letting Aaron know what's happening." Didi showed him the phone screen.

Shay nodded and sat down. "Takes things in his stride, I see. As you say, not the jealous type."

"He knows he doesn't need to be. I once had a boyfriend who was jealous." She pulled a face. "Not an attractive quality. And counterproductive because it just makes you think they know you could do better than them."

"So what happened? Or can I guess?"

"I finished with him."

Shay laughed. "Of course you did. Right, where are we eating? Any preferences?"

"Here, I think. Then no one can see us having dinner together somewhere else and think they've caught us out on some kind of clandestine meeting."

"Like a date, you mean? You'd rather be on display for all the world to see." He grinned. "Makes sense. Will we be able to get a table here? It's looking pretty busy."

"We'll get a table," said Didi. "I know the management."

Once they'd moved through to the restaurant and chosen from the menu, Shay said, "So when did the jealous guy feature in your life? Was he one of the fiancés?"

Didi shuddered. "God no, he was only around for a few weeks. We met at a hotel management conference. He was really keen on me, and the first couple of dates were fine. Then we went out for lunch in an Italian restaurant, and he got annoyed because he thought the waiter was being too friendly toward me. That was the first sign."

"And after that?"

"The next time, we were at a party, and he accused me of fancying one of his friends. I didn't," said Didi. "I was just being polite, but he wouldn't stop going on about it. I said I didn't think us seeing each other was working out, but he begged me to give him one more chance. So then we met up again a few days later in a park. There was a guy there throwing a ball to his dog, and one time, the ball landed at my feet. I teased the dog for a few seconds before giving the ball back, and that was when my psycho so-called boyfriend accused me of publicly humiliating him by flirting with the other guy and using his dog as an excuse."

"Nice of him," said Shay.

"So I told him it was over, walked out of the park, and caught a taxi home. And that was it. I never saw him again after that."

"Good. How about the ones you did get engaged to?"

Didi flashed a smile. "Have you been wondering about them ever since Sylvia told you about them on your first day back here?"

"Maybe. Just natural curiosity." He was maintaining a straight face, but there was a telltale glint in his eyes. Didi realized she was leaning across the table toward him, and Shay was mirroring the angle. She sat back and took a glug of ice water, adjusting her body language in case other people were surreptitiously taking note. Far better to look as if they were business acquaintances, all aboveboard.

Then again, no reason why she couldn't tell him about the fiancés. "Well, the first one was never meant to happen for a start. His name was Craig, and we got together in our final year at university. But it was one of those relationships that was always pretty casual, so once we graduated, I just assumed we'd go our separate ways. Except I didn't have the heart to break up with him, so it kind of limped on for a bit longer. When Craig came down to see me on the twenty-third of December, I'd already decided that as soon as Christmas was out of the way, I was definitely going to tell him it was over. It cost me a fortune," she added wryly. "I bought him a really expensive leather jacket because I felt so guilty about being the bad guy."

"Go on," Shay prompted, clearly enjoying hearing about her dating disasters.

"Well, my dad was throwing a big party here in the hotel that night, so it was full of friends, people we'd all known for years." Just the memory of the evening was making Didi's spine prickle with mortification. "Craig and I had already opened our presents to each other because the next morning, he had to drive up to Perth to spend Christmas with his family. He'd given me a really weird orange knitted dress that made me look like a frankfurter, and I had to wear it, even though it felt like my insides were being microwaved. But at least he'd bought me something that hadn't cost as much as the leather jacket. I was glad about that."

The conversation was interrupted by the arrival of their food. Didi picked up her knife and fork and continued. "Anyway, so all of a sudden, the music stopped, and there was Craig standing by the Christmas tree, asking everyone to be quiet because he had something important to say."

"And that was the moment you knew."

"It was the moment everyone in the room knew." Didi shivered at the memory. "It was like one of those dreams where you're walking down the street and suddenly realize you're naked. I wanted to run away and hide. I couldn't believe he was going to do it. But he was. He made me join him, then gave this whole speech about how much we loved each other and how I'd made him the happiest man in the world, and I wanted to faint with embarrassment. It just seemed to be going on forever. Then he went down on one knee, produced a ring, and asked me to marry him."

"And you said yes."

"I had to! He had that huge audience there, everyone whooping and cheering and clapping like seals. How could I say no? Well, I couldn't even speak," she amended. "I just nodded, and he put the ring on my finger, then he kissed me, and the crowd went wild. And that was it, I was engaged. Happy Christmas to me."

Shay looked amused. "Awkward. What was the ring like?"

Diplomatically, she said, "Oh, maybe I wouldn't have chosen it for myself, but I'm sure lots of girls would have loved it. Plus it was too big, so I had to keep my fist clenched for the rest of the night to stop it falling off."

"And how long did the engagement last?"

"Nine days. As soon as we'd gotten New Year's out of the way, I told him I couldn't do it and gave him back the ring."

"Was he upset?"

"Just a bit! But how could I have let it carry on? I let him down as gently as I could and said we'd always be friends. But Craig didn't want us to be friends, so that was that." She paused, remembering. "I've got a photo somewhere on my laptop of the proposal, sent to me by one of my dad's friends. You can actually see the terror in my eyes."

"Poor guy." Shay shook his head. "Do you know if he ever recovered?" He raised an eyebrow. "Or was he scarred for life?"

"Complete recovery. No scars." Didi smiled. "He's living in Cardiff now, married to a beautiful dentist named Alesha, twin boys named something and something"—she'd seen the photos on Facebook last year—"and a Maltese terrier named Digby."

They got on with eating their food before it was completely cold. Vestiges of her earlier dream were still flickering through Didi's brain, playfully taunting her and sending little rushes of adrenaline through her veins. She was still taking care to sit back and look as if this was nothing more than a pleasant casual dinner with an old friend, but her body knew better. Her body was more interested in wondering what might have happened in the dream if Sylvia hadn't burst into the room and woken her up.

"So that was the first one." Shay broke into her tumultuous thoughts. "How about the second?"

OK, concentrate. "You really want to know?"

"Of course I want to know."

She'd known he would. "Fine, then, but you mustn't laugh. This one doesn't do me any favors."

His eyes glittered in the candlelight. "I like the sound of this story already."

"His name was Pierre, he lived in Monte Carlo, and he came over to the UK to stay with his grandmother in Stow-on-the-Wold because she'd developed Parkinson's and needed someone to keep an eye on her. The family was wealthy, and his parents wanted to make sure she wasn't being taken advantage of, and Pierre was an artist, which meant he could work anywhere."

"A good artist?"

"Abstract." Didi pulled a face. "So who knows? Anyway, he brought Grand-mère here one evening for her birthday; that was how we met. Then he came back the next day without her and told me I was the one for him. It was a coup de foudre apparently, love at first sight. Was I single? Did I feel the same way? When could he see me again?"

"And when did you see him again?"

"That night. He was *French*," Didi emphasized ruefully. "He looked like a film star and had an accent to die for. I'd spent the last two years working flat out with no time to even think about boyfriends, and all of a sudden, here was someone volunteering for the job. Plus he was supercool and drop-dead gorgeous."

Shay's eyes flickered from her eyes to her mouth and back again. "So you went for it."

Why had he looked at her mouth? Did she have spinach in her teeth? And did he have any idea how that flickering glance made her feel?

She shrugged. "Everyone said I'd be crazy not to. So I did. And we had the most amazing time. It was one of those whirlwind relationships, and I really thought this was the one. His grandmother was a sweetheart too. Then after four months, he proposed to me."

"Four months?" Shay whistled. "That's pretty quick."

"I know, but it felt right. And this time, there was no audience. I said yes, and he gave me an antique diamond ring that had been in his family for generations. It even *fit*. I was twenty-four, and I thought this was it for the rest of my life."

"What happened?"

"Oh, he got fed up because I was working longer hours than he was happy with. So he started secretly seeing some woman who ran an art gallery in Oxford, and when I found out about it—because they didn't make much of an effort to keep it a secret—Pierre complained that it was my fault for leaving him on his own and caring about my career more than I cared about him. He said how else was he meant to pass the time? And I was devastated—I mean, properly heartbroken. I just couldn't believe he'd done this to me, but he still thought I was the one to blame." She shook her head and took another swallow of wine. "Finally, he offered me a deal. He agreed to give up his girlfriend in Oxford if I promised not to work more than forty hours a week."

Shay raised an eyebrow. "He sounds great."

"So I said no, I wouldn't do that, and he said fine, it was a shame, but if that was my decision, could he have his ring back?"

"I hope you at least threw it into the river," said Shay. "Or stuffed it down his throat."

"Except I couldn't because it didn't belong to him. It was his grandmother's."

"Were you really devastated?"

"Utterly. I couldn't eat, couldn't sleep, went through the next couple of weeks like a complete zombie. Because I just couldn't believe I'd fallen in love with someone capable of doing that to me. I felt gullible and stupid and furious with myself for getting it so wrong, but at the same time, I still missed him." She gestured helplessly with her fork. "Isn't that crazy? I'm telling you, it wasn't a happy time."

He was giving her that all-seeing look again. "But you got over him. Or did you? Maybe you still secretly dream about him?"

Didi shook her head. Enough talk about dreams. "Time heals. And it helped to hear that he had broken up with the woman from the art gallery. A week after that, he moved on to someone else, then another someone, then he got caught with a married TV actress, whose husband broke his nose. I suppose I finally saw him for what he was and realized he'd never be happy with just one woman in his life. And I decided to go back to concentrating on my career instead."

Shay tore off a piece of focaccia and pointed it at her. "Good for you."

"I can't believe I just told you that story. My greatest humiliation."

"Honestly?" A faint smile. "I liked hearing it."

Of course he would. She'd let Shay down when it mattered most, hadn't she? Having her heart broken by a charming, unfaithful Frenchman was karma in its purest form.

"So what happened after that?"

"I concentrated on my career. Again. Until Aaron came along and—"

"Swept you off your feet?"

Had there been sweeping involved?

"Until Aaron came along and made me realize there were good men in the world who weren't selfish and immature and only interested in sleeping with other women behind their girlfriend's back."

"Do you ever really know that for sure?" said Shay.

"I trust him. Completely. After Pierre, I didn't think I would ever trust again, but Aaron changed my mind. He won me over and ticked every box. He's the kind of man anyone would want to marry. Not a bad bone in his body..." *OK, stop now, before it sounds as if you're trying to convince yourself.*

There was such a thing as showering your fiancé with too much praise.

Shay searched her face for a second. "Well, good for you," he said as if he meant it. "I'm happy you've found—"

"Oh my God, it *is* you! Shay Mason, I can't *believe* it. Hello!"

chapter 17

Bossy Bella Carpenter had been two years above them at school, and her voice had always been loud. Now, as she approached their table like a ship in full sail, all heads turned, and Shay was forced to rise to his feet in order to be clutched in her embrace.

"How amazing, back at last—gosh, we have some serious catching up to do! And look at you two, having dinner together. Where's that handsome man of yours, Didi? Shay, it's so good to see you again, and looking so *well.*"

Alerted by the racket, Sylvia poked her head around the entrance to the restaurant and caught Didi's eye. Didi pushed back her chair. "Sorry, looks like I'm needed out in reception." Resting a hand on Bella's pillowy upper arm, she added cheerfully, "I was just telling Shay all about Aaron, so thank you for calling him handsome!"

Just as well they'd finished their meal; as Didi left the restaurant, Bella Carpenter was already sliding into her empty seat. Deciding to give them ten minutes together, Didi chatted for a while with Sylvia, and they agreed that Bella was both the noisiest and the nosiest inhabitant of Elliscombe. Through the doorway, they could hear and see her being her extravagant, cackling self.

"She's finishing your glass of wine." Sylvia was aghast.

"She's welcome to it. At least I'm not having to listen to her bellowing on about her precious holiday apartment in Cala d'Or." It occurred to Didi that if she was going to spend the rest of the evening in Layla's flat without Layla there to keep her company, she could do with something to read. "OK, I'm going to leave them to it. I'll just pick up a book, then head over the road. Don't worry. I'll text Shay and let him know."

"Ooh, have you tried that one I lent you last week? About the psychopathic granny baking severed heads inside birthday cakes?" Sylvia was hooked on thrillers, the more grisly and stomach-churning the better.

The book's blood-spattered cover design had been enough to put Didi off. "Is that a giant spoiler?"

"Oh yes. Sorry! It's still brilliant though."

"I don't think I'll read it. I don't know how you can enjoy stuff like that."

Sylvia winked. "Don't knock it till you've tried it."

"Fine, but I'm never going to eat any cake you've baked for me."

Upstairs, Didi headed over to the private quarters and let herself into her apartment. She found the novel Sylvia had lent her and read the blurb on the back cover: *The inhabitants of Upper Sisley are losing their heads. But who is taking them, and where are they being hidden? It's up to Marjory Buttermaker to find out!*

No need to bother with that one, then.

As she was sorting through her shelves of paperbacks, the half-open door was pushed wider, and Shay came in.

"You escaped," said Didi.

"Just about. One minute, you and I were having dinner together, and the next, you'd thrown me under the bus."

"Sorry. I didn't want Bella to think she was breaking up something… you know, *significant*."

"She finished your glass of wine."

"I know. I saw that. How did you manage to get away?"

"Told her I had to take a conference call with a company in New York." He paused. "I wasn't expecting to find you here."

"Just dropped by to pick up something to read." Didi waved the book currently in her hand, then realized it was titled *The One That Got Away* and hastily shoved it back on the shelf.

"We could go downstairs and get another drink if you want. Bella's left, so it'd be safe."

"I don't think so." Didi shook her head; even prior to Bella's arrival, she'd been aware of other diners keeping a surreptitious eye on her. Which was fine when you'd absolutely nothing to hide but less comfortable when the whole reason for sitting together in public was to convince your audience that this was the case.

Especially when—let's be honest here—it wasn't.

"I know." Effortlessly reading her mind, Shay said, "I felt it too. But there's no reason why we couldn't have another drink up here before you go over to Layla's."

Could he really not think of a reason? Did that mean she was the only one battling with her emotions? Teetering on the edge, she heard herself say, "OK, just one drink." Well, she hadn't been able to find a book that grabbed her attention. "There's a bottle of Vouvray in the fridge. Shall I open it?"

"I'll do a deal with you," said Shay. "Let me sort out the wine. You find that photo of you being proposed to by the first of the three fiancés."

He disappeared into her tiny kitchen, and Didi peered at the desktop. By the time he returned with two glasses, she'd found the incriminating photograph.

"I see what you mean about the outfit." For a moment, as he leaned in closer for a better look, Shay's forearm brushed against hers, and she didn't dare glance down because she could feel the little hairs on her own arm standing to attention.

"I really did look like a knitted frankfurter."

"The expression on your face," said Shay. "God, I'd love to have been there."

And for a moment, Didi couldn't speak, because if he *had* been there, if they'd stayed together and Shay had never left Elliscombe, she would never have gotten involved with Craig in the first place.

She gave herself a mental shake. "OK, now let's show you Pierre." She began scrolling forward at the speed of light, whizzing through the next couple of man-free years. "Here he is."

Shay slanted an eyebrow. "Looks like a smooth bastard."

He did too. Hindsight was a wonderful thing. Skimming forward again, Didi found the section containing recent photos featuring herself and Aaron. Out of a sense of pride, even though Shay had already met him in person, she wanted to find the ones that made Aaron look his best.

After a second, Shay nodded. "I hope he makes you happy."

"He does." And now her heart was thudding against her ribs, because while it wasn't a lie, it suddenly felt like one.

"Got any more?"

"Of Aaron? Loads!" She brought up the next one, of Aaron striking one of his Hollywood poses, then hastily slid past before Shay could pass comment.

"Actually, I meant photos of any more boyfriends."

"No." Was it embarrassing that there hadn't really been any others? Her dating history had been patchy to say the least.

"Not even the first one?" said Shay.

She turned sideways to look at him. "You mean you? We didn't have cell phones back then." It had been just before they'd become affordable for teenagers. Somewhere in the back of a drawer was a box containing random photos taken at parties using cheap disposable cameras, but that was as far as it went.

"Nothing at all from Venice?"

She shook her head. He'd had copies made of those magical snowy nighttime photos, and she'd treasured them, keeping them safe in the back of her purse so she could gaze at them whenever she wanted…until she and Shay had broken up and he had abruptly left town, and it had been just too painful to remember the night it had all begun in St. Mark's Square.

"Let me guess, you tore them into a hundred pieces and threw them away?" He was watching her, half smiling now, because he knew so well what she'd been like.

Didi smiled too. "I was going to do that, but Layla persuaded me not to. So they stayed in my purse. Until a few weeks later, when she took me to Cheltenham on a shopping trip to try and cheer me up. While we were queuing in Burger King, someone accidentally tripped and fell against me. Well, I thought it was an accident, but when we went to pay, my purse was gone from my bag."

"Were you devastated?"

"It was OK. Layla paid for my burger."

Shay laughed. "Well, thank goodness for that."

She'd always loved his laugh, had loved being able to make him laugh. After a moment, she said, "But yes, of course I wished I hadn't lost the photos. They were a part of our past."

Shay took out his phone, keeping the screen angled away. When he showed it to her, there it was, the photograph that had existed only in her mind for the last thirteen years. It was slightly yellowed and worn around the white edges, with a diagonal crease across the bottom left-hand corner, but otherwise exactly as she remembered. There they were, two teenagers, standing pink-cheeked and sparkly eyed alongside a snowman just a couple of hours old, laughing at each other while the elderly Italian man took their photo and snow fell like fat swirling feathers around them.

Seeing it again was surprisingly emotional. For a long moment, Didi had to concentrate hard on willing her eyes to stay dry. When she trusted herself to speak again, she said, "I never thought..."

"You didn't think I'd keep them? I almost didn't," Shay admitted. "I left them behind when I went to Australia. Then eighteen months later, while Dad was out of prison, I asked him to send me my five-year diary. When it arrived and I unlocked it, there were the photos."

She remembered the diary, fat and padlocked, which he'd kept beside his bed. He had filled it with little cartoons, random thoughts, addresses and phone numbers, funny stories, and plans for the future.

"So I kind of followed you all the way to Australia."

The creases deepened at the outer corners of his eyes. "You did. It was good to see you again. After that, I took you along with me wherever I went."

Didi was touched to hear it. And now, thanks to technology, there were digital copies of the photos that would last forever. Tapping a key on her desktop, she pointed to show him her email address. "Can you send them to me?"

Shay nodded, and a couple of seconds later, the photos arrived in her inbox.

Just like that, and just as they could have done all those years ago while they'd been on opposite sides of the world, if only they'd been speaking to each other.

Didi swallowed the lump in her throat. "Did you hate me?"

"No." He shook his head slowly. "I didn't hate you. I just realized you didn't completely believe me, and that was the worst part of all, the biggest kick in the teeth. I couldn't handle it."

It was terrible to hear him say it, and she couldn't even attempt to defend herself because it was the truth. His departure had broken her heart, and she couldn't blame him for disappearing.

Oh, but how different their lives might have been if the thing that had driven Shay to leave had never happened.

chapter 18

It had taken the others on the Venice trip less than a morning to work out what was going on. So much for believing they were being discreet.

"What's up?" Layla had demanded as they ran upstairs to collect hats and coats before heading out for their trip on a vaporetto. "You were being all weird during breakfast, and now you're looking all...*zingy*."

If she *looked* zingy, she felt even zingier on the inside. "It's the snow. It's exciting! It's your birthday, and we're in Venice! Who wouldn't be zingy?"

But Layla wasn't the only one who'd noticed something was up. The more normal Didi tried to be, the more impossible it became to remember what normal felt like. And Shay Mason had evidently found it just as tricky. All it had taken in the end was for their covert glances and resultant fleeting smiles to be intercepted by the rest of the group. By lunchtime, their cover was well and truly blown, and the inevitable torrent of teasing ensued.

Nothing more had happened that weekend, but everyone continued to be aware of the electricity crackling like invisible fireworks between the two of them.

"See?" Layla was gleeful and as proud as if she'd engineered the situation herself. "Aren't you glad I invited him now? I told you he was nice!"

And when they flew home on the Sunday afternoon, as the snow was melting in Venice, the situation between Didi and Shay was unmistakably heating up.

So that had been the start of it, and the following months had turned out to be the best of Didi's life, a giddy whirlwind of first love, studying for A levels, brilliant sex, more studying, loads more sex, spending every possible minute together, and basically feeling sorry for everyone else on the planet because they couldn't possibly be as happy as she was.

It just didn't get better than that. Didi had never expected to meet the love of her life at the age of seventeen, but it had happened anyway, and there wasn't a thing she could do to stop it. She loved Shay Mason with all her heart and every atom of her being. Nothing was ever going to tear them apart.

If her parents had been less than thrilled when they first discovered that their only daughter was involved with Red Mason's son, any concerns were soon allayed once they got to know him. Shay was warm, intelligent, charming, and trustworthy. He took his father's reputation in his stride and was even able to joke about it, which in turn enabled other people to relax and stop worrying about mentioning the elephant in the room.

By mid-June, A levels were behind them and school was over. With his pick of unconditional offers, Shay was all set to head off to university, but in the meantime, he took a job at the hotel, helping out wherever he was needed, either as a porter or behind the bar. Everyone loved working with him; he was cheerful and efficient, calm in a crisis, capable of dealing with any problem that arose. So when Dominic, the assistant manager, was knocked off his bike by a van and was signed off work for six weeks, Didi's parents decided to offer Shay the position.

The offer was made with one proviso. When David and Maura Laing called him into the office, they explained that they trusted him implicitly of course, but they did require his assurance that he would never at any time let the assistant manager's set of keys out of his sight, either on or off the premises. It had been an awkward moment, but under the circumstances, it needed to be said, and they hoped he understood.

Shay did, and he gave them his word that the keys would never be left unattended.

For the next ten days, he made himself indispensable, taking over Dominic's duties and making sure the Wickham Hotel ran as smoothly as it ever had.

Until the night an intruder let themself into the hotel and emptied the safe in the office, getting away with wads of banknotes, several passports, and jewelry and watches worth almost fifty thousand pounds.

This was before CCTV had been installed. The police dusted for fingerprints and eliminated the staff one by one, concluding that the burglar, unsurprisingly, had been wearing gloves. The hotel was in uproar, a hotbed of whispering and accusations. Antonia, the pursed-lipped housekeeper, was the first to come out with it. "So is it up to me to say what everyone else is thinking? Just after Shay Mason gets his hands on the keys, this happens. I mean, it's not rocket science."

When Didi heard what was being said, she hit the roof, but rumors were rumors, and there was nothing she could do to stop them spreading. To make matters worse, her mother had lost a significant item of jewelry in the burglary; David had bought her the fabulous emerald necklace the previous Christmas. Maura had been overcome with emotion when she'd opened it on Christmas morning; it was a stunning piece and by far the most extravagant gift he'd ever given her.

Now it was gone, and she was devastated. All they could do was hope and pray that at some stage, the stolen items would be tracked down and returned. The fact that the necklace was insured was of no consolation to Maura; as far as sentimental value was concerned, nothing else could begin to compete with the original item chosen for her by her husband.

While sympathetic to her mother's loss, Didi had more important things to worry about. Her father was now paying extremely close attention to Shay, and not in a reassuring way. Much as he liked Shay as a person, he evidently still found the coincidence and the timing suspicious. As did the police. Shay was spoken to on several occasions, along with his father. Red Mason flatly denied any involvement in the burglary. His house was searched, and friends who were known criminals were questioned too. Nothing was found, but Didi began to experience a creeping unease because other people's suspicions weren't going away. And deep down, scarcely able to admit it even to herself, she found herself beginning to suspect that Shay wasn't being entirely truthful either.

She wasn't imagining it; that was the thing. She knew him so well by this time, it was agonizingly apparent that he was hiding something.

And while at first she wouldn't have dreamed of suspecting him of any involvement, the longer he refused to admit that he was concealing some small detail from her, the more she found herself worrying about what it might be.

Not that she thought for one second that he could have had any deliberate involvement, but there had to be something to explain his behavior. Her number-one suspicion was that despite his vehement denials, he'd taken the hotel keys home with him and accidentally left them out somewhere, long enough for copies to be made or for the originals to be used on the night of the robbery.

If that was what had happened and he would just come out and admit it, she wouldn't tell anyone else and she wouldn't blame him either, because obviously it wasn't something he would ever have done on purpose. But his outright denial, coupled with the fact that she was categorically aware he was holding back something significant, made the sense of frustration almost unbearable. He knew who was behind the robbery, she was certain, but no way was he going to tell the police or even admit his suspicions. It was like honor among thieves, despite the fact that he wasn't a thief.

The crack in the relationship deepened.

Didi's father explained to Shay that he was sorry, but under the circumstances, he'd be hiring a replacement assistant manager until Dominic was able to return to work.

That night, the police arrived at Hillcrest and arrested Red in connection with a smuggled shipment of whisky. Still on parole following his most recent stint inside for illegal handling of a Lamborghini, he was returned to prison to serve out the remainder of his sentence.

About to finish her shift at the hotel that evening, Didi overheard Antonia saying to her mother, "Don't fret about the boy. He'll find another job soon enough. And at least we know the culprit is out of the way now, back where he can't do any more damage. Until the next time, that is."

"Maybe it wasn't him. Red's saying he had nothing to do with it." Maura still sounded concerned.

"Well, he would say that, wouldn't he? That man's spent his life lying to the police. And I'll tell you who isn't going to be happy about him being back inside." Antonia's tone was both conspiratorial and disapproving. "I heard he's been having a bit of a thing with Lena Barker for the last couple of weeks while her husband's up in Dundee looking after his sick mother. Honestly, Red Mason has the morals of a—"

"Mum? I'm off now." Didi had heard enough; she didn't like the fact that Antonia, who was prim and endlessly judgmental, could never resist making digs at other people.

"Oh, hi, darling. Yes, see you later. Will you be home tonight?"

"Shouldn't think so. I'll probably stay over at Shay's." She caught Antonia's headmistressy arched brows and loud sniff of disapproval.

"OK. Be here by seven tomorrow." Maura gave her hand a squeeze. "Busy day."

"I won't be late. I never am."

As she was leaving, she heard Antonia murmur, "Is that sensible, Maura, letting her spend the night in the house of a known criminal?"

Oh, do give it a rest, you witch.

When she reached Hillcrest, she found Shay working in the garden and relayed Antonia's words to him. She wrapped her arms around his waist. "Are you OK? Sorry about your dad."

"It's fine. I'm used to it." He held her tight and she closed her eyes, wishing everything could go back to how it had been a week ago. She breathed in the scent of his sun-warmed skin and ran her hands over his back.

"I love you," she said.

"Love you too." But when she opened her eyes, Didi saw from the reflection in the living room window that he was gazing into the distance in that distracted way she'd seen far too often over the past few days.

She took a step back, forcing him to look at her. "What are you thinking?"

"Nothing." He shook his head.

She hated that he was lying to her. "Something's bothering you. If you love me, you'll tell me what it is."

He wasn't budging. "There isn't anything."

"But that's not true," said Didi. "You shouldn't be keeping secrets from me…not *any* kind of secret. You know something, and you don't trust me enough to tell me." Her breath quickened as her frustration escalated. "*You don't trust me.*"

"And you don't believe me," Shay shot back. "You say you do, but you don't, not completely. You still think I'm lying to you."

They stared at each other, and that was the moment it happened. In a split second, everything changed. He'd never looked at her in that way before. She realized she was trembling, shock mingling with rising anger because he was accusing her unfairly, putting the blame on her instead of admitting she was right.

"I don't think," she said. "I know."

"Well, if you're so clever, why don't you tell me what happened?"

"Honestly? I think you're denying everything because you know you accidentally left the keys somewhere in the house and your dad got hold of them."

"My dad says he didn't carry out the robbery."

"Look, I like your dad, but he's a criminal." The words shot out like bullets. "He always says that."

"But this time, it's the truth. And I didn't leave the keys where he could get hold of them either. It wasn't him, and it wasn't me. But thanks for clearing some things up for me. It's good to know how you really feel, deep down."

"That's not fair! I'm on your side!" She could feel herself losing control now; the afternoon sun was burning the back of her neck, perspiration trickling down her spine.

Shay shook his head. "Maybe you think you are, but that's irrelevant. You still think I was involved in some way, and that tells me everything I need to know about us." He turned away, one palm raised in protest. "That's it."

Talk about overdramatic. "This is crazy. You're—"

"No, it isn't crazy. I've just learned a big lesson, and it's better that it happens now than years down the line. Go home," said Shay. "Go back to your family. We're done here. We're just…done."

He was looking at her as if she were a stranger. Didi couldn't believe it had come to this. Part of her wanted to stay and fight—OK, not *fight* fight, but carry on the argument until she could finally make him see sense. The other part of her had too much pride to continue arguing when he was the one being so unreasonable, and furthermore, she knew there'd be no changing his mind about anything tonight.

He'd lost his job and was feeling ganged up on. This was an over-the-top reaction, but she supposed he had a right to be upset. The best move now would be to leave him to think things through and let him get the pent-up anger out of his system.

But she was only human, so instead of leaving without saying anything more, Didi turned and called over her shoulder, "Fine. Give me a call when you're ready to tell me what's really been going on."

....

Thirteen years on, thinking back to that fateful moment, Didi could still remember every last detail of that afternoon: the dragonflies darting back and forth in front of her as she took the shortcut across the field; the long, dry summer grasses whipping against her bare legs; the way her T-shirt clung damply to her torso. She could also clearly recall each twist and turn of the argument she'd carried on having with Shay inside her head. By the time she'd reached the hotel, it was an argument she'd won, and he had apologized profusely, admitting he was the one in the wrong. He'd wrapped his imaginary arms around her once more, told her he knew when he was beaten, and confessed that yes, he'd meant to lock the hotel keys away but had dozed off on the sofa and forgotten. And she'd told him it didn't matter one bit, she was just glad everything was sorted out now, and there must never be any secrets between them again. Then they'd kissed, and kissed some more, before heading upstairs to Shay's bedroom to put the argument well and truly behind them.

Except that hadn't happened. Instead, she'd gone over to Compton House to see Layla. They'd spent the evening out in the garden, playing music, eating pizza, drinking cider, and complaining about boys. At midnight, gazing up at the stars flung like silver confetti across the sky, Layla had said dreamily, "I've never spent the night in a tent. I bet it's brilliant fun. There's a music festival in Bristol this weekend. Katie and Jo are heading down there tomorrow. D'you fancy going along with them? Their tent sleeps six, and we could get a lift in their car… Oh, sorry, I wasn't thinking."

Didi tilted her face toward her. "Thinking about what?"

"I just said it because I knew you had the next couple of days off work, but you and Shay'll be back together again by tomorrow." Layla tossed a Malteser up into the air and tried to catch it in her mouth. "No worries. Bum, missed."

Didi watched her launch another Malteser. This time, it hit her in the eye, causing Layla to say indignantly, "Ow, that *hurt*," as if the Malteser had done it on purpose.

Didi thought about those friends who were more than happy to go out with you when they were single, yet the moment they found themselves a boyfriend, you wouldn't see them for dust. It was selfish and infuriating, and she'd always made a point of trying *not* to be the kind of person who did that.

Which meant she wasn't about to start now. Layla was her best friend, they both had the weekend free, and Shay was the one who'd been unreasonable. A couple of days apart would do them both some good. Didi picked up a Malteser that had bounced off Layla's shoulder and landed on the glass-topped garden table and popped it into her own mouth. "If you want to go, let's go."

"*Really?*" Layla jackknifed upright, scattering Maltesers in all directions. "Are you sure?"

"Sure I'm sure. It'll be great. We'll have a laugh, a proper girls' weekend together."

"Hooray!" Layla waved her arms in the air.

"And don't let me forget to take a tape recorder."

"Why?"

Didi grinned. "I'm going to record everything you say in your sleep."

And it had been great, a properly raucous girls' weekend filled with laughter, fun, and wild dancing. The weather had stayed fine, an unidentified rodent had stealthily entered their tent on the first night and bitten a hole in their shared air mattress, and Layla had been captured on tape at four in the morning muttering, "No way. I can't get married to a boa constrictor." Which meant every time they saw a likely looking boy, the rest of them would murmur, "Well *hello*, Mr. Boa Constrictor..."

When the festival drew to a close on Sunday evening, they headed back up the motorway happy, sunburnt, and exhausted. Didi had missed Shay like crazy, but hopefully the weekend apart had done them both good. She couldn't wait to see him again.

Except it hadn't been a weekend apart. Arriving home, she'd casually asked if there'd been any calls for her. There hadn't, so she'd taken a long shower and had an early night. Finally, after finishing work on Monday evening and inwardly hating the fact that she was the one making the first move, she made her way over to Hillcrest. She found the house securely locked up. No one answered the door, and it felt empty.

The next day, one of her school friends told her he'd seen Shay at the train station on Saturday with a tightly packed haversack at his feet. When he'd stopped to chat, Shay had told him he was leaving Elliscombe in search of work. When their friend had asked him about Didi, he'd replied that she wouldn't miss him, that their relationship was over.

As the days and then the weeks passed, it slowly sank in that he hadn't been bluffing.

He really had gone.

chapter 19

Now, thirteen years later, all the old feelings—of regret, dismay, and disbelief—were as fresh as ever in her mind. Her first love had ended in desperate heartbreak, and it had been her own fault.

"I'm sorry," she said.

"I know." Shay nodded.

The crime had never been solved; Red Mason had continued to maintain that it hadn't been him, but plenty of people nevertheless assumed he'd been the one behind the robbery.

"And I don't blame you for being so angry with me." She wasn't about to stir up the argument about her deep conviction that he'd been hiding something. "I should have trusted you."

Shay nodded. "I overreacted, I know that now. Growing up, I loved my mum so much, I thought she'd always be there for me. Then she got ill, and I know it's completely illogical, but when she died, I suppose I felt…abandoned. So after that, it was just me and Dad, and I loved him but he kept leaving me too. I mean, I coped, because what else could I do? And I got used to putting on a brave face, but deep down, I guess I felt let down every time it happened." He paused, studying his hands. "It grew easier as I got older though. And all the people who said I wouldn't be able to cope, that I'd end up going the same way as my father…well, I *really* enjoyed proving them wrong. So that was great. And the better I did at school, the happier I was. Then you came along, and that was pretty good too." He smiled briefly and met her gaze. "OK, maybe better than good. You made life pretty much perfect."

Perfect. Didi had to look away. She wasn't going to cry, she *mustn't* cry, but the tightening was there in her throat.

"Then it happened," Shay continued, "and that was it. All of a sudden, everything changed. The people who'd decided I was an OK guy after all were no longer quite so sure. They thought maybe I'd been playing a good game, a clever game, just to win them over. Even if they didn't come out and say it, I knew what they were thinking. And then there were the ones who *did* come out and say it. Like your father." He took a slow breath. "What with everything going on, it was a bit of a nightmare. I was OK though; it might be grim, but I knew I could get through it because at least I had you on my side."

"Oh God." Didi's heart ached for the eighteen-year-old boy she'd loved.

"Discovering you had your doubts about me too, that was what did it. All of a sudden, I realized you didn't completely trust me after all. I suppose it felt like the final kick in the teeth. First Mum, then Dad. And then that."

He didn't need to say any more. The silence was enough.

"So you decided to leave me before I could leave you," said Didi.

Shay nodded. "I couldn't deal with the idea of it happening again."

"I'm sorry."

"Hey, don't. It was a messy situation. We were young," he reminded her.

"And now we're old." Well, old-ish.

"We've both changed. We're not the same people now as we were then. You've moved on, and so have I."

It was a statement rather than a question. Didi glanced down at her engagement ring, glittering in the reflected light of the table lamp. Aaron was her future now. Shay might have come back into her life, but he was a part of her past. Just because her thoughts and dreams were getting distracted by his return didn't mean they meant anything. It was like spending all day looking forward to a roast dinner, then finally sitting down to eat it…and all of a sudden being distracted by the sight of someone tucking into perfectly golden fish and chips.

Seriously, though, what would you do? You wouldn't tip your roast dinner into the nearest trash can, would you? No, of course not. You'd get on and eat it and bloody well like it.

In the bathroom, Didi checked herself out in the mirror above the sink. She splashed her face with cold water and blotted it dry. The trick was to get a grip and keep her emotions under control; talking about the past had swirled them all up like wading through a muddy pond, turning clear water opaque.

Back in the sitting room, she said, "Come on then. Fair's fair. You've seen my exes. Now it's your turn to show me yours."

Which ended up doing the trick in more ways than one, because her attention was diverted from the traumatic breakup of thirteen years ago, and in addition, studying the photos reminded her of the caliber of girlfriend Shay had become accustomed to since then.

Actually, it was a bit of a sobering experience, what with them being *so* incredible to look at. Didi had always been happy enough with her own appearance; she liked the fact that her eyes were hazel, her lashes were long, and her nose was OK. Her mouth might be a bit wide and a couple of teeth were crooked, but didn't that add character? Her body was good enough too; her boobs were on the small side, as bitchy Estelle at university had so enjoyed pointing out, but at least they didn't get in the way or give her a chronic backache. Plus there was a jagged scar down her left calf, and one of her toes was bent sideways, having never recovered from being broken when she'd jumped out of a window for a dare.

But overall, she'd never wasted time wishing she could be taller, thinner, and more like the perfect people on Instagram. Clothes were clothes, makeup was fun but not essential, and her hair was a slave to humidity, but wasn't that the case with most hair? At least she had plenty of it.

Shay's girlfriends, however, were in another league entirely, and unlike those Instagram photos you just knew had been filtered to death before being posted, these were in their natural state. And the girls were all the more stunning for it.

"That's Cara." Shay indicated a willowy blond in cutoff shorts and a bright blue bikini top, her long hair shimmering like a waterfall down to the small of her back. "We went out together for six months."

"She's so beautiful. What does she do?" Hopefully something that proved she was a complete airhead.

"Barrister."

"Right." Of course she was. Didi nodded politely and waited until he reached the next one, who looked like Thandie Newton only more flawless. "How about her?"

"Jess? She's an orthopedic surgeon."

Fuck.

"How long were you seeing each other?"

"Three, four months? She's volunteering in a hospital in Syria now."

"Is that why you broke up?"

"Kind of. Well, not really. It just ran its course." Shay scooted through more photos. "And this was my last girlfriend."

"Rebecca." Didi said it without thinking, then wished she hadn't.

"That's right. Well remembered."

"In this job, you need to have a good memory for names." She studied the photo of the gorgeous brunette with possibly the world's most spectacular bone structure. "You met her in a bank, then she waited for you to come outside and asked you out on a date. Don't tell me, she's a world-famous research scientist."

"Primary school teacher actually." Shay sounded amused. "But good guess."

"She likes spreadsheets. Which I still don't think is a bad thing."

"They're fine, within reason." He shrugged, then said drily, "But keeping a color-coded Excel spreadsheet of every item of clothing you own is a bit excessive."

"Maybe a tiny bit," Didi conceded.

"She also used them to keep track of what every online horoscope was telling her about her upcoming love life."

Didi laughed. "OK, you win. Well, fingers crossed you'll manage to find some half-decent girlfriend one day. I mean, someone a damn sight better than this bunch of scuzzy losers."

"Let's hope so." Shay was doing that enigmatic half smile again, the one that caused her stomach to do a dolphin dive. Through the open window, they heard a rousing off-key chorus of "Happy Birthday to You" being sung by a group of guests outside on the terrace. As they listened—"*Happy BIRTHday, dear Denzil*"—Didi glanced across at Shay and found herself picturing him naked. The next moment, as if someone had telepathically intercepted her thoughts and sprung into action, his phone lit up, and the name of yet another woman appeared on the screen.

Sophia.

She pointed to the phone as it rang on. "Aren't you going to answer it?"

"I'll call her back."

Meaning once he was alone. Didi finished her drink. "I need to head off anyway."

"You don't have to go."

Oh, I think I do. If only you knew what's been going on in my head.

His phone stopped ringing. Aloud, she said, "No, I must. I'll leave you in peace. Thanks again, though, for giving up your suite. You've made the anniversary couple incredibly happy."

"Well, I hope it's made you happy too," said Shay.

"It really has." Didi was on her feet now, retreating to the door, her knees like jelly.

"I'm glad about that. Anyway, it's not too much of a hardship."

"Seeing as you get to sp—" She froze, stopping the flippant comment in its tracks. *Oh my God, listen to me…*

"Seeing as I get to what?"

"I don't know. I've forgotten… Sorry, I'm exhausted. No idea what I was going to say."

"No?" The corners of Shay's mouth twitched. "I thought you were about to say seeing as I get to spend the night in your bed."

Mortified, Didi reached for the door handle and shook her head. "Oh no, it definitely wouldn't have been anything like that."

Across the road, having let herself into the empty flat, Didi changed into polka-dot pajamas and hopped into Layla's bed.

"Hi!" Aaron's face appeared on her phone screen, his voice raised so she could hear him above the sound of Freddie Mercury giving "Don't Stop Me Now" his all. "Hang on, let me turn it down. I'm just chopping..."

Didi watched as he propped her up on the counter, then moved around the kitchen wiping his hands, sweeping the neatly chopped garlic and onions into a frying pan and finally reducing the level of the music he always had playing at top volume while he cooked. And he *did* cook, no matter what time he arrived home from the office or the gym. Other people might grab takeout or maybe make do with something to go in the microwave, but Aaron liked to wind down by preparing a meal from scratch. He could chop vegetables like lightning. He even wore a proper chef's apron over his T-shirt and shorts while he was doing it. For Didi, who far preferred eating to cooking, it was yet another big tick in the list of things to look for in a fiancé.

"Right, done." He was back, smiling at her while simultaneously reducing the flame under the pan of chicken and stirring butter into the frying onions and garlic. "How are you? How's your day been?" He did a belated double take. "And whose bed are you in?"

"I'm glad you noticed." Didi's own bed was always made up with white hotel linen, whereas now she was lying against pillowcases that were neon pink, purple, and turquoise. "It's complicated. There was a mix-up at work, and the Midnight Suite got double-booked. Which means Shay's had to move out for the night. So he's over at the hotel in my room, and I'm here at Layla's, sleeping in her bed, while she's staying in Bourton with Harry."

"Definitely complicated. Poor you." Aaron deftly flipped over the chicken breasts, crossed the kitchen, and extended an arm like a game-show host, indicating the pots of herbs standing to attention along the windowsill. "Now then, let's see if you've been paying attention. Which of these should I add to the sauce?"

OK, this was one of his slightly less endearing qualities. He did love to test her on subjects in which she had zero interest.

"The one with the green leaves?" she suggested.

He grinned and wagged a finger at her. "Come on. I told you the answer the other week."

"I don't know. Surprise me."

"Tarragon." He picked up the pot second from the left. "This one. Beautiful."

"I had a quick dinner in the hotel restaurant with Shay," said Didi, because if she didn't mention it, someone else would be bound to.

"What did you have?"

"Shrimp and mushroom risotto."

"Nice. Right, my chicken's done, and I need to concentrate on the sauce. Shall I phone you back afterward?"

She shook her head. "Don't worry. I'm tired. Going to go to sleep now."

"OK, I'll give you a call tomorrow. Have a good night. Love you."

His smile was warm, but she knew he was longing to get on with constructing the sauce; as he was so fond of telling her, cooking was all about timing. She waved her fingers at the screen and said, "Love you too. Night."

It was kind of frustrating though. She'd made a point of FaceTiming Aaron so he could be reassured she was alone in bed in Layla's flat, and he didn't even seem to appreciate it.

chapter 20

A week later, Rosa was on her way back from the craft shop when a massive black cloud scudded across the sky, dumping its contents on Elliscombe in general and her in particular.

Urgh. Within thirty seconds, she was soaked to the skin, her thin dress clinging to her body. And she'd blow-dried her hair this morning too. Hastily, she hurried along Ravenwood Road, splashing through the torrential downpour. Two minutes later, reaching the Esso station, she heard her name being called and saw Benny Colette beckoning to her while he filled his car with gas.

"Where did this come from? Two minutes ago, it was sunny." He grinned, safely under cover, and removed the nozzle, replacing it in the holder on the pump. "Hop in the car, and I'll drop you home."

Some offers you couldn't refuse. Rosa hopped into the passenger seat while Benny went off to pay. Upon his return, she said, "When I get out, I'm going to leave you with a wet seat. Sorry."

"Hey, it's leather. It can cope. I'm just glad this didn't happen while I was still on the motorway. I was dropping Ingrid at Heathrow," he explained. "She's off on a business trip to Stockholm, back next weekend in time for her birthday."

"Oh, wonderful. I love birthdays. Will you be doing something nice?"

"Just dinner at Le Manoir." Benny peered through the sheets of hammering rain as he edged off the garage forecourt. "She's off again the following Monday to New York. You know what it's like."

"Well, not personally. Seeing as I'm not a fabulously glamorous jet-setting international businesswoman." Rosa laughed. "But I'm sure it's par for the course for those who are. Have you bought her something amazing for her birthday?"

"Funny you should say that. I was supposed to be getting it sorted today. Birgitte, Ingrid's daughter, was going to come with me, but she couldn't make it. The plan was to visit this new shop in Stow. I'm not sure I'm brave enough to risk it on my own."

"Why's that?" Rosa had to raise her voice to be heard above the thunderous drumming of the rain on the roof of the car.

Benny grimaced as they edged along the road. "Honestly? I don't have great taste. I used to think I did. I thought my taste was fine because it was fine for me. Until Ingrid explained that I was wrong and she's the one with taste. Which is why the plan was for Birgitte to be there to guide me. I just thought it'd be nice for once to give Ingrid something she actually liked."

"She is very stylish," Rosa acknowledged. "I mean, I'm not saying I know her that well, but she always looks stunning."

"I don't suppose…" He glanced sideways at her, then said, "No, don't worry."

Rosa burst out laughing. "Were you about to ask me to go with you, then saw the state of me and realized I had no taste either?"

"Absolutely not. I was about to ask, then told myself it was too much of an imposition and why would you want to come along when you have plenty to keep you busy here?"

Stow was only a few miles away. Rosa said, "It wouldn't take that long, would it? I can spare an hour or two."

"Really? That'd be brilliant. From the sound of it, the place has the kind of saleswomen who won't give up until you've bought what they want you to buy." Benny shuddered. "I can't handle pushy saleswomen. They scare me to death."

He drew to a halt outside Frog Cottage and waited in the car while Rosa dashed in, stripped off, towel-dried her hair, and changed into dry jeans and a stripy Breton top. Red was upstairs in his room, having his usual afternoon nap. By the time she raced back outside, the black cloud had moved on, and the rain had all but stopped. Throwing her umbrella onto the back seat, she said, "We might need it again by the time we get there."

But when they reached Stow, the sun was back out. Benny parked the car and they found the shop, which occupied three floors of a Cotswold-stone Georgian property on Sheep Street. Rosa had heard of Ellery Dove, which had opened with a flourish last December. It sold stunning things at mind-boggling prices, ranging from designer clothes to jewelry and anything you could possibly want for your home, so long as you could afford it. The lighting was exquisite, the decor was fabulous, and the walls were painted a dozen different jeweled shades of peacock blue, jade, and magenta.

The saleswomen were predictably elegant too, but finding herself in charge of Benny made it easy for Rosa to bat them away with a polite but firm *We're just looking*. Together they climbed the narrow flights of stairs to the top floor and began inspecting the clothes.

"She wears a lot of beige," said Benny. "Except I'm not allowed to say that word. We have to call it taupe."

"How about this?" Rosa ran her fingertips lightly over an ivory cashmere top and heard the saleswoman behind her give a sharp intake of breath. Flipping over the price tag, she saw that it said eight hundred pounds. *Yeesh, no wonder.*

"She's already got one like that. Oh, I like *these*..." Benny approached a narrow rail of dresses made from fine mesh over slippery silver silk, bound with strips of pink and lime-green leather around the neck and armholes.

"No." Rosa shook her head.

"Are you sure?"

"They might be expensive, but they look cheap." Whoops, another gasp from the saleswoman. "I mean...eclectic. Trust me, Ingrid wouldn't wear something like that."

In the end, they decided on a long honey-colored jacket made of the finest, softest suede before moving down to the beauty and accessories floor. Rosa picked out an eyeshadow set in silver packaging and various skin creams and potions that smelled divine. When Benny found himself entranced by a chunky necklace of turquoise and bizarre purple crystals in a rose-gold setting, she steered him away and chose an ethereal moonstone pendant on a long silver chain instead.

"You're sure it isn't boring?" Benny wanted to know.

"It's not boring; it's classy. And she'll love it."

On the ground floor, he was instantly taken by a wall hanging of a stag's head sculpted in black resin with tiny crystal-encrusted birds and butterflies perched in its gold antlers.

"It's the kind of thing you love," Rosa patiently reminded him. "And I love it too, but Ingrid would think it was garish."

"You're a cruel woman."

"But I'm right. You know I am. Look, how about something like this instead?" She led him over to the opposite wall and indicated a small original oil painting. "I mean, I don't know her taste in art, obviously, but it looks as if it could be her kind of—"

"I don't believe it. This is by Ulrika Nilsson! And I didn't even spot it there." Benny's eyes had lit up. "Ulrika Nilsson is one of Ingrid's favorite artists...but I thought she'd given up painting to look after her husband."

"He died," supplied yet another elegant saleswoman. "And she started painting again. This one came in just yesterday."

The painting was a cloudy, chilly-looking seascape in a pale gray wooden frame, not Rosa's cup of tea at all, but she'd managed to pick the right thing. Beside himself with delight, Benny paid for the various items and together they carried everything back to the car.

As they reached Frog Cottage, he said, "Really, I can't thank you enough. You made it so easy. All I have to do now is buy some fancy wrapping paper and I'm sorted."

"Are you good at wrapping?" Rosa couldn't help herself; she had to ask. Much as she'd adored her husband, every present Joe had ever given her had resembled a bag of potatoes frantically fastened with fifty meters of Scotch tape.

"I can manage." He didn't sound entirely confident. "I mean, it's not that hard, is it? Damn, I should probably have asked them to do it in the shop."

"Come in with me," said Rosa. "I can never resist buying beautiful paper. I might not be good at many things, but I'm an excellent wrapper."

In the living room, she introduced Benny to Red, who was in his favorite chair, simultaneously keeping an eye on the horse racing on TV and doing the *Telegraph* crossword.

"Hey there." Red nodded easily at Benny and handed Rosa an envelope. "Post arrived. Another begging letter."

He hadn't opened it. Recognizing the handwriting, Rosa said, "It might not be."

"Ah, but would you bet money on it?"

"I wouldn't bet money on anything."

"You get begging letters?" Benny was incredulous.

She tore open the envelope and skimmed the contents. Red said, "Come on then. Let's hear it."

Rosa cleared her throat and began to read aloud:

Dear Rosa,

Hello, it's me again, little Maisie's grandma. I haven't heard back from you, so I'm writing to say I have been saving my pennies by cutting down on my supermarket shopping and have now managed to save seven pounds fifty. I know it isn't enough, but I wondered if you could make a smaller doll? Maisie would still love it. Please, my dear, I beg you, don't ignore my letter just because I'm a widow and a pensioner with terrible rheumatism and a bad back. If I were rich, I would buy my Maisie all the dolls in the world.

Bless you again.
Yours sincerely,
Pamela Baker

She finished reading just as the horse race on the TV reached its climax. The commentator, hysterical with excitement, bellowed, "And the winner is Shady Lady!"

Benny said, "Bloody hell."

"I know. You should have heard the last letter." Red shook his head. "I told Rosa it was a scam."

"Talk about laying it on thick," Benny agreed. He looked at Rosa. "Does this happen often?"

"Not often. Well, sometimes."

"It's emotional blackmail. And this is your job. You mustn't give in to it."

"I know."

Red stood up, reached across, and took the letter from her hand. "Shall I do the honors?"

"Yes." She nodded and watched him tear it into small pieces before dropping it into the kitchen garbage.

"There, done. Now forget it," he said.

"You're right." Rosa nodded. "I will."

Upstairs, she double-checked that the first letter from Pamela Baker was still there in her sweater drawer before hauling the box of wrapping paper, tape, and ribbons down to the living room. "OK, here we are. Choose whichever kind you like."

Having picked out pale turquoise and silver paper, Benny watched as she cut it to size and expertly wrapped each of the presents in turn, then tied them with white ribbons and, using the blade of her scissors, began making curls and spirals out of the ribbon ends.

"That one," said Red, pointing at the TV as a horse was led out for the next race. "That's the winner right there. Number six, Paris Perfect."

"And this is what I call fate," Benny marveled. "I was just thinking I should take Ingrid somewhere for her birthday when I noticed the Eiffel Tower charm." He pointed to the bracelet on Rosa's left wrist. "And then Paris Perfect turns up on the TV. That has to mean something, doesn't it? Sorted!"

Rosa smiled because Benny clearly adored Ingrid and it was heart-warming to see a man wanting to make such a romantic gesture. She said happily, "Oh, she'll love it! Joe and I took Layla to Paris when she was eight, two days at Disneyland, then two days in the city itself, and we had such a fantastic time. In fact that's why she chose the charm… I mean, when she found the bracelet in the shop and saw that the Eiffel Tower was one of the charms on there… *Whoops!*" In her panic to cover up her mistake, Rosa dropped the scissors and almost speared her own foot.

"Twelve to one," said Red. "Pretty good odds. I'm placing a virtual ten-pound bet on Paris Perfect."

Rosa finished attaching the ribbons to the parcels. They watched the race unfold on TV. Paris Perfect finished in fourth place.

"And this is why I never bet actual money," said Red.

"Those look incredible," Benny told Rosa. "Thank you. For everything."

When he'd driven off, Red said, "Nice guy."

"He is." Rosa nodded as she rewound the unraveled ribbons and placed them back in the box.

"Were you being extra helpful so that when the time comes to ask him about visiting his garden, he'll be more likely to say yes?"

"No! Because I'm never going to ask him." Rosa shook her head vehemently. "I wouldn't even mention it. They sent the scary letter from their solicitors, and that was enough for me. Are you OK?"

Red nodded, but his eyes were closed, his face creased with pain. He breathed his way through it, knuckles clenched and white as he clutched the arms of the chair. After a minute or so, he opened his eyes once more and said wryly, "Never better."

He was still looking pale. "Can I get you anything?"

"Just some water, thanks. I might go back to bed, see if I can sleep through it until the next round of painkillers."

She hated seeing him like this but also knew he didn't want to be fussed over. "Well, if you want anything at all, just give me a shout."

After another nod, he rose slowly to his feet. She went into the kitchen to fill a glass with ice-cold water and carried it upstairs for him.

"Thanks." Wincing, he lay down on the bed. "God, I'm a barrel of laughs today, aren't I? Sorry. I try not to be, but sometimes this is just… shit."

Rosa's heart went out to him. "Don't you dare apologize. It is shit. But the pain comes and goes, and by this evening, you'll be feeling better." Hopefully.

Red looked up at her, then raised a hand and brushed his fingers against hers. "Thank you. And don't worry. I'm not planning on kicking the bucket just yet."

His eyelids closed once more, and Rosa left him to it. Crossing the landing to her own bedroom, she slid open the sweater drawer and took out the letter from Pamela Baker with the photo of her granddaughter attached.

Yes, she knew she was a soft touch and it was an odds-on certainty that Red and Benny were right to warn her she was being conned. But what if it was a genuine plea from a loving grandma desperate to cheer up an unhappy child?

How could she refuse to help if that was the case?

chapter 21

Two days ago, while Red was sleeping upstairs, Rosa had begun the construction of the doll she'd been instructed in no uncertain terms not to make. Paying close attention to the photograph of Maisie, she'd fashioned a paper template before cutting out the cream cotton material to create the head and body. Next, she'd drawn on the facial features with colored indelible felt pens, taking care to make the eyes bright and the mouth smiley. She then replicated in precise detail the outline of the birthmark on Maisie's neck and chest. By the time Red had rejoined her later in the evening, the first stages were complete, and the Maisie doll was packed away in one of her workboxes, hidden beneath plenty of wadding.

The next morning, thankfully feeling much better, Red had been collected by Shay to spend time over at Hillcrest and observe while work continued on the cottage. Rosa carried on with the doll, sewing the various sections together and stuffing each in turn before carefully stitching the hair to the head, then braiding the wool and fastening the ends of the braids with blue ribbons just like Maisie's.

The final stage had been the clothes, necessitating a trip to the high street on Monday afternoon to buy red T-shirt material and blue cotton for the shorts, plus a pair of oval-framed reading glasses from the pound shop, from which she needed to remove the glass before stitching Velcro to the frames so they could be attached or removed when required.

The church clock chimed midnight. Rosa sat back, eased her aching back, and surveyed the doll with satisfaction. After eleven hours of intensive sewing, stuffing, and accessorizing, she'd finally finished. She wrote out a label that said, *Hello, I'm Maisie's doll!* and fastened it with ribbon around the doll's wrist. If she said so herself, she'd done a good job.

Taking a fresh sheet of paper, she wrote a brief note to include in the package:

Dear Pamela,

Here is the doll I've made for Maisie—I do hope she'll like it. No payment is necessary. You have a beautiful granddaughter, and she's very lucky to have you in her life.

Very best wishes,
Rosa.

Having tidied up, she carried the doll and the letter upstairs and put them out of sight. Tomorrow, she would wrap the parcel and mail it off.

She paused and wished there were someone she could confide in about her tiny act of rebellion, someone who wouldn't shake their head and tell her she was gullible.

Actually, there *was* someone…

"Because even if Pamela *is* a con artist, Maisie still exists, doesn't she? And if she's that unhappy, a doll's going to help her feel better. I'm really glad I made it now. You don't think I'm crazy, do you? No, of course you don't, because you were even more of a big softie than me." Rosa ran her hands over the grass that she liked to think contained the essence of Joe. "Remember the time I came home and you'd bought six tea towels from one of those door-to-door sellers because the guy said his dog needed an operation? You paid ninety pounds for those tea towels, and then you found out he'd told the neighbors a completely different sob story about…"

The words died in Rosa's throat as she heard the sound of the french doors being unlocked, followed by the swish of them being opened. OK, no need to panic; this had happened before. All she had to do was keep quiet and stay still.

It was half past midnight, for heaven's sake. Whoever it was, why weren't they asleep by now?

There was no tap-tapping of high heels like last time. Rosa didn't turn around. She listened and waited, then held her breath as the faint sound of someone moving across the grass grew closer.

Moments later, the movement stopped and a low voice behind her said, "What are you doing?"

Bugger. Here we go. Rosa twisted around. "I'm so sorry."

"It is you." Benny gave a quiet bark of laughter. "I thought it was. What's going on? Is it something to do with the hedgehogs?"

"You have hedgehogs?"

"Ingrid said we did. Or possibly badgers."

"Oh. Well, they might have been me."

"Does that mean you come here…often?"

"Well, quite often. Yes. Sorry."

He took a step closer. "So if you're not here to see the hedgehogs, what's the reason?"

He was an intelligent man; could he seriously be asking that question? Rosa said, "To talk to Joe."

She could just make out his frown. "In our garden?"

"It used to be ours."

"Look, no offense, but couldn't you talk to him in your own garden?" He was sounding bemused rather than angry.

"But this is where he is. You know that."

"What?"

"His ashes. This is where we scattered them, under his favorite tree. I know it sounds stupid, but it's where I feel closest to him. If I'd known I was going to have to sell the house, I'd never have done it. I would've k-kept them…but by the time I found out, it was t-too late…" Oh God, and now, to her horror, she was choking up, teetering on the edge of tears. How mortifying. Hastily, she wiped her brimming eyes with the sleeve of her black cardigan.

"Look, shall we go inside?"

"I'd rather not."

"OK." Benny sat down on the grass a couple of feet away. "So how long's this been going on?"

"About a year. I didn't do it at first. But once I started, I discovered I couldn't bear to stop. It's kind of addictive."

He raised an eyebrow. "And it never occurred to you to ask if you could come over every now and again?"

"Of course it occurred to me! I did ask!" She took a shuddery, indignant breath. "You said no."

"I did? When?"

"OK, it was your solicitors. I sent the letter to you, and they wrote back. And it wasn't a polite no." Rosa sniffed and wiped her cheeks again. "It was a definite, scary, not-in-a-million-years kind of no." She glanced at him accusingly. "They must have sent you a copy of their reply."

Benny shook his head. "I haven't seen it. I didn't see your letter either. Who were the solicitors?"

"Not the ones you used when you bought the house. This was Berry and Bayliss in London." She heard him exhale slowly. In the distance, an owl screeched.

"Right. Well, now it's my turn to apologize. Maybe I was away at the time, but Ingrid must have dealt with it. I'm afraid she's quite into rules and regulations. She probably asked for legal advice and was told it wasn't a good idea, because…well, we didn't know anything about you. It could have turned into a tricky situation."

"Of course…I mean, it wouldn't have, but you weren't to know that. I'm sorry."

"Stop it. I'm the one who should be apologizing. I feel terrible."

"You really didn't know?"

Benny shook his head. "I swear I didn't. I'll have a word with Ingrid about it. As far as I'm concerned, you're welcome here anytime."

Rosa's spirits lifted. "Really? But what if she says no?"

"She can't do that. Ingrid doesn't own the house. It's in my name."

Well, she hadn't known that. "So…how was she able to get the letter sent?"

His smile was wry. "Trust me, Ingrid has her methods. Anyway, don't worry. I'll sort it out with her. From now on, you're an invited guest. Oh God, are you crying again?"

"In a good way." She brushed away the tears of relief before they dropped off her chin. "You don't know how much this means to me. It's been three years since Joe died, and I've kept going all this time without him, but it doesn't seem to get any easier. Sometimes I wake up in the night and think, haven't I suffered long enough? I just want him back now. And I'm not going mad. I know he can't come back, but anything that makes me feel better is worth doing, I think, and being here, talking to Joe, is the best thing of all. It cheers me up."

"Anytime you want," Benny told her. "How do you manage to get into the garden anyway?"

"Well, it's not by parachute." Rosa managed a smile. "Over the wall."

"With your dodgy knee? That's asking for trouble." A thought occurred to him. "Did you once leave a jar of Gold Blend coffee on the lawn?"

She nodded. "I did. Sorry, that was—"

"Because Gold Blend was Joe's favorite coffee?"

Rosa spluttered with laughter. "He preferred tea. Leaving the jar behind was an accident. I was looking for the charm bracelet I'd lost the night before."

"Ah, the charm bracelet…that happened to have an Eiffel Tower charm on it." The lines deepened at the corners of his merry blue eyes. "I'm enjoying putting all these puzzle pieces together."

"Layla gave it to me on my birthday, and by the next morning, I'd managed to lose it. That's why I was so desperate to get it back." He may as well hear the whole story. "When I fell off the bus, that was when I'd gone into Cheltenham to buy the replacement."

"I'm sorry. I've no idea what happened to the first one," said Benny. "Ingrid probably put it in the bag for the charity shop."

"It was my own fault for trespassing. I don't make a habit of going around breaking the law."

"Just here."

Rosa nodded ruefully. "Yes. And how did you know I was skulking around in your garden tonight?"

"I just happened to look out the landing window on the top floor. You were pretty much hidden from view by the tree, but I saw your hand stroking the grass. Well, I saw *a* hand," Benny amended. "I didn't have a clue what was going on. But now I do."

"I'm glad I don't have to feel guilty anymore." Rosa rose to her feet, anxious not to outstay her welcome. "Anyway, I should be going."

"There's a ladder in the shed. Would that be a help, to get you over the wall?"

"It's fine. I'm used to it." She brushed bits of cut grass off her trousers. "There are really good footholds between the stones. But thanks."

"You're welcome," said Benny as she made her way across the lawn. "And I mean it," he added. "Anytime."

chapter 22

Five days later, confident and pleased with himself, Benny nudged open the door to the master bedroom with his foot and carried the loaded tray through with a flourish. "Happy birthday to you, happy birthday to you, happ—"

"Thank you." Ingrid raised a hand. "It's OK. You don't have to sing that song to me. I'm not six."

"I always sing it to you," Benny protested.

"I know you do. I should have told you before." Ingrid gave him one of her forthright looks. "But I'm saying it now. The breakfast looks wonderful though. Thank you."

"And there are presents too." He placed the tray on the bedside table, handed her the glass of iced orange juice, and retrieved the parcels from his side of the fitted wardrobe.

"Goodness, look at those." Ingrid was visibly impressed. "Who wrapped them up?"

"Me of course." Well, it was only a white lie.

He sat on the side of the bed and passed her the first one. He loved making people happy, and watching them open presents was always a special pleasure. As Ingrid pulled off the ribbons and ripped open the turquoise-and-silver paper, he admired her ice-blond hair, her slender shoulders, and the lingering scent of the perfume she'd worn as long as he'd known her. The perfume had been something of an acquired taste in the first weeks of their relationship, but he was used to it by now.

"My God, I don't believe this. I *love* it." Having already opened the eyeshadow set and the face and body creams, Ingrid held up the silky-soft honey suede jacket. "You've never bought me anything like this before!"

Then came the moonstone pendant. "Benny, it's like you've turned into a mind reader!" she exclaimed. "This is so *me*."

Benny looked suitably modest. He was unused to such praise, more accustomed to being on the receiving end of Ingrid's disappointment. He passed her the next parcel and saw her eyes widen as the paper came off.

"It's a new Ulrika Nilsson? Oh my goodness, you're a genius. I can't believe you found this." She threw her arms around him. "My *most* favorite artist. And such a beautiful painting." She laughed. "A bit better than that terrible sculpture you gave me last year, remember? And those hideous candlesticks!"

He'd guessed she hadn't like the sculpture when it had promptly disappeared from the house. Come to think of it, he hadn't seen the carved marble candlesticks either. Passing her the envelope containing the final surprise, he watched as she tore it open.

"Oh, darling, you shouldn't have," she said.

Possibly inspired by the story behind the Eiffel Tower charm on Rosa's bracelet, he'd arranged to whisk Ingrid off to Paris tomorrow to stay at the George V overnight and fly back on Monday morning.

"Don't be daft, you're worth it. Happy birthday..." Just in time, he remembered not to break into song once more.

"I meant you *really* shouldn't have," Ingrid told him. "Not without checking with me first." She indicated the e-tickets on the duvet in front of her. "I promised to meet up with Hedda. I can't let her down."

Hedda was her Dutch friend, currently living in Oxford. "But...she wouldn't mind, would she? For something special like this?"

"Benny, that's unkind. Hedda's been feeling low recently, and she's looking forward to seeing me. I don't dump my girlfriends when I get a better offer. That would be an awful thing to do."

Of course it would. Benny shook his head. "Sorry, I didn't know you'd made plans."

"That's because you didn't ask."

"I wanted it to be a surprise."

"Well, it was a nice idea, so thank you for that. And it's my birthday today, so we're going to have a wonderful time. Tomorrow, I'll see Hedda and stay over at her house. Then on Tuesday, I'm off to New York."

She was a hard worker; he couldn't take that away from her. "Fine. I'll cancel the flights and the hotel."

"What time is our table at the Manoir booked for tonight?"

"Seven thirty."

"I'll wear this beautiful jacket." Ingrid lovingly stroked the butter-soft suede.

Benny said, "I lied about wrapping the presents. It wasn't me."

She looked amused. "Why am I not surprised to hear this?"

"I didn't choose them myself either. A friend helped me."

"Again, I thought there might have been someone else involved." Sitting back against the pillows, Ingrid began spooning up her favorite breakfast of granola and plain yogurt. "Who was it? Someone very beautiful?"

"Rosa Gallagher."

"Ha, really? The secret garden interloper who also fell off the bus? So I can relax and stop worrying that she might steal you away from me!" Ingrid flipped back her hair. "Still, I'm grateful to her. I wouldn't have thought she'd have such good taste. She found me some very nice gifts."

"And wrapped them up too."

"You mean she did all this for you in exchange for being allowed to sit in our garden at night and speak to her dead husband? This town is full of strange people."

"I don't think it's strange," said Benny.

"And now you're defending her." Ingrid's tone was playful as she tapped his hand with the back of her spoon. "Maybe I should be jealous after all."

....

"The thing is," Aaron said over the phone a fortnight later, "it's Jasper's birthday, and he's making a weekend of it. Racing at Ascot on Saturday, big party in the evening, then a picnic in the park with competitive games on Sunday afternoon."

Didi's heart had sunk at the mention of Jasper. It carried on plummeting as the details of the birthday celebrations were laid out. Jasper was one of Aaron's bosses; he was loud and boorish and drank like a fish.

"I don't understand why he's invited me along. I've only met him three times." And that had been plenty.

"His wife told him he needed to invite couples this time. I think it's her way of making sure they don't end up in a strip club again, like last year. Oh, come on. It'll be fun."

It wouldn't be. Jasper would leer at her boobs and make unfunny jokes about sex. "He's an ape," Didi sighed.

"I know, but he's my boss. And there'll be other women there to talk to."

"Is Tanya going?" Tanya was the girlfriend of another of his colleagues.

"She can't make it."

Typical. Tanya was the only one Didi actually liked.

After a couple of seconds, Aaron said, "You don't want to come down, do you?"

She felt mean, but it was true. It was one thing spending the weekend with Aaron, but his male coworkers were brash, overconfident, and difficult to like, and their wives and girlfriends tended to spend most of the time discussing fillers and Botox while scrolling through Instagram bitching about anyone who hadn't succumbed to either.

"Would you mind if I gave it a miss? It's just that we're rushed off our feet here. We've never been so busy, and I hate swanning off, leaving everyone to cope without me." This was true. They were almost halfway through August, and it was the height of the holiday season; Elliscombe was bursting at the seams with tourists, and both the hotel and its restaurant were fully booked for weeks ahead.

"You work too hard," Aaron chided. "Everyone needs a break. But OK, I know you wouldn't enjoy having to put up with Jasper all weekend. I'll tell him you can't get away, shall I?"

The relief was huge. "Thanks. You'll have more fun with your friends anyway, not having to worry about me being bored out of my mind."

"I'll miss you, but I know what you mean. How are things going with Layla and her chap?"

"All good, as far as I know. Haven't met him yet, but she's happy. Why?"

"I just remember her saying the other week how she always goes over to his place and he never wants to spend any time at hers," Aaron said lightly. "Sounds kind of, I don't know…familiar?"

"Oh no, that's not fair." Didi laughed. "You *like* getting away from London and spending time up here. And if it wasn't Jasper's birthday, I'd definitely be coming to see you. If you tell him you can't go to the racing and the party and the picnic in the park, I'll jump on a train and spend the weekend with you." As she said it, she wondered if he'd consider doing that.

"And wouldn't that be great? But I can't. This is Jasper we're talking about. He's the boss, and he doesn't take no for an answer."

"We'll see each other next weekend. And if you really want, I'll come down to you," Didi promised, because it was only fair.

"I may hold you to that. Right, I have to go now. Love you."

"Love you too."

"I'll call you tomorrow," said Aaron.

"If I don't call you first." This was a well-worn routine, the way their phone conversations always ended.

"Bye, beautiful."

"Bye." Didi ended the call and exhaled slowly. Mission accomplished. Jasper's dreaded birthday celebrations had been avoided, she was staying here in Elliscombe, and better still, she was free to enjoy the sunny weekend stretching ahead.

What a relief.

chapter 23

On Friday evening, instead of catching the train to London, Didi ended up working until midnight because one of the waitresses was stuck in Menorca thanks to a canceled flight home. On Saturday, she stayed around the hotel to help with a silver wedding anniversary celebration. OK, it was work, but it was still fifty times more enjoyable than having to spend hours in the company of Jasper and his cohorts.

By five, though, she was hot, tired, and ready for a change of scenery. After a quick shower, she changed into a khaki tank top and black shorts. As she dragged a brush through her hair, she glanced out the window and saw Shay leaving the hotel via the gate at the far end of the terrace. He was carrying a Nike bag, which meant he must be heading over to the sports center on the outskirts of Elliscombe.

OK, she wasn't going to go there, then. What if he thought she was following him like a stalker? She checked her reflection in the dressing table mirror. Makeup or no makeup? No, not this evening. A memory from the distant past was swirling up, and now that it had occurred to her, she knew what she wanted to do.

Yes, yes. Perfect.

Hestacombe was a twelve-mile drive away, through verdant Cotswold countryside. As Didi approached the village, situated in the dip of a bowl surrounded on all sides by big hills, she caught tantalizing glimpses of Hestacombe Lake glittering in the sunlight between the trees.

But as she reached the parking lot just up from the crescent of beach bordering the lake, her stomach gave a lurch of recognition at the sight of a car she definitely hadn't expected to see here.

Shit, *shit.*

But at the same time, if she was being completely honest… *Oh*…

The blue Audi was empty. Didi's head swiveled in the direction of the lake, but she saw only a couple of families with children splashing around in the shallows. If she reversed out of here sharpish and continued back up the narrow, winding lane, she could get away without being seen, and he'd never even know she'd been here. That would be the sensible course of action.

The next second, Shay's head broke the surface of the water twenty meters away, and she saw him register her presence. Oh God, what was she supposed to do now?

Finally, after a long moment, a smile lit up his tanned face, and Didi experienced a rush of relief. Of course she wasn't going to drive away; here it was again, their shared past drawing them together. She switched off the ignition and stepped out of the car, moving closer to the water's edge.

"Well." Shay's blond hair was slicked back from his face. "Fancy seeing you here."

She raised a hand, palm out. "OK, before you start thinking it, I didn't follow you. I've been working all day. I wanted to relax and cool off." She shook her head. "I had no idea this was going to happen."

"Fine, I believe you." He grinned. "Still a coincidence though."

"I saw you leaving, carrying a sports bag. I thought you were heading over to the sports center." Was this completely true? Had she subliminally wondered if he might have shared her idea to come to the lake? She genuinely had no idea.

"Hey, we both had a good idea at the same time. Are you getting in?"

"I don't know. Maybe I shouldn't."

"You've driven all this way. Seems a shame not to."

Didi hesitated, still torn. After a couple of seconds, Shay said easily, "I'll leave you to have a think about it." Turning in the water so he was facing away, he began to swim toward the other side of the lake.

Oh, just look at those broad, tanned shoulders, those powerful arms. She watched as he cut effortlessly through the water. Dragonflies with iridescent wings hovered and darted above the lake while birds wheeled lazily overhead. The glitter of the sun's reflection bouncing off the surface was almost blinding. Didi glanced over at the low wall to her left, her heart swelling as she spotted Shay's keys tucked away in a crevice between two rocks. It was where they'd always left any valuables, back in the day. She added her own car keys, then removed her T-shirt and shorts and left them on the sand beside his Nike bag.

He'd reached the center of the lake now. She launched herself into the water and began swimming out to join him.

"Just like old times," he said when only a few meters separated them.

"Well, not quite." During that long, hot summer thirteen years ago, they'd cycled over from Elliscombe, bringing food and spending entire days at a time here whenever work allowed. There'd been music and dancing, swimming and splashing, all interspersed with laughter and kissing.

A *lot* of kissing.

Not to mention the rest…

Oh God, was she mad to be doing this, feeling the way she did right now?

Then again, she'd only come here to have a swim. It wasn't her fault Shay was here too.

"No Aaron this weekend?"

"It's his boss's birthday. He has to be in London. Lots of celebrating to be done."

"And you don't mind?"

"I haven't been abandoned. I was invited."

"But you stayed here instead."

"It was going to last all weekend, and I can't stand his boss."

Shay's eyes sparkled. "Well, good for you."

"Plus the hotel's busy," Didi added.

"I've noticed."

"You've been busy too. How's the renovation coming along?"

"We're on schedule, just about. I had Dad over with me today, keeping an eye on things. Until he fell asleep on his sun lounger out in the garden. Then I stopped work for thirty seconds to refill my water bottle, and he came inside to see what was going on." Shay grinned. "Called me a lazy sod."

"Better stop skiving off then," said Didi, "and get a move on with that house."

He swept his hand across the surface of the water, sending an arcing wave into her face.

"Oh dear." Didi wagged a finger at him. "You shouldn't have done that." Scooping with both hands, she splashed him back, then shrieked with laughter and launched into an energetic crawl, heading for the far side of the lake where the branches of the willow trees bowed down and kissed the surface of the water.

They splashed, swam, and raced each other for the next thirty minutes before getting out, spreading their towels on the narrow sandy beach, and lying down to let the late-afternoon sun warm them up and dry them off. Just as they'd done all those years ago.

"We never did find out who lived in that place." Propped up on one elbow, Didi twisted around and pointed to the impressive Victorian property behind them, set in stunning grounds and with an uninterrupted view over the lake. All they knew was that it was called Hestacombe House, and back then, they'd occasionally glimpsed an elderly man at one of the upstairs windows. Now there were swings and a slide in the garden and a pair of yellow children's rubber boots lodged high in the branches of a well-established monkey puzzle tree.

Had the original owner died, or had he sold the place and relocated, perhaps to somewhere more exotic? Who knew? Either way, this view and the lake itself might still be unchanged, but life had moved inexorably on. They all had.

Hadn't they?

"I'll tell you who does still live here," said Shay.

They'd never known anyone from Hestacombe. She raised an eyebrow in disbelief. "Who?"

He pointed over to the right, and she followed his gaze. From around the bend in the lake, where low-hanging branches and thick reeds had previously obscured their view, a pair of swans now emerged. "Oh, wow." She sat up to see them better. "They can't be the same ones, surely?"

They certainly looked the same, but was that possible? Thirteen years ago, there'd been a pair of swans here, always together, invariably gliding along in unison. Didi and Shay had made up stories about their lives, their complicated families, and the arguments they had in private while maintaining a blissfully happy public persona for the benefit of visitors to the lake.

"Betty and Neville." Shay was shielding his eyes from the sun. "It definitely looks like them."

The pair drew closer, as elegant and synchronized as Torvill and Dean, and Didi spotted the mark on Neville's neck, the result of an injury sustained long ago. "It *is* them. See the scar. They're still together." Ridiculously, a lump had sprung into her throat, because it was so romantic. "After all these years."

"Are you about to *cry*?"

"Shut up. Of course not."

Shay's mouth twitched. "Glad to hear it. Because that would be weird."

He was just a man. He didn't understand.

They watched as Betty and Neville glided past, ignoring them completely, needing nothing but each other's company. Still raised up on one elbow, Didi closed her eyes and felt the sun warm her eyelids. How was Shay feeling about them being here together? He was wearing a pair of faded red board shorts, and she was in her old black swimsuit; his bare legs were just there and hers were here, right next to them. Was he remembering how they'd once lain on this beach with their limbs entangled, their bodies pressed together? Did he ever think about the kisses they'd shared? Was every detail of the sensation of her mouth on his still as fresh in his mind as it was in hers? What was going through his mind right now...and was she completely crazy to be asking herself that question, given what was going on in hers?

Because if Shay were to turn toward her now, touch her arm, brush her hair back from her temple with his hand...would she be able to stop him? Or even want to?

Her pulse quickening, she knew the answer would be no.

From a tree behind them, a blackbird was singing. She opened her eyes and gazed up at the cloudless sky, remembering that it had been Red who'd taught her how to recognize the songs of the different species of bird around the cottage. Tilting her head, she prepared to tell Shay—

Oh, what?

Seriously?

While she'd been lying beside him, awash with adrenaline, happy memories, and forbidden thoughts, he'd fallen *asleep*?

Didi exhaled, her ego crashing back to earth with a thud. She didn't know whether to feel crushed, cross, insulted, or relieved that her feelings clearly ran so much deeper than his.

Talk about a kick in the teeth. Then again, maybe it was just as well.

Oh, but how galling to realize that while she'd been secretly fantasizing about Shay, he'd been thinking of her as nothing more than an ex-girlfriend who'd once featured in his past.

Silently adjusting her position, she rolled onto her left side and studied his face. His thick dark lashes didn't flicker; he'd been working crazy hours over at Hillcrest and was obviously exhausted. His streaky blond hair was starting to dry in the sun. There was the narrow scar on his forehead that she longed to trace with her index finger, the familiar angles of his high cheekbones...his nose...his jawline. And there was the curve of his upper lip, which had always mesmerized her. What was that bit called, the tiny dip between—

Shay's eyes snapped open, and she jerked back, mortified at having been caught.

"Hello." The faintest of smiles hovered around the mouth she'd been caught inspecting.

"I thought you were asleep."

"Just resting. What else were you thinking while you thought I was asleep?"

"Sorry, it was driving me mad trying to remember what it's called." Didi touched the dip above her own upper lip. "I know it. My mind's just gone blank. I'm sure it begins with a *t*."

"It's your philtrum," said Shay.

"That's it!"

"Doesn't begin with a *t*."

"But there's a *t* in it. Don't be so pendantic."

He grinned. "Are you still saying that?"

"I'll never stop. I love the look on people's faces when they try to correct me."

Shay was shaking his head, his gaze taking in every detail of her own face. His expression might be unreadable, but it was having a considerable effect on her body. She hoped he hadn't noticed the increased rate of her pulse, hammering away in the base of her throat. Swallowing, she said flippantly, "I hope you're admiring my philtrum."

"You mean your philtrum with a *t*."

And now she found herself unable to tear her gaze away from *his* philtrum-with-a-*t*, wishing she could kiss it. Oh God, this was terrible. She really *really* shouldn't be thinking this, let alone wanting to do it. But this wasn't just any attractive man. It was Shay, and she'd never in her life shared such an intense connection with another person, not even Aaron, although heaven knows Aaron didn't deserve to be engaged to someone who was capable of feeling this way about another—

Drringgg. Her phone broke the spell, like a pantomime villain popping up with an evil cackle just when he was least welcome.

Didi turned away to reach for it on the other side of her beach towel. If it was Aaron, it would be fate's way of telling her to sort herself out.

But it was someone calling from the hotel. Answering, she heard Sylvia say, "Hi, look, we're getting no reply from the room, and he isn't answering his phone, but we need to get hold of Shay. Someone drove out to his house, and he isn't there either. I don't suppose you've any idea where he might be?"

"He's here." For a split second, Didi had considered pretending to contact Shay by other means, but the message was clearly urgent and could only mean one thing. "He's right here. I'll pass you over to him now."

The phone call was brief. Shay was on his feet before it even ended.

As he whisked his shirt out of his Nike bag and pulled it on, he said, "Dad was struggling to breathe, so Rosa called an ambulance. She's with him now at the hospital, and he's in a bad way. Shit, he was coughing more than usual this afternoon but nothing worse than that… I can't believe this is happening…"

"What can I do?" In her haste, Didi almost lost her balance as she shoved one leg into her shorts. "You can leave your car here, and I'll drive."

"No, I'll take mine. *Fuck.*" He was pale beneath his tan. "I left my phone in the car, and they've been trying to get hold of me for the last hour."

"You didn't know. It's not your fault."

But he shook his head, grabbing the Nike bag and making his way up the narrow path to the parking lot. "While we've been swimming and lying on the beach, he's been rushed to the hospital, unable to breathe. He probably thought he was going to die. Right, if anyone else calls, tell them I'm on my way there now."

The Audi shot off up the lane in a cloud of dust. Didi collected up the towels and headed back to her own car, feeling almost as guilty as Shay evidently did.

Please, God, don't let Red die.

Not now. Not yet.

chapter 24

Shay had spent the night in the waiting room outside the ward, dozing for only a few minutes at a time on the hard plastic chair. Now he listened to the muted sounds of the hospital as it came back to life around him and the rattle of the breakfast cart making itself heard farther down the corridor.

Finally, he was allowed back onto the ward. The nurses assured him that his father was doing as well as could be expected, but Red was still looking dreadful. His skin was ash gray, the lines around his mouth pronounced. Much of his face was covered by the oxygen mask. His arms lay at his sides, and Shay saw that the rose-gold three-diamond gypsy ring was looser than ever on the third finger of his right hand.

He pulled up a chair and waited, watching his father's chest rise and fall, hearing the effort it was taking him to breathe. There was a drip in his left arm and an oximeter fastened to his index finger. His skin was waxily pale.

But he was still alive. As a machine beeped in an adjacent room, Red's eyes opened, and he registered Shay's presence with the faintest of smiles. Lifting the oxygen mask, he said, "You still here? You should get some sleep."

"I'm OK. Do you need anything?"

"Wouldn't say no to a double scotch."

Shay knew this was to try and reassure him, but how could he be reassured? He'd left his phone in the car while he'd been swimming in Hestacombe Lake with Didi. There'd been increasingly concerned texts and voicemails left on it by Rosa, and he could only imagine how panicked she'd been as his father's condition had taken a sudden turn for the worse. While she'd been dialing 999 and calling the ambulance out to Frog Cottage, he'd been lying in the sun on the tiny lakeside beach, not even pausing to spare a thought for Red. His mind had been entirely occupied with Didi, with talking to her, longing to kiss her and run his fingers through her dark hair, to trace the curve of her suntanned cheek, to pull her into his arms and—

Red started coughing helplessly, and Shay stopped thinking about Didi. Once the coughing episode was over, he plumped the pillows, helped Red to take a few sips of water, and made sure he was comfortable once more. He *had* to stop thinking about her. His father needed to be his number-one priority at all times. The situation with Didi was impossible anyway.

"Go home now." Red's words were muffled by the oxygen mask. "I can't sleep with you sitting there watching me. It's putting me off."

"I'd rather stay here."

"I'm the sick one, so I get to decide. And you need to be getting a move on with the house." Indicating the ward doors, he creaked, "Off you go. I'll see you later. Tell Rosa I'm sorry I gave her a scare."

"OK." Shay gave his arm a squeeze. "I'll be back later. Be good."

"By the way, where were you when Rosa couldn't get hold of you?"

There it was, the question he'd been waiting for.

"I was over at Hestacombe Lake with Didi. Left the phone in the car."

Red nodded. "Thought it might have something to do with her."

"Don't look at me like that. Nothing's going to happen," said Shay.

Above the oxygen mask, his father gave him a ghost of a wink. "Sure about that?"

He couldn't. He mustn't. And Red wasn't going to persuade him otherwise.

"Quite sure," he said.

Didi remembered the couple well; she'd shown them the hotel back in March and been taken by their story. Beth and Phil were in their forties and had both been through the mill. Phil's wife had died four years ago, leaving him to bring up three small daughters. At around the same time, Beth's violent ex-husband had landed her in the hospital with severe internal injuries. Told that she was unlikely to be able to bear children as a result, she'd moved across the country from Norfolk to Oxfordshire to begin a new life. Two years on and working as a teaching assistant, she'd met Phil, whose children attended her school, and a slow, shy courtship had developed. Indescribably happy together, they were all set to get married next summer and had booked the Wickham Hotel for the ceremony and reception.

Except a problem had arisen.

"It's my mum," said Beth. "She's poorly and slowly getting worse. I asked the doctors if they thought she'd still be here next summer, and they said it was…very unlikely. Sorry." She wiped away a tear. "It's been a bit of a shock, although it shouldn't be. It's a brain tumor, you see. I just love her so much, and she's always been there for me, and she's been so looking forward to the wedding…"

Didi's heart went out to them; they'd been through so much, and now this.

"We just wondered if there was any way we could cancel the date we booked and bring it forward, but it'd still have to be a Saturday because so many guests are teachers… I know it's a long shot, but if there's anything at all before Christmas, we'd go for that."

"Oh, Beth, I'm so sorry…" Didi scrolled through the calendar on the computer screen, just in case there'd been some last-minute cancellation she'd somehow managed to miss. But there hadn't; with its reputation and history as one of the oldest hotels in England, the Wickham was a year-round popular venue for weddings. They were already taking bookings for eighteen months ahead.

"It's OK. We knew it wasn't likely. Everyone wants to get married here." Beth nodded at Phil and clasped his hand. "We'd have loved to get married here, but Mum comes first."

"We'll book the register office instead," Phil told her, "and we'll still have an amazing day. You'll have your mum there, and the girls can still be bridesmaids. Hey, look how lucky you are." He lifted Beth's hand

and kissed the back of it. "We found each other, didn't we? That's the important thing."

Beth's eyes filled with tears once more. To stop her own doing the same, Didi conjured up a mental image of ugly politicians wrestling naked in mud. It generally did the trick.

Phil turned to her. "Sorry to mess you around. We know it means losing our deposit, but that's OK. At least we—"

"Oh, will you look at that? It was there all the time!" Eyes wide, Didi jabbed at the screen, which was tilted away from them. "There *is* a free Saturday in December. I can't believe I missed it!"

"Really?" Beth's entire face lit up. She let out a squeak of excitement. "In December? A Christmas wedding! That would be *perfect*."

"December the seventh," said Didi, and this time, there was no escaping the lump in her throat as Beth and Phil clutched each other in delight.

"We'll take it, we'll take it!" Beth exclaimed. "Thank you so much! I can't believe we'll be getting married here after all. It's going to be the best wedding ever."

When they'd left, Didi slowly exhaled and marveled at what her subconscious had made her do. Was it wrong? She had no idea. It was fairly momentous, certainly. But it felt right. And it was without question the answer for Beth and Phil.

All she had to do now was work out how to explain it to Aaron.

chapter 25

On Friday afternoon, Didi drove to Moreton-in-Marsh to catch the train to London. Passing Hillcrest, she saw a couple of vans outside and some work being carried out on the roof, but no sign of Shay. His car wasn't there, which probably meant he was over at the hospital, where he'd been spending every spare minute. They hadn't seen each other since last weekend's afternoon at the lake, and if he was deliberately avoiding her, she understood why and didn't blame him one bit. She also knew that Red was recovering from the chest infection that had had such a terrifying effect on his body.

It rained all the way to London. Didi found herself sitting opposite a girl on the phone to a friend, sharing stories about her boyfriend, who was amazing in every way, honestly, and was really encouraging her to lose weight so she could fit into slinky dresses without looking like an overstuffed sausage. After twenty minutes, Didi longed to tell the girl that her amazing new boyfriend was a controlling gaslighter who was already skillfully isolating her from her own family. But the train stopped and the girl jumped off before she could intervene, her seat taken by a middle-aged man eating a tuna sandwich and slurping from a can of Foster's. Oh joy.

Finally, after almost two hours, the train pulled into Paddington station. All she had to do now was catch the Tube; Aaron was working late but would be home soon enough.

Except when she made her way along the platform and reached the main concourse, there he was. Wearing his navy work suit and looking boyishly handsome, like a TV ad for a perfect boyfriend. He was waiting for her with a huge grin on his face and a cellophane-wrapped bouquet of gold roses in his left hand.

Predictably, women of all ages were casting admiring glances in his direction.

"Surprise!" He held his arms out in welcome. "When I said I had to work late, I lied. Come here!"

Oh, help, and now everyone was watching. She had to go along with it as he enveloped her in a hug. He kissed her on the mouth, then said, "You came all this way. How could I not be here to meet you? Let me take your case… Wow, it hardly weighs anything at all!"

It hardly weighed anything because it was pretty much empty. And she'd come all this way because it would be unforgivable not to. How could she let him schlep up to Elliscombe in order to be told what she had to tell him? It was an unspoken rule that the breaker of bad news had to be the one doing the traveling. Her plan was to let him down as gently as possible, then collect up the few belongings she'd left at his flat over the last year, pack them into her overnight case, and catch the last train home tonight. Boom, sorted.

But it needed to be done in private rather than slap-bang in the middle of Paddington station, in front of an audience of women who would without question be on his side. And Aaron, who wasn't a fan of taking the tube, was already leading the way to the taxi rank.

Oh, it was hard to find the right moment, though, to take the plunge and start the conversation that needed to happen. In the taxi, they got themselves landed with a chatty driver who was bursting to tell them about his son having passed his driving test that morning. Then, when they pulled up outside Aaron's flat, Didi's stomach gave a noisy growl of hunger, and Aaron insisted on taking her across the road to his favorite restaurant.

"I was going to cook for you, but it'll take too long. We're both hungry. Come on. Let's eat." And when they entered the crowded restaurant, a group of friends who lived in the same apartment building beckoned them over to share their table.

It was like being a double agent, pretending to be one half of an idyllically happy couple while knowing what was going to happen the moment the two of them were alone together behind closed doors. Being polite to Aaron's neighbors, Didi felt like the ultimate fraud; it might not be the done thing to break off an engagement by text, but was anything more agonizing than this?

The cancer wasn't going anywhere, obviously, but at least the chest infection had cleared. The antibiotics had worked their magic, thank God, and tomorrow Red was being discharged from the hospital.

Having both spent the evening with him on the ward, Shay dropped Rosa off at Frog Cottage and drove back to the hotel. He hadn't seen Didi all week, but now he wanted to share the good news. When there was no sign of her either in the restaurant or outside on the crowded terrace, he stopped Sylvia on her way across reception and asked where she was.

"Oh, Didi's not here. She's gone to London to see Aaron." Sylvia, who was one of Aaron's biggest fans, made a swoony face. "To make up for missing him last weekend." She gave Shay a playful nudge. "I'm sure you know what I mean."

Shay knew what she meant; he just wished he didn't have to hear about it. With a nod and a brief smile, he prepared to head upstairs, but Sylvia put out a hand to stop him, her expression avid. "Ooh, have you heard who's staying here?"

Shay already knew the hotel was full. "Quite a few people?"

"It was booked last week under a pseudonym, so we didn't have any idea. A proper celebrity. I mean, I wouldn't tell you, but she's right opposite you in the Midsummer Suite, so it's best you know, just in case you spot anyone sneaking up the stairs to try and get a look at her."

"Who is it?"

"Caz Holloway." Sylvia's eyebrows did a little dance of excitement. "The actress and singer? You must know who she is," she chided. "She starred in *Call Me, Darling*. And the next year, she nearly married her costar, the one with the mustache who played Terry in *Our Favorite House*. Oh, you know who I mean. She's always in the papers!"

He and Sylvia probably read different sections of the newspaper.

Shay said, "The name rings a bell," mainly to be polite, but she had pulled out her phone and was evidently determined to educate him.

"Here she is. Now you recognize her. This was taken when she was starring in the West End as Éponine in *Les Mis*. I saw her in that! What a voice. She's a character all right. Oh, let me show you something else. What do you think of this?"

Instead of Caz Holloway, the phone screen now showed an emerald-green velvet hat with a swooping brim and an explosion of ribbons and feathers on one side. Sylvia waited expectantly for his reaction.

"It's…very dramatic," said Shay.

"I know!"

"Is this…for you?"

"Of course!"

"For a special occasion?"

"No, I thought I'd wear it while I'm scrubbing the kitchen floor." Her eyes danced. "Yes, it's for a special occasion. Didi and Aaron's wedding! Don't you think it's the most gorgeous hat you ever saw in your life?"

It was like a jab in the ribs, well meant but painful. Didi was marrying Aaron, and he couldn't be allowed to forget it. Preparing to make his escape, Shay nodded. "It's perfect."

Sylvia gazed lovingly at the hat. "Sometimes you clap eyes on something for the first time, don't you, and you just know you have to have it."

Since taking up residence, he'd grown accustomed to the creaking oak floorboards on the curved staircase leading up to the top floor of the ancient hotel. After a while, you barely noticed them. But as he made his way along the carpeted landing, it became apparent that the new guest had heard his arrival. The door to the Midsummer Suite opened a couple of inches, and a female voice said, "Are you room service?"

"I'm not," said Shay. "Sorry."

He heard a sigh. Half a face appeared in the slender gap, and one heavily made-up eye stared at him. "For crying out loud, where *are* they? I ordered a bottle of wine *ages* ago."

"They're pretty busy downstairs."

"And I'm pretty thirsty upstairs." Having checked him out, Caz Holloway opened the door wide. "Hello. Are you sure you aren't room service?"

"I'm sure." He pointed to his own door, across the landing. "That's me there. But if you want, I can go downstairs and get your wine for you."

She hesitated, tightening the belt around her white terry robe, then shook her head. "Thanks, but it's OK. If I say yes, you'll tell everyone I'm a right diva."

She shouldn't be having to wait though. Shay said, "How long ago did you order the wine?"

"Three minutes."

He nodded gravely. "Right."

"I know, I know, but I don't like having to wait." She broke into a grin. "See what I mean? Diva."

He held up his key. "If it helps, I've got some wine in my fridge. Would that keep you going?"

"You"—Caz waggled a finger at him—"are a lifesaver."

"Wait there."

When he returned with the half-full bottle of Picpoul de Pinet, she took it from him. "Is there anyone else in your room?"

"Not that I'm aware of. Unless they're hiding under the bed."

"Do you have a wife?"

"No."

"Girlfriend?"

"No."

"Boyfriend?"

"Not even one of those."

"And are you off out anywhere this evening?"

"No."

Caz tilted her head. "So if you wanted to come over to my room for a quick drink, you'd be welcome. D'you think you might fancy that?"

Shay hesitated. He might not be familiar with her shows, but he recognized her now, had seen her photo online, and had watched her being interviewed on TV. She was a character who wore her heart on her sleeve and was prone to speaking her mind when maybe it would be more sensible not to. Her romantic trials and tribulations endeared her to her adoring public, who treated her as a kind of impulsive, wayward surrogate sister or daughter.

Basically, Caz Holloway was a bit of a handful.

Which he really didn't need right now.

"Thanks," he said. "That's really kind of you. But it's been a long day. I'm pretty exhausted."

She looked stunned. "You're turning me down?"

"Not turning you down. Just saying no thanks, not this evening."

"Well, I'm crushed," said Caz. Her smile regretful, she turned to head back into her room. "But thanks for the wine. Night."

Minutes later, Shay heard the familiar creak of floorboards as Caz's room service request was delivered to the Midsummer Suite.

He took a shower, then put on clean jeans and began flipping through the TV channels. Mental images of Didi kept jumping into his head. Where was she now? What was she doing? Were she and Aaron out somewhere glamorous, meeting up with friends, maybe dancing and socializing at a party? Or were they back at his place enjoying the first night of a romantic weekend together, doing the kinds of things he definitely didn't want to imagine them doing?

Stop it. Don't think about Didi. Watch the TV or download a film and concentrate on that instead.

A knock came at the door.

chapter 26

Shay looked at the door. No, of course it wasn't Didi. She hadn't changed her mind about spending the weekend in London and come racing back to tell him—

"Hey, it's me, your neighbor. Tell me you haven't gone to sleep."

He opened the door, and the empty wine bottle was thrust into his hand. "First, thank you for the wine. I'm very polite, so here's your bottle back."

"Thanks." She'd changed out of her robe and into leggings and a thin cotton top.

"Second, I don't like the feeling of inviting someone over for a drink and being turned down."

"Sorry about that. You mustn't take it personally."

"Except I do." Counting on her fingers, she said, "And thirdly, I came here to relax, be on my own, and get my head straight, but I didn't realize how quickly the novelty would wear off, which is why it's half nine on day one and I'm so bored I could scream. Turns out I don't like being on my own after all."

"Better if you don't scream," said Shay.

"Will you come over and keep me company? If I ask nicely?"

"Let me just—"

"How about if I beg?" Caz blurted out. "Shamelessly."

At least she'd take his mind off Didi. "Let me just grab a T-shirt," he said.

Their suites were similar in size and design—thick carpet, squashy gray velvet sofa, one feature stone wall behind the king-size bed, antique furniture, with a dazzling chandelier suspended from the double-height beamed ceiling. Through the leaded windows, there was a view over the high street. The main difference was that whereas his own suite was pretty tidy, hers looked like a tornado had swept through an upmarket boutique and dumped its contents on every surface.

"Here." She handed him a brimming glass of Cloudy Bay and clinked her own against it. "Thanks for humoring me. You don't have to stay long, I promise."

"Don't be daft. Thanks for the invitation. I'm Shay."

"I know."

"Oh?"

"I saw that there were only two suites up here on the top floor. When the assistant manager showed me around, she told me your name and said I wouldn't bother you. She also said you were here for a couple of months."

"True." Shay nodded. "And your name is…?"

"Caz."

He grinned. "Correct. Well done."

She sat cross-legged in the center of the bed and scooped up a handful of salted almonds, spilling a couple on the carpet, then took a glug of wine. "Let's get started then, shall we? You go first. Tell me everything about you."

And Shay found himself doing it. He didn't tell her *everything*, obviously, but Caz got the story of his father wanting to come home and his work renovating Hillcrest. Against all expectations, she was an avid listener, interested in every detail and asking endless questions. Finally, he said, "That's enough about me. Now it's your turn."

She pulled a comical face. "Oh God, what d'you want to hear, the PR company's spin or the real version?"

"We don't have to talk about you at all if you don't want to."

"Which is exactly the way to make me want to tell you the truth." Caz grinned and splashed more wine into her glass. "I split up from my boyfriend a few weeks ago. It was kind of our specialty—we've had so many breakups in the last year, it's laughable—but this time, we're done for good. He's sleeping with his manager, and she's ten years older than me. She's not even that pretty."

"Are you devastated?"

"Oh, I can cry on cue if you want me to pretend to be. But honestly, it had run its course. According to my nan, we were like a low-rent Richard Burton and Elizabeth Taylor. Drinking too much, fighting nonstop, breaking up and making up practically every week. It was no fun, it was exhausting, and I knew deep down he was only with me for the money and the publicity. I spend my time working my socks off, and he does sod all. Story of my life," she concluded wryly. "Well, not my *whole* life, but it's been pretty much the same for the last ten years, ever since I got famous."

"Not much fun."

"Tell me about it. Got a thing for bad boys, that's my trouble. Time I sorted myself out." She shrugged. "That's why I came here, to have a break and get away from all the chaos."

Shay glanced around the suite, at the clothes and shoes chucked on the floor, at the makeup scattered over the chest of drawers, the glossy magazines and packages of candy spilling out of one of the expensive suitcases over by the window.

Caz followed his gaze. "I know, I know, but this is physical chaos, and I'm allowed to be messy in my own hotel room. I'm hungry," she announced. "Are you hungry? I don't want to go downstairs though. Shall we order loads of food? Oh, don't tell me you don't want to." She lobbed an almond at him when he hesitated. "I can't cope with rejection—I'm a diva, remember! Please say yes."

It had been one of those endless evenings, the nightmare kind where you found yourself trapped in a situation from which there was no escape. The table of friends from Aaron's apartment building were chatty and funny, and under any other circumstances, Didi would have loved spending time with them. Finally, dinner was over, and they prepared to leave the restaurant. The next moment, two people walked past the window, stopped abruptly, and tapped loudly on the glass to attract their attention.

"Hey, it's Raj and Kev!" Aaron's face lit up. "They're back from Ibiza!"

And that had been that. Raj and Kev had come bursting into the restaurant, and Aaron had said, "Come on. Let's go back to my place. We need to hear all about your holiday!"

Oh please no, we really don't. Didi attempted to mentally signal to Raj and Kev that this would be a terrible idea.

"Yeah!" Raj high-fived Aaron. "Got plenty of drink in?"

"Loads," Aaron promised.

"We'll probably miss the last train home. OK to crash at yours?" said Kev.

"No problem at all."

Didi silently exhaled; so much for telepathy.

"Brilliant." Raj was jubilant. "What are we waiting for? Let's go!"

It was one o'clock in the morning. Caz was singing along dreamily to a track from the new Lewis Capaldi album. She had an incredible voice, warm, husky, and fantastically expressive. As she sang, she caught Shay's eye and smiled. "Be an angel, pass us those tacos and that avocado dip."

Tonight had been an interesting experience in more ways than one. Shay hadn't planned on still being in her room this late, yet here he was. Caz had led an astonishing life and told great stories about and against herself, cheerfully admitting her flaws and failings. As a rule, whenever he met a new woman, within an hour or two, Shay would inevitably find a reason to be disappointed in some aspect of her personality. It was ridiculous, he knew, and a really annoying character trait to have been landed with, but that was just how it went, and over the years, he'd grown used to it.

Tonight, though, it hadn't happened. Against all the odds, getting to know Caz Holloway had exceeded expectations. She was self-deprecating and down-to-earth, and he was enjoying her company. She also seemed to be enjoying his.

"What are you thinking?" she said now.

"I'm thinking you've nearly finished the avocado dip."

"That's because my manager isn't here to give me grief over how many calories there are in it." She ran her index finger around the inside of the pot and stuck it in her mouth. "If you want more, we can phone down for some."

"I'm OK."

"Oh, I already know that."

He pointed out of the window. "Look at those stars."

"Why?"

"Because there are so many of them. It's a beautiful night."

"I mean, why did you change the subject when I said I knew you were OK?" She cocked an eyebrow. "Are you shy?"

"No."

"Well, that was me making my first move. Being a tiny bit flirty, showing you that I'm interested."

Here we go. This was what she'd been leading up to.

"It's just that you're bloody gorgeous, and I get the feeling you like me too." Caz searched his face. "I mean, am I wrong? And here's me, sitting all alone on this huge bed while you're over there in that chair. You seem quite a long way away, that's all."

Shay gave a tiny shrug. This wasn't how he'd expected tonight to pan out, but sometimes these things happened, and maybe this particular thing was happening for a reason. The last few weeks hadn't been easy, God knows. Right now, Didi was in London with Aaron. By this time, they'd be in bed together. She was marrying him in December, and that was that. If Shay had had any idea how seeing her again after all these years would make him feel, maybe he would have come back to Elliscombe earlier, preferably before Aaron had appeared in her life.

But instead he'd been an idiot, holding on to his pride and refusing to allow those feelings and emotions to rise to the surface. He hadn't come back in time, and now it was too late. Didi had been snapped up by someone else.

"You know what happens when you play it cool?" Caz slid down from the bed, her wide-necked top falling off one tanned shoulder.

"What happens?"

"It makes other people keener." She moved toward him. "It's quite a game-playery thing to do, but it does the trick. It makes them want to kiss you." Reaching his chair, she took hold of his hands. "I really want to kiss you, and I hope you want to kiss me too."

Shay looked at her. It was an offer not many men would refuse. He still had the picture of Didi in his head, but what was the point of even continuing to think about her?

"OK, I'll count to three, and if you haven't kissed me by then, you'll have to leave," said Caz. "Because that'll mean I've made a massive show of myself."

Shay rose to his feet and drew her to him until their mouths were almost touching. With a slow smile, he said, "No need to count. I'm not going anywhere."

"Phew." She gave a shaky laugh of relief. "Thank goodness for that."

chapter 27

If the timing hadn't been so terrible, it would be funny. Didi lay awake on her side of the bed, gazing up at the ceiling and listening to Aaron's low-level snores as he slept on his back next to her.

Aaron's snores weren't the problem. The reason she was unable to sleep was because of the epic Boeing 707–level noises emanating from the living room and reverberating through the thin wall separating them from their overnight guests.

She pressed the pillow over her ears, but it didn't help; Raj and Kev were quite the double act. Sometimes they snored in unison, but more often, they were out of sync. Plus there were all the random grunts, snuffles, and snorts to add to the chorus.

No wonder the pair of them didn't have girlfriends.

Sliding out of bed, she resisted the urge to creep into the living room and smother them with cushions. Instead, she crossed to the window and leaned against it to admire the view over the river. The stars were out in force, a crescent moon hung above the Tetris-patterned skyline, and even at this time of night, the roads far below were still busy with traffic.

Not like Elliscombe at all. Resting on her elbows, Didi pictured the main street outside the hotel, illuminated by the ornate vintage streetlamps casting pools of golden light at intervals along the sidewalk. The next moment—she couldn't help it—her imagination sent her rising from street level, soaring over the gabled roof of the hotel, then hovering in midair outside the windows of the Midnight Suite. Inside, Shay would be sleeping, and unlike Raj and Kev, his breathing would be regular, silent, and not annoying at all. Moving closer in her imagination, Didi saw that the diamond-leaded window on the right was ajar. If she wanted to see him, all she had to do was nudge it open a bit wider and swoop inside—

Back in nonfantasy land, there was a loud crash from the living room, followed by a muted bellow of, "Fuck...ow...get out the way."

Kev must have rolled off the sofa. Didi heard him stagger to his feet, curse as he banged into the glass coffee table, then stumble to the bathroom at the far end of the apartment. Where he proceeded to empty his bladder into the toilet bowl so loudly you'd think he was doing it through a megaphone.

When he'd returned to the sofa and resumed snoring, she went back to bed. It was OK. In the morning, Kev and Raj would wake up with raging hangovers, apologize profusely for having been nightmare overnight guests, and head for home.

And once they were gone, she would get on with the business of breaking up with Aaron.

Finally.

....

When Shay opened his eyes the next morning, Caz was lying on her side next to him, tracing light circles on his chest.

"I've been waiting ages for you to wake up," she murmured playfully.

"Ages. Does that mean two minutes or three?"

"More like one and a half."

"And now I'm awake. What happens next?"

"That thing we did last night. Can we do it again, please?" She moved closer. "I liked it a lot."

An hour later, Shay returned to his own room to shower and dress before popping back in to the Midsummer Suite.

Caz was sitting up in bed, tucking into the full English breakfast that had been delivered while he'd been across the corridor.

"Have a sausage," she offered, waving the one on the end of her fork at him.

"I'm fine."

She grinned. "I already know that."

He pinched a slice of toast from the tray. "Right, I'm off to collect Dad from the hospital."

"And I'll definitely see you later, once he's settled? Or am I about to get ghosted, now you've had your way with me?"

"I'll be back." He hadn't had that sinking feeling that so often made its presence felt the morning after the night before.

She reached forward for a kiss. "That's all I need to know. You just make sure your dad's OK before you leave him. He's the one who matters. I'll wait as long as it takes."

As he closed the door behind him, Shay thought what a nice, undiva-ish thing that was to say.

At the hospital, they had to wait awhile for Red to be checked over by the doctor on call. At last, he was given the all clear, and they were allowed to leave.

"Plenty of rest, remember," the doctor warned them. "No gadding about."

"My gadding about days are over," said Red. "Am I still allowed to drink?"

"In moderation."

Shay shook his head. "Why are you even asking that question? You know you're going to do it anyway."

His father winked. "Sometimes it's more fun to do things when they're forbidden."

As they drove back to Elliscombe, Red said, "Shall I tell you what's great about being this ill? Everything looks better." He pointed through the window. "The fields, those hills, the birds in the trees. They're all miraculous."

A pigeon flying overhead took the opportunity to drop a white splodge on the windshield. "Even that?" said Shay.

"Even that." Red chuckled and coughed. "Might not seem like it to you, but even pigeon poo is its own kind of miracle."

"Look, are you sure you want to stay on at Rosa's? If you moved into my suite at the hotel, you'd be more comfortable."

Red pulled a face. "No thanks. I'm happy where I am. Can we stop at the house to see how it's going?"

When they reached Hillcrest, Shay pulled up and gave him a brief tour. The roof had been repaired, the pointing completed, and the kitchen and living room both smelled of drying plaster where the walls had been stripped back to basics and completely redone. Red nodded his approval. "Coming along."

At Frog Cottage, Rosa came running out to greet them. Having carried his father's case inside, Shay laid out his various medications on a tray in the kitchen, along with a list of instructions as to when and how many needed to be taken. A chicken casserole was simmering in the oven, and a just-made Victoria sponge cake was cooling on the counter.

"See what I mean?" Red said happily. "Why would I want to move into some fancy hotel when I've got all this here?"

"Are you hungry?" Rosa looked eagerly at Shay. "If you'd like to stay for lunch, you'd be very welcome. I've made tons."

But Red was already shaking his head. "No need for him to stay. He's spent the last week sitting by my bed. Off you go. Do your own thing." He made a get-out-of-here gesture. "We'll be fine here, just the two of us."

"Are you sure?" said Shay.

"Completely. After a week stuck in that ward, I'm looking forward to a bit of peace."

Shay knew for a fact that his father couldn't possibly know about the night he'd just spent with Caz Holloway. But from the way Red was looking at him, you'd think he did.

Returning to the hotel at one o'clock, he encountered Marcus, the nervous waiter. In a stage whisper like a pantomime spy, Marcus said, "Did they tell you who's staying in the Midsummer Suite?"

"Caz Holloway." Shay nodded. "Yes, I heard."

"If you see her, don't ask for a selfie." Marcus shook his head seriously. "Sylvia said we mustn't do that."

"I won't, I promise."

As he climbed the stairs, Shay passed the corridor leading to Didi's quarters and deliberately averted his gaze. She was in London with Aaron; the time had come to accept this and get her out of his system once and for all.

Well, he'd already made a start.

He continued up to the top floor and tapped on the door of the Midsummer Suite.

"Who's there?"

"Room service," said Shay.

Seconds later, the door opened, and there she was, wearing nothing but a bath towel and a naughty smile. "Well, hello, room service. I hope you have something special for me."

He took a packet of red and black fruit pastilles out of his pocket. "Picked these up in the hospital shop. Will they do?"

"To be honest, I was hoping for something a bit more special than that." Caz snaked her bare arms around his neck and insinuated herself against him. The white towel dropped to the floor.

Shay moved her backward into the suite. "In that case, might be an idea if we close the door."

"Spoilsport," she said.

OK, it had felt before as if the fates were conspiring against her. But it was three o'clock in the afternoon now, and Didi was starting to suspect them of cracking up laughing while pointing at her gleefully behind her back.

Raj and Kev had carried on sleeping and snoring until midday before waking up and complaining about their terrible hangovers. When Aaron had made them cups of tea and offered to call them a cab, Kev had mimed vigorous retching and declared that he felt far too ill to get into any kind of moving vehicle.

Finally, *finally* they'd recovered enough to leave. There'd been mention of calling up friends and arranging to meet in a pub in Notting Hill for hair of the dog, and Didi had waved them off, sending up a silent prayer of thanks that she'd never have to see them again as long as she lived.

She and Aaron had still been watching from the window when another taxi pulled up outside the apartment building and a woman in a pink coat emerged from the back seat. Aaron said cheerfully, "Here she is then. She's early."

"Who's early?"

"It's Mum. She wanted to surprise you."

chapter 28

Oh what? Come on, fate. Give me a break, please.

Didi had been all geared up to getting The Conversation started. And now this. "What's she doing here?"

Aaron gave her shoulder a reassuring squeeze. "Hey, don't look so horrified. It's something nice!"

Aaron's mother, Kay, lived in Swindon and worked as an assistant in a pharmacy. Two years ago, she had lost her husband and her confidence, and today—of course—was the first time she'd felt brave enough to make the journey up to London on her own. She was a sweet and lovely lady, and catching the train had been an ordeal for her.

"But I gave myself a good talking-to and said it was time to get a grip," she told Didi. "Trips don't have to be scary. I just have to think of it as an adventure. And of course I wanted to see you again. Has Aaron told you where we're going? I booked it myself, as a special treat for the three of us." Her eyes bright, she added, "And we must take loads of photos because guess what else I've done? Joined Instagram!"

What could Didi do but go along with it? She wasn't a monster. Kay had organized for them to take a trip on a boat that traveled up and down the Thames while everyone on board enjoyed chicken and chips and jugs of sangria, and a bald man and a huge woman in a purple kaftan took it in turns to tell long-winded jokes and play mournful music on a harp.

For three extremely long hours.

After that, Kay said she'd always wanted to go on one of those topless buses to see the sights of London, so Aaron bought tickets, and they dutifully admired Buckingham Palace, the shops on Oxford Street ("Look, there's *another* Marks and Spencer!"), and the traffic careering around Hyde Park Corner. By the time they got off, Kay had taken over two hundred photographs and uploaded most of them to Instagram for the benefit of her six followers.

At 8:30, the taxi arrived to take her to Paddington. She hugged Didi. "Bye, love. It's been so lovely to see you again. Not long now till the wedding!"

This was awful. Didi hugged her back. "It's been lovely to see you too."

"Now that I've got the travel bug, we'll be able to meet up more often."

"Oh yes." Feeling like a politician who knows he's not going to be keeping any of his promises, Didi said, "We definitely will."

"Don't forget to follow me, will you?"

For a split second, Didi thought she meant follow her to Paddington, which was actually the plan just as soon as she'd finished finishing with Aaron.

"On Instagram." Kay nodded encouragingly. "Otherwise, you won't be able to see all the photos I post. I'm hoping to go viral!"

At last, she was gone, and it was just the two of them, alone together in Aaron's ultramodern eighth-floor apartment.

"Is there anything left to drink in the fridge?" said Didi. If Raj and Kev had polished off the lot, she was going to have to hire an assassin.

"There's a glass of white left."

A glass? She could do with a full bottle. "Fine, that'll do."

"Mum loves you," said Aaron. "I'm so glad you two get along so well together."

"OK, there's something I have to tell you." She didn't have time to lead into it gently. She reached for the glass he was holding out to her and took a giant gulp. "We need to talk."

He grinned. "Sounds ominous."

"Well, it is kind of…ominous. Sorry."

"Is this to do with Mum?"

"No, *no*…"

"About the wedding?"

She took a breath. "Yes, it's about the wedding." God, this was hard.

After a second, Aaron said, "If you'd rather elope, that's fine. We can change anything that needs to be changed. You want to fly to Vegas and get Elvis to do the honors? No problem."

OK, enough of playing twenty questions. Didi blurted out, "It's the whole getting married thing. I'm sorry. You're great, and you haven't done anything wrong. I just don't love you enough to go through with it."

Aaron was no longer smiling. She saw the confusion on his face morph into stony disbelief. "Is this a joke?"

"I wouldn't joke about something like this. It's just been a feeling building up and up… I realized I should be more excited about us spending the rest of our lives together." She spread her hands helplessly. "And I just wasn't."

"Because I'm not exciting enough? You mean I'm *boring*?"

"You aren't! Of course you aren't boring! This is nothing to do with you. It's all me!"

"Oh, give me *strength*…"

"I'm sorry. I can't help how I feel."

"And you've just this minute decided you need to break it to me," said Aaron.

"Well, no…"

He figured it out. "You mean it was the whole reason you came down here. And you've been waiting since last night for the chance to say it. Jesus."

"I didn't know we were going to have nonstop visitors." Didi's stomach squirmed with misery; she hated having to be the bad guy.

Aaron was looking at her as if she were a stranger. "So is it just the wedding that's off? Or the whole relationship?"

She swallowed. "Yes. I mean, the second one. Both of them."

"I don't believe this is happening."

"Sorry."

"Stop saying fucking sorry. Why are you sorry anyway? This is what you want." He paused suddenly, his eyes narrowing. "Oh, I get it now. There's someone else. You've found a replacement, some guy who's better than me, more *exciting* than me." His jaw taut, he said icily, "Now let me think, I wonder who that could possibly be."

Didi's heart was thudding like the hooves of a runaway horse. She shook her head. "There's no one else."

"No? I wonder why I find that so hard to believe. It's all been going on, hasn't it? The old boyfriend who came back, better looking and oh so much richer than before. And like an idiot, I trusted you completely because I thought you loved me as much as I loved you. Go on then, tell me. How long have you been shagging him?"

"Nothing's been going on, and I haven't been shagging him. Or anyone, because I'd never do that. I can't force you to believe me, but it's the truth."

"And I still don't believe you." Aaron took a step back and raised his hands. "I'm not the jealous type. Did you notice that I didn't say anything about him to make you think I was worried? That's because I wasn't worried."

"It's not you. It's not him. This is all down to me." Didi twisted the diamond ring off her finger and held it out to him. When he didn't move, she placed it on the glass-topped coffee table. Filled with sadness and suddenly overwhelmed with exhaustion, she said yet again, "I really am sorry. You deserve better than me."

"Too bloody right I do," Aaron snapped back.

She'd only said it to be polite, but fair enough. In a situation like this, it was no fun at all being either the finisher or the finishee.

It didn't take long at all to throw her few belongings into the overnight case. As she added the toiletries bag that had lived in the cupboard under the bathroom sink for the last year, he sneered, "So that's why you brought the empty case down with you."

When it was time to leave, she said, "Sorry. Bye."

"If you were actually sorry, you wouldn't be leaving." Aaron paused. "Have you really not slept with him?"

"I swear I haven't."

"Do it, then."

"What?"

A muscle was twitching in his temple. "Have all the sex you want with the guy for a week…or two or three weeks. Until the novelty wears off and the pair of you come to your senses. There you go. How about that for an offer you can't refuse? Because you can deny it until you're blue in the face, but I know it's Shay Mason. He's the one behind all this. So do it," he continued evenly. "You've got a free pass from me. May as well make the most of it. Get him out of your system."

Didi was on the verge of saying so many things, but in the end, her words deserted her. It would be wrong to deny his comments, seeing as the basic accusation was true. She looked at him and said, "I'm going now."

He held open the front door, and she walked past him, carrying her case. As she made her way down the staircase, she heard him head back into the flat, then come out again. When she reached the ground floor, he called her name, and she looked up through the rectangle of space that formed the central well of the stairway.

"Take this," said Aaron.

"Take what?" She saw him drop something small, then heard a tiny metallic clink as it hit the ground six feet away.

"I can't take it," she called out.

"Well, if you leave it lying there, it's just going to get stolen." He turned and disappeared inside the apartment, the door slamming shut behind him.

He wasn't wrong about that. Wearily, Didi picked up the ring, rummaged in her shoulder bag, and zipped it securely inside her blue leather purse. When Aaron was in a calmer state of mind, she would arrange to mail it back to him.

The tube journey back to Paddington was crowded and stiflingly hot. Reaching the concourse at last, Didi heaved a sigh of exasperation when she saw on the screens that her train was delayed.

An hour later, there was still no sign of one, thanks to major signal failure on the line. Everyone watching the screens was getting increasingly fed up. By eleven o'clock, there were no seats left anywhere, and last night's lack of sleep was catching up with her. After yawning so hard she almost dislocated her jaw, Didi gave up and dragged her case up the slope that led out of the station.

chapter 29

"Red's doing OK," said Rosa. "Well, as OK as can be expected. His chest infection's sorted out now, but he's had to increase the morphine. I made risotto tonight—you know the seafood one you like?—but he couldn't manage much of it." She paused to run her fingers through the back of her hair and let some air get to her neck. "Oh, and it's all still going well with Layla and her chap. Harry the fitness trainer, remember I told you? She sees him two or three times a week. I haven't met him yet, but I'm sure it won't be long now. I'll keep you posted and—"

"God, is this the kind of thing you talk about?"

Rosa jumped out of her skin. Usually Ingrid wore clattery stilettos, but this time, she was barefoot. "Sorry, I didn't hear you."

"When Benny told me about you coming here to chat to your dead husband, I thought you'd be having more interesting conversations than that." She gave a little laugh. "At this rate, if he were still alive, he might die of boredom."

What must it be like to be so blunt, to have that much confidence in yourself? Rosa wondered how Ingrid would react if she were to say, *How dare you be so fucking rude?*

Instead, she replied, "It depends on how much has been happening. But I want to keep him up-to-date with what's going on in our lives. Even the little things."

"Right. And am I allowed to ask when you might be finished?" Ingrid indicated the phone in her hand. "It's just that I came out here to make a call, and it's kind of inconvenient having to wait for someone else to talk for ages to another person who isn't even here."

"Sorry, I didn't know." Rosa scrambled to her feet with some difficulty; one of her legs had gone to sleep and was now fizzing like sherbet candy.

"I mean, it is *our* garden. It would be nice to be allowed some privacy."

With no time to say her usual goodbye to Joe, Rosa hastily crossed the lawn and climbed the wall. As she dropped down on the other side, she heard Ingrid say with another chuckle, "Let's hope your dead husband doesn't eavesdrop on my phone call. I think maybe he couldn't cope with so much excitement."

....

The air-conditioning on the train hadn't been working, which was always nice on what promised to be the hottest day of the year so far. After having spent Saturday night in a fairly grim hotel a couple of streets from Paddington station, Didi was just glad there was a train running at all. Arriving back at Moreton-in-Marsh, she unstuck her white T-shirt from her spine, opened all the car windows, and headed out of the parking lot.

At least she'd done what she'd set out to do. Who knew what might happen next? Whoops, police car… Hopefully the future didn't involve being landed with a speeding ticket. But no, today even the police were on her side.

As Didi drove back to Elliscombe, her spirits rose. She breathed in lungfuls of clean country air, and when she switched radio stations, there was her favorite Killers track playing as if she'd magicked it out of the ether. Singing along at the top of her voice, she pretended she wasn't holding her breath about what might lie up ahead. Then she rounded the final bend and abandoned the pretense, because there it was, Shay's Audi parked in the driveway outside Hillcrest. It was midday on Sunday, and he was here, still working.

Her pulse accelerated as her brain considered the options. On the one hand, she was hot and sticky, and her shirt was looking like an old dishcloth. On the other hand, would he really mind? Seeing that his car was parked outside, didn't that give her the perfect opportunity to call in and ask after Red before viewing the progress that had been made with the renovations? And if Shay did happen to ask her why she was back at this time on a Sunday, she could casually mention that the engagement was off. She'd be able to see in his eyes how he felt about that, and maybe an unspoken conversation would ensue. Then, who knew where it might go from there?

Her foot touched the brake, and the car began to slow down. She'd almost reached the house now, and a million possibilities were ricocheting through her brain…until a flash of pink appeared at the perimeter of her vision and an entirely new possibility presented itself.

The next moment, she was far enough along the lane to see the garden to the right of the house. The pink she'd glimpsed was a bikini top being worn by a female sporting a white sunhat, dark glasses, and a short khaki skirt. She was tanned, laughing, and worst of all running her hands over Shay's chest in a way that allowed no doubt as to the extent of their relationship.

It wasn't how you'd greet your mail carrier or the guy who'd come to read your electricity meter, put it that way.

Who was she? Didi felt sick. Where had this laughing, playful female sprung from? What was going *on*? Except the answer to that last question was blindingly obvious because Shay certainly wasn't objecting to being manhandled. Oh God, and now she was reaching up to kiss him…

Didi shuddered; thank heavens she hadn't stopped the car. Neither of them had noticed her slowing down as she drove past. Leaving them behind, she glanced into the rearview mirror and saw them kissing properly now.

While the cat's away…

What was extra frustrating was that she hadn't even known she was the cat.

....

"You're back!" Sylvia exclaimed as Didi carried her overnight case up the staircase. "Did you have fun?" Without waiting for a reply, she went on, "Ooh, bit of gossip for you. Guess who's in the Midsummer Suite?"

"Well, it was booked by a Marcus Williams."

"He made the arrangements on someone else's behalf. It's Caz Holloway! *Exciting.*" Sylvia was beaming with pleasure at being the one to relay the news. "You'll never guess what else."

And that was it. Like being hit in the stomach with a medicine ball, Didi knew. The woman in the pink bikini top had been wearing dark glasses, and her hair had been stuffed under her hat, but with hindsight, of course it was her. Careful to keep her expression neutral, she said, "What else?"

"Caz and Shay, swear to God! Inseparable! Pretty sure he's spent the last two nights in her room. Isn't that fantastic?"

"Wow, yes, great." What else could she say? Didi fanned herself vigorously. "It was so hot on the train, thought I was going to melt. I'm going to jump in the shower. Anything else I need to know about?"

"Nothing. All under control here," Sylvia said. "Everything's perfect."

Except it wasn't, was it?

Upstairs in her apartment, Didi showered, blow-dried her hair, and applied more makeup than usual. Then she looked at her reflection in the bathroom mirror—hello, Miss Try Hard—and removed the makeup, because what was she trying to do, compete with a BAFTA-winning actress who could sing and dance and was so beloved by everyone she was practically a national treasure?

An hour later, the blue Audi pulled into the hotel parking lot. Her stomach constricting with envy, Didi watched from her bedroom window as Caz and Shay made their way through the side entrance and across the terrace. Everyone else out there was watching them too, in that discreet British way, until one of the guests said something to Caz and held up her phone, evidently asking for a selfie. Caz stopped and dutifully posed for the camera, then said something that made the guests laugh. The next moment, she and Shay disappeared inside, but not before Didi had seen the look they exchanged, along with the brief shared smile.

They were so well matched, so in tune with each other. Like an actual perfect couple.

Making her mind up, Didi crossed to the bedside table and took out the engagement ring she'd put away after unpacking her case. She slid it back onto her ring finger. Just for now, life was going to be an awful lot easier if she carried on wearing it.

…………………………………………

"Oh, you're an angel," Caz whooped the next morning. "You're literally a lifesaver. Thank you so much!"

She'd called down to reception in a panic, and Didi had come to the rescue. "Well, it's a phone charger, not a kidney," she said with a smile. "But I know what you mean."

"Can't live without our phones, though, can we? My agent goes mad when he can't get hold of me." Caz was perched on the bed wearing shorts and a strappy top, painstakingly painting her toenails bright orange and seemingly unaware that she was holding the bottle of polish at a precarious angle. The brush slipped, and she said, "Oh bum."

"If you like, we can arrange for a nail technician to come to the hotel," Didi offered.

"Nah, too impatient. They take ages, and my feet are dead ticklish. Easier to do it myself. Whoops!" A drop of nail polish landed on her ankle. "Don't worry about the sheets—if I wreck anything, I'll pay for it. My mum calls me Mr. Bean!"

"I'm not worried," Didi lied, "but why don't you let me hold the bottle? Would that help?"

"See, didn't I say you were an angel? Come and sit down." Caz patted the space next to her on the bed and passed over the bottle. "Have a good laugh at what a pig's ear I'm making of painting my toes. You're Didi?"

"That's right." Didi wondered how much Shay had told her. "I hope you're enjoying your stay with us so far."

"Are you kidding? I'm enjoying every single thing about this place. I break into a cold sweat every time I remember that I almost booked a week in Barcelona instead. You have a gorgeous hotel."

"Thank you."

"And gorgeous guests." Caz giggled. "Well, one guest in particular. I'm sure you know which one I mean."

Didi nodded, firmly in hotel manager mode. "I did hear a mention of this."

"Oh God, though, isn't he amazing? *Total* babe." She clutched her free hand to her chest. "I'm like, what have I done to deserve this? Since Friday night, we've been together practically nonstop… I just can't believe my luck. He had to go to work this morning, and I'm already missing him like crazy. Can you imagine if I'd gone to Barcelona instead? We'd never have met!"

"There might have been someone even better in Barcelona." Didi attempted levity.

"Not possible. Shay's the real deal. I'm telling you, it's been like a complete whirlwind. I get giddy just thinking about him." Caz's face was glowing, the excitement clear to see. "After all these years of shit boyfriends who mess me around and sell stories about me behind my back, I've finally found a good one. About bloody time too. My luck's changed at last!"

Didi's cheek muscles ached from smiling. It was agony having to hear the sheer pinch-me happiness in Caz's voice. Caz clearly had no idea that Didi and Shay had once been a couple; he hadn't thought to mention it. Then again, why would he? It was evidently irrelevant.

"And the sex is out of this world," Caz went on cheerfully.

Thanks for that.

"Sorry, am I oversharing? I can't help it, I'm just so happy. Isn't it just the best feeling in the world though? Well, *you* know. You've got one of your own." She pointed with the dripping nail polish brush at the ring on Didi's left hand. "What's he like, your guy?"

"He's great! In every way." Didi marveled at her own acting ability. "We make a good couple. I'm very lucky."

"There, all done. Now I've got to wait for them to dry." Caz admired her glowing orange toenails. "Then I'm going to head over to the house Shay's doing up for his old man. I know it's crazy, but I just want to be with him all the time. I'm like his groupie! If I tell you a secret, will you promise not to laugh?"

"I promise." *Oh please God, not more sex talk.*

"I know it's only been three days, but it's never felt this right before. After he left this morning, I called my mum and told her I've found my happily-ever-after." Sliding off the bed and walking like a duck with her toes splayed, Caz crossed the room and began brushing her ash-blond hair. "I've been waiting to find someone like Shay my whole life."

chapter 30

"WHAT'S ALL THIS THEN?" WILL CLIMBED OUT OF THE TAXI ON Monday evening and eyed the sack of gift-wrapped presents on the sidewalk outside Layla's flat. "Working on the side as an out-of-season Santa?"

"Be gentle. Some of them are fragile."

He lifted the bulky sack and placed it in the trunk. "Someone's birthday? Lucky them."

Since he knew where he was taking her, it had to be pretty obvious whose birthday it was. Layla still got the feeling Will didn't approve, but this evening, she was too excited to care. "It's Harry's birthday… Well, it's actually tomorrow, but he's heading up to Sheffield to see his parents tomorrow morning, so we're celebrating tonight. I love buying presents for people."

"Well, you've certainly got plenty here." Will closed the trunk and opened the passenger door for her.

"I have." Layla beamed at him. "He's worth it."

Will said, "I used to love buying presents for my mum. And she always complained about them."

"Why?"

"She said I went over-the-top and spent too much." He smiled at the memory. "All she wanted was a card and maybe a small bunch of flowers, but nothing fancy. Anything else was a waste, that was what she told me, every time. And all I wanted to do was spoil her, give her lovely things to make her happy, even if she wasn't well enough to go out and wear nice clothes in public. It's hard trying to show someone you love them by buying them silk dressing gowns and bottles of their favorite perfume." With a rueful smile, he added, "Which they then refuse to wear."

"But she knew you loved her. You must miss her so much," said Layla.

He shrugged. "Of course I do. Then again, I was lucky to have her around for as long as I did. She could have died when I was a kid, like Shay Mason's mum. That would have been so much worse."

"Oh my God." Harry did a massive double take when he opened the door to his flat. "What's all this? You've gone completely over-the-top. Here, let me help you…"

Once they were up the stairs, he dropped the sack onto the sofa and pulled Layla into his arms. "Happy birthday to me, happy birthday to me…" And when he'd finished kissing her, he said sincerely, "You gorgeous, beautiful thing…you're the only present I want."

"Well, that's too bad," Layla teased as his hands roamed over her body, "because you have plenty more to unwrap."

"I'll get to those later." His eyes glinted as he led her through to the bedroom. "You first."

Afterward, he opened the gifts, admiring the effort she'd gone to with the wrapping and decorations. Before long, the bed was covered with discarded gold paper and caramel satin ribbons.

"A coffee machine." When the final present was revealed, he looked suitably surprised.

"This is the one that had the best reviews. And these are the pods that go in them. I've bought two hundred, so you won't have to worry about running out of coffee for a while." She patted the boxes of café au lait pods. "Or milk!"

"Great," said Harry. "Although if I run out of milk, I just drink it black."

Didn't she know it. Layla watched as he examined the bed linen she'd chosen for him, a matching set of sage-green Egyptian cotton sheets, pillowcases, and king-size duvet cover.

"Eight hundred thread count." She stroked the beautiful sheets, so much nicer to sleep on than the bobbly purple polyester ones currently in use on the bed.

He pulled a face. "Should we count them to make sure they're all there?"

"Only if you really want to." She gave him another hug. "Do you like everything?"

"You bought far too much."

"I love giving presents." Yes, maybe she'd gone over-the-top, but they were all things he needed, and they made life so much more enjoyable. Matching cutlery! A gorgeous cashmere sweater and delicious aftershave that didn't smell of toilet cleaner! Lovely new goose-down pillows!

"You're amazing. Thank you so much." He ran a finger over the outline of her mouth. "I love you."

Layla gave a shiver of joy; he'd said it at last.

"Is it too soon to be saying that? I can't not tell you." Harry shook his head. "It's the truth."

Her heart swelled like a marshmallow in the microwave. "It's not too soon. I love you too."

Later that evening, after they'd finished their pizzas, Harry took out his phone. "Have a look at this. What d'you think?"

She found herself gazing at a photo of a motorbike, a black-and-silver Yamaha according to the description beneath it.

"Five hundred CC, four years old, eight thousand miles on the clock. Three grand."

"I know nothing about motorbikes. Are you going to buy it?"

"I don't know if I can afford it. But it's definitely something I need. I mean, a pushbike's fine for getting around, but at the moment, I'm spending more time getting to my clients than training them. It just makes sense to be able to travel farther and faster than I'm doing right now." He grimaced. "The money thing could be a problem though."

"You could apply for a loan, get a finance agreement," said Layla.

"Except I'm self-employed. The only companies who'd take me on are the loan-shark kind, and no way am I doing that."

She knew all about his parents' problems; it was their dealings with one such company that had landed them in such massive debt last year. Harry had been forced to use up his entire savings in order to bail them out.

"Is that why you're seeing them tomorrow? Are they able to pay back some of the money you lent them?"

He shook his head. "They can't, and I wouldn't ask them. They had no idea they'd end up getting into such a mess financially. I'm going to see them because I love them, not to pester them for money. Mum'll have knitted me a sweater, and Dad will give me a ten-pound voucher for Top Man, and I wouldn't want any more than that."

He was fighting back the emotion; Layla knew how much he loved his parents. She gave him a hug. "They'll be so happy to see you."

He nodded. "They will."

"They sound great." Hopefully she'd get to meet them one day.

"They're amazing." He gazed once more at the motorcycle on the screen, then switched off his phone.

An hour later, he said, "I've got something to ask you. And I don't want to have to say it, but…well, it's kind of personal."

A sense of foreboding began to unfurl in the pit of her stomach. "What is it?"

"No, don't worry. Doesn't matter."

After a few seconds, Layla said, "Go on."

"You might not like it."

"Ask me."

"OK, but you can always say no."

Here it came. Layla braced herself. If it was a request to lend him the three thousand pounds for the motorbike, she would have to say no. It was too much, too soon… *Please* don't let him ask it…

"OK, don't hate me." His beautiful dark eyes were apprehensive, his thumb anxiously stroking the back of her hand. "But do you still have the receipt for the coffeemaker?"

Oh thank God. She gave a shaky laugh of relief. "Hello? I'm an accountant. Of course I've kept the receipt."

"I feel terrible, but would you mind if I took it back? It's just, I wouldn't really use it, and if I'm trying to get some money together for a bike, it'd be a real help."

Layla was filled with remorse. She'd known he might not want to use a coffee machine; it had been for her own benefit really. It was on a par with giving someone a kennel when they didn't have a dog. "I don't mind, I promise."

"Sure?"

She gave a reassuring nod and ran her bare foot along his shin. "I'm glad you said it."

Harry looked hopefully at her. "Are you?"

"Yes!"

"It's just that getting myself some transport has to be my number-one priority." He tapped the purple polyester that was so bobbly it drove her to distraction. "And I already have a sheet. So if you really mean it, maybe we could return the stuff for the bed too."

chapter 31

"I KNOW, DARLING. I'LL SEE YOU TOMORROW. LOVE YOU."

Benny was in the kitchen, and Ingrid was sitting outside in the shade with her laptop, preparing for tomorrow's meetings in Copenhagen. The windows were wide open, and he assumed she was speaking on the phone to her daughter, until it came back to him that Birgitte had called last night from Johannesburg.

He made Ingrid one of the tiny cups of espresso she always drank and carried it out to her. "Who was that you were talking to?"

"Hmm?" She flipped her ice-blond hair back from her forehead and tapped a few words into the document on the screen. "Oh, it was Birgitte."

"Was it? Just before you hung up, you asked which hotel the two of you were booked into."

She gave him a mocking look. "Benedict! Were you eavesdropping on my private call?"

"The windows were open. It was hardly private. And you weren't on the phone to Birgitte."

"Fine. You caught me out. Gold star for M'sieur Poirot." Her blue eyes regarded him with amusement. "And I think you can probably guess who I was speaking to."

The sensation inside Benny's chest was akin to a distant door closing. Not being slammed shut but being closed carefully and firmly. Overhead, birds sang, and as he stood and looked down at her, he heard a dog barking, a car beeping its horn over on the high street, small children shouting happily as they made their way to school.

"Sven."

"Correct." Ingrid took a delicate slip of espresso. "Two gold stars."

"You told me it was over."

"And when I said that, it was true. Oh, come on. You aren't stupid. You know. You've always known."

Had he? He'd suspected it, certainly. Had on occasion chosen not to ask a question he might otherwise have asked. Because he didn't want to be branded as jealous, suspicious, and too boring for words. *Suburban*, that was what Ingrid had accused him of being when the on-again, off-again affair had first come to light. *Bourgeois* was another word.

I've been such an idiot. Benny imagined a different kind of life, an easy, happy one without distance, deception, and a partner who didn't care much about anyone else at all, so long as she was able to carry on doing whatever she wanted to do.

Sometimes being suburban and old-fashioned seemed like a good way to live.

"You have fun in Copenhagen with Sven." He paused. "When you get back, you can move in with him."

Ingrid heaved a sigh of annoyance. "I would, like a shot, if only he'd leave his hideous, whining wife."

....

The best thing about afternoon naps was the dreams, Red had discovered. These days, he almost always woke up remembering them. And they often featured Mel, which was a bonus.

He opened his eyes now, his beloved wife still fresh and vivid in his mind. In his dreams, they were both young and healthy—another bonus—and the connection between them was as strong as it had ever been. Was she appearing more frequently these days because he was thinking more often about her? Or could it be that she was paying him these subliminal visits to let him know that she was waiting for him and would be there when the time came for him to join her?

The phone at his side buzzed to remind him that Shay would be here any minute now and that he'd be bringing someone with him. Right, better get downstairs. Rosa had gone over to see Layla, so he needed to unlock the front door.

The knock came just a few minutes later. And there on the doorstep, with Shay standing behind her, was the new girlfriend, the one off the telly.

"Hi, I'm Caz! I've been dying to meet you!" She gave him a hug, then let out a yelp of dismay. "Oh God, I can't believe I said that. I'm such a klutz. Sorry, it's just that I'm in love with your son, and my brain's gone doolally. I can't think straight anymore. Oh, but look at you. I know you've been through the mill, but there's still a twinkle in your eye. Shay's told me so much about you! My uncle Eddie was always in and out of prison too—he was a naughty boy just like you. I can't wait to hear all your stories!"

By the time they left an hour later, Red was exhausted. Caz could talk, he'd give her that. And she was clearly besotted with Shay.

He poured himself a small glass of Valpolicella and switched on the TV for company, allowing the day's news to wash over him. One good thing about dying was not having to worry about world events that might take place years from now.

The bad thing about dying was knowing you'd never find out what happened to family and friends after you'd gone. He wouldn't live to see Shay settle down and hopefully have a family of his own. He'd had the idea in his head that he could give fate a nudge in the right direction, but it wasn't showing any sign of working out the way he'd planned. It had been a long shot, admittedly. In his mind's eye, he'd even conjured up the end result and imagined himself telling the two of them that this had been his master plan right from the start.

So much for wishful thinking.

Caz seemed like a nice girl at least. A bit noisy and over-the-top, but with a good heart. And who knew? She might end up being the one for Shay. Maybe they'd have beautiful blond-haired children and be as happy together as he and Mel had been.

He tilted his head back and closed his eyes, picturing a future that was yet to happen. If Shay stayed on in Elliscombe and had kids, and Didi and that fellow of hers did the same, maybe their children would all attend the same school. And just occasionally, every now and again, Shay might cast a glance in Didi's direction, and she might do the same… and the two of them might wonder if things should have turned out differently.

Maybe, twenty-odd years down the line, when their children were grown and their marriages had crumbled, they might finally figure out where they'd gone wrong and do something about it.

Better late than never, eh?

Red exhaled. Except he wouldn't fucking well be here to see it and tell them he'd been right all along.

chapter 32

A week later, Rosa bumped into Benny Colette as she was leaving the co-op with three bags of shopping.

"Hi!" He beamed at her. "How have you been? Haven't seen you in the garden recently. Not that I've been looking… God, sorry, that makes me sound like a right nosy parker. I wasn't trying to spy on you, I promise."

"It's fine. Don't apologize." Rosa laughed at his mortified expression. "I haven't been over for a while." She hesitated, wondering whether to tell him about her humiliating encounter with Ingrid. Maybe not. "Everything OK with you?"

"Everything's great. Well, Ingrid's moving out, but that's fine too."

"*What?* When did this happen? What went wrong?"

He shrugged. "Who says it went wrong? Maybe it's all gone right." He paused. "Look, d'you fancy a coffee? Would you have time?"

"Plenty of time." Red was over at Hillcrest with Shay and Caz. "We could try the new café on the square."

"OK, though I'd prefer my place." He was already backing out of the shop.

"Didn't you come in to buy something? May as well pick it up while you're here."

But Benny shook his head. Wryly, he said, "I only followed you inside so I could accidentally bump into you."

Rosa hid a smile; from the way he'd acted, she'd kind of guessed as much.

Back at Compton House, by mutual agreement, they didn't attempt to do battle with the complicated coffee machine. When they were seated at the kitchen island with their mugs of Gold Blend, Benny said, "Does it feel weird, being back here?"

"A bit. But it's all completely different now. It *feels* different." All the walnut fittings had been ripped out, replaced with ultramodern units in shades of palest gray. "Is Ingrid definitely not here?"

"She's visiting a client in Madrid. Back tomorrow night. Coming back," he amended, "and moving out the next morning. Can't wait."

"You might change your mind."

"I won't." Benny was firm.

"What happened?"

"She's been seeing someone else."

"Oh *no*. I'm so sorry."

"These things happen. It's not the first time." Benny grimaced. "Or the second or the third. Sven's an old boyfriend. They've been sleeping together on and off for years, but he's married. When Ingrid first moved in with me, I think she only did it to teach him a lesson, to make him jealous and realize that he needed to leave his wife. Except it didn't happen. I was an idiot, I know that now. I thought she needed to get him out of her system and then she'd be able to settle down with me." Drily, he added, "Because that's how gullible I am. But the last couple of years haven't exactly been great. And that's an understatement."

"This is so sad." She might not be a fan of Ingrid, but Rosa's heart went out to him.

"Sad in one way," he admitted. "On the bright side, it means I've had plenty of time to get used to the idea that sooner or later, we'd be going our separate ways. Honestly? It's kind of a relief."

"Well, in that case, maybe we should celebrate. If I had a bottle of champagne right now, I'd open it." Rosa held up an imaginary glass and clinked it against the imaginary glass in Benny's hand. "Cheers! Here's to you and to the start of your fabulous new life!"

"There's a bottle in the fridge." Benny made to slide down from his stool. "Shall I open it?"

"Oh gosh, I'm supposed to be working this afternoon. I have a doll to finish."

His eyes twinkled. "Just one glass wouldn't hurt, would it?"

"Go on, then. You're a terrible influence."

He fetched the bottle and a pair of noninvisible glasses. "Who's the doll for?"

"A three-year-old boy in Singapore. Poor little chap was born without arms."

"Did you ever hear from that woman again? The one with the granddaughter?"

"Oh, for heaven's sake, get away!" Flustered, Rosa batted her hand at a wasp that had landed on the table. She'd mailed the doll off to Pamela Baker by recorded delivery and had kind of expected to receive a thank-you letter, but nothing had arrived. Oh well.

"I know what we said to you at the time, but I did feel a bit bad about it afterward." Benny's smile was rueful as he tore the foil off the top of the bottle and loosened the wire cage. "It's a shame you threw those letters away because I kept thinking afterward, what if it *wasn't* a scam? If you still had the address, I'd have paid you to make the doll and send it to her."

Pop went the cork; they both jumped as it ricocheted off the ceiling, and Rosa clapped her hands in delight.

"If Ingrid were here now," said Benny, "she'd be shaking her head. Apparently letting the cork pop is what common people do."

"It's my favorite sound in the world." Rosa beamed at him. "I love it. And if Ingrid were here now, I wouldn't be here at all." When the champagne had been poured, she said, "Here's to happier times ahead."

"Cheers." Benny's eyes crinkled at the corners.

"And I'm so glad you said that about the doll. It's nice that you wanted to pay for it."

"Why are you looking at me like that? Do you still have her address?"

She nodded. "I have her address."

"Yes!" Benny was delighted. "I'll give you the money. Let's do it."

He really was a lovely man. Warmed by his change of heart, Rosa took a sip of Veuve Clicquot and confessed, "I already did."

He started to laugh. "You sent it? I might have guessed. I bet the grandmother was over the moon."

Rosa shrugged and broke into an unrepentant grin. "Let's hope so. I haven't heard back."

He winced. "You're kidding."

"I know. Don't tell Red. I'll never hear the end of it."

"And don't you tell him what I said either." By way of a pact, Benny touched his glass against hers. "He'd call me a bloody soft touch."

It was the second day of September, and their time together was up. For now at least.

"Your car's waiting outside." Shay attempted to disentangle himself; Caz was clinging to him like a baby koala.

"I don't want to go. Don't make me!"

But it was kind of necessary that she did. Filming was due to begin the day after tomorrow in Toronto, and the director wouldn't be thrilled if his lead actress was a no-show.

"Come on." He led her down the centuries-old oak staircase. "You'll love it once you're there."

"I won't! I want to stay with *you*..."

"I'm going to be working sixteen hours a day."

"Will you miss me though?"

Shay's mouth twitched. "Of course I'll miss you."

She kissed him on the staircase, then again on the sidewalk outside the hotel. The chauffeur opened the door to the car, and Caz gave Shay one last desperate kiss before clambering inside and loudly proclaiming that life was unfair and she was so miserable she just wanted to superglue her mouth shut so she couldn't even act.

"Now do you have your passport?" said the chauffeur.

"No." Caz gave him an innocent look. "Lost it. Oh dear, now I can't go."

The chauffeur, who had evidently worked with her often enough before not to be alarmed, checked her handbag. "Yes, it's in there."

"I hate you. OK, let's go." She clutched Shay's hand through the open window. "Don't you dare do anything naughty while I'm away. Definitely don't sleep with the next person who moves into the Midsummer Suite."

Shay said, "I'll try not to."

The car moved smoothly off down the high street. When it was out of sight, he turned back and saw Didi behind the desk in reception.

She looked up. "It probably won't happen."

"Sorry?"

There was a flash of diamond as she reached up to smooth an errant lock of dark hair behind her ear. "Just a couple of hours from now, a big burly American named Myron is going to be moving back into the Midsummer Suite."

Myron, owner of the troublesome electric toothbrush.

"Well"—Shay managed a faint smile—"never say never."

He answered his ringing phone and heard Red's voice. "Are we going over to the house? I thought you were coming to collect me at ten."

"Caz was late leaving for the airport." She had kept the driver waiting outside for twenty minutes. "I'm on my way now."

"I'll just do a couple of hundred star jumps while I'm waiting," said Red.

Five seconds after he ended the call, Shay's phone rang again.

"Are you missing me already?" said Caz. "Because I miss you."

Was she even a mile away yet? "I'm just heading off to the house."

"Do you miss me though?"

He glanced across at Didi, who was frowning at her computer screen but doubtless also listening to his conversation. "I will just as soon as I get the chance."

"Do you love me?"

"Yes."

"Say it then!"

"I can't speak now. I'm driving."

"I don't have to catch my flight," Caz reminded him. "I could always come back. Unless you say it."

In her world, it was practically meaningless, Shay knew. Onstage, on TV, and on social media, she regularly told her audiences how very much she loved each and every one of them from the bottom of her heart.

He murmured, "I love you," and heard Caz's whoop of delight.

"See? I knew you could say it!"

By the time he ended the call, Didi had disappeared. Shay wondered if she'd overheard him.

Well, so what if she had? She and Aaron must say it to each other all the time.

chapter 33

"All OK?" Benny greeted Rosa when she joined him in the kitchen at Compton House the following week.

"Great, thanks!" She pulled out a stool at the marble-topped island and helped herself to two of the shortbread biscuits from the tartan tin. "It feels strange being out there talking to him, knowing I don't have to skulk around anymore. Strange but nice," she amended. "Being allowed to be here."

"You always would have been allowed if only I'd known."

"Ah, well, I didn't tell you before, but I had a bit of a run-in with Ingrid the other week too."

"You did?" Benny looked horrified. "What did she say?"

Rosa provided him with a brief recap of the mortifying encounter in the garden. "She didn't approve of you letting me be there. And she told me my conversations with Joe were dull."

"God, I'm so sorry. I used to tell myself she was just a plain speaker. But that was me trying to convince myself that she was a decent person deep down. Whereas in reality," said Benny, "she's just a bitch who enjoys making other people feel small." He ran his fingers through his rumpled brown hair. "I don't know how we stayed together as long as we did. It's my own stupid fault."

"It definitely isn't your fault. Don't ever think that!"

"I meant for getting involved with someone I knew wouldn't be easy to live with. I'm just not great at choosing the right women." Benny sighed. "I've never had a relaxed relationship, d'you know what I mean? One where you don't have to mind your step and watch out for problems the whole time. All I want is an easy, *happy* life with no arguments and no drama."

"I know." Rosa was already nodding in agreement. "I was very lucky. I had that with Joe. He was always cheerful; I never had to wonder if he'd be in a mood when he came home. We just loved being a couple, doing nice things for each other, and having fun. If ever we were making dinner and a good song came on the radio, we'd start dancing together, and it was just so lovely."

"In here?"

"In our first little flat in London and then yes, in here too." She smiled at the memory. "When Layla was little, she used to clap her hands and join in. Then she turned into a teenager, which put a stop to that. But Joe and I always carried on, even when she was rolling her eyes and going, 'Eww, gross, old people getting sexy.' Joe always told her that even when we were ninety, we'd still be dancing in the kitchen."

"Sounds wonderful," said Benny.

"It was. And maybe we didn't get to carry on doing it until we were ninety, but it was brilliant while it lasted. I was lucky to have him for as long as I did." Rosa gestured to her face. "And look at me now! It goes to show, time really does heal. I used to burst into tears just thinking about it. Even last year, I'd break down if I tried to talk about it. But here we are, and not a tear in sight. It's become a happy memory."

"That's good. I'm glad. Were you amazing dancers?"

She doubled up with laughter. "Oh, no, not at all. We were terrible! It just didn't matter, so long as we were having a ball and being terrible together."

....

When Rosa arrived back at Frog Cottage three hours later, she found Red stretched out on the most comfortable sun lounger in the shade of the willow tree. She observed him for several seconds, holding her breath until reassured that his chest was continuing to rise and fall.

The next moment, without opening his eyes, he said, "Why are you watching me?"

"I thought you were asleep."

"Or were you checking I was still alive?"

"Don't say that."

He chuckled and opened his eyes. "Why not? It's true, isn't it? Where've you been anyway?"

"Compton House."

He checked the angle of the sun in the sky. "For three hours?"

"Sorry. I didn't mean to be away for so long."

"No worries. Shay only dropped me back an hour ago. Been drinking?"

"What is this, the Spanish Inquisition? No, I haven't been drinking. Why would you say that?"

"You told me you had champagne last time."

"Well, we didn't today. Do I sound as if I've had a drink?"

"No. Your face looks kind of lit up, that's all." He was studying her with interest. "Almost…sparkling."

"We were sitting outside in the sunshine," said Rosa. "It's probably sweat."

"That must be it." Red sounded amused. "But you had a good time."

"We did. We were just chatting away about all sorts. I didn't realize it was so late. By the way, what are you up to tomorrow, any plans?"

"Not sure. I'll probably be over at the house again. Why?"

"Benny's driving to Westonbirt Arboretum. He wondered if I'd like to go along, and we thought you might be interested too." Hastily, because walking more than a hundred meters would be too much for him, Rosa added, "We checked online, and it's completely wheelchair friendly. You'd love it."

"Trees. No thanks."

"You like trees!"

"I like *some* trees. But there's such a thing as too many. They get a bit samey after a while."

"They wouldn't be samey," Rosa protested, but he was already shaking his head.

"Not my thing. You two go without me. Tell Benny thanks for the offer, but I'd rather spend the time with my boy."

…………………………………………

The trouble with missing breakfast was it gave your stomach delusions of grandeur when it was time for lunch, like it deserved a reward for having waited so long. Instead of grabbing a sandwich or a pot of pasta salad from the bakery just up the road, Layla found herself heading instead for the French café on Comer Street.

Sometimes only a cheese soufflé and triple-cooked fries would do, and no one made them better than Bettine.

Reaching the café, she saw through the window that it was busy. She also spotted Will sitting at one of the tables, oblivious to his surroundings, tapping away on his iPad. As she watched, he paused to take a mouthful of tomato soup and thickly buttered bread. She'd asked him several times what he was working on, but he always said it was nothing special.

By the time she'd placed her order at the counter, all the other tables were occupied. As she hesitated, a toddler made a grab for the hem of her yellow polka-dotted dress, and the sudden flash of color and movement caused Will to look up.

"Hi." He glanced around when he saw that she was searching for somewhere to sit. "You can share my table if you like."

The iPad was swiftly switched off and moved to one side. Layla pulled out the empty chair and sat down opposite him.

"Help yourself to chips." Will nudged the plate toward her. "They're amazing."

She took one. "I know. They're half the reason I'm here."

"What's the other half? Oh, have you ever tried the cheese soufflé? Out of this world."

"And that's what I've ordered." Layla felt herself relax. "Looks like we're soufflé twins."

"With excellent taste." Will paused. "Why are you looking at me like that?"

"Doesn't this feel a bit weird to you?" Layla gestured at him, then at herself. "We've sat together hundreds of times, but it's always been side by side. We've never sat facing each other before. You look…different!"

"You mean having to see my whole face is an ordeal?" He raised an eyebrow in protest. "Would you prefer it if I stayed in profile?" He turned his head to the left, then to the right. "Like this?"

"I'm sure I'll get used to it. And don't let me disturb you when you're busy." She indicated the iPad. "If you want to carry on doing what you were doing, go ahead. I'll be quiet, I promise."

"It's fine. I've finished for now." As ever, Will evidently had no intention of letting her see what had been occupying his attention.

"Is it poetry?" said Layla. "Are you a top-secret spy? Ooh, are you an anonymous restaurant critic? Is that why you're always so secretive?"

"You got me." Will grinned at her across the table, utterly relaxed. "Here comes your lunch now."

As they ate, he chatted about his job and the weirder encounters that took place with people in his cab, including this morning's foreign tourists who'd been outraged when he'd explained that he couldn't take them on a guided tour of Scotland this afternoon. No, not even a quick one.

"Thank goodness I'm not weird." Layla tipped her head from side to side, jangling her oversized flamingo earrings. "Apart from my outfits, that is."

"I'd never call you weird. You're one of my best clients."

"Best as in favorite? Or because I spend the most money?"

"Both, of course." He hesitated. "Can I ask you a personal question? Why don't you drive?"

He'd never asked before. Layla experienced the familiar twist in the pit of her stomach. "I don't like it. I don't want to. This is actually the world's best cheese soufflé." She cut into the crisp golden-brown crust with the side of her fork and inhaled the steam from the swiss-cheese melted center.

"But why don't you want to?" He was looking at her steadily. "OK, you don't have to tell me. Let's change the subject."

"No, I will." She put down her fork. For years, her mind had skittered away from the memory, like a squirrel in a panic. It was an experience she only wished she could wipe from her brain. "I almost killed someone once. And that was it. I couldn't handle the guilt. After that day, I never drove again."

His expression softened. "I'm sorry. I did wonder if it was something like that."

"Yes, well. It's not as if it's a secret." Layla shrugged, adrenaline stirring in response to the inevitable flashback now that she'd said the words aloud. "Some people are better off staying off the road, and I'm one of them."

"But this person didn't die."

"No."

"Were they driving too?"

"No. Pedestrian." She exhaled slowly, willing herself to keep the fear at bay.

"But it's not as if you did it on purpose. You didn't set out to mow them down. It was an accident, an honest mistake."

"It wasn't," said Layla.

He gazed at her in horror. "What do you mean?"

"I don't mean I did it on purpose. It wasn't *my* mistake," she clarified.

"Oh. So why…?"

"I was twenty. I'd been driving for three years. And I had a boyfriend I was crazy about. We were in my car, heading over to his parents' house so I could meet his family for the first time. I was driving down the street when this older woman stepped out into the road without looking." Layla swallowed; the sound of another human being thudding against the side of the car would live with her forever. "I wasn't going fast, but I couldn't stop in time. It was the most horrific moment of my life. And then it got even worse." Her voice cracked with emotion, and she was forced to compose herself. "Because it was my boyfriend's grandmother."

"Oh God."

"Lying on the ground in terrible pain with a fractured pelvis and three broken ribs. She hadn't been looking where she was going because she was on the phone to her friend, telling her about how she was heading over to her son's house to meet her grandson's new girlfriend for the first time."

Will shook his head in sympathy. "Go on…"

"Ambulance. Police. I was breathalyzed. Luckily, I hadn't had a drink in days. My boyfriend called his parents, who arrived and screamed at me. Then he joined in and started yelling too while a crowd of people stood around gawping at the whole thing like it was something off the telly. Anyway, the family blamed me. Luckily, there were enough witnesses to prove it hadn't been my fault, but it didn't stop me feeling guilty. Because if I hadn't been there, driving down the road at that moment, it would never have happened. So that was the end of the boyfriend, and it was the end of driving too. I never want to risk having that feeling again. And I won't, so long as I have you." OK, that sounded wrong. Hastily, Layla went on, "I mean, you and any other taxi drivers who pick me up and take me wherever I want to go."

"Well, now I understand," said Will. "It's a terrible thing to happen. No wonder you were traumatized."

Layla nodded, relieved she'd told him, glad he'd asked. "Have you ever had an accident?"

"No. Did the grandmother recover?"

"Yes, thank goodness."

"Did the family ever apologize for blaming you?"

"No."

"That must have been horrible too. If you don't mind me saying so, you had a pretty crappy boyfriend."

It was nice sitting here like this, talking to someone who was on her side. Layla said ruefully, "Oh, he was just one of many. I've been involved with a long line of crappy boyfriends over the years."

Will's eyebrows rose. "You mean…?"

"Until Harry, of course." She felt herself breaking into an unstoppable smile. "He came along and broke my losing streak at last. About time too." The eyebrow thing was happening again. "Why are you doing that?"

"Doing what?"

"Looking dubious. He makes me happy. I've finally got myself a lovely boyfriend. It's good news!"

"OK."

"And you're still doing it. Do you know something I don't? Have you seen him with someone else?" She flung the question out with a mixture of challenge and fear.

"No, I haven't—"

Layla's phone began to ring. She said to Will, "Well, I'm glad to hear that," and whipped it out of her bag. "Hi, we were just talking about you! What time am I seeing you tonight? Oh right, no, that's fine, I have a ton of work actually. Tomorrow's much better. Yes! Love you too!"

Talk about bad timing. She put her phone away, silently cursing the demanding client who'd just insisted on booking Harry for this evening because now Will was bound to have jumped to the wrong conclusion. Cheerfully, she explained, "He's really building up his client list. This year, the Cotswolds, next year, the world! Are you OK to drop me over to Bourton tomorrow evening at seven?"

Will nodded. "No problem."

"You should try dating apps. They're great. Honestly, download Fait and give it a try. You never know who you might meet!"

It was the turn of Will's phone to burst into life. He glanced at the screen, finished his tumbler of sparkling water, and rose to his feet. "Customer waiting. Have to go. I'll see you tomorrow."

There was a single triple-cooked chip on his plate. Reaching across because she just knew he'd left it on purpose, Layla said, "Bye," and popped it into her mouth. So what if she already had her own? You could never have too many chips.

Only lukewarm now, but still delicious.

He grinned. "I knew you'd do that."

He was about to leave, but a grandmother with a double stroller was struggling to do a three-point turn in the cramped café. Out of nowhere, Layla heard herself say, "You don't trust Harry, do you?"

Caught as off guard as she was by the unexpectedness of the question, Will hesitated. "I don't really know him."

Had she been subconsciously wanting to understand why he seemed to have taken against her boyfriend? "Are you sure you haven't seen him with another woman?" It was a possibility after all, given Harry's job;

maybe Will had spotted something and jumped to the wrong conclusion. If so, she could explain and put his mind at rest.

"No." He shook his head.

Oh, thank goodness.

"Sorry, sorry to hold you up. I need learner plates for this thing!" The grandmother had managed to reverse her stroller into a space between tables. She stood back and gestured energetically for Will to squeeze past. "Better escape while you can!"

"See you tomorrow," he told Layla. "I'll be at yours by seven."

He would be. He always was.

"Is that your boyfriend?" said the grandmother, having wrestled the baby out of one half of the double stroller. "Hasn't he got a lovely smile?"

Layla scooped up a spoonful of soufflé. "He isn't my boyfriend."

"No? Sorry, when I saw you pinch his last chip, I thought you must be together. Oh well." She waggled her eyebrows in approval. "He still has a gorgeous smile."

chapter 34

Benny's heart was racing as he left Compton House. The last time he'd experienced this much of an adrenaline rush had been when he'd misread the price tag on a watch Ingrid's daughter had asked for; instead of four hundred euros, it had turned out to have cost four thousand. And of course a week later, she'd lost it on a beach in Saint-Tropez.

OK, calm down and stay focused. It was speaking to his cousin Mary last night on the phone that had prompted today's plan of action. Then again, she'd met her husband when she was sixteen and they'd both joined the drama club at school. Forty-five years, emigration to America, seven children, and eight grandchildren later, they were still ridiculously happy.

He hadn't meant to confide in her about Rosa, but that was another of Mary's talents; she had a way of wheedling those details out. It was her cozy voice that did it, Benny reckoned. Before he knew it, he'd found himself telling her everything. And Mary, who was addicted to Hallmark movies, couldn't have been more delighted. She'd only met Ingrid briefly two years ago during a family visit back to the UK, but the two of them hadn't taken to each other at all.

"Well, this one sounds wonderful," she had declared happily yesterday evening. "You have to tell her how you feel!"

Just like that. Because of course it was that easy. Backpedaling out of sheer fright, he'd said, "Ingrid only moved out two weeks ago. It's too soon."

"No, it isn't," Mary scoffed. "You told me yourself you're glad she's gone."

"Wouldn't it look bad, like I'm moving on too fast?"

"Benny, listen to me. You've been out with this Rosa a few times now. You had a great time together at the arboretum and at that fancy manor house place you took her to for lunch. If you know something feels right, you need to take action."

"But—"

"Shall I tell you what looks bad?" Mary effortlessly steamrollered over his objections. "You being miserable for the rest of your life because you were too slow to let this one know how you felt, and while you were hanging back going 'It's too soon, it's too soon,' some other guy jumped in and waltzed off with her. Think how annoying that'd be! Imagine how much you'd wish you'd done something about it. If she's as wonderful as you're telling me she is, who's to say there isn't some other fellow out there just waiting to snap her up? It'd be like really wanting something on eBay, then at the last second getting outbid!"

He'd tried to protest at this point that it wasn't anything like that, but Mary had launched into the long story of how she'd longed to own a nineteenth-century patchwork quilt and had thought her bid would be enough to secure it, but some other complete monster had swooped in and won it with a single second to spare, and she'd regretted it ever since. Before hanging up, she'd said, "Do something romantic, Benny. Make an effort and win her over before someone else does. You snooze, you lose."

Which was a slightly surreal expression for a sixtysomething grandmother from Wisconsin to use. Benny blamed Netflix.

But her words had stayed with him, niggling away. As far as he'd been aware, there was no other rival for Rosa's affections. When he'd pointed this out, however, Mary had replied, "What about that lodger of hers?"

"He's dying of cancer."

"So was Pastor Mike at our local church. Then the prayers of the townsfolk worked, and he made a miraculous recovery. The next thing we knew, Pastor Mike left his wife of thirty years and ran off with the schoolmistress. People can get better, and then you never know what they'll do. It makes them reckless. Is he a good-looking chap, this one?"

Benny said, "Well, he's pretty sick. But I suppose…yes."

"There you are, then. Don't be complacent. You can't guarantee he's gonna die."

And crazy as it was, it had been this last warning that had prompted him to act. Because people did sometimes making astonishing recoveries from serious illnesses, and if anyone was capable of springing a surprise like that, it was Red Mason, with his quick wit, dry humor, and that irrepressible twinkle in his eyes.

Benny continued on down the lane. At least he knew, because Rosa had mentioned it in passing yesterday, that Red would be over at Hillcrest today, keeping an eye on things while the new kitchen was installed.

Outside Frog Cottage, he paused to catch his breath. The kitchen windows were open, birds were chirping in the trees, and he could hear Rosa happily singing along to Robbie Williams while dishes clattered in the sink.

OK, let's do this.

To make sure everything went according to plan, he switched off his phone. Being interrupted by a call from Ingrid to fix a time when she could collect the remainder of her belongings was the last thing he needed.

Now he just had to hope that the radio DJ would play something half-decent next.

Rosa was scrubbing away at her oval glass casserole dish and swinging her hips along to Robbie Williams when there was a tap at the front door. Holding her sudsy arms up, she went to open it.

Her heart lifted when she saw it was Benny. "Hello! What brings you here today?"

"No reason. I just happened to be passing."

She laughed because it was fast becoming their in-joke. "Excellent!"

"Plus, Ingrid might be dropping by to collect her things, so I'm keeping out of the way."

"Well, that makes more sense. Come on through. I'm just finishing the dishes. There's beer in the fridge if you fancy one. We can sit out in the garden as soon as I'm done."

Benny followed her into the kitchen, where Robbie Williams had finished and the presenter was now burbling on about Speedos. "Thanks. A beer would be great."

She plunged her hands back into the sink and decided to be brave. "I was telling Layla about the arboretum and how gorgeous it was." She glanced over her shoulder and saw him wince slightly. Raising her voice to be heard above 50 Cent's latest release, she said, "Oh, sorry, was it boring for you? Did you not enjoy it?"

"No, no, I did." He nodded rapidly. "It was great. In fact, if you're free this Sunday, there's a country fair over in Frampton on Severn. If you think you might fancy heading over there, checking it out. With me, I mean. Not on your own."

"Brilliant!" Rosa flushed with pleasure. "Thank you." Oh dear, her crush on Benny was growing by the day. She loved his company and had the sense that he enjoyed spending time with her too, but the prospect of making a fool of herself and thinking he liked her more than he did was terrifying. She was so out of practice, she'd completely lost the knack of tentatively building a new relationship. And Benny had made no moves of his own, so did that mean he liked her just as a friend?

They continued to chat about the country fair. When the dishes were done, they leaned against the counters and opened their bottles of lager. On the radio, 50 Cent gave way to the news and weather, then the DJ played an old Sex Pistols track, and Rosa heard Benny give a sigh of irritation.

She said, "Is something wrong?" and saw him shake his head. It was as if he was waiting for something that wasn't happening.

The next moment, it came to her. As Benny gazed out the window and Johnny Rotten screamed and bellowed his way through the track, realization hit her like a brick, and the sense of relief was overwhelming. Wanting to laugh, she heard herself say, "Is it the music you don't like? You can change to another station if you want."

He looked at her, unsure as to whether she was saying it because she knew. Returning his gaze, Rosa gave him a tiny encouraging nod. Benny crossed to the radio on the window ledge. When he began pressing buttons, she noticed that his hand was trembling.

The strains of a military band came blasting out, making them both jump.

"Maybe not," Rosa murmured.

He pressed again, reaching Classic FM. Elgar's "Nimrod" was playing. The last time Rosa had heard it was at her father's funeral.

"No." She shook her head again.

Benny had another go. Silently, she prayed the third time would be the charm. Elgar was replaced by…

A medical phone-in, oh joy. A man was saying earnestly, "The thing is, Doctor, I *want* to wear open sandals, but the fungus is just so—"

"We don't want to know," Rosa blurted out as the button was hastily pressed again.

"This isn't going to plan at all." Benny was shaking his head, starting to smile. "Story of my life. Every time I try to do something, you can guarantee it'll go wrong."

"And now," said the DJ, taking pity on them at last, "here's one of my mum's favorite tracks: 'The Winner Takes It All'!"

The familiar opening bars filled the kitchen, and Benny's sigh of relief matched her own. He said, "I thought he was never going to play anything decent."

Rosa felt herself relax. "And now he has. Thank God for ABBA."

He held out his arms, the tension broken. "Would you care to…?"

A smile was spreading unstoppably across her face. "I thought you'd never ask."

Benny reached for her, and for the next three minutes, they danced together in the kitchen. His hands were around her waist, hers were on his shoulders, and maybe they weren't the best dancers in the world, but it didn't matter. They were having the best time, and that was the important thing.

When the song came to an end, Benny said in a low voice, "I know I'm not your Joe, but I'd always be up for a bit of kitchen dancing with you."

Rosa's heart was racing in a way she'd thought it would never race again. He was a lovely man, nice looking but not off-puttingly handsome, with untidy hair, a cheerful smile, and a bit of a belly. Since her own stomach was also on the rounded side, she was glad of this. They might not be model perfect, but they were middle-aged and normal.

And being normal was fine.

"It doesn't just have to happen in the kitchen," she said. "There's garden dancing too."

"I've really enjoyed these last few weeks getting to know you." He seemed to be searching her face for clues, still anxious in case he might be overstepping the mark.

"Same." To reassure him that he wasn't, Rosa found herself smiling and nodding and moving imperceptibly closer. It was going to happen; he was about to kiss her, and she was able to admit to herself at last that this was something she'd been wanting to happen for ages.

And now he was moving closer too, oh so slowly, and at any second, his mouth and hers would make contact… Oh, she couldn't wait—

DRRRINNNGGGG went the doorbell, and they both froze.

"Who's that?" said Benny.

"I don't know. I'm not expecting anyone."

He took a step back. "God, I hope it's not Ingrid."

"Why? Did you tell her you were coming over?"

"No. But she wanted to know if I was seeing someone, and she definitely wasn't happy about me letting you come into our garden."

DDDRRRINGGGGG.

chapter 35

Rosa said, "OK, no one knows you're here. I'll answer the door and get rid of them."

"Where can I go? What if they want to come inside?"

She thought fast. "Upstairs. Wait in Red's room. And don't worry. I'm not letting anyone into the house. They'll be gone in two minutes."

Someone began hammering on the front door. A vaguely familiar voice shouted, "Hello? Are you there? Can you answer the door please? *Hellooo!*"

Alarmed, Benny hastened up the stairs. Rosa went to see who was making all the racket. At least the voice didn't belong to Ingrid.

Once he was safely ensconced in Red's bedroom, she opened the front door and got the shock of her life.

"Yes, she's in! Phew, I was starting to panic for a minute! Rosa Gallagher? You're Rosa, yeah? Hello, and please don't swear. You're live on *Every Morning*!"

The unexpected visitor on the doorstep was blond and curvy and crazily vivacious. She was also clutching a microphone and flanked by two men wielding television cameras. Rosa had watched *Every Morning* often enough to recognize her from the daily show, during which she was regularly sent out to surprise members of the public in their own homes.

Even as she struggled to take in what was happening, the woman, whose name was Carol and who was wearing epic quantities of perfume, was squeezing past her while shouting, "Can we come in, Rosa? Is this your living room? Ooh, look at that mural on the wall. Isn't that fantastic? Now, face this way so the viewers can see you. We're here because we've got a big surprise for you!"

Her home had been invaded, and both cameras were focused on

her. Carol's voice was so loud that even from upstairs, Benny must have been able to hear everything. Baffled, Rosa said, "I think there's been a mistake. I haven't entered any contests, so I can't have won anything."

"Oh, bless ya, my darling! You might not have entered anything, but you've still won! You were nominated for our Lovely Person award, and you're today's winner! So what d'you have to say to that, my darling?"

Rosa blinked. "Um…I'm not lovely though."

Carol let out an earsplitting shriek of laughter. "Oh my, you're hilarious! Never mind. Here's a little reminder… Chuck it over here, Bob!"

Another assistant appeared from behind one of the cameramen and tossed something through the air to be dropped and hastily scooped up by Carol. "Whoops, butterfingers! What's this, Rosa?"

The situation was becoming more surreal by the minute. "It's…um, a doll."

"And you made this beautiful doll, didn't you? Because a lady named Pamela wrote to you, desperate for a doll that looked like her precious granddaughter!"

Rosa found herself zoning out as Carol went on to explain to the viewers at home what had happened. She held up a photograph of Pamela and little Maisie, keeping her other arm draped around Rosa's shoulders. While she was talking, Rosa heard the front door being pushed further open. The next moment, Red appeared in the increasingly crowded living room. He looked at Rosa and mouthed, "What's going on?"

"Hello, hello, come on in. The more, the merrier!" Racing across to shake him by the hand, Carol bellowed, "You must be Rosa's husband! I'm Carol from *Every Morning*! And we're here to give your wife a Lovely Person award!"

The cameras zoomed in on Red, who said, "I'm not her husband."

Cue another screech of laughter from Carol. "Well, in that case, can I have your phone number? I must say, babe, I bet you were quite the looker back in the day… In fact, you're not so bad now! What's your name?"

Watching TV in Derby while she vacuumed her living room carpet, a woman named Christine, who'd never quite gotten him out of her system, did a double take and exclaimed, "It's Red!"

In Marbella Old Town, almost dropping her glass of fresh orange juice, Didi's mother, Maura, laughed out loud. "This is hysterical. Look at his face! Oh, but he's so *thin*..."

In a flat close to the Gloucester docks, a prison officer named Maeve turned to her sister and said, "Bloody hell, that's Red Mason. Remember him? Had a fling with Paula the week after getting out on bail! God, he looks ill."

And lying in bed in his trailer overlooking Perranporth Beach in north Cornwall, Big Gav almost dropped his can of Stella on his hairy bare chest at the sight of his old mate Red. Fucking hell though. The poor sod was looking rough, skinny, drawn, and like death warmed up. Not that it was stopping that bloody screaming creature on the telly from batting her eyelashes at him. Then again, what was new? Red had been a magnet for women his whole life, so why would they stop now?

All over the country—and in some cases outside it—people recognized Red Mason for a variety of reasons. He was one of those people who, once known, wasn't easily forgotten.

Back in the living room of Frog Cottage, Red was extricating himself from Carol's enthusiastic grasp. Politely, he said, "Sorry, I came home because I need to get some rest." Excusing himself, he left the room and made his way carefully up the narrow staircase.

....

Upstairs in Red's bedroom, Benny had been watching the shenanigans going on downstairs on the small TV perched on top of the chest of drawers. Hearing Red's approaching footsteps, he briefly considered rolling off the bed and sliding out of sight beneath it.

But no, he wouldn't do that. The current situation might be pretty bizarre, but the first hurdle had been cleared.

The bedroom door opened, and Red appeared. Having taken in Benny's presence, he calmly closed the door behind him. "Well, this is unexpected. Have you come here to seduce me?"

Benny gave a snort of quiet laughter. Feeling suddenly brave, he said, "I came here to seduce Rosa. But we kind of got interrupted." He gestured to the television, where the show was heading into a commercial break. "When they rang the doorbell, we didn't know who it was."

Red's eyes widened. "How much did they interrupt?"

"We were dancing in the kitchen. I was about to kiss her."

"Oh well, at least they didn't interrupt you mid-shag. Still, good on you." He gestured for Benny to budge up so he could join him on the bed. "She's a fabulous lady. How she hasn't already been snapped up is beyond me."

"It's taken her a while to get over losing Joe."

"But now she's ready to give things another go. You're a lucky guy."

In a burst of honesty, Benny said, "I was worried you might be the one to snap her up."

"*Me?*" Red laughed, coughed, and clutched his chest until he was able to speak again. "In the state I'm in? I've got as much chance of seeing Christmas as your average turkey. I'm on my way out, whether I like it or not. If I hadn't been," he added drily, "maybe you'd have had some competition. But as things stand, well, I'm out of the running. What's going on downstairs anyway?"

At that moment, the commercials ended, and the jovial male host back in the studio said, "Hello again, welcome back, and we're taking you straight over to rejoin Carol and Rosa, the recipient of this week's Lovely Person award!"

"The woman who couldn't afford the doll for her granddaughter," Benny explained. "The one we said was a con artist. Turns out she wasn't."

Red tut-tutted. "Damn, I hate it when I'm wrong and other people are right."

Benny sat up and peered out of the bedroom window. "They're bringing someone else up the path."

On the TV screen, the doorbell rang, and Carol answered it, ushering in a tiny woman in a droopy peach cardigan and a flower-patterned dress. "And here she is. This is Pamela, come to thank you in person for being so lovely!"

Benny winced as Pamela gave Rosa an awkward hug and blurted

out, "I'll never forget your kindness. You're an angel from heaven," then promptly burst into tears.

"Ah, bless ya, my darling! I know, it's emotional! Here, you have a cuddle of your granddaughter's doll, and I'll tell Rosa what we've got for her!"

"God, this is embarrassing," said Benny.

"Right, first off, we have some lovely flowers for you." Carol collected them from an assistant and presented them to Rosa. "And a big bottle of champers, my favorite! And best of all, we're sending you and a friend on an all-expenses-paid three-night break in Paris!"

"Gosh." Rosa was wide-eyed.

"You could take that handsome chap you've got tucked away upstairs!" Carol gave another parrot screech of laughter.

In the bedroom, Red looked at Benny. "If only she knew there were two of us up here."

"So that's it from me and from this week's *lovely* Lovely Person," shouted Carol. "And now it's back to you lot in the studio!" Grabbing Rosa's hand, she forced her to wave into the camera. "Bye-eeee!"

Within five minutes, the TV crew had departed, and it was as if they'd never been there at all, apart from the ostentatious bouquet, the champagne, and the phone ringing with messages from Rosa's friends exclaiming that they'd just seen her on the telly.

"Sorry." Turning off her phone, Rosa looked at Benny and Red as they came downstairs. Her cheeks were pink. She was gorgeous.

Benny said, "It's all fine. We watched you on Red's TV."

"I might have known you'd make that doll," said Red.

She grinned. "What can I tell you? I'm a sucker for a sob story."

"And it paid off. You're officially wonderful. Except we already knew that." He coughed, clutched his rib cage, and sat down on the sofa.

"You should be resting," Rosa told him. "What can I get you? Cup of tea? Glass of scotch?"

"Nothing, thanks. I might have a doze. You two carry on without me."

Benny hid a smile because Red was teasing and Rosa was looking flustered. He held a hand out to her. "I told him about us dancing in the kitchen. Now I think we need to leave him in peace and have a dance over at mine."

"Oh." Rosa looked relieved.

"And with luck, this time, we won't be interrupted." Benny clasped her soft hand in his, inwardly marveling at how wonderful it felt; it was as if they were a perfect fit. "Shall we go?"

"To your house?" Rosa glanced at their intertwined fingers. "What if people see us?"

Red gave a croaky bark of laughter. "You're single. He's single. Who cares if they do? Besides," he added, "plenty of people are going to see you when you take him with you to Paris."

chapter 36

Hillcrest was ready. For the last week, Shay had been working all hours of the day and night in order to make the house perfect. And now it was done.

Watching from the doorway, Didi bit the inside of her lip and concentrated on the pain. *Mustn't cry, mustn't cry.*

"Amazing." Red finished gazing around the immaculate kitchen, decorated in the shades of cobalt blue and cream he'd chosen himself. Addressing his audience, he said with characteristic candor, "I was worried I might kick the bucket before it was finished. But I didn't. I'm still here, back where I wanted to be. And my boy's done a brilliant job. As I knew he would."

"Thanks, Dad. But you didn't have to make a speech." Shay shook his head, his expression wry.

"I know I don't have to. But I want to. You didn't have any intention of coming back to Elliscombe, I know that. You certainly didn't want to spend your summer slogging your guts out rebuilding the old family home. But you knew it was what I wanted, so you did it. You're the best son any father could wish for, let alone a terrible old reprobate like me. And you'll never understand how much this means." He suppressed a cough and waved his free hand in the air by way of an apology. "Anyway, I'll shut up now, but you get the gist. It's been wonderful staying with Rosa, and we've had a great time, but this is my home now. For the rest of my life."

It hadn't been planned, but the twenty or so people gathered in the kitchen broke into applause. As Didi worked hard to maintain her composure, someone in the doorway directly behind her gave a huge gulping sob like a honking goose.

"Oh God." Caz clutched her arm. "I haven't even got any tissues on me, and I'm a total wreck."

Didi dug a pack of Kleenex out of her shoulder bag and handed them to her. "I didn't know you were here."

"Just arrived. Flew in from Toronto and got my driver to drop me outside. Managed to wangle a couple of days off. How's everything with you?" She nodded at the diamond ring glittering on Didi's left hand. "All good?"

It wasn't wrong to lie, was it, when you were doing it for the right reason? "Great, thanks. Does Shay know you're back?"

"Nope! But when I heard all this was happening today, I couldn't resist putting in a surprise appearance. Except I didn't expect it to be this emotional, and now I look like a melted clown."

"Here, let me help." Out of sight of the rest of the gathering, Didi took a clean tissue and carefully wiped away the nonwaterproof mascara sliding down Caz's cheeks. "There, all done."

"Sure? Am I presentable?"

"You look gorgeous."

"Thanks, darling. What would I do without you?" Caz gave a little showbiz shimmy, then made her big entrance through the doorway, exclaiming, "Well, this was worth flying back for. Looks like I got here just in time!"

Heads turned. Everyone was clearly delighted to see her. Including Shay, Didi observed with a pang of envy.

Red said, "Cazzy!" and with a squeal of joy, Caz raced into his open arms.

Of course people couldn't help going *aaahh* and taking photos of the happy reunion as Caz gave Red a gentle yet heartfelt hug.

"We weren't expecting to see you," he said.

"Oh, babe, this is your big day. How could I stay away? Look at you, in your dream home! I wouldn't have missed it for the world." She embraced him again and stroked his thin face. "How are you feeling?"

"Happier than I have any right to be. And not so bad, not so bad." They all knew he was playing down the ever-present aches and pains. "Although I'd better sit down now."

It was time for Caz to turn to Shay. Watching them, Didi found herself experiencing a wave of desolation as she held him tight and kissed him full on the mouth, prompting a flurry of good-natured whistles from the crew of builders, decorators, and plumbers who had worked alongside Shay to get the house ready on time. When one of the electricians called out, "Get a room," Caz turned to flash him a cheeky grin and said, "Don't worry. I already have."

....

Didi was working in her office the next day when the door was pushed a little way open and Caz's face appeared in the gap.

"Hi, are you crazy busy?"

"Just medium busy. What's up?"

"Could you spare five minutes for a chat?"

"Of course." Didi closed her laptop and gestured for her to pull up a chair. She tried not to wonder how many times Caz and Shay had had sex last night. Then again, maybe the answer was zero and their relationship was on the rocks. *No, don't even think that.* "Everything OK?"

"Don't look so worried. Me and Shay are fine!" Caz's eyes danced. "He's still amazing."

OK, too much information. "So what's the problem?"

Caz sat cross-legged on the chair, pushing up the sleeves of her striped Breton top. "Well, the thing is, my agent just called about a part in a movie that's going to be filmed in New Zealand. Apparently the director really wants me to take it. And normally, I'd be dead flattered, but it means spending three months over there, plus I have to let them know right away if I'm up for it." She looked anguished. "The thing is, what about me and Shay? That's a long time to be apart, and if his dad's still around when filming starts just after Christmas, I know he wouldn't leave him..." She gestured helplessly as the words trailed away.

"You can't ask me," said Didi. "You need to talk to Shay, see how he feels."

"But you know him better than I do. He might feel obliged to say the right thing. God, it's just so hard. I'm rubbish at working out what men really think. All the ones I've been with before have been complete bastards."

"Shay isn't a bastard."

"I know. That's why I'm so desperate for us to work out. Well, and he's drop-dead gorgeous too. It all helps." Caz flashed an appreciative grin, then went on, "But what's your honest opinion about us? Could I trust him if I was over in New Zealand and he was here? Should I ask him to come out and stay with me? Or if he won't do that, should I just turn down the film? Maybe he'd prefer me to stay here. What do you think?"

Oh God, this was agonizing. "OK, you still have to ask him," said Didi. "But for what it's worth, he seems to really like you. And you're lovely, so why wouldn't he? It all depends on what happens with Red, basically. If he's still alive, I'm sure you could trust Shay while he was over here. If his dad is...well, then he might want to fly over to New Zealand and be with you. And it could do him good to be away from here."

"Really?"

"Really." It wasn't what she wanted to say, but it was the truth. She had to be honest.

"Thank you." Caz nodded, then said, "You're lovely too. And it's so good to know you're on my side. You're not...you know, jealous."

Jealous? Didi's mouth went dry. "Why would I be?"

"Oh, don't look like that. I'm not saying you're desperate to get your hands on him again! It was just something the assistant manager mentioned yesterday evening... I hadn't realized you and Shay were once a couple. He'd never mentioned it, and neither had you. I was surprised, that's all. And she didn't say anything bad," Caz added hastily. "It was just about the time you built a snowman together in the middle of the night in Venice, so I asked her about it, and she explained that was how you two first got together. It's a cute story!"

"We only saw each other for a few months. It was so long ago." Didi felt the back of her neck prickling; she was getting hot. "We were still at school."

"I know. Shay told me. I asked him last night."

"It wasn't meant to be a secret. It's just...we don't think about it anymore." What else could she say? "We've moved on."

"I know. Of course you have... You've got Aaron now. You're getting married soon! Honestly?" Caz's tone was earnest. "If Shay had come back here and you'd been single...well, then I might have thought twice about swanning off and leaving him behind with someone as gorgeous as you around. Because that's when things can start happening, isn't it? And then I'd have been the one who was jealous. I'd be in a right state, stuck on the other side of the world, imagining what could be going on without me here to keep him on the straight and narrow." She sat back, raking her fingers through her hair and pulling a regretful face. "Sorry, should I even be saying this? I can't help it. I just blurt out whatever's going on in my head. But the thing is, I know I don't have to worry because you're happy with Aaron, *and* you're on my side. So that's great!" Her eyes were bright, and she was beaming with relief. "When's the wedding?"

"Um...the seventh of December." Didi attempted to look like an excited bride-to-be; so much for thinking that the time had probably come to stop wearing the ring and let people know the engagement was off. It looked as if she'd be keeping it on for a while longer after all.

"Fabulous! If I can make it, are me and Shay both invited?"

Again, how else could she respond? It was probably one of those flippant don't-really-mean-it remarks anyway.

"Of course you are."

Caz's bangles rattled as she clapped her hands like an excited child. "Yay! And if me and Shay get married, you and Aaron are definitely invited to ours!"

chapter 37

Maura had meant to call in on her daughter first, but on impulse, she instructed the airport taxi to drive on past the Wickham Hotel and head out to Hillcrest instead.

Get it over with.

Red had been in his refurbished home for over a week now. It was certainly looking good from the outside. She rang the bell and waited. How long would it take him to reach the front door?

Not long at all evidently. Maura heard footsteps and mentally braced herself.

But when the door opened, it was Shay Mason she came face-to-face with. Caught off guard, she said, "Oh, hi!"

"Maura." He glanced at the overnight case by her feet. "This is a surprise. Have you come to stay?"

"No, of course not. How are you, Shay? I'm here to see your father if he's here?"

"He is." Shay paused, which was unnerving.

"I happened to see him the other week on that TV show. And of course Didi's kept me updated, so I know how poorly he is. I just thought while I'm back over here, it'd be nice to meet up again before, well…"

"You and plenty of other people." Shay's tone was dry.

"Is that OK?"

"Let me just check that he's feeling well enough for a visitor. Won't be a minute."

What he meant was, would Red actually want to see her? Maura waited on the doorstep until Shay returned and beckoned her inside.

"Dad's in the living room. Go on through." He had his car keys in his hand. "I'll leave you two in peace and be back in an hour. Any problems at all, my cell number's on the notepad next to the landline."

The front door closed behind him, and Maura took a slow, steadying breath before entering the living room. They say you never got over your first love. Well, Red might not have been her first, but he'd been her third. Which just went to show, you never got over that one either.

He was lying on a daybed in front of the french windows that gave an uninterrupted view of the garden at the rear of the property. His hair was still dark, if tinged with gray, and his skin was tanned, but the pallor of illness was evident beneath it. There were violet shadows under his eyes, but the eyes themselves were as bright and observant as they'd always been. He was thin, though, very thin.

"Oh, Red." Her smile wobbled.

"It's OK. I know I look terrible. How are you?"

Maura bent over him and he greeted her with a brief, dry kiss, the fine stubble on his jaw grazing the corner of her mouth.

"I'm fine." She breathed in the scent of him, a mixture of almond soap and a hint of mint. "I had to come. You know why."

"I could probably hazard a guess. Here, sit down. If you want a drink, you'll have to help yourself."

Maura sat. Of course he knew what was on her mind; he wasn't stupid. She said, "I've spent years trying not to think about it. But then I thought, if you die, I'll never find out."

"And imagine how annoying that would be." Red looked entertained.

"So tell me. What happened to it?"

"Nothing. It's still here."

"In the garden?"

Red nodded and pointed through the french windows. "Well, that's where I buried it. Over there under the mulberry tree. I mean, I suppose someone could have come along and dug it up while I was away, but no one else had any idea it was there."

"So you don't know for sure that it's still there?"

He gave her his wicked gambler's smile. "I quite like the idea, don't you?"

Was he mad? "Not really, no. I thought you'd have gotten rid of it long ago."

Red shook his head. "And kept the money, you mean? That would have made me an accessory."

She changed the subject. "I saw you on that TV program the other week."

"And when you saw the state of me, you thought you'd better get in touch pretty damn quick."

"Not only for the other reason. I wanted to see you again before…" A lump was expanding in Maura's throat; she'd loved him after all. Even if it had turned out to be unrequited.

Reading her mind, Red reached for her hand. "I know. It's a bugger, isn't it? Shall I tell you something?"

"Go on."

"Remember how I told you I didn't love you? Well, that was a lie."

Maura looked down at his thin hand clasping hers, then up at his face. "What?"

A fleeting smile crossed his features. "I did love you. But I couldn't tell you that. Because I couldn't let it happen."

There was probably a complicated German word for wanting to sob with relief while simultaneously wanting to murder someone. Although Maura already knew the answer, she said, "Why not?"

Maybe hearing him say it would be enough.

"I was single; you were married. You had your fancy lifestyle; I had my unfancy one." He paused, then said steadily, "And we had your girl and my boy to consider."

So that was it.

Maura knew she'd always been a selfish kind of person, had tended to put her own needs before others. All those years ago, she and Red had been aware of each other in an interested kind of way. Nothing had happened, but she'd always sensed that it would at some stage. She'd enjoyed the anticipation and had looked forward to the right opportunity presenting itself.

Then Didi and Shay had gotten together on that trip to Venice, which had put the kibosh on her happy plan. Red had withdrawn his attention, and frustratingly, this had made Maura want him *more.*

She hadn't given up, obviously. Had continued making opportunities to bump into him. There was an almost palpable chemistry between them that she'd known wasn't just a figment of her imagination.

It was powerful, all-encompassing, and growing by the day. More than that, it was mutual.

But Red had continued to play the relationship down. "We mustn't. It wouldn't be right. Not when Shay and Didi are making a go of things."

It was such a pointless argument. So what if her daughter and his son were currently seeing each other? They were only teenagers; it wasn't as if their relationship was ever going to last. Yet Red had maintained that it might, which meant he'd steadfastly refused to allow anything to happen between them.

Even more annoyingly, after the robbery at the hotel, Didi and Shay had—inevitably—broken up, and just when she'd thought the way was clear at last, Red had been arrested and carted off back to jail.

It was like a fairy tale with no eventual happy ending. There'd always been some obstacle or other in the way—their children, the law, her own unhappy marriage. And it was never going to happen now. She would never know what it could have been like.

"I definitely need that drink," she said. "Are you having one?"

"No thanks." His smile was crooked. "See? That's how you know I'm ill."

In the kitchen, she found an unopened bottle of Cloudy Bay in the bottom of the vast American-style fridge. Spinning off the lid, she took a crystal flute down from the wall cupboard and poured herself a full glass. Then she took a couple of big swallows and topped it back up. What an unholy mess; what a lesson she'd learned from one impulsive mistake and how she wished she'd never made it.

She gave a shudder of regret. Selfishness aside, she had always thought of herself as an essentially decent person…well, at least an honest one. It had been David's fault for buying her a birthday present he should have known she wouldn't like, from a store overseas that had no truck with returns. Despite twenty years of marriage and knowing perfectly well what she liked, he'd managed to choose a ridiculously ornate emerald necklace, the garish stones mounted in a modern tangle of too-yellow gold. It had genuinely been the polar opposite of her taste in jewelry, and she'd hated it, wearing it only once—under sufferance—before putting it back in its velvet-lined leather case and chucking it into a drawer.

Then, six months later, the robbery had happened, and although it had been completely out of character for her, the idea had arrived fully formed in her brain. The emerald necklace might be horrible, but it was worth thousands of pounds. And it was insured.

Well, why not?

Hearing herself tell the police it had been there in the safe, she'd half expected to be struck down by a lightning bolt. But nothing had happened. Everyone had believed her. She'd shown them a photo taken on the one occasion she'd worn the necklace.

She had also, needless to say, found a much safer hiding place for it than her bedside table.

In due course, the insurers paid out, but by then, the guilt had well and truly kicked in. With the money, she'd bought a stunning diamond bangle, but the joy of owning it had never materialized. Each time she saw it on her wrist, it reminded her of the bad thing she'd done. But it was too late: she'd learned the hard way that crime didn't pay. It just made you feel hideously ashamed of yourself.

Red might have been able to do it—found it fun, even—but she definitely wasn't cut out for that sort of life.

Then, three years after the robbery, her marriage had come unstuck for good. There came a stage when you both had to admit defeat, accept that the relationship had run its course, and move on. David had stayed in Elliscombe, training Didi to take over the running of the hotel, while Maura had found herself a beautiful apartment in Marbella Old Town and embraced the expat lifestyle. Before leaving, though, she'd come to Hillcrest to see Red.

Now, having topped up her glass for the second time, she carried it back through to the living room. She paused to take in Red's profile against the window: the carved cheekbones, those long, dark lashes, the curve of that clever mouth she'd never stopped wanting to kiss.

Sitting down next to him, she said, "We'll never know who did it, will we?" Red had always maintained it hadn't been him, and she'd believed him.

"Oh, I can tell you the answer to that if you want."

She stared at him, saw a flicker of a smile. "You mean it *was* you?"

He simultaneously coughed and laughed. "No. But if you really do want to know, you need to keep it to yourself."

Maura nodded; she'd had enough affairs over the years to become an expert at keeping secrets. "I won't tell anyone," she said fervently.

"It was Big Gav."

"What? Your *friend*?"

"Yes."

"But...but how did he get hold of the keys to the safe?"

"Remember Antonia?"

Maura frowned. "Antonia Webb?" Antonia had worked as their housekeeper for five years. She'd been Scottish, dour, disapproving, and fond of tweed. "What about her?"

"She and Big Gav had a bit of a thing going."

"Are you *serious*?"

"I know, but it's true. She's the one who gave him the keys."

"I can't believe that." Maura shook her head; you could search for years and not find anyone more prim and proper. "Did Gav tell you himself?"

"Not at the time. His wife did, when she found the photos on his phone."

Her eyes widened. "What kind of photos?"

"The bondage kind. She made copies and brought them over here to show me." Red grimaced. "Not the prettiest of sights, Antonia in stockings and a basque, and Big Gav with a—"

"Stop!" Wine slopped over the rim of Maura's glass as she waved her arm in protest. "For God's sake, why would she even show you?"

"Because she was mad as hell. Have you ever met Big Gav's wife?"

"I don't think so."

"She's bloody scary. Gav was terrified of her. When she found out what he'd been up to, he dropped Antonia like a brick, couldn't get away from her fast enough. That's why she left the hotel."

Maura remembered Antonia leaving suddenly, but so many hotel employees did. "She told us she'd been offered a fantastic promotion at a five-star in London."

"She got out in a hurry before Big Gav's wife turned up and knocked her block off."

"Wow." Maura shook her head in wonder.

"He came up from Cornwall last week," Red said easily. "Caught me on the TV, just like you did. It was great to see him again."

"But he let you take the blame for something he did!"

"Well, these things happen. Can't be helped. He was a dodgy guy, but then we both were. And Gav was a good mate. I only ended up back in jail because I broke the terms of my parole," Red reminded her. "That was my fault, not his."

There it was, honor among thieves. Maura took another gulp of wine. "Is he still with his wife?"

"He is. Still scared of her as well, I'm sure."

"So nothing ever happened to the photos?"

"He knew she'd taken copies and put them somewhere. She told Gav any more funny business and she'd post them all over the internet. Kept him in check, I suppose."

"Do you know where they are?"

"Certainly do." Red flashed that wicked smile of his. "They're buried in the same airtight box as your emerald necklace."

"Have you been crying?" Didi searched her mother's face; there were telltale signs of redness beneath the freshly applied eyeliner.

"No. Well, maybe a bit."

"Why? Oh my God, are you ill?"

"Not ill. I popped in to see Red on my way here, that's all. It's a strange feeling, saying goodbye to someone with both of you knowing you're never going to see each other again."

Didi nodded. "I know." That was the thing about Red; despite being no saint, so many people thought of him with genuine affection. "Is that why you flew over? To see Red?"

"Not the whole reason. I came to see you. Whenever I call you about the wedding, you tell me everything's under control." Maura was giving her one of her unnerving looks now. "But you never raise the subject yourself. It's as if you're not even excited to be getting married. Most brides-to-be can't talk about anything else. I mean, I know it isn't a big wedding, but…" She trailed off meaningfully and waited.

Oh well, at least they were in her private quarters. There was no one to overhear their conversation. Didi said, "There isn't going to be a wedding. Well, there is, but I gave my booking to someone else. Aaron and I broke up."

A slow nod. "But you're still wearing the ring."

"I know. It's complicated."

"Whose idea was it to not get married?"

"Mine."

"Well, that's something. And am I allowed to ask why?"

"It wasn't feeling right. He didn't do anything wrong," said Didi. "I just don't love him enough."

"I see. Anyone else you do love?"

"No." But she'd said it a split second too soon.

"Who is it?"

"No one." Some daughters told their mums everything, but Didi had never been able to do that, not since the disastrous robbery and her mother's instinctive reaction to Shay.

"Married, I'm guessing. I'd have thought you'd have known better." Maura raised a disappointed—and somewhat hypocritical—eyebrow.

"He's not married."

"Not single either."

Didi shrugged; let her think what she wanted. "Anyway, you won't have to fly over for the wedding."

"Did you ever even buy a wedding dress in the end?"

"No."

"I knew it. Oh, darling, be careful. It's all very well being a career girl and letting the hotel take over your life, but work isn't everything. Love's important too."

"I'll be OK. I'm fine." This wasn't true; the only person she loved was someone she couldn't have. Shay was involved with Caz Holloway, and she had a horrible feeling theirs was a relationship that was going to last. Caz was crazy about Shay, and why would he want to finish with someone as adorable as her?

"You don't look fine." Her mother's gaze was frankly appraising. "You've lost weight."

This time last year, Maura had informed her that her bum was too big. Didi said, "Isn't that supposed to be a good thing?"

"Not when it doesn't suit you. No one likes a scrawny woman."

Her mother had always been honest to the point of bluntness. By way of retaliation, Didi pointed at her normally immaculate french manicure. "Nobody likes dirty fingernails either. What have you been doing, Mum? Don't tell me you've taken up gardening in your old age."

"I was helping Red with a potted plant." Maura quickly hid her less-than-immaculate nails from view. With a touch of asperity, she said, "And I'm not *old* either."

chapter 38

"Oh, hello!" Harry looked taken aback when he opened the door and saw Layla on the doorstep. "This is a surprise."

"I had a meeting with a client in Cheltenham and thought I'd drop by on my way back." She hopped from one foot to the other. "I'd have called to let you know, but my phone's died. And I'm bursting to use the loo… Can I come in?"

For a split second, she wondered if he had another girl with him. Then he broke into a smile. "And here was me thinking you couldn't wait to seduce me. Of course you can come in." He moved aside, and Layla raced up the stairs ahead of him. As she reached the landing, she couldn't help pausing to glance through the half-open door into his bedroom. No, of course there was no naked woman in his bed; there was just a metal box lying on top of the crumpled duvet, next to an open notebook with writing on it and…hang on, was that her own name? She faltered, but Harry was behind her, and he had a bit of a thing about privacy, plus her bladder had sensed she was within seconds of finally being allowed to pee, and once it knew that, there was no stopping it.

By the time she emerged from the bathroom two minutes later, there was no sign of either the metal box or the notebook.

"Did I catch you in the middle of writing your diary?" she teased Harry. Maybe he'd been saying lovely things about her.

"Oh, you mean the blue notebook?" He shrugged easily. "No, I just use it for work to keep track of my clients' training schedules."

But that night, lying beside him in bed, Layla found herself unable to sleep. Yesterday morning, over a coffee and a catch-up, Didi had asked to see the photo of Harry on her phone. Having studied it, she'd said with an air of triumph, "Yes, that's him. I knew it. I saw him going past in a red Mercedes on Saturday evening. So he does come to Elliscombe occasionally."

Layla had been startled. "Was he driving?"

"No, he was in the passenger seat. I couldn't see who was behind the wheel."

"And it was definitely him?"

"Yes. Well, ninety-nine percent sure."

But when Layla had asked Harry the next day, he'd laughed and said, "I must have a doppelgänger, because it wasn't me. I told you, I was up in Sheffield."

And when he'd said that, she'd ninety-nine percent believed him. Because he was *so* believable. But deep down, she'd begun to waver and wonder and take a metaphorical step back in order to focus more clearly on the tiny inconsistencies that over the weeks had begun to add up. Maybe it was time to acknowledge them.

In his sleep, Harry shifted his hold on her, moving his arm from around her waist and rolling onto his other side. When his breathing had settled once more, Layla slid out of bed and silently searched the room. There weren't many places to hide something the size of the box she'd seen, and it didn't take her long to find it, hidden in the back of the wardrobe beneath an old sports bag. It was secured with a hefty padlock. Lifting and tilting it, she could feel the notebook sliding around inside.

Returning it to its hiding place, she covered it back up. Finding the key that would fit the padlock would be a far trickier task.

She crept through to the kitchen, noiselessly slid open the junk drawer, and found the spare front door key tucked between a ball of string, several pencils, assorted batteries, and a penknife. When she'd gotten here early the other week and been forced to wait outside for an hour until Harry arrived home from work, she'd wondered if he might give her his spare key. But he hadn't.

Stealthily, she closed the drawer and dropped the key into her shoulder bag. Seconds later, Harry's voice called out, "Where are you?"

"Just getting myself some water. I'm thirsty." She ran the tap and filled a tumbler. "Do you want one too?"

He sounded sleepy. "No. I missed you, that's all. Come back to bed."

....

In the morning, they left the flat together at ten to eight. Having apparently borrowed the money for his new motorbike from a friend, Harry now headed off on it, and Layla crossed the road to where Will was waiting in his cab.

"Morning." He smiled at her, returning his iPad to the glove compartment.

"Hi." She double-checked that the motorbike was out of sight. Harry was on his way to visit a client in Chipping Campden. "Actually, I've forgotten something. I'll be back in two minutes."

"Fine," said Will, unruffled.

Her hand shook as she fit the stolen spare key into the lock. Not stolen, *borrowed*. Up the stairs, into the bedroom, pull out the metal security box. It was too big to fit into her handbag, which meant she'd have to put it in a supermarket plastic bag. Luckily, whenever she'd brought food over here, she'd left the bags in the cupboard under the sink so they could be reused.

And now one of them was finally getting its chance.

Back downstairs, hyperventilating with the stress of what she was doing, she let herself out of the flat and hurried back to where Will was waiting with the engine running, for all the world like a getaway driver.

As she was clambering into the passenger seat, a small rip in the bottom of the plastic bag suddenly expanded, and the sharp-cornered box tumbled out onto the sidewalk.

"Whoopsy!" A woman in her sixties hurried over, picked up the box, and handed it to Layla before she could reach it herself. "Can't trust a plastic bag, can you? There you are!"

"Thanks." Scarlet, Layla wondered if the woman lived here in Bourton. Did she know Harry, and was she likely to say something to him in all innocence?

"Get yourself a canvas bag. They're much better!"

"I will."

They drove off. When they'd left the village behind them, Will said mildly, "All OK now?"

He'd seen her pale complexion, her trembling hands. "Fine."

"Given you a key to his place, has he?" His tone was light.

Layla looked at him as he pulled up at the traffic lights. "No. No, he hasn't."

There was no point in trying to deny it. Will knew. Of course he knew.

God, she'd make a terrible international spy.

"Want to tell me what's going on?" He paused. "I wouldn't say anything to anyone. I'm good at being discreet."

"I don't trust Harry as much as I used to." Layla's neck prickled with shame; it wasn't a comfortable admission. It made her feel like a failure.

"What's in the box?"

"I don't know, but I think it might have something to do with me. And he keeps it well hidden, so he definitely doesn't want me to see it."

Will nodded. "All the more reason to find out what it is, then."

Since she might as well tell him the rest, Layla said, "Didi thinks she saw him in a car in Elliscombe on Saturday night. But Harry told me he was up in Sheffield for the whole weekend."

"Right." A hedgehog was ambling across the road, and Will veered around it. When they were safely past, he said, "When we were in the café and you asked me if I'd seen him with someone else, I said no. But I'm pretty sure I saw him in the upstairs window of a flat overlooking the market square."

"Really?" Layla's heart sank. Incriminating details were piling up at a rate of knots.

"Sorry."

"How sure?"

"It was him. He could have been with a client though."

"Did he look as if he was with a client?"

"I don't know. But his top half was bare."

"What about the bottom half?"

"Couldn't tell."

"Oh, fuck. Which flat?"

"The one above the hairdresser's."

Layla took out her phone.

"Mum?" she said when Rosa answered. "Where are you?"

"I'm at Hillcrest with Red. I told you I'd be over here this morning."

"How is he?"

"Not too bad. Better than yesterday."

"If I drop by, could he help me do something slightly illegal?"

"I don't know. Let me ask him." Muffled whispers, then Rosa was back. "He says if he can do it sitting down, fine. He's not up to breaking and entering."

"Great. I'll be there in two minutes."

Red was on the sofa, looking through an old photo album and drinking tea. His eyes went instantly to the security box she was carrying like a baby in her arms.

"Sorry, I don't know who else to ask. And I'm a bit desperate." She placed it on the coffee table in front of him. "Do you think you could get into this?"

"No problem."

"Really? It's a hefty padlock."

"Padlocks might look hefty, but they're often simple enough to open." His eyes gleamed. "When you know how."

"OK, I have a confession to make." Rosa looked at him. "I threw away those lock picks of yours. I just thought you didn't need them anymore."

"I don't need them. Lock picks are for the tricky ones." Resting his hand on the metal security box and giving it a fond pat, Red said, "This one's straightforward. All I need is a couple of paper clips."

Rosa found them, and Red fashioned them into the necessary shapes; he might have no longer had much strength, but he was still capable of bending a paper clip.

Within ninety seconds, the padlock clicked open.

"This is a life skill I need to learn." Layla's air of flippancy was an attempt to conceal her rising dread. Red handed her the box, and she lifted the lid.

There was the blue notebook she'd seen on the bed. As soon as she turned the first few pages, it was apparent what it was.

"Oh, darling." Rosa's hand was on her back, rubbing comforting circles.

"Even I never did this," said Red.

Harry was thorough, she'd give him that. Each of the women he'd targeted was described in meticulous detail. How and when they'd met, the tricks he'd used to make them feel special, the stories he'd told them about his life. Then there were the amounts of money they'd lent or gifted him and the estimated potential for further gifts. There were details of each woman's age, assets, and earning ability.

Layla paused when she came to her own page. There was her name, in his handwriting, and her relevant details. Aged thirty, single, no car, two-bedroom flat in the center of Elliscombe. Accountant, own business, embarrassing clothes, pretty but needy. Contribution to motorbike—zero. Bed, seven out of ten. Hastily, she turned the page before either Red or her mum saw. Seven out of ten? How *mortifying*. Her face burned with shame; how dare he? Worse still, all this time, she'd told herself how great he was, and it wasn't even true. He might look fantastic, but in bed, he was actually very average. More like a five than a seven. *Bastard.*

Oh well, that was all in the past now. She forced herself to concentrate on the next entry. Molly Kendrick was forty-one and lived in a five-bed detached house in Shipton-under-Wychwood worth—according to Harry—megabucks. She'd been divorced for the last three years, had twin seventeen-year-old sons, and drove a brand-new red soft-top Mercedes. Lucky old Molly.

Determined not to look at the rest of Molly's details in case she scored ten out of ten in bed, Layla flipped to the next page.

Angel Black, twenty-eight, single, silver BMW, one-bed flat (rented), senior hairstylist, new to Elliscombe, fantastic body, designer outfits, rich grandmother died in February. Gifts: £2K so far. Had promised more when the inheritance came through. £50K??

OK, this wasn't funny. Within the space of a minute, Layla realized, she was feeling sorrier for the girl called Angel than she was for herself.

"Oh, sweetheart, you don't deserve this." Rosa had leaned across to look at the page.

"None of us do." Flicking back through the notebook, Layla found a dozen or so women who lived in other parts of the country and evidently predated Harry's move here. She said to Red, "Thanks for opening the box. If it hadn't been anything bad, I'd have put everything back where I found it. But I don't think I need to do that now."

"Good girl." Red nodded his approval as she rose to her feet.

Rosa was looking worried. "Where are you going? What are you going to do?"

"I think other people might be interested to see this." Layla slipped the book into her shoulder bag.

"Do you want me to come with you?"

"I'm OK. I'll be fine."

Will was waiting for her outside the house.

"Where to?" He put away his iPad and started the engine, then glanced sideways at her. "The place where I saw…?"

"Yes."

chapter 39

There were three people working in the salon. One was a middle-aged woman in a cardigan and a flowered frock, one was a snake-hipped man in white jeans and a fashionably ripped Freddie Mercury T-shirt, and the third was Angel, tiny and beautiful with spiky white-blond hair and wearing a truly microscopic pink Lycra dress.

Layla lurked outside until the stylist had finished blow-drying her client's hair, then made her way in and asked if she could have a quick word.

"Oh, I'm sorry," said Angel. "I'm fully booked all day. But if you're really desperate, Matt could probably squeeze you in."

Matt said good-naturedly, "Our Angel has a way with words. You don't have to be *really* desperate."

"I'm not here about my hair," said Layla. "Do you know someone called Harry?"

Angel's eyes lit up. "He's my boyfriend!"

But Matt was looking at Layla's face. His grimace let her know that he had an inkling as to what might be about to happen. "Come on, babe. Let's go into the back room and hear what she has to say."

Two minutes later, Angel let out a shriek of fury and hurled the notebook across the back room. "That absolute fucker. All he was ever after was my gran's money."

"Oh, babe," said Matt.

"He told me he loved me!" She turned to Layla. "Did he say it to you too?"

Layla nodded.

"He has a busy schedule," Matt said. "From the look of that list in there, I'm about the only person he hasn't said it to."

"You told me there was something iffy about him." Angel heaved a sigh of frustration.

"He never wanted to go anywhere with you, doll. All that ever happened was he came over to your flat, and then the two of you'd stay in and have sex nonstop. Oh, sorry." He gestured apologetically to Layla. "But it's what he did."

"Not even very good sex," Angel said with an air of defiance.

"*What?* You told us he was fantastic!"

"It's what you have to tell people when it's your boyfriend," Angel retorted.

"Oh, babe. At least you've found out the truth before you gave him any more money."

Angel checked the time on her phone. "This is *so* annoying. I want to go and tell him exactly what I think of him, but I'm stuck here until six and can't let my clients down."

Layla said, "Why don't we meet up this evening? I think we need a plan."

On the way to Shipton-under-Wychwood, she studied the rest of Molly Kendrick's details. Molly's contribution to the Harry fund had initially been five hundred pounds, then last week, she'd added to it with a further three-thousand-pound payment.

"She might not even be there," said Layla as they entered the village.

Will's tone was reassuring. "No worries. We can always come back later."

He was being so nice. If anything could bring her to tears, it was his calm manner and the fact that he hadn't said *I told you so* once.

"Should I even be doing this? Maybe it's none of my business and I ought to just let him get on with it."

"Don't even think that," said Will. "My mother got taken in by a confidence trickster after my dad died. It broke her heart, and she never recovered."

And then her physical problems had begun, leaving her practically housebound for years. Layla was appalled. "Oh, Will, I didn't know. How awful. I'm sorry."

"Looks like she's at home." He braked as they reached the address Harry had listed, a detached Cotswold home smothered in wisteria. And there, parked at a jaunty angle in the graveled driveway, was the red Mercedes.

"OK, here we go again. Wish me luck."

"You've got this," said Will as she climbed out of the car. "He's the one who's going to need the luck."

Molly Kendrick had been mowing her lawn; she was a busty brunette with crystal-encrusted talons for nails and a big welcoming smile that faded as soon as Layla mentioned Harry by name.

"Come in. Tell me why you're here. Oh God, is this bad news? If you're his wife, I swear I didn't know. He told me he was single."

"I'm definitely not his wife. But I did think I was his only girlfriend." Layla passed her the notebook. "Looks like he's been telling all of us a few lies."

In her manicured back garden with its stunning flower beds and half-mown lawn, Molly Kendrick read the relevant pages in silence. Finally, she looked up and said, "Just when you think you've found someone decent at last."

"I know the feeling."

"If we went to the police, he'd just say we'd given him the money. He didn't steal it."

Layla nodded; she had realized that too.

"Three and a half grand he cost me. *And* a brand-new iPhone, the bastard."

That explained the flashy new phone, the one he'd apparently won in an online contest. "I wasn't sure whether you'd want to know," said Layla. "But I had to tell you."

"I just wish it weren't too early for a drink. I could murder a gin and tonic. Actually, I could murder bloody Harry." Molly's hoop earrings rattled as she shook her head. "But I won't, because how would I ever find a good man in a women's prison?"

....

"I like this place," said Angel. "I can't believe I've never been here before. It's gorgeous!" They were in Bourton-on-the-Water, and the church bells had just chimed six. Harry would be home soon. The three women sat on the wooden bench at the water's edge, just across the road from his flat.

"He kept us compartmentalized," said Molly. "He told me he lived in his grandmother's cottage and she was always there. That was why we spent all our time at my house."

"Same." Angel nodded.

Layla said, "Which was why he never came to my place. Because he was already seeing you, and I only live a few hundred yards down the road. I had to come here instead."

"Is his flat nice?" Angel was curious.

"No! Horrible bath towels." Layla shuddered at the memory of them and the ghastly bed linen. "And he never had any fresh milk in the fridge."

"Can I just say?" Molly touched the sleeve of Layla's purple satin shirt. "I don't think your clothes are embarrassing. I think you look great."

"We all do. We *are* great," Layla declared. She'd already resolved that Harry's snide comment wasn't going to stop her wearing the outfits she loved.

"Here we go." Angel sat up straight as the sound of a motorbike made itself heard. "I'm looking forward to this now."

Layla was too. The three of them were currently shielded from view by the huge weeping willow tree overhanging the river. They watched through the low-hanging green fronds as Harry parked the motorbike—his pride and joy—and climbed off it, then removed his helmet. When he turned to head toward his front door, Layla jumped up and hurried across the strip of grass separating them.

"Surprise!"

He swung around. "Hello! Another surprise? You should call before you come over."

"Why?"

"Why d'you think? Because I might not be here."

Behind him, Molly and Angel were making their two-pronged approach. Layla said cheerfully, "Oh, I thought you meant because you might be meeting someone else."

He looked taken aback. "What d'you mean?"

"Hiya!" sang Angel, materializing to the left of him.

Harry's smile vanished.

"Hello, darling!" Molly appeared to his right.

"Oh, for fuck's sake," said Harry, realizing he was trapped.

"You could say that." Molly beamed.

His eyes darted between the three of them; he was like a cornered wild animal.

"Oh, Harry. What a pathetic creature you are," said Molly.

"Seriously? You think *I'm* pathetic? Look at all of you." He was sneering now, the charming, charismatic personality a thing of the past. Except it had never existed, not really. It had, Layla reminded herself, all been an act. "How did you find out anyway?"

"A woman from Sheffield contacted me," Layla told him. Not true, but it was worth a try.

"Which one? Was it Estelle? She's a fucking bitch."

But she was a fucking bitch who'd lost her husband three years ago and had been persuaded to lend Harry four thousand pounds he'd evidently had no intention of ever repaying. Had he been doing this for years, moving around the country each time he was found out? *What a way to live your life*, thought Layla.

"Actually, I found this." She took the notebook out of her oversize sequined shoulder bag.

Harry's face darkened. "How did you get hold of that? It's mine. You can't take things that belong to other people."

Molly snorted with laughter.

"I just borrowed it," Layla said innocently.

"Like you borrowed three and a half grand from me, remember?" Molly gave him an encouraging nod. "But you haven't managed to start paying any of it back."

"Oh, give me a break. You're loaded." He glared at her.

"And you're a liar and a cheat. Never mind. I've spoken to my solicitor—"

"For fuck's *sake*." Harry let out a howl of outrage, suddenly spotting Will standing a few yards away, filming the encounter on his phone. "What d'you think you're doing? Fuck off, the lot of you, and leave me alone."

"Oh, don't be like that," Molly protested. "You told me you loved me!"

"You told me that too," said Angel.

"And me." Layla shrugged as Harry turned and stormed off toward his flat. "Oh well. Bye!"

The front door almost bounced off its hinges as it slammed shut behind him.

"Dammit, that's annoying," said Molly. "I forgot to tell him he was a four."

Angel shook her head. "That's too generous."

"Did you get the whole thing?" Layla asked Will.

He grinned and pressed the button to stop recording. "Absolutely. Got it all."

"I'll send him a text before I block him," Molly said with satisfaction. "Let him know that if we ever hear he's been up to any more nonsense, we'll post the video on YouTube and send the link to every fitness club in the land."

chapter 40

SHAY WAS SITTING BESIDE HIS FATHER'S BED IN THE LIVING ROOM, listening to the sound of his breathing as he slept. How much time did they have left?

Not long now.

It was the third week of October. Summer had ended abruptly a fortnight ago, and autumn had swept in with a vengeance. The trees had turned orange and ochre as the temperature dropped, an almighty storm had shaken the first swathes of leaves from their branches, and squirrels had darted to and fro across the lawn, collecting and burying fallen nuts.

Not at this time of night though. Outside, an owl was hooting peacefully, and in the far distance, a fox barked.

Red opened his eyes. "What are you doing here?"

"Nothing. Just sitting."

"What time is it?"

Shay checked his watch. "Ten past four."

"Now I know what you're doing."

"Go on then, tell me."

"You heard that thing on the radio about sick people being more likely to die at this time of night."

He was right, as usual. Shay said, "What are you, some kind of mind reader?"

"Yes. And I'm not going to die tonight, so you can go back to bed."

"Bossy as ever."

"I'm feeling pretty good, if you must know."

He was certainly sounding brighter than he had for the last couple of days. He'd been sleeping more, but the pain was under control. When the hospice nurse had paid a visit over the weekend, she'd asked him if he wanted to come into the hospice, and Red had explained that he'd really prefer to spend his remaining time here at home.

Shay said, "Can I get you anything?"

His father nodded. "Wouldn't say no to a Drambuie."

"At this time? Are you sure?"

"Hey, I didn't die tonight. We may as well celebrate."

Fair enough. Shay poured the drinks and brought them back to the bed next to the french window. One of the security lights had come on; a hedgehog was ambling across the patio.

"Cheers," said Shay, and they clinked tumblers.

"Good health." Red smiled slightly. "That's a joke."

"Don't give up the day job."

"What's going to happen after I'm gone?"

"I have no idea."

"Will you stay here?"

"I don't know."

"What about Caz?"

"What about her?"

"I want to know what I'm going to be missing. Do you think she's the one for you?"

Shay shook his head. "Dad, you're asking me questions I can't answer."

"Fine, then. Tell me what you most want to happen. Best-case scenario."

Right now, there was no best-case scenario. Avoiding the question, he said, "It's way too soon to be making plans for me and Caz."

"When I met your mother, I knew right away she was the one for me. By the end of that first evening, it was a done deal. I told everyone I'd found the girl I was going to spend the rest of my life with." Red covered his mouth to cough, then said, "Do you ever wonder what she'd look like now? I do. God, I wish she were still here." He gazed out through the window at the night sky, speckled with stars. "Maybe she is. Maybe she's waiting for me, giving me a nudge and telling me to get a move on."

Shay said, "You were lucky."

"When you know, you know."

"It's not always that straightforward." As he'd found out to his cost.

"Do you know why I wanted to move into this house?" Red asked. "Because I thought getting you back here might sort you out."

"Sort me out in what way?"

"You're thirty-one. I've met plenty of your girlfriends over the years, seen the way you are with them. And they've all been great girls in their own way." Red coughed again, then took another swallow of Drambuie. "But you've never been as happy with any of them as you were with Didi."

Tell me something I don't know.

Shay's heart thudded. "We were kids."

"I know. So was I when I met your mum."

He sat forward. "Are you seriously telling me you emotionally blackmailed me into spending the whole summer working seventy hours a week all because you thought it might help to get me and Didi back together?"

"Well, that was the plan. Didn't bloody work though, did it?"

"She's about to get married."

"You could have persuaded her to change her mind."

"It's too late."

"Never too late." Red's breathing was becoming more labored.

"Just because you want something to happen doesn't mean it's going to," said Shay. "Maybe if she hadn't met Aaron first, things might have been different. But she did, and I'm not going to try and break them up because that'd be a shitty thing to do. And it's not my decision to make either. Didi's the one who chooses whether or not she gets married."

"You and your morals. I don't know where you get them from." Red summoned a brief smile. "Anyway, I'm sorry I ruined everything for the two of you."

"It wasn't your fault," Shay reminded him. "You didn't break in and empty the safe."

"Ah, but I'd done enough other stuff to make people assume I had. If I'd had a proper job, led a decent life, Didi's parents would never have thought it was me in the first place."

"It doesn't matter." Time to change the subject. "Can I ask you something?"

His father chuckled and coughed. "Before I die, you mean?"

"It would help if you're still around to give me an answer." Both their glasses were empty; Shay reached for the bottle and refilled them.

"Go on then. Fire away."

"Did anything ever happen between you and Maura Laing?"

Red raised an eyebrow. "Why?"

"I always wondered if it did."

"Well, nothing happened."

"Really?"

"No need to sound so surprised."

"I thought you were going to say yes. After all, you had more than your share of adventures."

"I did." Red nodded, shifting his legs into a more comfortable position. "But not with Maura."

"OK."

"Guess why not."

"I have no idea."

"She wanted to. Well, we both did. But I said no. Because I didn't want to risk doing anything that might make the situation awkward for you and Didi."

Shay looked at him, silhouetted in the dim lamplight. "Are you serious?"

"Completely. It's one of the few honorable things I've done in my life."

"Dad." Touched, Shay said, "I can't believe you did that. I'm impressed."

"So you should be. Waste of time though, wasn't it? You two broke up anyway."

Which meant this had happened—or rather *not* happened—prior to the robbery. Casting his mind back to the days after it had taken place, Shay recalled the oddness of Maura's reaction to it, her discomfort and awkwardness, the distinct feeling he'd had that she was hiding something or at least knew more than she was letting on.

Oh well, if you couldn't ask a tricky question mere days or weeks before your father died, when could you ask it? He said slowly, "Do you think Maura was involved in the robbery in some way? I mean, I'm not saying she *did* it. But had she been persuaded for one reason or another to give someone the keys?"

Did that sound crazy? Maybe, but it had lurked in the back of his mind for years.

"Shay, she wasn't involved. I can one hundred percent guarantee it. Maura had no idea who was behind the robbery, and that's the truth."

Right. Shay exhaled. That had come as even more of a relief than he'd expected. It felt like a weight slipping from his shoulders. "OK. That's good."

"I know who did do it." Red tilted his head. "Want me to tell you?"

"Was it anyone…significant?"

"No one from your family. Or Didi's."

Shay considered this. "Fine. No need for me to know, then." Sometimes it was easier not to.

"If you're ever curious, ask Maura. I told her when she came to see me the other week." Red yawned; his eyelids were starting to close now. The tumbler of Drambuie was tilting in his hand.

Removing it before it spilled over the bed, Shay said quietly, "No one can say you haven't lived an interesting life."

The corners of his father's mouth lifted. "It's been good. And now it's your turn to carry on."

"I'll try to stay out of prison, if that's OK."

"You do that." Red's eyes flickered open, and he rested his hand on top of Shay's. "Did I ever tell you I love you?"

"Several hundred times." It was Shay's turn to smile. "I love you too, Dad."

"Be happy," Red murmured.

Shay swallowed hard. "I will."

....

A woman in an emerald-green coat was waiting outside Hillcrest, lurking beneath a navy golfing umbrella, when Shay arrived back from the funeral home a fortnight later. Red had left strict instructions that he wanted to be buried wearing a black suit, white shirt, and crimson tie, because that was what he'd worn on his wedding day.

Having delivered the clothes, Shay had been half tempted to stop off at the pub for lunch on the way home. Seeing as it was raining hard and his visitor was looking pretty sodden, it was just as well he hadn't. He pulled into the driveway and climbed out of the car.

"At last," Maura Laing exclaimed. "I've been standing here for ages."

He unlocked the front door and led the way inside. Once she'd peeled off her sodden coat, Maura threw her arms around him. "Darling, I'm so sorry about your father. He was one of a kind."

"He was," Shay agreed. "Thank you." Maura had always been the sort of person who called everyone darling, but it still felt weird coming from someone who'd once sacked him.

"As soon as Didi told me he'd gone, I knew I had to fly over for the funeral."

"That's good of you."

"Such a lovely man." She hesitated. "The thing is, the *other* thing is, there's something I need your help with."

Here it came. "In what way?"

"Red left something here for me, and I need it. Kind of…today."

Shay nodded; Red's actual words to him had been, "If Maura turns up asking for something, let her have it."

Whatever *it* might be.

"You'll have to tell me where it is," he said. "I'll go and get it for you."

She turned and gestured through the window. "It's out there."

The rain was now hammering down harder than ever. He frowned. "I'm going to need more of a clue than that."

"It's in the garden. In the ground," Maura elaborated. "Under the mulberry tree."

What the hell?

"And you really want it now?"

"Yes please."

The thing about growing up with a father like Red was you learned to expect the unexpected and take it in your stride. Thankfully, this section of the garden was hidden from view of any passing cars. Having instructed him where to dig, Maura was now hovering next to Shay like a flamingo, holding the golf umbrella over her own head rather than his.

After digging for a while and finding nothing, he said, "Are you sure this is the right place?"

"Red said it was here. He came out and showed me. I did try to get it myself, but the ground was rock-hard back then. You should have seen the state of my nails." She grimaced. "They looked terrible afterward. Gardening really isn't my thing."

Minutes later, the garden spade struck something hard. After that, it didn't take long to unearth the cookie tin swathed in heavy-duty plastic. The lid of the tin was securely sealed, wrapped around a dozen times with duct tape.

Back in the house, dripping mud and rainwater at every step, Shay rinsed off the tin and dried it with a towel. Handing it to Maura, he said, "Do I get to see what's inside?"

"No. Sorry."

"Are you worried it's something that might make me think less of my father?"

Maura shook her head. "Not at all."

"Well, that's good. Although just so you know, it wouldn't have made me think less of him."

"The reason I don't want you to see it is because I don't want you to think less of *me*." Maura spoke with what seemed to be genuine regret. "I try to be a good person, Shay, but sometimes I fail. Can we leave it at that? By keeping this buried in the garden, your father was helping me." Tears brimmed in her eyes as she tucked the tin under her arm. "At least he was honest about being dishonest. In so many ways, he was a better person than me."

chapter 41

By the next day, the storm had thankfully passed. The sun came out, and a blustery wind caused playful havoc with hats and dress hems as the mourners emerged from the church and gathered around the open grave.

Didi was glad she was wearing trousers. At her side, Maura was struggling to prevent the flimsy silk of her pineapple-yellow frock from flying up and revealing her Spanx. Didi murmured, "Why don't I hold your handbag for you?" but her mother shook her head firmly.

"I'm fine. I can manage."

Didi took her at her word. She still had no idea why her mother had been so determined to visit Shay yesterday afternoon. It had made her yearn, suddenly and overwhelmingly, to be with him herself, just the two of them together, so she could tell him how sorry she was about everything and they could reminisce fondly about Red. But as she'd been preparing to drive over, her mother had announced that she needed to see Shay, and no, it couldn't wait, so Didi would just have to be patient and wait her turn. And that had been it. By the time Maura had returned two hours later, Didi had been too busy sorting out a staffing issue to get away, and when she was finally able to escape, it was too late. Having managed to get time off from filming on location in Cape Town, Caz had arrived back in Elliscombe.

Now, in the graveyard, a broad-brimmed black hat flew off the head of an elegant brunette and cartwheeled between a row of gravestones. In fact, now that Didi was paying attention, it was noticeable that among the two hundred or so mourners, there were quite a number of attractive older women attending without partners.

Well, Red had always been popular with the ladies.

Small white clouds scudded across the sky as the vicar began to speak. The attractive older women dabbed carefully at their eyes with hankies, attempting with varying degrees of success not to wreck their makeup. As the coffin was lowered into the ground, the sound of muted sobbing was audible.

Didi saw the lines of grief drawn on Shay's face and longed to be able to comfort him. But it wasn't her place; he didn't belong to her. At his side, a single tear slid down Caz's left cheek as she rested her head against his shoulder. She was looking beautiful, holding his hand supportively and gazing with ineffable sadness into the open grave as he now stepped forward to drop a handful of earth onto the lid of the wicker coffin.

The ceremony was concluded and the invitation issued for everyone to come back to Hillcrest. People began to drift away from the graveyard. Shay stayed where he was, with Caz beside him. Didi wondered if he was imagining that Red had finally been reunited with Mel, the wife he'd loved more than all the other women who'd subsequently danced in and out of his eventful life.

Hopefully they were now together forever, and Shay could add his father's details to the black marble gravestone commemorating his mother. Watching him, Didi's eyes misted over.

"Come on." Maura tugged at her arm. "We don't want to be the last ones there, do we? I need a drink."

....

Most of those who'd attended the funeral went back to Hillcrest for the wake. Luckily, the blustery wind died down, enabling people to mingle both in the house and outside in the sunny garden. Drinks and canapés were served, tales were told about Red, and Didi found herself recognizing people she hadn't seen for years. There was Big Gav and his wife, both knocking back the cider and helping themselves to sausage rolls. Over on the other side of the garden was Barbie, who'd once owned the florist's shop on the market square before moving away over a decade ago.

"Who's that?" Maura pointed at a dumpy woman in a tight-fitting cream trouser suit.

"Haven't the faintest," said Didi.

"What about her over there?"

"Mum, I'm not Google! I have no idea! Red knew people from all over the place."

Slept with most of them too.

"I recognize the woman with the wobbly chins." Layla joined them, having overheard the conversation. "She has a dear little jewelry shop on Garrett Street in Cheltenham. I bought Mum's charm bracelet from there for her birthday."

"Ah, that's right." Maura nodded a bit jerkily, her cheeks reddening. "That's how I recognize her. I knew I knew her from somewhere."

It was a while later that Didi turned and caught Shay's eye across the garden. Caz was otherwise occupied chatting to the elderly couple who ran the funeral parlor, and Shay was briefly alone. When he half smiled and began to move toward her, she met him halfway.

She greeted him with a fleeting kiss on the cheek—oh God, it might be fleeting, but it still played havoc with her heart rate—and said, "How are you doing?"

"Be glad when it's over." Again the crooked smile. "Except it won't be over, will it? He's not coming back."

"He loved you so much. And you've done him proud." She longed to hug him, but what if she started and couldn't stop? Imagine how embarrassing that would be, in front of everyone. "At least he got to spend time in his old home. I was so worried he wouldn't have the chance. He was so happy to be back here too."

"I know. It meant the world to him." The expression in Shay's eyes was unreadable as he glanced at her then looked away. "Thank goodness we managed to get the place finished in time."

People were watching them; Didi could feel their gazes. Living in a small town where everyone knew you had its drawbacks. "And how about you? Any plans for the next few weeks? You need to relax, take things easy." As she said it, Caz managed to escape from the elderly couple and crossed the lawn to join them.

"Can you believe it? They asked for a selfie. Hello, you!" She gave Didi a big hug. "God, all this being nice to strangers is exhausting."

"I was just telling Shay, he needs to take time to unwind."

"You're absolutely right." Caz slid her arm around Shay's waist. "I said the same. He has to get away for a proper break. One of my mates has a place in St. Lucia, and she said we can stay there for as long as we like, but Shay's not sure he wants to." She gave Didi an encouraging nudge. "Come on. Back me up here. Tell him he needs to go."

Here it was, one of those situations you didn't want to find yourself in. Not wanting him to go at all but unable to say so, Didi nodded at Shay. "It'd do you good."

"Thank you! See? Didi agrees with me. You've been through a shit time, and now you have to take a few weeks off. As soon as I've finished in Cape Town, we could spend a fortnight in St. Lucia, then fly on to New Zealand before I start my next job…if it goes ahead."

"I don't know…" Shay was raking his fingers through his hair, clearly still unconvinced.

"Babe, take it from me, it's what you need. And I'll be there to look after you, won't I?" Reaching up, Caz kissed him tenderly on the mouth. "All I want to do is make you feel better, then—"

"Didi, found you!" Sylvia had finished her shift and belatedly come to pay her respects. Waving and hurrying toward them in her purple dress, she exclaimed, "Why haven't you been answering your phone?"

"I turned it off in the church." It was a fairly basic requirement when you were attending a funeral, although Red would probably have found it amusing if a comedy ringtone had suddenly blasted out during the eulogy. "I didn't get around to turning it on again. Why, what's happened?"

"You've got a surprise." Sylvia's eyes danced. "Waiting for you back at the hotel. *Oh…*" She turned apologetically to Shay. "So sorry about your dad. Was it a lovely service? Looks like you're giving him a wonderful send-off."

Shay nodded. "Thanks."

After an awkward moment, Didi said, "What kind of surprise?" Well, she had to ask. Maybe a Michelin inspector had just paid a visit to the restaurant and been so bowled over by his lunch that he'd cast off his anonymity in order to shower praise on—

"It's Aaron!" Clearly over the moon, Sylvia clapped her hands with delight. "I told him you were here, but obviously it wouldn't be right to have a wonderful romantic reunion at a wake. So he's waiting for you at the hotel! Isn't that just the most fantastic surprise? He's flown all the way back from New York because he missed you so much! And let me tell you, he is handsomer than ever!"

What the hell?

"Look at her. She can't believe it," Caz exclaimed. "She's stunned!"

That was certainly true.

"Your face is a picture," whooped Sylvia. "Oh, we should have videoed this!"

"Love's young dream." Caz did a comedy swoon and turned to Shay. "I hope you're always going to be this romantic with me."

"Shall I call the hotel, let him know you're on your way back?" Sylvia already had her phone out.

"I can't leave yet." Didi recovered the power of speech. "This is Red's wake."

"Of course you can," said Caz. "Red wouldn't want you staying here. He'd be the first one to tell you to get yourself back to the hotel. Wouldn't he?" She turned to Shay for confirmation.

He nodded, clearly distracted by more urgent concerns. "Caz is right. It's fine. You should go."

chapter 42

In the past when she'd been busy at work and Aaron had arrived at the hotel by taxi, he'd always greeted her exuberantly in front of a crowd, for maximum impact. This time, he was waiting for her in the otherwise empty hallway, and as soon as he caught sight of her, hope flared in his eyes.

"Didi." He hurried toward her and gave her a quick hug. "Can we go up to your flat?"

She nodded; he wasn't the only one who didn't want an audience.

Up the polished wooden staircase they went. As soon as her door closed behind them, Aaron blurted out, "I've missed you so much. Oh God, you have no idea."

"Is that why you're here?" Didi shook her head. "I'm confused."

"You're not the only one." He took a step closer. "Sylvia seems to think you and I are still getting married in December and that I've flown back from New York to see you."

"Ah." She'd invented his secondment to the New York branch of the company to explain his absence.

"Show me your hands."

"What?"

"Please."

Didi held out her hands, and Aaron's gaze flickered over them. "OK, the reason I'm here is because I was at a business meeting in Leeds yesterday, and one of my colleagues showed me a photo he'd seen in the paper."

Still none the wiser, Didi said, "A photo of what?"

"Of you. I don't make a habit of reading the tabloids, obviously, but this was pointed out to me." He opened his phone and held it up to show her the screenshot. It was a recent photograph of Caz returning to the hotel. Spotting her climbing out of a taxi, Didi had gone outside to welcome her, whereupon someone on the other side of the road had captured the moment on camera. As they'd greeted each other with enthusiasm, Didi's left hand had been outstretched.

And there, clearly visible on her third finger, was the diamond, glittering away in the bright sunlight.

"So you're still wearing my ring. And you don't appear to have told anyone here that we broke up." Aaron tilted his head. "Which leads me to think you've been regretting what you said to me and trying to pluck up the courage to admit you made a massive mistake. Am I right?"

Didi's heart was sinking ever lower. She'd landed herself in this mess, and now, somehow or other, she had to get out of it.

....

It took a while. Aaron had never been one for admitting that he might have gotten hold of the wrong end of the stick. Didi was forced to invent an overeager suitor with a bit of a crush on her who'd made it necessary for her to pretend she was still engaged. Aaron wanted to know who the suitor was, but she refused to tell him. He then asked if anything had happened between her and Shay, and she was able to assure him truthfully that it hadn't.

"But I told you, you could go for it. I gave you my permission." He seemed frustrated that she hadn't taken advantage of his generous offer.

"Shay's seeing Caz. Plus, I didn't want to sleep with him."

Aaron gestured with frustration. "But how are you going to get him out of your system if you don't?"

Twenty minutes later, a text from Sylvia arrived on Didi's phone:

> So so sorry to interrupt, but the Walker-Dunns are here. They want to book the hotel for an eightieth birthday party and are insisting they speak to you about it.

"I have to go," she told Aaron. "Something needs sorting downstairs."

"Work, work, all you care about is this bloody hotel." He gave a snort of disgust. "If you'd come down to London more often, none of this would have happened, and we'd still be together."

Didi was pierced with a mixture of sadness and relief. Maybe that was true. All she knew was that if Shay hadn't returned to Elliscombe, remembering what real love felt like might have passed her by. But he had returned, all the old dormant emotions had come surging back, and she'd realized just how important those feelings were in order to live a complete life.

She might not be able to spend that life with Shay, but nor could she stay in a relationship with someone she now knew she didn't love nearly enough.

"We still could be together," Aaron persisted. "If you change your mind, I could make you happy."

And in some ways, he probably could. But again, not happy enough.

Didi swallowed. "I'm sorry. Please take the ring back."

As if recognizing finally that her mind was made up, Aaron said, "Are you sure?"

"Quite sure." It came off her finger with ease; she'd lost weight without even being aware of it.

He zipped it into his wallet and gave her a hug, which was a far nicer way to end it than last time in London.

"There's more to life than just this place, remember." He regarded her sympathetically. "I hope you come to realize that."

Didi nodded. "Thanks. I'll sort myself out. You be happy too."

The Walker-Dunns were waiting for her downstairs. For the next two hours, closeted with her in the office, they went through a long and elaborate list of requirements for the birthday celebrations to be held in January. By the time they left, having discussed everything in exhaustive detail, Didi had developed a killer headache.

"You look exhausted," said Sylvia.

"I am."

She winked. "Not surprised. Sorry about interrupting the big reunion. What a shame Aaron couldn't stay any longer."

"Just a flying visit. He had to get back to London." Didi winced, her brain feeling as if it were being squeezed in a vice. "Look, I don't want this headache to turn into a migraine. I'm going to catch up on some sleep."

"Oh, you poor thing! That's the trouble with these romantic reunions," Sylvia said with a grin. "They do take it out of you."

....

Back at Hillcrest, there were still a hundred or so mourners determined not to leave. The wake was turning into a proper party as tradition dictated, with music and dancing and wild stories from the old days being retold with relish.

It had taken Maura this long to pluck up the courage, but now the time had come. Knocking back the rest of her glass of white wine, she saw that the wobbly chinned woman in the tight trouser suit had collected her handbag and was starting to say her goodbyes.

Maura tracked her progress around the house, then stealthily followed her outside. There were cars parked the length of the lane, and the woman was jangling a set of keys as she trotted along the verge. There would be CCTV in the jeweler's shop; it was far safer to do it out here.

"Hello?" Maura quickened her pace, calling out to attract the woman's attention. "Sorry to bother you. Is your name Pat?"

Pat turned and nodded. "It is, my love. And you're the one from the hotel. Maura, am I right?"

Maura nodded, feeling sick. "I used to live at the hotel. I have something… I asked Red, and he said you'd help me…"

"Yes, he gave me a call, mentioned someone might be in touch. Didn't say it was you though." Pat's chins wobbled as she gave a knowing smile. "Got it with you?"

Maura's hands shook as she took the tightly wrapped package out of her bag. Glancing back over her shoulder at the house, she said, "I just want it gone, OK? Red said you could break it up, retrieve the stones, and melt down the gold."

"I can do that, yes. Let's just have a little look, shall we? See what we're dealing with."

"Could we sit in your car?" Maura blurted out. "Would that be easier?"

"Fine. I'm just up here." Pat sounded amused.

Once inside the green Nissan, Maura unfastened the package and took out the emerald necklace.

"I'm giving the money to charity."

"Of course you are."

Pat could blackmail her, Maura realized. She watched as the woman reached across, took a jeweler's loupe from the glove compartment, and held up the necklace in order to expertly examine the stones.

"Nice." She nodded. "We'll say fifty-fifty, shall we?"

"Sorry?"

"There needs to be something in it for me, love. I don't handle stolen goods for nothing, do I?"

"It's not stolen. It's my necklace." As she spoke, the rear passenger door was yanked open, and she jumped a mile.

Pat said easily, "All right, you two? Just doing a spot of business before I give you a lift to the station."

"What you got there then, Pat?" Big Gav leaned forward and took the necklace from her. Oh fuck, and his wife was with him too.

"This lady's asking me to break it up for her. Seems a shame really. Lovely bit of workmanship. Cost a few bob, I'll be bound."

Fuck fuck *fuck*. Maura twisted around in horror to look at Big Gav, the man who'd committed the robbery in the first place.

"Well, well," he said cheerfully, "I always wondered what happened to that necklace. Because I sure as hell knew I didn't have it."

"I'm giving the money to charity," Maura stammered.

"Well, don't expect me to do that with my share." Pat's cackle of laughter resembled a crumpled chip package. "Because it's not gonna happen!"

Big Gav gave Maura's shoulder a prod from behind. "How much is she asking for, then?"

"Half." She just wanted to be gone. He reeked of cider. This was like being involved in some terrifying gangland TV drama. They could murder her right now and throw her body in a ditch, to be torn apart and eaten by foxes.

"Hey, be nice to her," chided Big Gav's wife. "It's Red's funeral, yeah? Do the decent thing and give her the cash. He's done both of you enough favors in his time."

"Yeah," said Big Gav, "pay her the money and let's get out of here. We've got a train to catch."

Maura blinked as Pat opened her bag and burrowed in it before pulling out several rolls of twenty-pound notes. "Fine then, take it. Six grand and count yourself lucky I'm in a good mood."

"Thanks," Maura mumbled, opening the passenger door and almost falling out in her hurry to escape.

"Make sure it goes to a good cause," said Big Gav.

Maura just wished she could wipe the photographic images of him naked from her brain. "I will," she croaked.

"And I never want to see you near my shop neither," Pat yelled as she fired up the engine. "I've got a reputation to think of. Don't need it being ruined by bloody amateurs."

When Didi woke up the next morning, it was six o'clock and still dark outside, but the sound of suitcase wheels rumbling across the sidewalk indicated that at least one guest was checking out early.

Peering through the diamond-leaded bedroom window overlooking the high street, she watched as a driver hauled the case into the back of a taxi. The next moment, Caz came into view, emerging from the hotel's front entrance in a pale sweatshirt, fuchsia-pink leggings, and flip-flops. So wherever she was heading, it was warmer than here.

The *next* next moment, a tall figure dressed in black carried out another case. Didi's stomach clenched in recognition, just as it did every time she clapped eyes on Shay. He'd clearly stayed here last night with Caz, escaping the postwake chaos at Hillcrest.

Was he going with her to the airport just to wave her off? It looked like it. As Didi rested her forehead on the cold glass, Caz looked up, spotting her in the window. She nudged Shay and pointed before waving madly and blowing Didi a kiss. After a moment, Shay raised his hand too, forcing her to smile down at them and wave back.

Then together they climbed into the taxi. Didi's smile fell away as the gleaming black car headed off up the high street. If Shay was accompanying Caz to the airport just to see her off at this time of the morning, he must love her a lot.

Lucky, lucky Caz.

But when she made her way downstairs an hour later, showered and dressed and ready to start work for the day, Sylvia said, "Caz Holloway checked out early."

"Right." Didi nodded.

"Back to South Africa. Taken Shay with her."

Taken him with her? For how long?

"Won't she be working?"

"Only for the next couple of days, she said. Then they're heading off to St. Lucia, imagine that! Caz decided he needed to get away from it all, have a proper break, so she booked everything last night. All right for some! Oh dear, apart from losing his dad. Of course he deserves a break after that." Changing the subject, Sylvia said hastily, "Ooh, did you see that photo of you and Caz in the *Mail* yesterday? Didn't she look gorgeous in it?"

"I did see." Didi nodded. "Aaron showed it to me."

Sylvia beamed at her. "Ah, and wasn't it a great photo of the front of the hotel? What a shame you weren't wearing any makeup!"

chapter 43

"There!" Angel whipped off the navy nylon cape with a flourish and stepped back to admire her handiwork. "Like it?"

"*Love* it." Layla tilted her head, her hair swinging from one side to the other; it made a nice change, being happy with the end result rather than struggling to hold back tears. "You're brilliant!"

"I know."

"You're going to be stuck with me from now on. I hope you realize that."

"Great. Speaking of being stuck with someone, your admirer's just turned up."

"He's not my admirer." Layla felt her cheeks heat up. Through the plate-glass window, she saw Will expertly reversing into a parking space on the square.

"OK, your driving instructor."

"Not that either."

"Fine then. The nice man who's helping you get your confidence back so you can start driving again." Mischievously, Angel added, "The handsome man who's too shy to admit he fancies you rotten."

"Oh, don't say that. He doesn't."

"Does too."

Layla hesitated. "Do you really think he's handsome?"

"Who, Will? Yes!" said Angel.

"*God*, yes," exclaimed Anthony, one of the senior stylists. "And in that understated way, which is what makes him so much more attractive."

"I know what you mean." Matt joined in. "It's those V-neck sweaters he wears over button-down shirt collars, and those eyes behind his glasses. He's like Elliscombe's answer to Clark Kent."

The older woman whose hair he was highlighting said, "Matt, all these years, and I never knew you were gay."

"I'm not. But I can still appreciate the way he looks."

"Like a sexy chemistry teacher," Anthony chimed in. "I wish *he* were gay. I'd be after him like a shot."

"He only has eyes for Layla." Now wielding a giant can of extra-hold hair lacquer, Angel said, "Spray?"

And Layla, who always found herself politely saying yes to spray even when she didn't really want it, had a sudden vision of herself and Will together in the car, kissing passionately. She blinked. "No thanks. Let's leave it as it is."

It had been just over a month since her relationship with Harry had come to an abrupt end, but it felt more like a year, and she hadn't missed him for so much as a minute. But maybe, just maybe, she'd been missing out on someone else…

This was her fourth lesson in getting her confidence back behind the wheel. Somehow, because Will drove for a living and was always so calm and in control, she'd found herself for the first time considering the possibility that maybe she could do it after all. Except the first attempt had been a giant failure; all she'd done was shake and try hard not to burst into tears before giving up after twenty minutes and jumping out of the driver's seat at a traffic light.

But the second time had been less disastrous, and during the third lesson, she'd managed to drive for a whole hour. Despite it still being stressful, the waves of panic were starting to come under control. And while anyone else might have lost patience long ago, Will continued to be a saint, understanding and endlessly patient and… OK, full disclosure, she'd been finding him more attractive with each passing week.

It just went to show, didn't it? You never knew what might happen next, what surprises could be just around the corner.

But it certainly seemed to be happening now. Now that she was no longer on the defensive, feeling the need to protect the so-called boyfriend Will had been right about from the start, Layla was able to appreciate his easy manner and dry humor. And maybe also his body, actually quite toned and athletic beneath those Clark Kent outfits.

What would he do if she suddenly launched herself at him in a frenzy of lust and kissed him right there in the car in the middle of the market square on a Tuesday afternoon in November?

Well, the answer to that was nothing, because she wasn't going to do it. She'd need at least six gin and tonics before anything like that could happen.

"Afternoon." Will gave a nod of approval. "You've had your hair done."

"Angel did it." She gave her head another tilt to make the ends swish. "You like?"

Because how could he say no when she was looking this fabulous?

"Very nice. Do you want to drive?"

"Not yet." It was too daunting coping with this many cars and pedestrians; so far, she'd only taken the wheel once the center of town was behind them.

A few minutes later, Will pulled into a driveway and they swapped seats. Layla instantly felt her pulse begin to race; was it the prospect of driving or the faint but delicious scent of his aftershave as they crossed paths in front of the car?

"You're allowed to look at your phone now," she told him, because texts had been pinging up since they'd left the salon.

"No need. It's fine."

"It might be important." Layla felt guilty enough as it was, knowing he was giving up an hour of taxi work just for her.

"If people are that desperate for a cab, they can call Darren instead. Now, deep breaths and relax. Off we go."

Layla did as she was told. As they traveled along the winding country lanes, Will gave her gentle encouragement. A rabbit hopped out into the middle of the road, and she managed not to scream, simply braking and swerving around it without crashing through a hedge. They chatted about work and clients and people they both knew, including her mother and Benny, whose relationship was going great guns.

"She's so happy," Layla told him, "and it's so lovely to see them together. They're off to London this weekend to catch a couple of shows, because Benny's never seen *Hamilton*, and it's Mum's favorite musical. It's like they were meant to be together." She paused as Will's phone began to ring, and without even looking at the screen, he switched it to silent. "What if it's an emergency?"

"Shush, it won't be. I'd rather concentrate on you. Now, we're coming up to Moreton… Fancy a turn around the station parking lot?"

"Not now. It'll be busy." Too many people stepping out suddenly, more concerned about their suitcases than the prospect of being hit by an oncoming car. Indicating left, Layla said, "Let's just stick to quiet roads for now."

"OK, fine. How's Didi getting along?"

This was what she liked about these times in the car with Will, the complete absence of pressure. If she said no, she didn't have to justify her decision. Relaxing once more, she heard his phone vibrate on silent. When he continued to ignore it, she said, "On the surface, not too badly. As far as she's concerned, she and Aaron weren't suited and calling off the wedding was the sensible thing to do. But I don't know. Deep down, she's still not happy. She's not eating properly, and that hasn't happened before. Nothing ever puts Didi off her food."

"Is she regretting breaking up with him, d'you think?"

"She says not, but I don't know. All she's doing at the moment is working nonstop."

"And how about you?" As he asked the question, a gust of wind sent a swirl of orange leaves skittering across the road in front of them. Layla let out a squeak of fear, because they looked like autumnal mice, but she managed not to do an emergency stop. She was making progress. "Me? I'm great."

"You don't miss Harry?"

"Ha, definitely not. None of us miss Harry."

"So you're happy being single?"

"Being single's fine. I'm used to it. I have a great life." Layla was concentrating on the road ahead, but inside her brain, the earlier fantasy was taking hold. What if she were to stop the car and say, *I want to kiss you*? Just like that?

Or *Do you want to kiss me?*

Actually, maybe not. He might say no thanks.

"What are you thinking?" said Will.

Oh God, was he reading her mind? "I'm thinking your phone is driving me nuts. I'm thinking you should answer it."

"Not yet. Once you've finished driving."

"Is it a girlfriend?"

"No."

"Do you *have* a girlfriend?"

"Again, no."

Layla pressed her foot on the brake and pulled up at the side of the otherwise deserted road.

"What are you doing?" said Will.

"I've stopped driving."

"Why?"

"So you can answer your really annoying phone." Switching off the ignition, she turned to face him properly and took a deep breath. "And so that I can kiss me."

"*What?*"

Oh God, oh God. "So that I can kiss you. Or you can kiss me. One of those." Now her skin was prickling with mortification. "Either of them, you choose. Or none. If you don't want to, that's fine."

Silence. Will stared.

His phone buzzed again, like an angry, trapped wasp.

He pressed the button on the passenger door, and the window slid open. He lobbed his phone out onto the grass verge, then turned back to look at her. "Really?"

She'd started, so she'd finish. "Really."

"I've wanted this to happen for months. I never thought it would."

So Angel had been right after all. Her voice unsteady and her adrenaline in chronic overdrive, Layla said, "Really?"

He was on the verge of smiling now. "Oh yes. Really."

"Right. Well, that's good."

"I was jealous of Harry." Will paused. "I knew he was a player. But I also knew you didn't want to hear it from me."

"He's gone. We don't have to talk about him anymore." Although in a way, it was thanks to her terrible taste in online dates that they'd arrived at this point now.

"It might help if you take off your seat belt," said Will.

"You might want to take yours off too."

Click.

Click.

Will said, "I've never kissed anyone in this car before."

Layla knew what he meant; it would be like her kissing a client in her office, over a pile of invoices and tax returns. "Do you think it's going to feel weird?"

His eyebrows tilted very slightly in that inimitable way they did when he was amused. "I think it's going to be amazing. And I can't wait to find out."

He was so lovely. How on earth had it taken her this long to realize what a good, decent man he was? Except deep down, she'd always known but had suppressed her feelings because she'd been so sure he would never be interested in her.

She leaned across, took his face between her hands, and kissed his beautiful mouth. His lips were warm, he smelled wonderful, and she could feel his heart thudding against her chest almost as wildly as hers. She felt dizzy with joy because it just felt so perfect, so right. Now that his fingers were gliding through her hair, she was extra glad not to be wearing hairspray—

"WA-HEYYY!" yelled a male voice from the driver's window of a passing van. The horn toot-tooted as he roared off down the road.

"That's not going to stop me," Will murmured with a grin.

And it didn't. They carried on kissing…and kissing…and kissing some more…

Until a knock on the window made them both jump and spring apart. An elderly woman with a face like a wizened walnut was staring in at them, alongside an elegant, silky-haired Afghan hound.

Impatiently, the woman tapped her gnarled knuckles against the glass again. Layla buzzed down the window. "Can I help you?"

"No, but I can help you. Word of warning, first of all." The woman eyed Will beadily before returning her attention to Layla. "Don't you go giving yourself away, my girl. I know what men are like, mark my words. No bugger's ever going to buy the cow if they're getting the milk for free."

Next to her, Layla heard Will stifle laughter, disguising it as a cough.

"Thanks, I'll bear that in mind." She raised her eyebrows. "What else do you want to help me with?"

"There's one of those infernal buzzing machines over on the other side of the car, in a patch of dandelions. So if it's yours, you might want to move it, because that's where Bert likes to do his business."

Bert wagged his tail in apologetic agreement.

"Right. Thanks." Polite as ever, Will opened the passenger door. He collected his phone, thanked the woman, then climbed back into the car.

"You're lucky Bert didn't piddle all over it." She shook her head. "Why does it keep doing that anyway?"

"Someone's trying to call me," said Will.

"Why aren't you answering it then?"

"I had other things on my mind." As he said it, Bert began to pee all over the dandelion patch.

"Want me to answer it for you? Tell them to bugger off?"

"That's very kind of you, but no need."

Bert finished his business, then he and the elderly woman set off up the road. Layla and Will watched them go.

"She was right about one thing," said Layla. "You definitely need to answer your phone."

chapter 44

"I don't want to," said Will.

"Why not?"

"It might be bad news."

Her blood ran cold. "Are you ill?"

"No. Not that kind of bad news."

He was holding the phone in the palm of his hand, gazing down at the name on the screen. Layla's imagination was going haywire. Was it a long-lost relative? An extortion attempt? An ex-girlfriend calling to tell him she'd just given birth to his child? She said, "Who's Esther Richmond?"

Whatever she'd been expecting, it hadn't been that Will would heave a sigh, put down his phone, and say, "My literary agent."

Layla blinked. "Sorry?" She knew what a literary agent was because a client of hers was a novelist who wrote impenetrable science-fiction and fantasy and was always forcing his latest books on her, urging her to read them, then asking complicated questions afterward to check that she had. But the reason Vincent had a literary agent was because he was an author.

Will was a taxi driver.

"Esther's my literary agent. She took me on a fortnight ago."

"I didn't even know you *liked* books." There'd never been so much as a battered paperback in the glove compartment.

"I love them."

There was so much she didn't know about him. "I've never seen you reading, not once. You're always on your…you know…iPad." As she mimed typing, her brain finally caught up with her fingers. Staring at him in disbelief, she said, "You've written a book?"

Will nodded. "I have."

"So all the time you were working on your iPad, that's what you were doing?"

"Yes."

Layla shook her head. "Am I the only person who doesn't know about this?"

"The opposite, actually. You're the only person who does."

"What? Are you crazy? You've written a whole book and gotten yourself an agent and you haven't told anyone? If it were me, I'd be marching up and down the high street with a giant megaphone. I'd be telling the whole *world*."

"You're you, and I'm me." Will managed a wry smile. "And getting an agent doesn't guarantee you'll find a publisher."

"But your agent's been calling you! Why aren't you answering your phone? She might have amazing news."

Will said, "And she might not. I know she emailed the manuscript to six editors at the top publishing houses. What if they've all said no? What if she's sent it out to more people and they've rejected it too? What if she says she's sorry, but she's changed her mind about representing me, it was all a terrible mistake, and my manuscript just isn't good enough to be published? What if—"

"Stop!" Layla held up both hands. "Oh my God, I don't believe this. You have to call her this minute. Seriously, just do it." She grabbed his phone and pushed it into his hands.

Will blanched. "I can't. I feel sick."

The phone began to buzz again, and he shook his head. Layla took it back and answered it.

"At last," said Esther Richmond. "But you aren't Will."

"He's right here next to me."

Will covered his face with his hands.

"And the reason he hasn't been answering his phone…? Is he asleep? In a coma?"

"He's scared you're going to tell him his book's no good and no one wants to buy it."

"You mean he's telling me I don't know how to do my job?" Esther Richmond gave a bark of laughter. "Put him on."

"Oh God." Will was as white as a sheet.

He took the phone and listened, and Layla tried her hardest to listen too, but he had it pressed so tightly against his ear that all she could make out was a brisk murmur of conversation punctuated by Will going, "Right… OK… Yes… Right," at intervals while looking dazed. Finally, he said, "I know. Sorry about that," and ended the call.

"Sorry about what?" said Layla.

"Not answering my phone while she was trying to set up a meeting with an editor." He exhaled, and she saw that his hands were trembling. Cool, calm Will was in a state of shock.

"And? Does that mean someone wants to buy your book?" Her heart began to skitter; it was like betting on a horse and seeing it move into the lead at the final fence.

"No." Will swallowed audibly and hesitated, then said, "Four editors want to buy it."

"My God, are you *serious*?"

He frowned. "Unless she was playing a trick on me."

"You know she wasn't. Oh, Will, this is amazing! It's incredible!" She flung her arms around him and kissed him again, hard. "Congratulations!"

"I have to go up to London to meet them. So I can see how I feel about the different publishing houses and their plans for the book. Esther says she's going to run an auction…and there's interest from a big American publisher too."

"You idiot," Layla said fondly. "You could have known all this an hour ago if you'd just answered your phone the first time she called."

"Ah, but I was with you. Which was pretty great to begin with. Then it turned from being pretty great into one of the best days of my life." Will reached for her hand and threaded her fingers between his. "Then you forced me to speak to Esther and it got even better."

Layla's heart expanded. "I don't even know what kind of a book you've written. I'm just so happy for you."

"It's about a space cowboy who travels the universe solving crime with his pet monkey."

She blinked. "I wasn't expecting that."

"Just kidding. It's about a taxi driver who takes off on a road trip around the UK in search of his long-lost family. According to Esther, it's quirky, comedic, and blissfully beguiling. She also said it made her cry, and she *never* cries."

"That definitely sounds more like you. It sounds like the kind of thing I'd love to read. Can I?" As she said it, Layla belatedly realized that she'd restarted the ignition, performed a three-point turn in the lane, and was now driving back toward Elliscombe. Well, they couldn't stay sitting parked up in the middle of nowhere forever.

"Where are you taking me?" said Will.

"I don't mind. Your place or mine? You choose."

He grinned. "This day's getting more amazing by the minute."

"Tell me more about your book."

Ten minutes later, they reached Elliscombe. So enthralled by what he was saying that she forgot to panic about the traffic around them, Layla drove through the town and pulled into the lane behind her flat. There was the allocated parking spot that had stood empty ever since she'd bought the property two years ago. Without even pausing to wonder if she could do it, she reversed the car into the narrow space. It wasn't quite straight, so she moved forward before reversing again, better this time. Her palms weren't damp and her heart wasn't racing; it was as if one of those TV hypnotists had cast their spell on her and quite literally siphoned all the terror from her brain.

"...and that was it. She called to tell me she'd stayed up all night reading the manuscript. Well done," said Will.

"I know. I think I'm cured." She held out her hands and admired their steadiness.

"Excellent. Do you have any clients to see this afternoon?"

"Not a single one."

"Even more excellent."

"How about you?" said Layla.

"If anyone needs a taxi, they can call someone else. My phone's staying switched off."

As they made their way around to the front door, Will took her hand once more, and the sensation of his fingers interlocking with hers was the best feeling in the world. Every bit of her body was tingling with anticipation now; *this* was what she'd been waiting for for so—

"Layla, perfect timing!" Malcolm Painter, who ran the garage repair shop, was hurrying up the road toward her, waving a fat gray folder fastened with several elastic bands. "I need to go through these with you, and it's urgent."

Was he mad? "It'll have to wait till tomorrow, Malcolm."

He looked horrified. "But it can't wait! Come on, love. You always fit me in when I'm in a rush. Can't we do it now?"

Honestly, you could tell he'd been married to his wife for forty-two years. Couldn't he see that she was holding hands with Will, on her way into her flat with him, and that now simply wasn't the time?

At her side, Will gave her fingers a reassuring squeeze, and she knew he was letting her know that if she did want to go through Malcolm's mountain of disorganized paperwork, it was fine by him. He was prepared to wait.

But Layla wasn't. Sod that. She didn't want to waste another minute standing out here on the sidewalk. In a firm but pleasant fashion, she said, "Sorry, Malcolm, but it's a no."

As soon as she'd closed the front door behind them, she pressed her body against Will's and kissed him again until her entire body was ablaze with excitement. Then she said, "There's something I need to tell you. Well, warn you about."

"Oh, great, here we go. You have a husband. You have six children. You keep baby alligators in the bath."

"I talk a lot in my sleep."

"You do?" Will lifted a strand of hair from her cheek and tucked it behind her ear. "In that case, there's something I'd better warn you about too. You're not going to be getting any sleep."

chapter 45

"Well, this is a surprise! I didn't know you were coming back."

Didi's face had lit up at the sight of her. Caz, dragging her overnight case across the ancient flagstones of the reception hall, inwardly melted with happiness, because it was this kind of genuinely warm welcome that made you choose to return to a hotel. She'd had enough practice over the years learning how to distinguish between those who put on a good show and those who actually meant it.

Didi was the real deal.

It was also lovely to know that someone you liked and admired liked you back and wasn't merely being polite.

"Another flying visit." She hugged Didi, breathing in the rose scent of her shampoo. "I'm meeting up with a director tomorrow morning who's working at the RSC in Stratford."

"Well, you're looking fantastic. Is Shay with you?"

"No, there was no point in him coming too. I'm heading back tomorrow, straight after the meeting."

"D'you have anything arranged for this evening? If you're free, we could have dinner. Only if you want to," Didi went on hastily.

"Oh, hooray, I'd love that! How are things with you?"

"Great. Though I'm not as tanned as you."

"This is what happens when you spend three weeks frying yourself on a Caribbean beach."

"And how's Shay doing?"

"Pretty good. Well, considering. He misses his dad."

"Of course he does. Look, I'm so sorry, but I have people waiting to see me. Can I leave you with Sylvia to check in? Shall we say eight this evening?"

"Perfect," said Caz.

Didi gave her another hug. "Can't wait. We'll have a proper catch-up."

They had dinner in Caz's room. Neither of the suites was available, so she'd been allocated one of the smaller doubles on the first floor, but it didn't matter a bit.

"It's been all fancy stuff and seafood for the last few weeks," she said by way of apology, "so I've been craving pizza and chips. Is that OK?"

"My favorite." Sitting cross-legged opposite her on the king-size bed, Didi opened the lid of the cardboard takeout box and swooned as a garlicky cloud of steam rose up to greet her. "Our restaurant's great, but we don't have a proper pizza oven. Carlo's do the best ones for miles."

"Shay told me about them last week. He also said you always used to order pepperoni with mushrooms and chilies."

"He's remembered that from years ago." Didi grinned and shook her head. She lifted out a slice and took a bite. "Ow, *hot*..."

"What was Shay's favorite?"

"Spicy meat feast with extra olives and peppers, which used to cost eighty pence more than mine. Funny how these things stick in your mind. I've never understood how people can like olives."

"And how about Aaron?" Caz watched as Didi expertly twirled a string of melted cheese around the index finger of her ring-free left hand and popped it into her mouth.

Didi put down the half-eaten slice of pizza. "Tomato and mozzarella. But we broke up."

"I know. I'm sorry." Didi's eyes widened, and Caz explained, "When I was checking in, I mentioned something about the wedding to Sylvia, and she told me it was all off."

"It's not a secret. And I'm not heartbroken. Sometimes you just realize these things aren't going to work out."

"If his favorite pizza's a margherita, I'm not surprised you couldn't marry him. Sorry again." Caz waved a hand by way of apology. "But it's definitely the most boring one. So when did you break up?"

Didi shrugged. "It was more of a gradual fading away."

"According to Sylvia, it happened a while back. But you carried on wearing the ring, making out everything was fine. And now you're looking kind of awkward," Caz said mildly. "Which is…interesting."

Didi shook back her hair and picked a slice of mushroom off her pizza. "I thought I might change my mind."

"You wouldn't do that though. So that's a lie, isn't it?" Caz gave her foot a gentle nudge to show she wasn't angry and saw the faint wash of color rise up Didi's neck. "See, the thing is, I got kicked out of school at fifteen, so I never took any exams, and because of that, people tend to assume I'm a bit dim. And when it comes to math and physics and geography, they're probably right, but where other things are concerned, I'm pretty on the ball." She paused significantly. "And when it's anything to do with emotions, I'd say I'm top of the class."

"OK, I just thought there was enough going on around here without me adding to the drama. I didn't want people to think I was trying to divert attention away from Red dying."

"You see, that's another good answer." Caz pointed a triangle of pizza at her. "And it's *almost* believable. But I think the real reason you kept quiet was because you didn't want me to worry or because you didn't want to give Shay something to think about."

Bingo. Didi's shoulders slumped in defeat. "God, how do you even do that? Honestly? OK, you're right. But you have to know, all I want is for you and Shay to be happy. You've found each other, and that's what's important. And I swear on my life, I'd never do anything to try and come between you; I just wouldn't. I'm not that kind of person. I couldn't live with myself."

Caz nodded. All these years, she'd been adept at fooling herself when it came to the men in her life, pulling the wool over her own eyes and believing what she'd so badly wanted to believe. But now it was time to grow up, get a grip, and pay attention to her subconscious instead of sticking her fingers in her ears and going *la-la-laaa*.

"I know you'd never do that." For a moment, she thought she was going to cry; thankfully, the heat at the back of her eyes dispersed in the nick of time.

"You have to believe me," Didi insisted.

"I do. I completely trust you." Caz reached for her hand and held it. "You're a good person."

"So are you. And if you two ever fall out, I'll always be on your side."

"That's good to know." Dammit, now she really might cry. "And can we always be friends too?"

"Definitely." Didi raised her own wedge of pizza in a toast and solemnly touched it against Caz's. A piece of pepperoni slithered off and landed in the lap of her white shorts.

"Shall we get a bottle of red sent up to celebrate?"

Didi gave her a warning look. "You've got an interview and an audition with a world-famous director in the morning. So I'm going to be a good friend and say no."

Could she make herself do what she knew deep down she needed to do? Caz wondered. Did she have it in her to act like a mature adult for possibly the first time in her life? She reached for her can of Diet Coke and playfully flicked a few drops in Didi's direction. "You can go off people, you know."

....

Twenty-four hours later, as the plane was nearing the end of the nine-hour flight, Caz removed her eye mask. The woman in the business-class seat next to her exclaimed, "Oh, thank goodness. I thought you were never going to wake up! Can I have a quick selfie to show my friends I sat right by you? Otherwise, they'll never believe me."

Caz was known for always being nice to people when they stopped her in the street for a chat and a selfie. She sat up, waited for the woman to come and crouch beside her, performed the obligatory smile, then said, "Can I just check it's OK?" and reached for the phone.

Yes, as she'd guessed, the woman had been taking sneaky snaps for hours. Over a dozen of them while she'd been wearing her eye mask.

"Sorry, couldn't help myself. It's OK though. You weren't snoring or dribbling. You look lovely even when you're fast asleep!"

"Well, that's something. Sorry, you'll have to excuse me." Switching on her phone and popping in her earbuds, Caz said, "I need to learn some lines."

The woman looked overjoyed. "Ooh, how exciting. Why don't I help you? I'd love to do that!"

"Thanks, but it's something I need to do for myself."

Caz hadn't been asleep. All the way across the Atlantic, she'd been weighing up everything she knew and wondering if she could bear to go through with it. Would she regret it forever if she did or struggle to live with her conscience if she didn't? Could she ever be genuinely, deep-down happy knowing what she did?

"Ladies and gentlemen, could you please return to your seats and fasten your seat belts" came the announcement over the speaker. "We're now beginning our descent..."

And there was Shay, waiting for her at the arrivals gate, deeply tanned and handsome in jeans and a sea-green cotton shirt. Caz's heart flip-flopped with yearning as she took in the easy stance, the windswept, sun-bleached hair, and that beautiful smile.

Maybe he really does love me.

She wrapped her arms around his neck and kissed him. Oh, that familiar, irresistible mouth. "You didn't have to come and meet me. I could have gotten a cab."

"No bother. I wasn't doing anything." He rested his hand on her waist as they headed toward the exit. "So how did it go, meeting him? When will you hear if you've got the part?"

That was Shay; he always asked the right questions and listened to the answers. To anyone else watching, he seemed like the perfect boyfriend. Behind them, Caz became aware of the telltale click of a camera phone and turned to see the woman from the plane giggling with her friend. The woman waved and called out, "Bye, Caz. Lovely to meet you!" The next moment, they heard her stage-whisper to her friend, "Blimey, is that her boyfriend? Wouldn't kick him out of bed!"

OK, enough was enough. Spinning around, Caz said, "Let's face it. He wouldn't be in your bed in the first place."

The woman reddened and hurried away with her friend.

Shay frowned. "Why did you do that? She didn't mean anything by it."

"I know. I'm stressed. She was taking a load of photos of me on the plane. Sometimes people can be really annoying."

"Let's get you back to the villa." He led her out to the parking lot where the rented four-by-four was waiting for them. "You'll feel better after a sleep."

Caz said nothing, pretty certain she was going to feel a whole lot worse.

chapter 46

Three hours later, after a fitful doze and a long, cool shower, she joined Shay outside for dinner. Bright stars studded the sky, and a crescent moon hung over the sea like the hook in one of those grab-a-teddy machines. As they ate their red snapper, she told him all about the meeting with the director and what it would mean workwise if the job was offered and she accepted it.

"I'd have to spend six weeks over in New York. How would you feel about that?"

"It's your career. I'm not going to tell you what you should do." He was relaxed, unaware that this was one of the easy baseline questions before the real ones got started in the lie-detector test.

Caz said easily, "I had dinner with Didi last night." And there it was, the fractional but unmistakable zing of adrenaline through his body, only experienced by proxy but there nevertheless. She'd known it would be; it always was. Without even being aware of it himself, Shay became that fraction more alert whenever Didi's name was mentioned or she appeared in the vicinity. It was like pressing the Enhance button on a photo on your phone. He had no idea he was giving himself away and no control over it either, but once you'd learned to look out for the signs, there was no mistaking it.

The Didi effect was always there.

But since she needed to prove it to herself for the thousandth time, she continued, "It was great to see her again."

"In Stratford?"

"No, I changed my mind, booked into the Wickham last night instead. It's nicer staying with people you know."

"Well, good." He reached for his glass and took a swallow of wine. "So you had fun."

"We had pizzas from Carlo's. Remember you told me about them? You were so right. They were the best. And I asked her how the plans were going for the wedding. You know, I really thought they might have invited us. Did you wonder about that?"

Shay forked up a piece of snapper. "It's not a big wedding. It's up to them who they invite."

She shrugged. "I suppose. Well, it doesn't matter now anyway because it's all off."

He froze. Caz found herself trapped in the twin headlights of his gaze. "What's off?"

"The engagement, the wedding, the whole shebang." She noted the single muscle twitching in his jaw, the increased heart rate visible via the pulse in his neck. But it was the look in his eyes that really gave it away.

"Whose decision?"

"Didi's. She said he didn't do anything wrong. He's a nice guy. It just wasn't enough. She couldn't go through with it."

"When did this happen?"

"Weeks ago. Before your dad died."

Shay said nothing. He looked away, absorbing this information. Finally, he said, "Wow."

"Better to find out sooner than later and do something about it. Didi's fine. She's relieved to have it sorted." Building herself up to it, Caz refilled her own glass for Dutch courage. "No point wasting other people's time, is there? That doesn't help anyone."

"I guess not."

"Good. I'm glad you think so."

Shay was so deep in thought he didn't even pick up on the comment. She took a gulp of wine and said, "Anyway, never mind them. We need to talk about us."

Now she had his attention. "What about us?"

"Oh, come on, Shay. You know what I'm saying."

He grew still. "What are you saying?"

"You and me. We should have done this before. But it was never the right time, was it? To begin with, your dad was ill, then he got really sick, and only a complete cow would waltz off and leave you while that was going on, and when he died...can you imagine how the public would have reacted if I'd broken up with you then? I'd have been labeled the heartless bitch from hell. But it's been long enough now. We both know this isn't going anywhere, not really."

"Okaaay." Shay took in what she was saying. "I didn't know you were thinking that."

"Come on. Think it through. I'm pretty and you're gorgeous. We look great together, we fancied each other from the start, and we get along well...but we're basically incompatible. I'm messy, I'm selfish, we don't like the same movies or books, you think my actor friends are shallow, you don't like it when I slurp a drink through a straw or sing when you're watching TV." She took a breath; now that she'd gotten going, the reasons were tumbling out. "It annoys you when I spill things. It annoys me when you talk about stuff like what politicians are up to, because I don't care about any of that kind of thing."

"Right." Shay nodded slowly.

"You're cleverer than me. I find that quite annoying too. Basically, we've had fun, but this is as far as it's going to go. Long-term, we're a terrible match, and I'd drive you insane. So we need to call it a day. I won't say anything bad about you," she concluded in a rush, "and I hope you won't say anything bad about me. How does that sound?"

Shay said drily, "It sounds like you've made up your mind."

But he was already looking more relaxed. *Relieved.* She'd just handed him his get-out-of-jail-free card. "See? You're taking it so well. I'd like it if we could stay friends. I mean, I won't be around much, what with work and stuff, but it'd be good to keep in touch. Same with Didi if I'm in the Cotswolds, I'd love it if we could meet up. And I'll always want to stay at my favorite hotel." She smiled the kind of delighted smile you were obliged to summon up when the emcee announced that the award was going to someone else.

"Of course we can stay friends," said Shay.

"Have you decided yet what you're going to do? Will you live in Elliscombe? Or move back to London? Or there's always Australia!"

"Who knows?"

Well, I know. I'd bet a million pounds on it.

Hiding her grief as efficiently as Shay was hiding his relief that the decision had been taken out of his hands, Caz said, "Anyway, there's no hurry, is there? You've got plenty of time to make up your mind."

....

The next morning, Shay loaded the turquoise suitcases into the back of the rented four-by-four and drove Caz back to the airport.

"Here we are again." He handed her the printed-out tickets they'd booked online last night. "And here's your passport. Try not to lose it."

"Thanks for looking after me. I'm going to be all kinds of jet-lagged by the time I land at LAX." She'd been shrieking with frustration an hour ago, searching for her mislaid passport, until Shay had found it outside in the garden beneath one of the sun loungers.

"And try to get some sleep on the plane this time." He loaded her cases onto a cart.

"I must. Sandy's taking me to a party tonight. She says it's going to be full of A-listers."

"You see, that's my idea of hell." Shay pushed the cart through the sliding doors into the air-conditioned airport. "Want me to help you get your luggage checked in?"

"It's OK. Even I can manage that." Caz stopped walking; it was time to let him go. Never again would she sleep with Shay or properly kiss him or feel his lean, finely muscled naked body next to hers. She held out her arms and said, "Sorry. Are you going to be OK?"

He smiled. "I'll be fine."

"Have you ever been dumped before in your life?"

"Never."

"Hey, it's character forming. You'll get over it." She held her breath and hugged him hard. Keeping her face buried in his shoulder, she said, "I know you're heartbroken right now, but shall I tell you what I think would be good? If you and Didi gave things another go."

She wasn't telling him what to do. He had a mind of his own after all. She was just letting him know that she'd be happy for the two of them if it did happen.

"You have fun in LA," said Shay. "And in New Zealand." He was loosening his grip on her now, preparing for them to go their separate ways.

Caz didn't bother to tell him about this morning's call from her agent, letting her know that the New Zealand film had fallen through. It no longer mattered anyway. She reached up, gave him one last fleeting goodbye kiss on the corner of his mouth, and marveled at her own skills because he had no idea that she was making the most honorable sacrifice of her life.

As she turned and pushed the luggage cart away, she murmured to herself, "Give me my Oscar now, please. God, I'm a brilliant actress."

chapter 47

It was Saturday afternoon on December 7, and Didi was standing at the back of the hotel's Bingham Suite watching as two people who weren't her and Aaron said their marriage vows.

She was glad it wasn't her, and so was Aaron. Earlier, on the morning of what should have been their wedding day, he'd sent her an email to make her aware of this. He'd met someone else, he informed her, and this time, it was a girl who truly appreciated him, who actually wanted to spend time in his company. But the reason he was contacting her was to let her know he forgave her and wished her well for the future.

Finally, because this was Aaron after all, he'd attached a photograph with the caption *Me and Amy on an afternoon walk*. Which had made Didi smile, because it was a very Instaworthy photo, apparently casual but in fact carefully staged, with the two of them looking absolutely perfect while walking in orange-shaded woodland, laughing together as they threw handfuls of autumn leaves into the air.

Yes, like confetti. The tiny dig wasn't lost on her. Well, as long as they were happy, good luck to them.

Anyway, here she was, witnessing the wedding of Beth and Phil, two people who genuinely did love each other for better and for worse, and she hadn't regretted booking them in here today for a single second. Some of the guests were struggling to contain their emotions as the celebrant spoke movingly about the events that had led to today's ceremony. Beth's mother was in the front row, frail in her wheelchair but clearly delighted to be there and dabbing at her eyes with a lace-trimmed handkerchief. Phil's three daughters were bridesmaids, wearing matching red dresses and tiny flowered hairbands, and when the youngest one tripped over her own shoe and asked to be picked up, Beth lifted her easily into her arms and planted a kiss on her cheek, then continued to balance her on her hip while the celebrant carried on speaking.

As she watched the little girl's fingers curl instinctively around Beth's neck, Didi felt her own throat tighten and found herself having to picture politicians wrestling naked in mud, because she mustn't wreck her makeup, not while she was on duty. It was her job to make sure every minute of this wedding went smoothly and the guests had a wonderful time. She took a surreptitious glance at her watch and saw that it was 3:30. Only another seven hours to get through before she could head to Benny and Rosa's, keeping her fingers crossed that the party wouldn't be over before she got there.

....

At Compton House, Slade's "Merry Xmas Everybody" was blaring out of the speakers, red and green helium balloons bobbed against the high ceiling, and Rosa, her cheeks aching from laughing, was being whirled around the kitchen by Benny.

They might never win on *Strictly*, but could the actual winners be any happier than she was right now? She doubted it. The last three months had brought changes to her life that she could never have imagined. Benny Colette made her heart sing, and every day, she loved him more. At first, she'd felt guilty, worrying that people would think she'd forgotten Joe, but friends had hastened to reassure her that no one thought that. They were glad she'd found someone who made her happy. And as Layla had pointed out, if Joe had ever met Benny, the two of them would have gotten along together like a house on fire. They were both glass-half-full people, outgoing and good-natured. If Joe could have chosen a replacement for himself, he would have chosen Benny, no question about it.

The song on the radio ended, Benny and Rosa simultaneously yelled, "It's Chrissstmaaaasss!" and hugged each other, then Rosa picked up the wooden spoon and returned her attention to the pan of chili simmering on the stove. The house was ready for this evening's party. Pared-back Scandi chic had been replaced by the more-is-more approach: there were fairy lights galore, three fragrant Christmas trees, and multicolored decorations throughout the ground floor. All they had to do now was finish preparing the food. Benny had suggested getting caterers in, but she'd insisted home cooking was the key to a happy and relaxed atmosphere. Tiny fancy canapés were all very well, but giant dishes of pasta puttanesca, cottage pie, butter chicken, and Mexican chili were better.

"If you keep on trying the curry," Rosa told Benny as he took yet another clean spoon from the cutlery drawer, "there isn't going to be any left by the time everyone gets here."

He gave her bottom a playful pinch. "It's your fault for being such a good cook."

"Only meee!" The door banged shut behind Layla as she burst into the kitchen, pulling off her silver sequined beret and stripy pink-and-green gloves. "Yeesh, it's freezing out there! This smells good… Ooh, my favorite. Can I try some?" She greeted Benny with a kiss on the cheek.

"If you've come to help, you can start peeling potatoes." Swatting Layla away from the pan of puttanesca sauce, Rosa said, "What time's Will going to be able to get here?"

"He's working till eight, then coming straight over." Flinging her purple fake-fur coat over one of the high stools, Layla trawled a chunk of focaccia through the sauce, then tried it and swooned. "Heaven. Oh, and Estelle called earlier to tell him she's just sold *Taxi Man* to a Dutch publisher, so that's seven translations now. Isn't that amazing?"

"Wonderful." Rosa meant it. Will's secret had taken all of them by surprise, and they were still getting used to the idea that he'd written a book that was being talked about in the publishing world with such anticipation. Film rights had been snapped up for an impressive sum, but Will refused to consider giving up the job that had inspired the story in the first place. Instead, he was carrying on driving and was writing in his free time. It was still exciting though. Having never been allowed to meet Harry, it was lovely to genuinely approve of her daughter's latest boyfriend. Fingers crossed this one might turn out to be a keeper.

"Right, where's the potato peeler?" Having washed her hands, Layla was ready at last to get started. Her phone went *ding*, and she pulled a face. "Oh no. It's Will. Don't say he's going to be late."

"What is it?" said Rosa as Layla opened the text and frowned.

"I don't know! He says can I ask you if it's OK for him to bring a guest along to the party tonight. But he's not telling me who it is."

Rosa said, "Well, we've got enough of a crowd coming that one more isn't going to make any difference."

"Tell him it's fine by us." Benny thought for a moment. "Just so long as it isn't Ingrid."

"Or Harry." Layla mimed horror.

"Or noisy Carol off that TV show," said Rosa. "Oh, will you look at that?" She gave a squeak of delight and gazed out the kitchen window. "It's starting to snow!"

Eight o'clock. Only another two and a half hours to go. Over at Compton House, Benny and Rosa's party would be in full swing by now. Not that Didi was feeling in a particularly party-ish mood, but sometimes you just had to make the effort, put on a good front, and force yourself to have fun.

Anyway, today had been a success, and the wedding party was finally preparing to leave. She came out from behind the reception desk and produced her sunniest smile as Phil pushed his new mother-in-law's wheelchair out of the Bingham Suite and into the hallway.

"Thank you so much." Beth's face was shiny with joy as she hugged Didi. "For everything. You made our day perfect, and we'll never forget it."

"You're welcome. It was our pleasure." Didi grinned at the three small bridesmaids, one fast asleep in her stroller and the other two with their headbands askew. "I'm glad you've had a good day."

Beth said, "If anyone had told me three years ago that I could be this happy, I wouldn't have believed them. Life's amazing, isn't it? You never know what's going to happen." Her hand came to rest on the middle girl's head. "And now I've got everything I could ever want."

Phil, nodding in agreement, beamed at his new wife. "We both have."

The wedding party dispersed in a convoy of cars, and Didi stood outside on the sidewalk, waving them off as they disappeared down the road. The temperature had dropped this afternoon, and early flurries of snow had caused great excitement among the hotel guests. Now the flurries had settled into a steady fall of tiny dancing snowflakes, the kind that were in no danger of causing disruption. But the effect was gorgeous, as if Elliscombe had been liberally dusted with icing sugar. The festive feel was enhanced by the shops displaying their Christmas decorations, their higgledy-piggledy white roofs reflecting the glow of the fairy lights strung in the trees along the high street.

Didi couldn't say she was looking forward to Christmas, but at least there was always the hotel to keep her busy.

She watched as a taxi made its way along the street. Recognizing the car, Didi raised a hand in greeting as Will drove past, no doubt finished for the evening and now heading up to the market square, ready to join the party at Compton House.

About to dive back into the warmth of the hotel, she heard the taxi slow to a halt a couple of hundred yards up the road. A car door slammed, then Will set off once more.

Didi paused, some sixth sense prompting her to turn around. And that was when she saw the tall figure silhouetted on the sidewalk over on the other side of the street. Her heart skipped several beats. The figure was standing outside the florist's, with its spotlit window display of holly wreaths, winter roses, and lollipop bay trees in wrought-iron pots. She held her breath because, his face might be in darkness, but she already knew who it was, just from the familiar, easy stance.

Of course she did. Every inch of his body was imprinted on her brain; she knew it better than she knew her own.

Shay was back in Elliscombe. Well, it had to happen eventually. And he was on his own, which must mean Caz had work commitments elsewhere.

OK, he was making his way across the road now, heading toward her. All she had to do was act normal and pretend to be pleased to see him *as a friend.* Not so easy, though, when the snow was falling all around you, the cold air was squeezing your rib cage, and your teeth were starting to chatter.

Never mind. She'd done it often enough before. She could do it again.

chapter 48

A fox darted past in the shadows, and Didi almost jumped out of her skin.

When Shay reached her, she said, "Hi. You're back."

"I am." He was wearing a thin leather jacket over a black shirt and jeans. "Well spotted."

"We weren't expecting you." She mentally kicked herself; why would he need to give them advance warning? "Where's Caz?"

"She's in LA."

"Oh, working? What a pain."

He shook his head. "Not working. Just catching up with old friends."

"And how is she?"

"Great. As far as I know." Shay looked at her steadily. "We're not together anymore."

Didi did a double take. "What? Why not? What happened?"

"Amazingly, we broke up. Caz decided we didn't have a future. She said we were incompatible."

Didi didn't know how to react. Stunned, she said, "God, I'm sorry. Are you devastated?"

His mouth curved up at the corners. "Devastated? I guess I should be. She's an amazing person, and we had a great time together. But she was right: we would never have lasted. She also thinks I'd be better suited to someone else."

"You mean she's going to fix you up with one of her famous actress friends?" Didi was speared with envy. Would he go along with that just because it was another celebrity?

"You seem to have hold of the wrong end of the stick here." The expression in Shay's silver-blue eyes was enigmatic. "Anyway, how's today been for you? Your wedding day, am I right?"

She couldn't feel her toes. "It didn't happen."

"I know. Caz told me about you and Aaron." Another pause. "That's why I'm here."

Didi felt her breathing quicken. She could *see* it quickening, the clouds of condensation emerging from her lungs like a steam train. "When did she tell you?"

"Almost three weeks ago. The night we broke up. Coincidentally, also the night before she told me who she thought I should be with."

Almost three weeks ago…

Didi swallowed, her mouth dry. "So why aren't you with them?"

"Hey, it's cold out here. You're shivering. Do you want to go inside?"

If they went inside, guests and staff would start pestering her with work-related questions. Didi blinked snow from her lashes and shook her head. "No."

Shay smiled. "Never stop being stubborn. It's what I love about you."

"What does that mean?" She didn't dare to guess; this was feeling like an out-of-body experience. A freezing-cold one at that.

"OK, it's one of the things I love about you. One of the many, many often completely infuriating things." He took off his leather jacket and draped it around her shoulders, and Didi closed her eyes, faint with longing because the jacket was warm from his body heat and it smelled of him. "Listen to me. I spent years trying to get over you. And I almost managed to convince myself that I had, until I came home this summer and saw you again. Dad persuaded me to stay and fix up the house because he wanted to see us get back together. Did you know that?"

She stared at him. "No."

"But you were with Aaron, you were happy with Aaron, and the wedding was all arranged." Shay shrugged. "Which kind of wrecked that plan."

Didi was light-headed with cold and warmth and confusion and the first tentative shoots of joy. "Then I broke up with Aaron, and when I got back here, you'd met Caz."

He lifted an eyebrow. "That same weekend? Our timing was terrible."

"Did she really say you should be with me?"

"Caz? She did. I think she knew all along."

"And she said it almost three weeks ago. So where have you been since then?"

"In the villa in St. Lucia. On my own. Thinking things through, making sure I knew how I wanted the rest of my life to go. Except I didn't really need the three weeks because, since coming back here six months ago, I've known exactly how I wanted the rest of my life to go. I just didn't think it could ever happen."

"And I thought you'd never be able to forgive me for not believing you about the robbery. I'm so sorry about that," Didi blurted out. "I know what happened now. Mum told me everything the day after your dad's funeral. I wanted to believe you, so much. But I just knew you were hiding something."

Shay nodded. "I was. I was hiding the fact that I was sure your mum was involved in some way. I knew she was guilty of something. And that was the one thing I couldn't tell you. But you knew me so well… God, what a complete mess."

"You broke my heart." Didi couldn't control the wobble in her voice. "When you left back then."

"But I came back."

"Then you went off again, with Caz." She took a step toward him. "And now you're back. Again."

"For good this time. Well." Shay's voice softened. "Only if you want me to stay."

Sometimes you just couldn't wait a single second more for the other person to make the first move. Didi closed the gap between them, wrapped her arms around his neck, and parted her mouth to meet his. Fourteen years of longing was compressed into one wild, heaven-sent kiss, and a surge of adrenaline fizzed through her veins, almost knocking her off-balance with its power. There were fireworks exploding, drums drumming, and angels singing. Nothing else mattered in the world other than the joy of being back at last in Shay's arms and the magical sensation of his never-forgotten lips on hers.

"I tried so hard to forget you," he murmured when they finally came up for air. "Never could. You were always there." He pressed his hand to his chest. "In here. Wrecking my chances of finding someone else."

Didi traced the scimitar curve of his cheekbone with an index finger. "I can't believe we wasted all this time when we could have been together."

"Don't think about it. Maybe this was the way it had to happen. And now it has." He held her face in his warm hands as a million tiny flakes of snow danced around them in the otherwise-deserted street. "I love you. And after all these years, we know it's not going to go away. You're stuck with me now, for good."

Didi was still trembling, but not from the cold. Had anyone even noticed she was missing from the hotel?

"I can't wait to be stuck with you." Belatedly, a thought struck her. "Did you come straight from the airport?"

"Yes, Will collected me. Why?"

"Where's your luggage?"

"We stopped at the house to drop it off. Then he waited while I visited the graveyard." He touched her cheek. "You left fresh roses on the grave. When I saw you'd done that, it felt like a sign."

Didi hugged him. "You must miss him so much."

"I miss being able to let him know he managed to get us together in the end." Shay smiled briefly. "Then again, this is Red we're talking about. He probably knows."

"Everyone's at a party tonight. Benny and Rosa's," she remembered. "I promised I'd go."

His eyes glinted. "Me too. Will told me about it and added me to the guest list." And when she looked at him, he shook his head. "No, don't say it. We can't not turn up."

"We don't have to stay long." Didi molded herself against him. "We can just say hello to everyone, then sneak off." The great thing was, she didn't have to wonder what Shay was like in bed. This was something else she'd never forgotten.

"We'll do that. And then what? Your place or mine?" His mouth brushed her ear, making her shiver with anticipation. "I'm telling you now, mine's pretty cold."

Didi tilted her head to indicate the hotel, filled with warmth, golden light spilling through the diamond-leaded windows. "Seems only right to spend the night here with the man of my dreams." She gave him a lingering kiss, melting the snowflakes on his mouth. "It is my wedding night after all."

epilogue

Fifteen months later

FIFTEEN YEARS AGO, ST. MARK'S SQUARE IN THE CENTER OF VENICE had been covered in a blanket of snow.

And now they were back, on the anniversary of that magical night when they'd sneaked separately out of the hotel, made their way here to the square, and ended up—after a dodgy start—working together to build a snowman.

"Call yourself a romantic?" said Didi. "If you really loved me, you'd have arranged for the delivery of six inches of snow."

Shay shrugged. "It was here this morning, waiting for you. Then the sun came out and it melted!"

"You're a liar, but I'll let you off. Just this once." She reached up and kissed him, the soccer ball–sized bump beneath her red wool dress making it harder to achieve these days. It had always been Shay's idea that they should come back to Venice on their honeymoon, but by then, she'd be thirty-eight weeks pregnant and not allowed to fly, so they'd brought the trip forward. The weather was mild and the sun was out, the cloudless sky an almost luminous shade of cornflower blue.

As Didi surveyed the scene around them, a group of nuns hurried past, scattering pigeons. The church bells were ringing out in the Campanile, and a string quartet was playing outside Caffè Florian. She reached for Shay's warm hand and felt him give her fingers an answering squeeze.

A month from now, their wedding would be taking place—at the Wickham Hotel of course. And shortly after that, fingers crossed, their baby was due to arrive. Or maybe before, for added drama and because babies apparently weren't great at sticking to schedules. Sylvia was running a sweepstake among the staff, and everyone had found it hilarious when Didi had managed to draw her own wedding day as the date her first child would make its entrance into the world.

Would it matter though, really, if it did? Not at all. Whatever happened on the day or whenever their baby arrived, Didi knew she was already happier than she'd ever been before in her life. The last fifteen months with Shay Mason had been perfect.

"Anyway, I've got something for you." With his free hand, he was taking a small envelope from his inside jacket pocket.

"What is it?"

"I always told myself I'd never show you this until it happened. But now we're here and I'm jumping the gun. Because I'm pretty sure it's going to happen now anyway."

"What *is* it?" Bursting with impatience, Didi tried to make a grab for the envelope, but he whisked it out of reach.

"And it seems only right to do it here." His eyes were sparkling in the sunlight. "Plus, I think you'll like it."

The baby chose that moment to give an almighty kick, the outline of its foot visible through the front of her red dress.

"Show me," Didi insisted, pressing the flat of her hand over the tiny protruding heel. "We can't stand the suspense."

Shay passed her the envelope and watched as she opened it. Inside was a folded sheet of paper, creased and yellowed with age. Unfolding it, Didi saw that it was headed notepaper from the Hotel Ciati, where they'd stayed all those years ago.

The short note written in black pen was in Shay's unmistakable hand. Dated fifteen years ago to the day, it said: **Tonight I built a snowman with the girl I'm going to marry.**

She gazed at it in silence for several seconds.

"I kept it in my diary," said Shay. "Even after we broke up, I couldn't throw it away."

Didi broke into a broad smile. "I always did like a man who knows what he wants. Especially when he wants me."

"Oh, I do." Shay wrapped his arms around her. "Always did. Always will."

Can't get enough of Jill Mansell's funny,
feel-good stories? Take a look at this classic:

two's company

Available now from Sourcebooks Landmark

chapter 1

Cass Mandeville, gradually stirring from sleep, stretched out an arm and encountered warm, bare flesh. She gave it a light tap. When the warm, bare flesh in turn shifted and its owner mumbled, "OK, OK," Cass raised herself up on one elbow and dropped a playful, nuzzling kiss on the back of her husband's neck.

"Forty-one today," she sang quietly. "Forty-one today…"

Jack, rolling over onto his back, prodded her in the ribs. "I'm forty."

"I know, but it doesn't scan." Cass prodded him back. "And forty's quite shameful enough. Should an old man like you be lying in bed naked anyway? Are you sure you wouldn't be more comfortable wearing stripy pajamas and a mesh tank top?"

Jack pinched the tender flesh at the top of her thigh. "Great idea. And you can parcel yourself up in one of those frilly flannel nighties with a drawstring around the hem to stop dirty old men like me taking advantage of tender spring chickens like you. Cass, it's my birthday," he wheedled. "I don't ask for much. Just a kiss from my lovely wife and a cup of tea in bed."

Cass giggled as he began trailing kisses up her arm. "Is that all?"

"Well, toast and marmalade would be nice." The kisses reached her elbow. "Then maybe a bacon-and-mushroom sandwich or two and a few newspapers to keep me company."

"I could keep you company."

The kisses, having reached her shoulder, abruptly stopped. Jack gave her a sorrowful look.

"You'll be too busy making the bacon-and-mushroom sandwiches. Besides, what would I want with a thirty-nine-year-old woman? We older men prefer nubile young beauties, not a day over twenty-three, to tell us how wonderful we are."

"How gray, you mean." Gleefully, Cass ran her fingers along his temples, where the first flecks of silver mingled with the unruly, swept-back black hair that always seemed to need cutting.

"Cass, my angel." Jack was reduced to begging now. "I'm starving. It's still my birthday. Cup of tea, bacon sandwich…?"

"Aaargh!" In answer, she reached across and seized the alarm clock, giving it a frenzied shake. "Shit, it's stopped! Jack, what's the time?"

"Don't tell me we've slept through my whole birthday," he grumbled, seeing no reason to panic. His own watch, an unglamorous but infinitely reliable Sekonda, rested on the table next to his side of the bed. "Nine forty-five. Is that so desperate?"

It was, actually. With a flash of guilt, Cass remembered that she hadn't quite been able to bring herself to tell him about this morning's interview with the people from *Hi!* magazine. Having been forced to put them off last week at embarrassingly short notice because she'd forgotten she was supposed to be presenting the prizes at Sophie's school sports day, she hadn't had the heart to say no when *Hi!* had suggested rescheduling the visit for this morning.

Hi! was one of the numerous magazines cashing in on the phenomenally successful formula initiated by *Hello!*, a formula mocked by many but devoured by millions. Cass, who read them herself, enjoyed seeing how other people lived. Appearing in them—she had been "done" by *Hello!* years ago—was both lucrative and painless because you knew there was no way in the world the saccharine-penned journalist would write a single unflattering comment about you, your family, or your choice in pink-and-green tartan wallpaper.

The drawback was Jack, who thought all such magazines were nauseating beyond belief, an insult to journalism, and completely crappy to boot. Jack had been away working for a month in Australia when the *Hello!* people had interviewed Cass. On his return, she had eased the pain of presenting him with the fait accompli with a new conservatory already in situ and paid for with the magazine's ludicrously generous fee.

They had made Cass an offer she couldn't refuse. The trouble was, as Jack so acidly pointed out, she could never refuse anyone anything anyway. She would have said yes if they'd offered her fifty pence to swim the Channel.

Oh dear, thought Cass, her heart racing slightly at the prospect of having to tell him now. *And this time, I've said yes for even less than that.*

"What?" Watching her, Jack frowned. "You're twitching. You look guilty. What is it?"

"Ah…"

"Mum! Dad! Someone downstairs to see you," bawled Sophie on the other side of the bedroom door. She sounded as if she was yelling through a mouthful of cornflakes, which was entirely likely.

Jack raised his eyebrows. He turned his gaze back to Cass. "A strippergram? I'm so old and in need of humiliation, you've gotten me a *strippergram*?"

Cass hesitated, still wondering how best to word it.

"Sophie!" shouted Jack. "This someone. Is she by any chance wearing stockings and garters?"

"I don't know. I haven't looked." Even through the closed door, they could hear their fourteen-year-old daughter's prosaic sigh. "It's possible, I suppose. D'you want me to ask him?"

It was no good. Cass, as incapable of keeping guests waiting as she was of saying no in the first place, grabbed a pink-and-white striped satin robe with yellow butterflies on it and threw it on.

"I'll make the tea. He's a journalist, come to do a piece on us. I got kind of bamboozled into it," she went on hurriedly as, with a loud groan, Jack began to slide down under the duvet. "We had a phone-in on the show about the best ways to fundraise, and this sweet girl called in to say she's never seen us interviewed in a magazine, so why didn't we do it and donate the fee to charity?"

"My God…" Jack had by this time disappeared from view.

"So I said what a good idea, because what else *could* I say on live radio?" Cass protested. "And within minutes, this editor-in-chief from *Hi!* was on the phone pledging ten grand to the charity of my choice if I took her up on it."

The groans increased in volume. "And who was the sweet girl, her secretary?"

"Oh, now that isn't *fair.*"

Jack raised his eyebrows in disbelief at his trusting wife's gullibility. Cass was about as streetwise as Bambi.

"Maybe not, but I'll bet it's true."

"You're so cynical," Cass protested.

"That's because I'm so old." He smiled slightly as he hauled himself back into a sitting position. "You go ahead, sweetheart. This is your problem. You deal with it. All the more reason for me to stay in bed."

....

"Hi, hello! So sorry to have kept you waiting like this!"

Gushing and breathless, Cass arrived downstairs to find her visitor waiting in the kitchen. Sophie had been joking. It wasn't a male visitor with transvestite leanings but a friendly-looking girl in her midtwenties, wearing a dark-green fitted jacket and a short red skirt that clashed wonderfully with her streaky orange hair.

To make matters even worse than they already were, she was sitting at the kitchen table, which was strewn with the debris of Sophie's haphazard breakfast together with last night's supper dishes. Belatedly as usual, Cass remembered that Mrs. Bedford wouldn't be in until midday because her husband needed her with him to make sure he didn't pass out at the dentist's.

"Really, it's no problem." The girl rose to her feet, smiled, and shook Cass's hand. "It's my fault anyway. I'm early. It's a failing of mine."

"And I'm always hopelessly disorganized," Cass admitted with a sigh. "I forgot to set the alarm last night, so I'm afraid we overslept. Oh dear, this is terrible. What must you think of us? Did Sophie even offer you a cup of tea?"

She was getting into a flap. As she frantically attempted to clear the worst of the mess on the table, the loose sleeve of her dressing gown caught on the handle of the milk jug shaped like a cow, a ghastly monstrosity given to them for Christmas by Mrs. Bedford. Before Cass knew what was happening, a tidal wave of milk shot up her sleeve and down her front. The cow skidded with its feet in the air across the table.

Like lightning, the girl in the smart outfit put out an elegant hand and caught it before it hurtled over the edge.

"Oh, I say. Well held," Cass gasped. Then she gazed down in dismay at the milk dripping down her front. "Eurgh. Just like breastfeeding."

"Look, why don't you sit down?" To Cass's amazement, the girl was taking control of the situation, piling up dirty plates and transferring them briskly to the sink. The kettle was switched on, the milk jug refilled. At this rate, Jack was in danger of having his breakfast cooked for him by someone far more efficient than his own wife.

"Sorry, it looks as if it's going to be one of those days." All Cass could do was sit and watch and look suitably appreciative. It seemed safer somehow.

"You've only just woken up. I'm exactly the same." The girl gave her a reassuring grin.

"But you've come here to do an interview, and look at the state of this place..."

"Let me tell you, it makes a nice change." The girl laughed. "All I usually ever get to see are glittering showhouses where you're scared to step on the carpet. It's so much more reassuring to know the people you're interviewing are human. Now, milk and sugar for you? Is this strong enough?"

Cass, accepting the cup of tea, was almost pathetically grateful. "You're being so kind. I still can't believe Sophie didn't offer to make you one earlier," she fretted. "She's usually quite good."

The girl sat down opposite her. "Well, she did ask me if I was wearing stockings and garters."

Cass groaned and clutched her head. "Oh God."

....

Over the course of the next fifteen minutes, the girl from *Hi!*, whose name was Imogen Trent, made more tea, helped Cass stack the dishwasher, and regaled her with discreetly scurrilous stories of other celebrities she had interviewed over the past year. Cass, enchanted by her friendliness and unaffected, down-to-earth manner, forgot all about Jack lording it upstairs, waiting for his breakfast to be brought to him in bed. Only when they had polished off five croissants between them—somehow, the flaky crumbs didn't plaster themselves around Imogen's mouth as they did hers—was Cass jolted into remembering by the clunk of more mail than usual being shoveled through the mail slot.

"Hell, instant divorce." Hurriedly, she drained her own teacup, refilled it from the pot, and began heaping in the sugar. Jack drank his black and hideously sweet.

Imogen grinned. "Can I quote you on that?"

"It's Jack's birthday. I was supposed to take this up twenty minutes ago." Even as she spoke, Cass heard the sound of bad-tempered footsteps on the stairs.

"Ah," said Imogen when the kitchen door opened. She didn't seem at all intimidated by the look of irritation Jack shot her. "Mr. Mandeville. Many happy returns of the day."

In one hand, Jack was clutching an assortment of mail. Some were cards, and others were evidently bills. With his free hand, he took the cup Cass held toward him and swallowed the lukewarm contents in one go.

"Sorry, darling. This is Imogen Trent." Cass silently willed him to smile. "She's been wonderfully understanding about all the mess. Now what was it you wanted, bacon and mushrooms?"

Jack, who was wearing a pale-pink sweatshirt and gray tracksuit bottoms, took his car keys down from the hook on the dresser.

"I'm going to the club for a swim. Maybe a game of squash."

There wasn't any point protesting; he had clearly made up his mind.

"OK. See you later." Cass signaled apology with her eyes.

"You will be here tomorrow afternoon for the photographer, won't you?" Imogen swiveled around in her chair to look at him.

Jack, in return, glanced at her skirt. He didn't smile. "No."

When he had gone and Cass had quickly changed into a white T-shirt and jeans, Imogen said, "Right," and prepared to get down to business. She took a small tape recorder from her bag and placed it on the table between them.

"Promise you won't say anything about Jack being touchy," Cass begged her. "He really isn't like that as a rule. I don't want you to think we're one of those nightmarish couples who only pretend to be crazy about each other."

"Please," Imogen protested. "This is *Hi!*, remember? You and your husband could be flinging grenades across the sitting room at each other, and we'd still say you had the happiest marriage in London. Apart from anything else," she added with a widening smile, "you *do* have one of the happiest marriages in London. You're famous for it...wonderful husband, terrific kids, brilliant career. Let's face it, all-around bliss."

"Well, it's nice of you to say so." Cass hesitated, embarrassed by such an accolade. "I suppose I've been very lucky..."

"Come on, don't be modest," chided Imogen. "It's a fairy-tale thing, isn't it? How many women really and truly have it all? And what's so great, *I* think, is the fact that people don't resent you for it. They're pleased for you because everyone likes you." She paused, then said, "You give them hope."

Cass looked amazed. "Hope?"

"Yes! Think of all your fans: the housewives, stuck at home with the kids, listening to your show," said Imogen eagerly. "The thing is, that's how you were, once upon a time. And now you're here, but you haven't let it go to your head. You're still wonderfully natural. So they can listen to you and dream of making a success of their lives, just as you did." She shrugged and concluded brightly, "Well, that's my theory."

Laughing, Cass said, "Is that what you're going to put in the magazine?"

"That kind of thing." Imogen beamed at her. "The works, really. I mean, I know most of it, but if you could just run through the early days for me, how you got involved with radio in the first place and how it escalated from there. That's what the readers love most of all, isn't it? The humble beginnings."

about the author

With over thirteen million copies sold, *New York Times* and *USA Today* bestselling author Jill Mansell writes irresistible, funny, poignant, and romantic tales for women in the tradition of Marian Keyes, Sophie Kinsella, and Jojo Moyes. She lives with her partner and their children in Bristol, England.

MAYBE THIS TIME

When you visit the Cotswolds with international bestselling author Jill Mansell, you'll never want to leave!

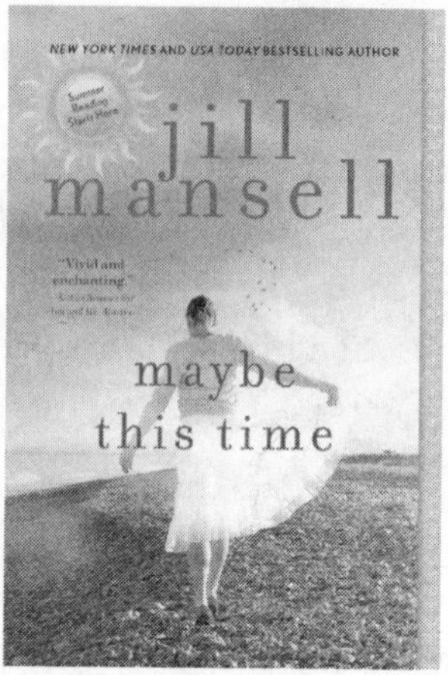

When Mimi Huish first visits her dad's new home in the Cotswolds, she falls in love with Goosebrook and the people who live there—especially Cal Mathieson, who's as welcoming and charismatic as he is gorgeous. Though Mimi loves her city life and her career, she'd be very happy to return to Goosebrook if it means seeing more of him…

"Full of heart and surprises, this novel will captivate readers."

—*Booklist* for *Three Amazing Things About You*

For more info about Sourcebooks's books and authors, visit:

sourcebooks.com